THE ITALIAN ROSE II MAFIA SERIES

THE SINNER

THE SINNER

THE ITALIAN ROSE MAFIA SERIES

C. R. Mitchell

COPYRIGHT

First Edition Copyright © 2021 by Papillon Publishing, LLC.
Second Edition Copyright © 2025 by Papillon Publishing, LLC.
All rights reserved.
Published in the United States by Papillon Publishing, LLC.
No part of this document (to include, but not limited to, its characters,
concepts, and items derived from this book) or the related files
may be reproduced or transmitted, OR RESOLD in any form, by any
means (electronic, photocopying, recording, or otherwise) without
the publisher's prior written permission.
1080 NW South Outer Road Blue Springs, MO 64015
Jacket Design by C. R. Mitchell
Published in the United States by Papillon Publishing, LLC.
Available through
www.papillonpublishing.com,
and other licensed and authorized resellers.
Paperback ISBN: 978-0-9961282-7-8
eBook ISBN: 978-0-9961282-6-1
www.PapillonEBooks.com
www.TheItalianRose.com
MANUFACTURED IN THE
UNITED STATES OF AMERICA
First Edition 2025 .

TheItalianRose
TheItalianRose
@TheItalianRose
TheItalianRose.com
papillonebooks.com

DEDICATION

To the strongest woman
I have ever known:
My Mother.
Vita R. Berg

IN LOVING MEMORY

My Papa
David A. Berg, Sr.

My Godfather
Steve Barber, Sr.

ACKNOWLEDGMENT

Four individuals make up the concrete pillars of support. Each person, in their own unique way, inspired me to continue writing. By pushing, dragging, and sometimes carrying me through rough patches, they helped me to the publishing finish line, for which I am eternally grateful.

I am very blessed to be married to my best friend and soulmate. Every day, he is the one person who consistently makes me happy. David is more than the love of my life, though. He is my editor, my creative consultant, and the reason I started writing. A million words could not express my appreciation for his abundant love, support, and the countless little (and big) things he does for me.

I have many friends, a handful of best friends, but only two Bestest Best-Friends who are blessings from God. Cindy Ellis and Lori Briscoe played an enormous part in this novel's creation by reading rough draft after rough draft. I appreciate their extraordinary friendship, unconditional love, and candid critiques.

From the moment she held me in her arms, my amazing mother has believed in me longer than anyone. We have traversed this life as mother and daughter, business partners, collaborators in writing and teaching, co-workers, and confidants. I have an abundance of gratitude for her.

I thank my readers and these encouraging individuals: David Berg, Sr., Jack, Luke, and Katie Chandler, Liz Mitchell-Busby, Jan & Jean Beyer, Steve Barber, Haley Dingfelder, Joanne Mariano, Sandra Lane, Doreen Scarborough, Kim Collier, Maria Robertson, Gladys McCoy, Joyce McCoy, Frances Brocato, Stephanie Block, Angela Dimmel, Jeanne Stephenson, Terri Marcase, Susie Gillam, Betty Witt, Father Opoka, Marita Casey, Rachelle Appleberry, Jessica Lajoie, Danielle Easley, my PEO Chapter KH sisters, and my *positive-energy* family from Ozark Research Institute. Your excitement and hunger for this sequel propelled me to continue writing. Thank you!

CHAPTER 1

"I tried to run from my inescapable fate. I should have stayed." Angelina placed the bruised hand against her cheek. "I was foolish, and for that, you suffered his abuse."

The memories of the past month filled her heart with unbearable pain. This was not the homecoming she wanted. But *wants* did not matter anymore. Only *musts* and *needs* reached the level of priority.

"You are not the only one who has paid a heavy price. In our time apart, I, too, have suffered."

With a sigh, Angelina bowed her head, and her tears crashed onto the white linen. The piercing gaze from the crucifix hanging above the bed fed the festering guilt in her soul. Frothing at the mouth, lungs gasping for air, she growled an unearthly cry of hatred that left its mark on her throat.

"I am no longer an innocent girl. *They* made me a wolf." She pounded her chest. "They made me a wolf just like them! I have done horrible things. Things that God *cannot* forgive."

Angelina gripped the sheets and allowed her pain, her victimhood, and her sorrow to escape.

The path of transgressions began the morning she witnessed the massacre. A horrid bloodbath that ripped her brothers from a happy life. The days following were filled with perpetual evils. Each monstrous act carved a black mark on her heart and slowly consumed her. Which caused the harshest sting, the night Giorgio attacked her or the sins she committed since?

It did not matter. Holy water, blessed by the Pope, could not cleanse her bloodstained soul. She was a sinner now, just like the wolves that tore the flesh of her family apart.

A chapel bell tolled in the distance. She removed a white lace handkerchief from her sleeve and wiped the stains from her emotional collapse. By the final gong of the nearby bell, Angelina had tucked her feelings and her handkerchief away.

"I will not give the wolves the satisfaction of knowing the damage they inflicted. They cannot - *will not* control me!"

She brushed a strand of hair from the swollen eye and exposed another long gash. Angelina bit at her free hand to suppress the overwhelming urge to curse the bastard who inflicted these wounds. She snarled, and her nostrils flared as her gaze swept down the body entombed in white linen.

"But they *will* pay for this! For *all* of this! I will make them *suffer*!"

CHAPTER 2

Maximus Fiori rarely allowed his ego to bask in material forms of vanity. Today was a special day. Today, he expected a telegram confirming a lucrative business deal.

He leaned back in the leather chair and propped his feet on the desk. With a sigh of satisfaction, he admired the expensive décor. His eyes roamed the room, noting the finery he had amassed. The hand-carved furniture, gold coasters, ivory statues, fresh-cut flowers, and the Waterford Crystal dancing with the sun's golden beams warmed the room. A smile curled his lips. He had done well as a young mafia boss. Better than the old guard—much better.

The recessed bookcases held copies of the greatest novels ever written. Among Maximus's favorites was *Pragmatism*, by William James, *Enchiridion*, by Epictetus, *and Meditations,* by Marcus Aurelius. Each book offered a new perspective and a reminder every choice has ramifications. A mindset not adopted by many mafia bosses. In Maximus's eyes, his adherence to these principles expedited his success.

The three famous paintings adorning the walls took him back to the day he made Freddy his right hand. Maximus leaned further back in his chair as he recalled their humorous conversation about the art.

"Any guess why I picked Ruben's *Consequences of War*?" Maximus asked Freddy as they walked around the room.

Freddy looked at the terrified faces and shook his head.

"Boss, I don't know any cat named Ruben."

"Ruben was a proponent of peace."

"That's an odd way of showing it."

"It looks like chaos." Maximus raised his brow. "The beautiful naked woman you are eyeing is Venus. She is trying to stop Mars, the 'god of war.' Next to Mars is Alecto, who punishes the moral crimes of humans."

"Ain't that an odd thing to have for...our line of business. You know, with the...*fates*...we control."

"Perhaps. But this reminds us there are limits to every action. Faint grey lines you never cross. To do so provokes chaos. *Uncontrollable* chaos." Observing the man's reaction, Maximus asked, "Tell me, are the tortured faces in the darkness unnerving or stir a guilt within you?"

"I don't think about those things. I do what must be done."

Maximus sipped his bourbon, pleased with the response.

"*La Primavera*, by Botticelli," Maximus said. "The Medici dynasty adopted the orange grove as a symbol of family."

"Who's the dame in the middle, the Blessed Mother?"

"No, that is Venus."

"Popular gal."

Maximus chuckled. Freddy could make any chat a humorous tête-à-tête. A refreshing quality and much appreciated in tough times.

"When you are the goddess of love, sex, and beauty, you tend to get all the attention."

"To the beautiful ladies and their skills!"

"And the ones who are foolish enough to love us."

"Boss, handsome cats like you attract love." Freddy squeezed his cheeks with one hand. "My face...only a mother could love!"

"Your self-awareness is astounding." Grinning, he patted his shoulder. "Here, she represents the benevolence of men."

"My benevolence was used up before the third grade."

"Precisely what made your resume stand out. And, of course, your size."

"My brains, too." Freddy puffed his chest.

"My friend, that is a hard, *no*." Chuckling, Maximus shook his head.

"Who painted the one above your desk?"

"Uccello."

"A good Italian name."

"A dragon plagued a town. After eating the livestock, it began feasting on the people. The king's daughter would be the next victim. St. George, astride his horse, spears the dragon's head."

"My kind of guy, rescuing the damsel in distress."

"Careful, you might be mistaken as a benevolent man."

Grinning, Freddy shrugged. "Hanging this one behind your desk makes you more intimidating."

"Well, now, forgive my previous misjudgment. You are a man of wisdom." Maximus gave a slight bow. "Per conoscere un furbo, ci vuole un furbo e mezzo."

"To recognize a fox, it takes a fox and a half!" Freddy translated, raising his glass.

As Maximus finished his tale of St. George, Freddy made them another drink, occasionally nodding as he listened.

"St. George's reward for slaying the beast was the hand of the king's only daughter."

"Always about a woman, Boss. It's *always* about a woman.

"To my captain, may he always be a fox and a half. Salute!" They clinked glasses and drained the golden liquid.

The memory made Maximus chuckle. Freddy's loyalty, wit, and unique perspective made him Maximus's favorite. He had achieved much since that day with Freddy. But he still yearned for a greater achievement.

He ran his hand through his thick black hair and gazed about the room again. Each item stirred a memory along his path. The casual jaunt of the last decade surfaced pleasant events and ones he wished he could forget.

The stench of World War II was fading, giving a much-needed respite from death and poverty. Now that peace reigned, people could enjoy the spoils of victory, and Maximus had done his part to earn an enormous pile of cash.

His empire was built with strategic steps that started in Italy, continued in Kansas City, and now, back in Italy. Intelligence and determination were not the only reasons for Maximus's rapid ascent. One man hastened his rise to the top. He met Peter Berg at Harvard. Their friendship was the catalyst for Maximus's success.

Every summer, Peter's parents traveled the world. Rather than spend the sunny days alone, Peter stayed with Maximus's family in Kansas City. Their friendship grew into a brotherhood by the time they graduated from Harvard. Both were driven, intelligent, and strong-willed. Even with their headstrong ways, they only fought about one thing. That one thing caused an irreparable divide between them.

"You don't respect me, do you?" Peter's face was fire red.
"That is not true, Peter! You damn well know it!"
"Then, why? Give me one *good* reason your answer is no?"

A gentle knock broke Maximus's reverie, pulling him back to a professional posture. "Come in."
"Sorry to bother you, Mr. Fiori, but this telegram says urgent!" Clara said, peeking her head around the door.
"I have been expecting it."
With a wave of Maximus's hand, Clara entered the room, tugging the grey fabric of her tight pencil skirt. Maximus rolled his eyes and groaned. *Not again.*
Clara crossed the room in four-inch stilettoes. She attempted to stroll like a seasoned runway model, but each wobbly step proved she was nothing close. The ultra-thin spikes barely supported her long legs, much less her massive boobs. Her perceived runway ended at his desk. She leaned over, providing a spectacular view of her cleavage.
Clara's employment was part of a business agreement with her father. When she arrived in a short skirt and low-cut blouse, Maximus regretted the arrangement. She was the bait in her father's trap to gain leverage over Maximus. By falling prey to her seduction, Maximus would be vulnerable. Firing her would violate the terms of the agreement, costing him a sizeable sum of money. Plus, her father would punish *her* for failing. Her termination was not worth the price either would pay, so she remained under his employment.
"Miss Clara, this is the third time we have discussed your appearance." Maximus snatched the telegram from her tiny hand. "You have worked here for *one* month. This is the last time we discuss your attire. Unless being fired is your goal!"
She flushed bright red, and a pool of tears welled.

"Are you dressing like a tramp because *you* want to, or are you following your father's instructions?"

"Mr. Fiori...I... Um...I...."

Miss Clara's thin form trembled under his dark, roving stare. Her beauty was not natural. She needed the thick makeup. The provocative attire accented her only arousing feature, her tits. Men at the bar fought over her for a chance to fondle them. With enough alcohol, he, too, might make his bid for the same reason.

He undressed her with his eyes. If she had an ass, he *would* consider bending her over the desk. But he could rent a woman with natural beauty, an ample chest, and a fine ass for far less expense and hassle.

"What do you want? Why do you dress like this? Do you want me to seduce you? Perhaps I should bury my head in your blouse. Or would you prefer I force myself on you?" He tapped the telegram against his desk. "You are an easy target, Miss Clara. Your father plays in the game of kings. He will never stop using you as a pawn. Is that what you want? I would think a bright woman like you would wish to fall in love and marry a man who appreciates you as someone more than your breasts."

Teary-eyed, Clara bit her lip and nodded.

"Your employment with me will help you gain experience and improve your skills as a secretary. However, the only way to break from your father's control is to become an educated woman and marry an educated man!"

He held up his hand to silence her excuses.

"I will cover the cost of school. If your father protests, tell him I insisted you need an education to be useful to me. Tell me if he continues interfering, and I will take it up with him myself." Maximus ran a hand through his hair and sighed at the terrified woman before him. "Become someone, Miss Clara. It is the only way to break this abusive cycle."

Maximus waved her dismissal. He watched her wobbly exit and shook his head, more in pity than disgust.

He stretched his neck and drew a deep breath before returning to the long-awaited telegram. Throughout his childhood, Maximus heard many tales about the man who saved his father's life. These stories of Rosario Beretta made him a hero in Maximus's eyes. As a wealthy and powerful man, Maximus could finally repay Rosario for his heroic acts.

During a recent tour of Northern Italy, Maximus offered Rosario a lucrative business opportunity. He hoped this telegram was Rosario's acceptance. An exhilarating tingle zoomed up Maximus's spine as he unfolded the telegram.

"Ah, the sugar that will make today sweeter than the rest. How *is* life in sunny Italy, Signor Beretta?"

His hands trembled. This was not the response he expected. The memory of Rosario sitting at the small table outside Bella Anna's Caffé stole his breath.

"Rosario, you hesitate. Have you changed your mind?"

"I must admit, my feet are cold."

"The purpose of our meeting is to assure you, face to face, of my sincerity. I will always be an advocate for your family."

"Maximus, you mean well, this I do know. You are your father's son. But my fears reach beyond sincerity. If word reaches Don Salvatore. We would be dead before you even had a chance to help us. I will tell no one about this meeting...until I am confident we are safe...I hope you understand the reasons for my concerns."

"I will send a few men to live nearby to help *if* an issue arises. Remember, Don Salvatore is *my* problem, not yours."

An immense pressure crushed Maximus's chest. He dismissed the man's concerns without hesitation, insinuating that the financial gain outweighed any risk.

Staring at the prophetic painting *Consequences of War*. Maximus's warm olive complexion faded. Five minutes ago, he basked in a gluttony of wealth. A greedy dragon, rolling in the mountainous piles of gold.

"I am a fool. How easily I forget your lesson. Every single day, the wisdom of this painting is here, before me. I examine its beauty and ponder its message. Yet, I allowed greed to blind me. Now, Alecto punishes others for my moral crimes."

Each letter in the telegram plunged Alecto's dagger deeper into Maximus's heart. Guilt replaced the morning's joy and eagerness.

"I promised to protect you." Maximus dropped the telegram on his desk, unable to look away from the message.

```
        Beretta attacked.
         Sons murdered.
    Daughters survived. Orders?
```

Maximus's greed put Alecto to work and caused the death of innocent people. He released a growl of fury and slammed his hand against the desk. The person he promised to protect the Berettas from was the only one ruthless enough to order such a heinous act. Failing his hero was soul-crushing.

"A man's family is sacred unless you desire a war! Even I abide by this unspoken rule!" He crushed the telegram, and his guilt turned to rage. "Don Salvatore, you want a war? I *will* bring it to you! I *will* crush you!"

Maximus paced, collecting his thoughts. He would gladly go to war with this tyrant. He mulled over his strategy. A painful memory of Rosario, a proud Papa, showing his children's portraits quelched Maximus's fury.

"Anger blinds a man from wisdom," Maximus said to his reflection in the window.

His obligation to secure Rosario's daughters took precedence. Retribution must wait until they were safe.

"Miss Clara?"

"Yes, sir?" She replied, trembling in fear of him.

"Get Peter Berg on the line. Then call Figgy. If he does not answer, keep calling until he does!"

Maximus fondled the coins in his pocket and paced the hardwood floor. The click of his shoes and the clinking coins blended into a rhythm as his plan formed. Maximus was sure Peter could supply what he needed; the challenge was convincing him to help.

"I have Mr. Berg on the line, Mr. Fiori."

Maximus did not respond to Clara. He snatched up the receiver and did what he did best, take control.

CHAPTER 3

Maximus stormed out of his building and headed toward the street. His driver, Figgy, stood next to a highly polished car. The early morning sun danced across the black hood of the Sixty-Special Cadillac. As Maximus approached, Figgy removed his cap and smoothed back the few strands of hair on his head.

"Mornin' Boss," Figgy said, opening the car door.

Each morning, without fail, Maximus's driver appeared with a level of glee that should be illegal. One time, after an arduous night, Maximus asked what he put in his coffee that made him so damn happy. Figgy's reply was a fifteen-minute explanation of the exact technique for brewing the perfect cup of 'joe.' He also said what he wore, or rather did *not* wear, to invigorate himself.

Maximus regretted asking because every morning, the unpleasant image of the chubby driver, shirtless, in baggy boxer shorts, flashed in his head.

"Youse gots to stimulate the body each morning with cold air, Boss," Figgy explained, slapping his overly round belly. "When youse cold and drinks the hot joe. Bam! It's like fireworks or somethin'."

Maximus rubbed his temples. The telegram caused his foul mood, but Figgy's peppy morning glee made his head throb. The man's cheerful disposition was only part of the agitation. Figgy's abundant energy was accompanied by an unending monolog. The enthusiasm usually pulled Maximus from his grumpy state. But today, he wanted him to be silent.

"Where too, Boss?"

"Union Station."

"Youse gots it!"

Figgy cheerfully strolled around the car and plopped into the driver's seat. His stocky body made the car pitch side to side as he situated himself behind the wheel.

"It's a beautiful day! I was at the coffee shop chattin' with Daniel, the cat that broke his leg jumpin' out that plane?"

"Chatting *with*? I doubt the man had the chance to speak." Maximus mumbled.

"That cat's a nut. Don't get me wrong, he's like a war hero or somethin', but jumpin' out a plane? The only thing I'm jumpin' for is to get the door for a beautiful gal! How's that for heroics!" Figgy chuckled. "Anyways, he was complainin' his leg hurt real bad. When it aches, it's a sign of rain. I told him he's nuts! The sun is out, and aint's no cloud in the sky!"

Maximus sensed Figgy's gaze in the rearview mirror, asking for an opinion. The order, *'just drive, damn it,'* danced on the tip of Maximus's tongue but never passed his lips. Figgy was a jovial man. Barking about his cheerful nature was like whipping a happy child on his birthday. For Figgy, *every* day was his birthday.

Turning onto Wyandotte Street. The sunlight illuminated Maximus's reflection on the perfectly polished window. Now, two pairs of eyes watched him, Figgy's and his own. The black stubble along his sharp jawline and dark bags under his bloodshot eyes emphasized his pale olive complexion. His driver had good cause to eye him. Maximus looked like a homeless drunk spiraling toward unconsciousness.

"Youse alright?"

Maximus flashed a glare and returned his pensive gaze out the window. His rough appearance answered the question.

Blocking Figgy's chatter from his mind, Maximus reviewed his plan. The necessity to act quickly forced him to rely on too many people. Reliance on another man's actions opened the door to the two things that ignited Maximus's temper; errors and failure. Neither, however, enraged him as much as *asking* for help. He would rather have the hair on his balls plucked, one by one, over asking for a favor. Unfortunately, this job would require several favors and the reliance on others. At the train station was the first of several requested favors.

"Anyone special at the station?"

Figgy's interruption of Maximus's contemplation was inevitable. Figgy did not know *how* to be quiet. If he were a salesman, people would buy because they believed him or, more likely, wanted him to shut up. Today, the cost was a name, and it would not purchase silence.

"Boss, youse alright? Is the muffler too loud? I gots a new one put on yesterday."

Maximus nodded. "I can hear you fine."

"Oh. Ok. I wasn't sure since youse didn't answer." Figgy glanced in the mirror. "No problem, Boss. I ain't gots to know nothin'. I was just, youse know."

Figgy's curiosity was equal to a toddler's, continually asking *why*. Expecting him to remain quiet for the short drive was unrealistic. Sighing, Maximus locked eyes with his driver's reflection. Against his better judgment, he spoke the one word that *always* unleashed a rushing river of jabbering.

"Freddy."

The news froze Figgy's gaze in the mirror, causing him to swerve onto the shoulder. The car pitched left, then right, as he tried to regain control. Horns blared, and curses were shouted at the terrible driver. Eventually, he merged back into the traffic. Dazed, Figgy glanced over his shoulder to give his Boss a quick look.

"Freddy?"

Figgy's bubbling excitement exceeded a kid with a giant rainbow lollypop. The door opened to his favorite pastime, recanting stories about his best friend, Freddy. They were partners on at least a hundred jobs. Figgy was the only man Freddy allowed to jabber endlessly and never complained about the incessant noise.

"Boss, I ain't so good at math."

"No....you are not."

"But I was thinkin'."

"Don't think, Figgy. Just drive!"

"Right. Sure thing, Boss." Five seconds later, Figgy's mouth erupted. "Not that I'm complainin', or nothin', but ain't he gots another six months?" He asked, counting on his stubby fingers. "Yeah! Like after the holidays."

Maximus wondered if Figgy was ever silent for a minute.

"Probably not even ten seconds," he muttered.

He tried to tune his driver out but eventually relinquished his desire for silence. He would enjoy Figgy's tale for the fiftieth time. Or, possibly, the first time hearing this version of the same story. Maximus smiled inwardly. Figgy always believed a story would cheer his Boss up, and there were no better stories than ones about Freddy.

"He was in solitary for what he did to that guy's mouth! He ain't been in there a few days before he told Jones to shut it."

Maximus chuckled. At that moment, he could relate.

"Youse know how Freddy gets when he's tired and hungry. Boy, that's a dangerous combonation. Anyways, this Jones guy was thinkin' he was tougher than our Freddy. On the counts, they was the same height. I saw the guy. He was big. But he ain't our Freddy big!"

A car zoomed past Figgy, cutting him off.

"Hey! Watch what youse doin'. Geeze! Damn, kids! Anyways, as I was sayin' before I was so rudely interrupted. That Jones cat, he don't shut up. Freddy don't take kindly to being ignored. So our boy, he grabbed the back of Jones's head and squeezed. I seen him do that! It makes the eyes bulge out, and the arms flop like a catfish straight out the Missouri River. Like he did to Ol' Philly-six-fingers?" Figgy laughed. "Oh man, good times."

Maximus gave a reassuring nod to Figgy when he checked the mirror.

"Juniors...he's the guy that told me about the mess. He says Jones's head made this loud thud against the wall. They thought the fight was over since he crumpled in a heap on the floor. Ha! Not *our* Freddy! He had to make a point! Juniors said that Jones screamed the loudest he ever heard a man. But I would, too, because of what our boy did next. But I wouldn't be so stupid as to piss Freddy off in the first place."

Figgy slowed the car and his mouth to a stop before turning onto Grand Street. His foot pressed the accelerator, the engine purred, and Figgy's mouth shifted back in gear.

"I can see 'Stone-Cold Freddy' hoverin' over Jones like a hungry grizzly. Freddy's a scary guy, especially when he's mad! But youse know that! Anyways, Juniors said, Freddy grabbed

Jones's lips in one hand. Out of no wheres, Freddy flashed three thin nails. Ha! Nobody can pull off what our boy can! Anyways, he pushed them nails through the guy's lips! The blood squirted all over, includin' all over Freddy. It was a big mess! Junior said Jones was sobbin' worse than a kid on the play-yard who got his nuts kicked!"

"Well, long story short, the guys parted like the Red Sea so Freddy could pass. He got six months of solitary. Hard to miss the man who done the crime when he is wearin' the evidence! Ha! Freddy said, solitary ain'ts so bad. He enjoyed bein' alone. He said it was worth it because when he got out of solitary, he could stare at someone, and they move to the other side of the room," Figgy laughed, and his belly jiggled. "Bet no one pissed 'Stone-Cold Freddy' off no more." Figgy turned his head to look at Maximus, "Ain't nuttin' likes stories about our Freddy, huh Boss?"

As if timed perfectly, Figgy pulled into a parking space at the same time he finished his story.

"Youse want me to wait here?"

"No!" Maximus replied harsher than intended.

"Sure, no problems. Youse want a coffee or somthin'?"

"No."

"That new donut shop, Lamar's, opened up. Our boy, Jack Taylor, and his boy, Jeff, run the joint. They make the *best* donuts in town. Ain't sure why they called it Lamar's. If they ain't too busy, I'll ask. Freddy likes the glazed. I'm gonna get him a dozen. Ain't no surprise, I like them all. Youse like the round ones with puddin' in the middle and the chocolate on top."

"Figgy! The train arrives at ten. We have no time to waste!"

"Alright, Boss. No problem! I'll get a variety. Youse like a cup of joe would do ya good, too."

CHAPTER 4

Waddling into the train station, Figgy scanned the massive foyer. The sunlight streaming through the stain-glass windows cast tinted cubes of light onto the sea of people meandering about—some in a rush, others on a carefree stroll to a sunny spot. A young couple walking hand in hand stopped in an illuminated patch on the marble floor. Her pillbox hat twinkled like the night sky when she turned to kiss her love one last time. Figgy thought it was a touching sight, something right out of a movie. After a teary goodbye, the couple parted, and the man became engulfed by the wave of dark suits mindlessly winding their way across the station.

The herd made no effort to show compassion for fellow passengers. An older gentleman with a hooked cane tried to pass through the swarm of black suits. He could barely take a full step without being mowed over.

"Youse need some help, Mister?" Figgy asked the man.

With a grateful smile, the elderly man's arthritic hand gripped Figgy's arm for stability. Figgy puffed his chest and forged a path through the crowd. He elbowed the torso of several men who tried to cut past. An egotistical man with an upturned snoot and a fancy suit headed toward them. He was focused on something across the way, pushing past everyone in his path.

"Youse ain't too good for us!" Figgy grumbled at the blatant arrogance.

Figgy, grinning, stuck his leg out. The arrogant man stumbled into the arms of a tall, burly worker in overalls. The guy growled and flexed his muscles, straining the seams of his white shirt. The arrogant man's attitude crumbled as a slur of apologies flew from his mouth.

The older man's laughter encouraged Figgy to continue using subversive tactics to clear the path. On the opposite side of the foyer, a middle-aged woman waved. The older gentleman acknowledged her with a smile.

"Thank you for helping my father, Sir."

Patting Figgy's arm, the elderly man smiled.

"Splendid chap, Splendid chap, indeed!" Grinning, he tapped his nose. "Careful for those falling snoots, son."

A garbled announcement of the inbound train from Chicago cued Figgy to disengage from his good deed. He backed away with a tip of his hat to the grateful pair before plunging back into the sea of strangers. His excitement on high, Figgy became the unstoppable salmon swimming up the stream of people, intent on his quest to find the platform for Freddy's train.

"Hey, Freddy, over here!" Figgy waved at a barrel-chested man wearing a black trench coat.

Freddy nodded and sliced his way through the crowd. His long stride made the hem of his coat pop against his legs, giving a sound to his ominous presence.

Figgy admired Freddy's appearance. It had been several years since they had been together. Freddy's four-year sentence was extended a year because of his occasional violent outbreaks. Judge Jack added a special gift to the end of Freddy's twelve-month victory lap. Freddy had to do community service for an additional year. This was Judge Jack's way of cracking Maximus's nuts. The judge didn't like how Maximus always slid by because of a procedural issue. When confronted about the delay tactic, Judge Jack expressed he intended to allow Freddy time to be reformed. A notion to which everyone laughed.

Freddy didn't squawk. Twelve days, twelve months, it was all the same to him. In his mind, he had to spend the time doing something.

"How's youse trip?" Figgy asked with a big grin.

Freddy shrugged his shoulders, "Alright."

His response was what Figgy expected, body language and all. A smile dimpled his chubby cheeks; it was like old times.

"Boss said it was urgent. What has happened?"

"Whatever it be, its got to be pretty bad! Specially since he called in a favor to get youse out early."

"Who hit first?"

"Huh? Naw, nuttin' like that. But Boss ain'ts right. Somethin's got him real worked up. Wait till youse seen him. He looks like shit. He's in the car."

Freddy nodded. The deep lines above his brow furrowed, and his dark eyes glazed. To an outsider, he looked kin to the Grim Reaper. For those who knew him, it meant Freddy was ready to get back to work.

Figgy couldn't suppress his excitement bubbling inside. He had a bouncy spring in his step until Freddy gave him a disapproving glare. Figgy winced. He cleared his throat, straightened his tie, and puffed his chest to show Freddy he wasn't weak. Fixing his own 'tough look,' Figgy kept his eyes straight forward.

Strutting side-by-side, the two sharply dressed men walked in unison. Figgy was about 3 inches shorter than Freddy but made up for it in the waistband. They were a dark wall pressing through the concourse, forcing the other passengers to shuffle around them. No one dared to step between them, much less look up to make eye contact.

Figgy and Freddy were partners and distant cousins, both descendants of great-great-grandmother Josephine. Figgy descended from Josephine and her first husband, Vincent, an older man from Northern Italy. Five years after Vincent's death, Josephine remarried. Her second husband, William, was from Hülben, Germany. From Josephine and William came the blood in Freddy's veins. The similarities between Figgy and Freddy started with Josephine. They ended with two traits: black hair and a love for going to the club.

"I ain'ts the only one happy youse home. The guys wanna take youse out for the tree 'F's—Food, Fun, and Fillies! Let me know what time, and I'll make the arrangements."

Freddy grunted his acceptance and said, "I gotta piss."

A loud thump echoed off the marble floor when Freddy dropped his bags in front of Figgy. The thud startled nearby passengers, but the sight of the Grim Reaper hovering above made them scurry out of his way.

Effortlessly, he flowed through the remaining passengers that separated him from the restrooms. The thud of his giant feet and the pop of his trench coat echoed around him. Out of habit, Freddy inventoried the surroundings. Under Maximus's employ, Freddy honed the skill to perfection. It made him invaluable to his partner and to Maximus.

Freddy's gaze fixed to the left. It was a distinctive look that meant someone had stepped out of line. A teenage boy bumped into an old woman at the fountain outside the bathroom entrance. It was a decoy move so the kid could snatch the woman's purse.

Figgy chuckled as the boy ran from the scene of the crime. The kid crooned over his shoulder to see if the woman would scream, but he should have watched where he was going. Freddy fluidly stepped to his left, intersecting the boy's path. The looming presence caught the kid's attention, but not soon enough. Clamping his hand on the kid's throat, Freddy slowly lifted him off the ground. A wicked smile curled Freddy's lip when the terrified boy dropped the caramel-leather handbag.

"Smart boy. Besides, it doesn't match your overalls."

A rapidly growing splotch of darkness appeared on the boy's left leg. Within seconds, a yellow stream trickled onto the boy's worn-out shoes. The kid's ragged appearance and repulsive odor confirmed the level of poverty the boy suffered. Now, the aroma of urine added to his pungent lack of social status. Freddy contemplated hurting the boy, but life appeared to be torture enough.

Five similarly dressed teenage boys near the main entrance laughed at their friend's fate. Freddy snarled and flashed his teeth at the young band of vagrants. They froze like terrified, beady-eyed mice caught by a bright light. Coming to their senses, they bolted. Only one braved a glance back to confirm the angry giant was not in pursuit.

Satisfied his lesson would remain a prominent memory in the boy's mind, Freddy tossed him to the side. The nimble form flopped in the air and barely touched the cold marble floor before springing upright to run to the exit.

Holding the purse, Freddy gently tapped the woman's shoulder. "I think this belongs to you, Miss," Freddy said with a pleasant smile.

Her eyes widened as she took in his size, but Freddy's charm instantly soothed the startled mare.

"Why, yes, it does!"

A healthy pink flush brightened her pale complexion and enhanced the pure white of her hair. Her feeble arm extended her delicate gloved hand to pat her gentle giant on his cheek. Freddy bent closer, shortening the distance so she did not strain her frail frame.

"Thank you, my dear! Let me give you a reward."

Her hands trembled like her voice as her long, thin fingers fumbled to open her purse.

"The pleasure of assisting a lovely young lady, such as yourself, is reward enough." He tipped his hat and bowed.

"Oh, my!"

Her pink cheeks brightened to red as she giggled and batted her eyelashes at her kind hero. For all his piss and vinegar, Freddy had a sweet side. He loved women, regardless of age, and could charm even the crankiest hellcat.

"Well, that cell ain'ts soured youse none. Youse buffer and charmin' as ever. Man, I'm gonna lose a load of bills." Figgy's grin widened. "Just like ol' times!"

Freddy shrugged and reached for his bags, but Figgy grabbed them first. He strained to get the long, leather duffel bags off the ground. Freddy glared at him.

"I ain'ts got soft. Let a brother be of service. Geeze!"

They sauntered toward the large arched doorway. Figgy continued his excited rambling about nothing important.

Before Freddy shipped off, he and Figgy would peruse the local bars on Friday night. The bet was the same on every outing. Whoever got a girl to laugh till she cried would get the first pick, and the other guy got the check. Figgy always lost, but it was a small price to pay to have the prettiest girls in the room sitting at their table.

"All the pretty girls hang out at the Hotel Phillips, Cabana Club. Oh, and we got to go to the Golden Ox's. Jean Beyer runs the joint now. He's a real cool cat. Makes the best martini, too. He'll fix youse up! The steaks, I can almost smell them sizzlin' ribeyes now."

Figgy babbled on without a breath while Freddy kept his eyes moving, evaluating every person in sight.

"It ain'ts cheap, but we know whose payin' the bill. I ain'ts been out much since youse left. The bar life ain'ts the same. Youse the chick magnet! So I stashed away some bills for when youse got back." He jabbed his thumb into his chest with pride. "Even if I'm lucky enough to win our bet, I gonna pay the tab!" Figgy puffed up his chest more. "It's my way of welcomin' youse home. We gonna paint the town up and make G-Gma Josephine proud!"

"Figs, you ain't changed either," Freddy grumbled.

Figgy, winded, grinned. "Geez, what's in here, a body—?"

Glaring down with an arched eyebrow, Freddy growled.

"Got it. this way."

Figgy tucked his chin and walked the rest of the way to the car in complete silence.

CHAPTER 5

Angelina watched her hometown quickly fade into the distance. The steady sound of metal on metal and the chug-chug from the engine whisked the locomotive deeper into the mountains. Under different circumstances, she would have enjoyed the symphony of sounds and the picturesque views as the train waddled down the track. To travel was a dream come true, but her dreams never included assassins.

Her mind juggled the pieces of her situation, one of which haunted her the most.

How could they follow her to this train? She thought.

She did not know which direction to pick, so how did these four souls find her. Francesca was the last person Angelina spoke to before heading to the station, making her presence the easiest to comprehend.

The night before, Carlos, her father's driver, stopped their conversation because he felt they were being watched. He had warned her about The Don's assassins, Antonio and Bruno. Francesca had first-hand knowledge of the devilish deeds these men rejoiced in performing. She was the cobbler's wife who had eluded them.

The assassins' smug faces of satisfaction angered Angelina as much as they frightened her. Their jubilee was spurred by the pleasant surprise of finding the *two* ladies together and the prospect of the train being a venue for Antonio's torture.

With little effort, Angelina could conclude the high probability of these three people following her. But the fourth pair of eyes on the opposite end of the train puzzled her the most. Fifty feet away sat the one person who could help her and Francesca escape. Instantly, her heart named the friendly smile her angel.

Her confidence, however, came laced with doubt. Each tree that ticked past her view sent her back hour by hour as she questioned her every step.

"Well, ladies. What shall we talk about?" Antonio mused. "The weather? How about your recent travels? Yes, I think you, Francesca, have traveled the most recently. But then again, what is the point? Don Salvatore doesn't care *where* we found you. Or how, for that matter. I think he is more interested in knowing the job is completed." Grinning with delight, Antonio pulled a long drag on his cigarette. "But he has special plans for you, Signorina Angelina."

Her empty stomach's revolt rose up her throat. At her brothers' funerals, Don Salvatore did not mince words describing her future role. With his hand on her lower back, The Don spoke with a satisfied smile. Each word forged another heavy iron link to the shackle he effortlessly clasped around her neck. As he explained the physical activities he intended to enjoy, he exuded the pride of a hunter displaying the carcass of a prized kill.

"If you behave, you will be treated well," Don Salvatore said with pleasure. "Do not think I wish for you to lose that feisty nature. It is what excites me the most! Yes. I will enjoy breaking in a beautiful, wild filly."

Don Salvatore's portly figure, glistening beads of sweat on his brow, and the slobber that dripped from a serpentine tongue made Angelina cringe. He was the devil walking upon the earth.

"But we have other matters to discuss, don't we?" Freshly wet from a slurp of wine, he smacked his lips.

"You cannot force me to do anything."

Angelina's resistance encouraged him. Even though his rage frightened her and his playfulness would dissipate, Angelina remained stalwart in her stance.

"Feisty, feisty!" His grubby paw gathered the fabric against her lower spine and growled. "My Little Dove, you will tell me what I desire or be punished! Unless you enjoy being whipped? I have heard some women are aroused by such aggression. Might you be one of these rare Unicorns?"

Clenching her jaw, she kept her gaze forward. With an organized trail of events, the demon ripped life into pieces. The past week of events could defeat the most resilient spirit, but she refused to comply. She would *not* become a rat, a snitch on a leash, finding sanctuary in Don Salvatore's palm.

"No."

"Very well. You are right. I will enjoy beating it out of you."

While he wet his lips with wine, Angelina imagined Don Salvatore bludgeoning her face with his fist.

"See how well you know me already! Yes, you will be an enjoyable conquest with the desirable traits for my heir!"

Confused, she said, "I thought Giorgio—a"

A devilish thunder spewed spit from his lips.

"Do *not* think! *I* will tell you *what* to think and *when*!"

She crumbled as the vision of hell became clearer. Don Salvatore's power was a gale wind, stirring all about him and destroying what resisted him.

She shivered at the thought of his chubby hand trailing up her leg and his fat body looming over her, sweat dripping from his red, puffy face. It was sickening.

No! She mumbled as a tear rolled down her cheek. *Only one tear. One and no more. My life is before me, not behind.*

"Now, now." Antonio noticed the tear and offered her his handkerchief. "There is no need to cry!"

She glanced at the satin cloth and turned away, repulsed.

"I can see you are still frightened by me. Only natural. I've had the same response from many women." Antonio smiled, revealing his yellowed teeth. "Especially the ones who know their lives are, well...in my hands!"

Angelina recoiled as Antonio reached up to wipe her face.

"Now, don't exaggerate, My...Hmm? What did Don Salvatore call you? Oh yes, his *Little Dove!* An endearing pet name. I see why he desires you. You are prettier than your mother at this age! Don't you think, Bruno?"

Bruno was a larger and somewhat quieter version of Antonio. His grin was as eerie as his gaze, and his deep, haunting voice rattled with ignorance.

"Much prettier!" Bruno grunted.

"Remember visiting little Sofia's family, Bruno?"

"How do you know my mother?"

Angelina did not remember any of Sofia's childhood tales, including those of Don Salvatore's henchmen. She recalled nothing, not one story, in her quick spin through the past.

"Sofia's mom was quite the ride."

"Now Bruno, don't embarrass the girl with tales of her sweet Nonna. It might upset Little Dove." Antonio mocked, jabbing his elbow into his partner's ribs. "Little Dove. Has a nice ring to it, Ehh?"

Antonio's boisterous laughter overpowered the train's loud chug-chug, causing several nearby passengers to cast scornful glares at them. However, Angelina was too distressed to care about the assassins' public spectacle.

"Yes, we officially name you Little Dove. Do you like your new name, Little Dove?" Antonio asked.

Bruno's massive figure bounced as he laughed, and Antonio's eyes twinkled with delight. She was repulsed by their mockery.

Lies and tormenting games. She thought. *I am not a moody feline, easily provoked with catnip-laced words!*

Angelina snapped her gaze out the window in reproach. She counted each passing tree, but the hyenas' delirious cackling pulled at her attention. Soon, the sights faded behind deadly versions of how the assassins would enjoy two helpless women. It was not *what* they would do, only *when*.

Angelina was grateful for Francesca's bold choice. They were two prisoners under the thumb of the same master. It was a small glimmer of light in the darkness of despair. With a sigh, Angelina reached out to hold her friend's hand.

"Francesca?" She removed her glove to palpate her friend's cold hand. The assassins' laughter grated her nerves.

"Stop laughing! She has a weak heart!" Francesca's lack of response rocketed Angelina's desperation to complete panic. "Francesca!"

CHAPTER 6

"Where is she?" Don Salvatore demanded.

His evil glare was a scalpel, slowly slicing through each layer of Carmella's eyes. Mustering all of her confidence, she puffed her chest. She would not back down, not in *this* house.

"I do not know. She was gone before I awoke!"

Don Salvatore growled at her. Knowledge was his battle axe, a monstrous tool he wielded masterfully. He persisted, but Carmella refused to satisfy his hunger. His mounting frustration fed her confidence.

Earlier, in the fading darkness, the engine's muted purr and the tires slowly crunching the gravel pulled Carmella from her sleep. She did not need to climb out of bed. Her heart already knew it was Angelina in the driver's seat.

Carmella urged the precious Angelina from Sofia's womb and spent time with her every day since. The young woman's absence bore another hole in Carmella's heart. A hole next to the cluster caused by the Beretta sons' death. Nevertheless, Angelina made the right decision. It was too dangerous for her to stay. The Don's presence was proof of it.

He slammed his fist on the table. "Do not test me woman!"

The loud percussion made Carmella jump, exciting her already rapid heartbeat. The Don had set his mark on her, a ravenous wolf stalking his prey. The intensity of his gaze prevented Carmella from looking directly at him for more than a second. His fat sausage fingers channeled the flames of hell, burning his wickedness into all he touched.

"I cannot tell you what I do not know!" Carmella roared.

Don Salvatore dug his fingernails into the table. Inches away, the wood carried the scar of tragedy. The divot made by the blade that stole an innocent boy's soul.

A flood of tears burned at Carmella's lashes. If even one fell, the beast won the match. That was not an option. She forced out all her agony and sadness in a raspy scream.

"Leave this house, you... you..."

The devil loomed closer, hovering over a precious space. His ominous presence grew with every word he hissed. She yearned for him to leave.

"You want me to go? Then tell me where I can find her! She is mine, and I will take her! Perhaps I should take her here. Right here! On this table!"

Carmella gasped at the thought. This table had been marred enough by this man. A young boy who had not reached his teens drew his last breath here. His warm blood seeped into the fibers of the table. Her eyes traced the faint lines etched by the pooling crimson. She plucked the boy from the table as she had done the day he was born.

Carmella's enemy leaned forward, his sour breath hot against her face. He pressed his hands against the wood, blanching his knuckles white. He was touching a sacred altar. The Don soiled the very space on which a loving family, one she loved as her own, dined in a blissful ritual every night.

As a child, Carmella's mother told her a man could never understand the maternal instinct. It was a gift God only granted to women. No man could match a mother's power. Don Salvatore was just a man, driven by his pride and the undoubtedly small sausage below his belt.

In the absence of the Beretta's matriarch, The Don's foul presence stirred the cauldron of Carmella's motherly prowess. He had done what no man should ever do. He killed the cubs from a den Carmella shared in love and loyalty. She would never divulge any information to this devil.

"Where is her room?" He demanded, releasing her from the bondage of his glare.

"Leave! Get out of this house at once! Or—"

"Or what?" A rumble rolled from his core, and his tongue slithered an evil hiss. "Will you call the Police? You are a smart woman. You have lived in this town most of your life."

Reflexively, her head nodded.

"How old were you? I think...yes...your parents came to Brusnengo when you were about four. Or, perhaps five. A fat frump of a girl with dark, unkempt hair. Your parents, so deep in poverty, couldn't feed you *and* your brother."

Don Salvatore's dark eyes lasered on Carmella. Slowly, he moved closer, forcing her back towards the kitchen. Carmella's manipulative opponent effortlessly shifted her from mother bear to a frightened child.

"Did they ever tell you why your brother died?"

The second blow from Don Salvatore's battle axe opened the forty-year-old scar. Carmella's battered heart shuddered. She didn't know, and she didn't want to know. Her parents were buried next to her brother. That part of her life was over. Carmella found love and had a son of her own. The vineyard, the Beretta's, Carlos and Fernando, were her family now.

"What do you want from us?"

The question was not asked with maternal strength. It was the meek voice of Carmella's terrified inner child.

"Us? Who is us? I thought you said you were alone?"

The fires of hell radiated a palpable heat from Don Salvatore. She took another step back and bumped into the cabinet. Licking his lips, Don Salvatore drooled, and a gleam of excitement flashed in his eyes.

A tickle of fear scurried up her spine. The massacre was only the beginning of the war. Don Salvatore would not stop until Angelina was back under his thumb. Everyone else was another victim awaiting their turn for slaughter.

"No...No...No one else is home." Emotionally paralyzed, Carmella could barely speak. The wolf had cornered his prey.

"If she is not here, then where did she go?"

Her tears flowed freely. The Don had secured a noose made from fear around her neck. He would continue his chokehold until she fed him what he craved. So she did what any good mother would do; she lied.

CHAPTER 7

"Mother Superior! Mother Superior! Wait!" She Sprinted across the marble floor, her long black skirt billowing.

"What is it, child?"

"She is gone!"

Mother Concetta's lips pursed with irritation as the young woman, barely fourteen, barreled down the hall with the grace of a bull on ice skates.

"Mother... Concetta," The girl shouted between breaths.

"Calm yourself, child. Who is gone?"

"Francesca!"

Mother Concetta peered down her nose. "Is this another of your tails, Margaret? We have discussed this at length!"

"No. On my honor Mother Concetta," She said breathless.

"Humph. *Your* honor? I will be the judge of that! Continue."

"On my way to morning service, I heard another woman tell Francesca she was leaving. I don't know for certain, but I think the other woman was Angelina!"

Under Mother Concetta's threatening gaze, the young girl rubbed her sweaty palms against her skirt.

"Margaret!"

"I was not eavesdropping, I promise! I remember our conversation from yesterday *very* well." Margaret tucked her chin and rubbed her backside.

"Humph! As you should! Go on."

"Francesca's door was open as I passed by, and her light was on. I couldn't see *who* was with her, and I did not pry. After mass, I went to the kitchen to attend to my morning chores. That is when I found this letter on the ground."

The young woman dug in her right pocket. Along with the small note came her rosary, a piece of candy, and a holy card with an image of St. Teresa, the Little Flower. Peering through her long eyelashes, she handed the Nun the note.

"Did you read the letter?"

"No!" Margaret subconsciously rubbed her behind.

"Then tell me, why do you believe Francesca is gone."

Margaret hesitated.

"Never mind. It is not important. Return to your duties."

Margaret raised her head to speak, but Mother Concetta's arched brow, emphasizing her discontent, halted the words in Margaret's throat. Instead, the young woman gave a slight bow and quickly disappeared around the corner.

Once alone, Mother Concetta released a heavy sigh. Usually, her discontent stemmed from Margaret's constant lack of compliance. Today, it was out of fear for the safety of the letter's author. A fear that began after the horrendous attack on the Beretta family shook the abbey's walls.

All the Beretta children attended the abbey's school. In those days, she was only Sister Concetta, one of the school's many instructors. Most of the time, the Beretta children were a pleasure to teach. The Nun's connection with the childrens' mother, Sofia, deepened her love for them. Mother Concetta helped form the sons into respectable young men. Learning they were murdered it shuddered her core.

The man's name who destroyed this family was never spoken, but Mother Concetta did not need to hear it. Don Salvatore's signature was a permanent scar on the hearts of dozens of innocent souls. Two of those souls convalesced down the hall. She contemplated demanding a confession from Catalina and Angelina as a condition for Rosario and Sofia's care. Hearing the family's sins could reveal the reason for the barbaric strike. It may also prepare her for any future attacks. After all, there were more than two souls to protect.

The jangle of Mother Concetta's large cross and beads was the only sound as she marched down the empty corridor. Her black skirt, a silent wave in a moonless night, rippling as she prayed.

"Heavenly Father, please protect your flock as they have gone astray from my reach, and I fear for their lives."

CHAPTER 8

Two days before their wedding, Giorgio led Catalina around her future home. A villa owned by the Salvatore family for over a hundred years. It was built when money flowed into the region faster than the wine ran out. Nothing passed hands without paying a handsome tax to the Salvatore Family. Every detail of the expansive estate was a masterpiece. The villa remained vacant for over two decades, but the structure and land were meticulously maintained.

"I guessed at what you might like. If you do not like it, you may redo any or all of it."

"You have impeccable taste. I am sure I will love it. So far, there is not one thing I would change about the whole place. It is a castle, and you are my king!" Catalina's eyes twinkled.

"Zio maintained it all these years for his heir. It was an expensive endeavor. I will repay his generosity!"

She bowed her head and stepped away.

"What is wrong?"

"Nothing."

Giorgio stepped closer to her and lifted her chin.

"Don't lie to me. We are to be wed. You must tell me everything. How else will I be able to spoil you!"

"Your Zio terrifies me."

"He should!"

Catalina jumped at the blatant and emphatic response.

"You cannot lie to me, and I will not lie to you. My Zio is a wicked man and has done many evil things."

"Will he not make you do evil things, too."

"Mario raised me, not Don Salvatore. I owe more to Mario. That is why I will not change my name to Salvatore." Giorgio held up his hand to silence her rebuttal. "Close your eyes."

His gentle and tender nature immediately soothed her concerns. Mildly displeased, she teasingly crinkled her nose.

"You are adorable when you do that."

"Do what?"

He placed her hands over her eyes.

"Close your eyes, or we will not look at your rooms."

"Room-s?" She uncovered her eyes.

"Close them!" He placed them back over her face.

Her bubbling excitement made her wiggle more than a child waiting for sunrise on Christmas morning. The jingling keys and the click of the lock added to her eagerness.

"Don't peek!"

"I will not."

Catalina rocked back and forth on her feet, waiting to see the space he described as *hers*. Living in a home of six children, finding *her* space was impossible. When her eldest brother, Marcus, left for the military, Catalina finally had her own room. She was sixteen.

"Why do I have my own... what did you call it?"

"Private Chambers."

"Yes, *Chambers*. Why are we not sharing a room?"

"All queens need a quiet place away from everyone!"

"Will I have a lady's maid, too?" Catalina giggled.

"You can open your eyes and see for yourself!"

Catalina's hands immediately covered her mouth.

"Giorgio!"

"My heart desires to make you the happiest woman alive."

She walked around the large room in awe. The gold crown molding accented the maroon wallpaper with a scrolling black velvet pattern. Her hand grazed across the hunting scene on the back of the settee. But all the finery seemed small next to the enormous fireplace.

"A pony could live in there!" Catalina giggled.

"If you wish, you may change it to a stable, My Love." Giorgio chuckled. "However, I would encourage you to keep it as a fireplace. The villa is old and drafty at night."

Catalina wrapped her arm in his and nuzzled his shoulder.

"I love to see those beautiful brown eyes dance with excitement."

"The first time I met you, I did not think you a romantic. You acted like an arrogant jerk in a fancy suit."

"There will be times, My Love, when I must act a certain way. I do it for business and for my Zio. Do not judge me by those times. I am a pawn in a game of kings. I grew up poor, and to provide a good life for you and our children, I must make a grand performance."

"You are different when it is just the two of us."

"With you, I can be my true self. Remember how I am with you, no matter what anyone says about me."

Catalina nodded and snuggled under his arm. Giorgio kissed her head and held her close for a few minutes. Gently, he encouraged her to continue looking around the room.

"Well?" Giorgio asked, "Do you like your private chambers, my queen?"

"Oh, Giorgio, I have had none of this!"

"Good! Get used to it, My Love."

He plucked her like a feather from the ground and twirled her. Catalina giggled with delight.

"I plan to give you everything you never had but always deserved. And for once, your sister will be jealous of *you*!"

Catalina rolled over in her bed, remembering the day Giorgio showed her their future home. His warning that others, especially her sister, would say and do things out of jealousy haunted Catalina.

Is envy the basis for Angelina's accusations about Giorgio? Catalina thought, staring at the ornate ceiling.

The sun crept above the horizon, trickling warm rays onto Catalina's face. The light was bothersome in the early hours of the crisp fall day, as was the memory of her conversation with Angelina.

"I am telling you the truth. I saw it with my eyes!"

"If it was true, you would not be alive to say such things. They would have killed you too!"

"I told you I was in the cellar, watching through the crack!"

"How can you be sure? That is such a small view!"

"You defend him, after what he has done to you! Do you so easily forget your bruises?"

"He has a temper, yes. But only after he suffers the abuse of his Zio. When we are left alone, he is different. I am sure, with your judgmental eye, you cannot see how he loves me."

"Oh, I see it and spit at the falseness! He mistreats you and apologizes with fancy things!"

"Everyone has their faults! Even you!" Catalina held her ground. "But jealousy was not something I thought you would ever succumb to, especially so easily."

"I am not jealous. You sleep in the wolf's home!"

Catalina needed her sister's support through what had to be done next, so she allowed the issue to fall to the side. But what she had seen that night in her chambers haunted her.

"Err! *No!* I do not want it to be true! It *cannot* be true!"

Frustrated, Catalina buried her face into the pillow and screamed several times before her aggression shifted to tears. A gentle tap-tap-tap came from her door. She refused to acknowledge it or the world outside her bedroom.

"Go away!"

"It is Constance, Signora. I have brought you breakfast."

The thought of food was revolting to Catalina.

"You must at least drink something hot. It will calm your nerves." Constance pleaded through the closed door.

Rolling her eyes at the door, Catalina groaned.

"Go away!" She collapsed back on her soft mattress.

Outside her window, in the beautiful hues of light, the birds rejoiced for the morning sun. Usually, the contagious joy of their songs tickled her soul and brightened her day. Today, however, it was a prickly spur digging at her nerves.

Constance knocked again, and Catalina growled at the maid's persistence.

"Must everyone disturb me today!"

Crawling under her thick white comforter, Catalina tried to hide from the world. But Constance's knock escalated to pounding her fist on the door.

"Fine, come in!"

The smell of hot coffee trailed into the room, rousing Catalina's stomach into a growl.

"Even you are against me!" She huffed at her abdomen.

"Signora?"

"No, no. Not you!" Catalina said, waving her hand.

"It is a beautiful morning, Signora."

Sliding out of bed, Catalina grumbled her way to the settee. A comment about the conditions outside was Constance's way of easing into a delicate subject. Catalina looked at the fireplace in defiance, refusing to encourage the maid to speak freely. She had no desire to confer over recent events, not even with the only woman Catalina trusted.

"Signora, if I may ask. What is your plan?"

"Plan for what? There is no plan except for me to stay in bed and cry until the world ends!"

"Do not say such things, Signora!"

Catalina rolled her eyes and sipped the hot coffee.

"Did you speak with your sister after the funerals?"

"We disagree," Catalina replied

"Signora, how can that be?"

"Lina is a big girl and will take care of herself." Mumbling into her cup, Catalina added, "As she always does!"

Nervously, Constance glanced around the room before kneeling beside her employer.

"We should leave before Giorgio discovers what you did."

"What *we* did!"

"Shh!"

Catalina looked at the open door and scoffed at the maid's irrational behavior.

"Only you and I know the truth. My husband will not beat it out of me. If you are not of the same mind, you may resign your post."

Catalina, arching her brow, handed her empty cup to the maid. In silence, she waited for Constance to choose her fate.

After replenishing Catalina's cup, Constance rubbed her hands against her thighs and bit at her lip.

"Signora, I am worried about our safety. These are dangerous times, and our enemy is led by a dangerous man!"

Catalina sipped the hot liquid and eyed Constance but did not speak. Constance sighed and bowed her head for a moment before answering.

"I am not as strong as you, but I will not leave your side."

"That is good to know."

"Are you not afraid of his Zio?"

Catalina considered the question. If she were honest, the answer would be a resounding *yes*! But honesty would not help her survive. She placed the cup and saucer on the table, smoothing her nightdress across her thighs. After a few moments, she cleared her throat.

"Constance, fear is a dangerous adversary. Allowing it to rule your choices, you will lose every time. I shall use what I know about Don Salvatore to my advantage. I shall not allow him the satisfaction of believing he can frighten me into submission. Even if he uses Giorgio as a tool for such things." Catalina narrowed her brows. "He will not win this fight!"

"If we leave alive, we will win."

"Do you really think Don Salvatore would let that happen? He wants my family's vineyard and the wealth that making great wine brings. For now, the business is under his control. However, without me, he cannot make *Beretta* wine. I know how to produce it from vine to bottle. If he kills me, he will lose what he does not possess, the knowledge in my head."

"What about Angelina? She knows how to make the wine, too. What if he decides he does not need both of you?"

"Then I may be forced to choose her life or mine?"

"Oh, Signora, this is a dangerous game you play!"

"Only if I lose."

CHAPTER 9

His back slightly hunched, Don Salvatore slowly padded forward like a wolf. Carmella was a cornered lamb, ready to be devoured. He watched her eyes dart back and forth. The pungent aroma of fear was enticing. This part of the hunt was almost as exciting as the final blow that ended the prey's life. The Don licked his lips, imagining how to begin his torture.

Rape destroys a woman's mind. Don Salvatore mused in silence. *But some women are not enticing enough to bring a tickle to the sword. This frump is one of them!*

Carmella was plump with streaks of grey in her dark hair, her sun-aged skin sagged from her arms, and her face was a canvas of wrinkled leather. Her appearance was revolting, so he quickly discarded the idea of rape.

Forcing you to submit would scar my mind more than yours. Don Salvatore thought.

The sunlight streamed into the kitchen, illuminating the countertop, but the darkness moved with Don Salvatore's body. Looming closer, a shimmer to his right captured his attention. A maniacal grin curled his lips. The large butcher knife twinkling in the morning light was nearly within reach.

Maybe the sight of blood squirting from the stump of your finger will loosen your tongue. The Don licked his lips again. *Perhaps using the knife's sharp tip to slowly pry off your nails, exposing the nerves, would refresh your memory. Oh, how I will enjoy watching you writhe in pain.*

Other options of torture coursed through his mind, each as tantalizing as the last. He imagined slashing one deep gash after another across Carmella's chest. It had been many years since he felt a knife slicing through human flesh. Yet, the memory of the sensation instantly tingled in his palm.

I have allowed Antonio and Bruno to have all the fun. I shall claim the occasional thrill. He decided.

As destructive and evil as Don Salvatore could be, he was mild compared to his assassin, Antonio. Known as *Demone di Fuoco*, Antonio's eyes were said to be a direct gateway to the flames of hell. However, he was called the *Fire Demon* because he used fire as his primary means of torture.

Don Salvatore stood sentry to Antonio's barbaric executions *once*. He had no interest in seeing the heinous act, but Antonio insisted.

"The sound of flesh popping and the smell of burning flesh gives me a hard-on," Antonio said with a lascivious grin.

"Ha! No one is that deranged!"

Antonio brought a woman to The Don's villa to prove he was not lying. He threw her before The Don's feet. The naked, beaten woman cried for mercy, but she was ignored.

"Do what you came to do and be done with it!"

Antonio's eyes danced with excitement as he poured gasoline onto her hair. He struck a match and watched the flames engulf her head. Instantly aroused, Antonio bent her over the desk and assaulted her squirming form.

The smell of singed hair and the blatant display of arousal nauseated The Don. He left the revolting scene. There was no need to watch his deranged assassin enjoy the woman's struggle with the dual method of torture. The prey's scream echoing through the air was as haunting as the act.

Don Salvatore grabbed the knife off the counter. The wooden handle seated perfectly in his chubby hand. His body tingled with excitement as he drew the blade up the side of Carmella's shirt. A bit more pressure, he would feel it cut her flesh. Don Salvatore's eyes danced with excitement. For a moment, he understood how Antonio could become turned on by a slow, sadistic torture. Inwardly, he chuckled; this fat frump aroused him, after all.

"Be glad I do not send my assassin to deal with you!" Don Salvatore growled at Carmella. "He would light you on fire just to watch you die. I, however, will only torture you and let you live!"

Carmella was motionless except for the tremors of fear that shook her limbs. Part of him wanted her to resist, to push him away and run. It would add to the excitement and make the kill more challenging.

A car door slammed, pulling Don Salvatore from his fantasy. Out of the corner of his eye, he saw Carlos and Fernando racing to the kitchen door. Any man with half his wits knew this was not a time to attack. Even at Don Salvatore's age, he could take down one of them and possibly render the other unconscious. Still, the old woman might snap free from her terror to assist in the retaliation. No, this was not the time to fight. Besides, he needed all three of them. They were still part of his plan.

Don Salvatore tossed the knife to the side and grumbled a curse before spitting at Carmella's feet.

"This is not over! Find her!" The Don grabbed his hat as he stormed toward the door. "Find her and *bring* her to me! Or you will find *your* son's corpse next!"

Every action was propelled by lust and revenge. It intensified the madness that ruled Don Salvatore. He had to find Angelina. She was an added element in his elaborate plan. She aroused him and intensified his desire to finish what he had started. Forcing his adversary's daughter to bear his heir became the crowning facet of his vengeance.

Pounding his fist against his steering wheel, Don Salvatore growled and floored the gas pedal. Gravel spewed from under the tires, and plumes of dust billowed behind his car as he raced past the rows of green vines.

"I will have this land! *And* all the sweet fruit that it produces, including your daughter! You will pay for your sins, Rosario Beretta! You shall pay the highest price!"

CHAPTER 10

The color in Angelina's face faded, and the lines across her brow deepened as she held Francesca's icy hand. All the stress had been too much for Francesca. Angelina did not want to admit her friend's death, but the lack of pulse and cold, limp limbs spoke the truth.

"She passed?" The conductor asked in a deep voice, tinged with a German accent.

Angelina's lungs stopped, and a dizzying whirl engulfed her head. She was not overthinking the situation. Even the conductor thought her friend was dead.

Crouching down to her level, the conductor looked into Angelina's eyes. "Signorina? Are you unvell?"

Unable to speak, Angelina looked helplessly at the conductor and nodded.

"Cüme. I have ün' empty private bünk you cün use."

"We can take care of them. Find someone else to bother!" Antonio's brow furrowed.

"But," Angelina squeaked in desperation.

Leaning forward, Antonio placed his hand on her knee.

"Now, *Little Dove*, I know it is your first time on a train."

Angelina recoiled.

The Conductor stood, allowing his tall figure to loom above Bruno. "I do not recall you two on ze platform."

Raising his eyebrow, the conductor puffed his chest, expanding his broad shoulders.

"Show ze tickets!"

Antonio's temper flared. As he reached for his gun, Bruno gave him a look of caution. The conductor outweighed Bruno by at least fifty pounds. The additional weight and the only one standing tipped the odds in the conductor's favor. In the small area, only one giant could find a solid footing. The other would be encumbered by the packed rows of seats. Antonio released an almost silent growl before moving his hand away from the butt of the gun. His partner's nonverbal warning was prudent.

Angelina glanced toward her angel. She needed to see that soft, reassuring smile. Yet, instead of hope, a pain pierced her heart. The comforting, familiar face was no longer at the other end of the car. The apparition vanished, taking the genuine love exuding from her angel's eyes. The oasis in her desert of fear was nothing more than a mirage. A dirty trick that moments ago bolstered her strength. Now, it was the harshest form of cruelty.

Offering his hand to Angelina, the conductor shot Antonio and Bruno an authoritative glare. His size was intimidating enough, but the look of fearlessness turned the conductor into a frightening giant.

"Diz way. We shall get you and ze, young lady, into a more comfortable place."

Angelina gulped at the wedge of frozen terror lodged in her throat. She never recalled a time when her choices produced one disastrous situation after another. In just twenty-four hours, she squared off with Don Salvatore and lost. Her goodbye to Francesca tempted the woman into a quest that rendered her dead.

Don't forget you placed your own neck on the chopping block by trapping yourself in this prison on wheels. Angelina scolded herself.

Doubt seeped into every crevasse of thought, blinding her rational decision-making ability.

Should I stay with known assassins or be isolated by a stranger? Either way, I will die. Angelina thought.

Floating alone in an agitated sea of uncertainty, Angelina continued her ping-pong match of choice. She could leave one dangerous situation for another. Yet, 'how' Antonio dealt with his targets urged her toward the unknown.

He may be a gentle giant, not a raving, sadistic killer like Antonio. Angelina told herself.

Gently, the conductor nudged Francesca several times.

"Signorina? Signorina?"

Admitting the truth pushed Angelina into a bout of sobs. Her voice cracked. "She is...dead?"

"No, no." The conductor scratched his head. "She passed."

Unable to contain themselves any longer, Antonio and Bruno launched into a roar of laughter, gaining the attention of the entire car of passengers.

"Yes, passed."

Angelina pointed to Francesca's blue lips and ashy complexion.

"See...Morta!"

"She thinks...hahaha... Bruno, she thinks...!"

"I know," Bruno added between bursts of laughter.

"Stop! Please, stop!" Angelina begged, sobbing.

Angelina wanted to slap Bruno for his exaggerated laughter and enormous foot slapping the floorboard. But, the assault would only make things worse.

"No, not gestorben, Signorina. She haz...Perhaps I say incorrectly. She haz passed..."

"Out!" Antonio roared.

"Oh, yes. Passed out." The conductor repeated. "I am sorry to alarm you, Signorina."

In another roar of laughter, Bruno stomped Francesca's foot. The jolt made her suck in a deep breath. The return of oxygen instantly sent color to Francesca's blue lips and grey cheeks. As much as Angelina wanted to chastise Bruno for his clumsiness, she felt the urge to thank him. Gratefully, the conductor interrupted the notion by offering to take them to another car.

Angelina encouraged Francesca to accept the conductor's proffered hand. Bruno brought her back to life, but his partner would take it as soon as he could. Even though her angel was a figment of her imagination, Angelina's dear friend was not. Francesca was alive, perhaps not well, but she would recover best in a private car.

Once Francesca was stable on her feet, Angelina considered sticking her tongue out at Antonio and Bruno. But it could instigate an attack from behind. She would have to be satisfied with the idea of mocking them.

Angelina gathered their bags and followed the conductor down the aisle. The beautiful wood grain walls shined in the morning sun. They passed through two sets of doors and stopped halfway down the car. He reached into his jacket and removed a set of keys.

"Here ze go, Signorina Beretta." The conductor smiled. "I believe you will be—"

A voice pulled his attention away from Angelina and Francesca. In that second, they exchanged worried looks. How did he know her name?

"I be with ze in a moment." The conductor said politely.

"As I vaz saying." He returned to his damsels in distress.

"Signore, I do not want to sound ungrateful, but how do you know my name?" Angelina asked.

A smile curled across his lips, and his blue eyes danced with delight. He had not meant to use her name. Angelina felt a lump form in her throat. She wanted to ask again, but fear had tied her tongue.

An impatient voice called the conductor again. For many, it would have caused a wave of irritation, but the conductor took it in stride. He nodded toward the passenger, signaling he was on his way. Before he closed the door, he replied.

"I know more about you than you could ever imagine, Signorina, Angelina Rose Beretta."

CHAPTER 11

Don Salvatore's visit terrified Carmella and enraged the two men who loved her the most. This was only the first of many visits by the tyrant, adding to Carlos and Fernando's fury. Don Salvatore saw them as pawns in his game, easily discarded for sport. They had survived many tragedies, but could they endure The Don's control over all of them. When the preditor's car was racing away, Carlos ran to Carmella.

"Did he hurt you?" Carlos asked, grinding his jaw.

Carmella sobbed into his broad chest. She was too distraught to verbalize her condition. Carlos pulled away, searching for any injuries. Finding no physical damage, he wrapped her tightly in his arms, gently stroking her hair.

Watching the loving embrace of his parents, Fernando felt a pang of jealousy. His entire life, he observed his parents and Rosario and Sofia enjoy a deep love and compassion with their soul mate. The tender displays dug at his wounded heart. He desired deep-rooted love with Angelina, but recent events robbed him of his dreams. Now, he felt buried under the mountain of emotional rubble.

When he was young and stayed the night with Anton, he would sneak down the hall to Angelina's room. Sometimes, he would go in, and they would talk for hours. On the nights she was asleep, Fernando would stand silently in the darkness and gaze upon her for over an hour. Her olive skin, accentuated by the white embroidered blanket, always entranced him. She was a beautiful angel in peaceful slumber upon a heavenly white cloud. From an early age, he vowed his heart was hers, and only hers, forever. She was the love of his life. He would wait patiently for her to return his love, even if it took an eternity.

In his pocket, Fernando's fingers gripped the only remnant of his relationship with Angelina. He was a fool to not go to her room when he heard someone stirring. Even now, the smell of the extinguished candle that hung heavy in the air of Angelina's room burned his nostrils and reminded him of his stupidity.

The night before, from Anton's room, Fernando listened to the wood creak as Angelina paced her room. She was angry at life and afraid of the future, as was he. His heart willed him to her side, but his mind talked him out of it. A car door shutting made him leap from the bed. Fernando peered out the window, but a tree obstructed the view.

His first thought was of Angelina's safety. Fernando's heart pounded as he sprinted down the hallway. He feared the footsteps were not Angelina's but someone sent by The Don to take her away. In the fading darkness of the early morning, Fernando could barely see the car through the cloud of dust in its wake.

His heart jumped into his throat when his mind conjured up a tragic picture, an image of destruction that seized his muscles. The soft white blanket, stained in Angelina's crimson blood, her perfect facial features bludgeoned, and the smile on her cherry red lips gone. He tried to suppress the horrid vision of her sprawled out in a pool of blood. He had seen enough blood in the past week. The gruesome scene where his friend drew his last breath continually punished his mind. Now, slaughtering a chicken left Fernando feeble.

His hand shook as he reached up to push the door open. Yet, he remained frozen in terror. His hand trembling an inch from the barrier between him and reality. The inner turmoil threatening his resolve made his heart race. The world spun, and darkness slowly narrowed his vision. Before he passed out, his mind posed the possibility of Angelina lying on the floor, her life in peril as it hung desperately on the edge of death's cliff. The thought of her alive and the knowledge whoever was here a moment ago fled, melted his frozen form.

The solid wood door slowly opened enough for the smell of smoke to fill his nose. The thick, green drapes were drawn closed, making the room eerie and dark. His lungs barely drew in air while he waited for his eyes to adjust to the darkness. He hesitated in total silence, listening for a sign of life, but the air was a vast chasm of hushed blackness.

He stepped cautiously, avoiding the loose floorboards as he did when he and Angelina spent hours talking about everything and nothing. At that moment, however, it was an unnecessary habit. The car door did not wake his parents. A small squeak would also go unnoticed.

He reached her desk and turned on the lamp. In the yellow glow, he noticed his name neatly scrolled across the cream-colored paper. Under his note was a letter to his parents. Both notes were sealed by a dark red wax impressed with her elaborately engraved rose signet ring.

Tracing the imprint with his finger, Fernando remembered the day her grandmother gave her the ring. It was her ninth birthday. Her cheeks were red and squished by the broad smile that exposed her white teeth. Her long, thick black curls bounced with every exuberant step. When Angelina showed Fernando her beautiful gold treasure, she twirled with delight. He had never seen her so happy. At that moment, he silently pledged to give her a ring that made her dance with the same level of joy.

Fernando's heart sank at what the note might say. With a sorrowful sigh, he felt the void of grief expand. Angelina was gone, and the ache in his heart said she would not return. He lost his best friend and his love in one short week.

Making sure he was alone, he turned to examine the room. The bedspread's white lines of embroidery were perfectly symmetrical, with stitching on the matching pillows. The thin fringe of dangling limp tentacles stretching for the dark wood floor hung evenly along the sides of the bed.

The slightly opened closet door was the only thing unusual. Without opening it further, Fernando could see a dozen empty hangers. He looked in the drawers of the dresser and nightstand. Tears stung his eyes as he opened the first drawer; it was empty. As was the second. However, the third remained full of her work shirts. Although each was stained with varying shades of pinks, reds, and purples, they were folded perfectly.

A tear fell, crashing helplessly on the fabric. Fernando shut the drawer before more escaped. Each empty space confirmed his fear. She was the driver of the car.

The nauseating dizziness returned, and his vision blurred into darkness. He forced his lungs to expand as he stumbled to the bed. Fernando's head landed on the soft pillow. The scent of her hair filled the air; it was intoxicating yet depressing. Never seeing Angelina again seemed like a death sentence. The crushing pressure pushed Fernando deeper into sorrow.

"Face it, she is gone! Anton is gone!" Fernando mumbled.

He allowed his tears to flow. He had no one to talk to, to hold him, or to comfort him. He gripped the pillow, drawing in Angelina's scent. It triggered a wave of sobbing convulsions to quake through his body. He released his grief until exhaustion won, giving him what he needed; sleep.

A beam of sunlight pierced through the tiny slit in the curtains, illuminating his face. The sweet chirping of birds sounding the morning's arrival filtered into the quiet space. He enjoyed the soft serenade until he remembered talking with Angelina until dawn's first light.

He pushed himself up and sniffed back the drainage. Out of spite, he imagined using the blanket to blow his nose. But that was not his nature. Even though Angelina's choice crushed his heart, he still loved her, so he used his shirt.

After a few minutes of collecting himself, Fernando tapped the letter against his knee. He wanted to open it and savor the perfect loops of her elegant script. Her handwriting reflected her essence, beautiful and without flaw. Yet, he could not read the letter. He feared it contained her feelings against him or a list of reasons their relationship could never work. The potential for her rejection always caused him anxiety. With his head hung low, Fernando slipped the letter under her pillow, picked up the one left for his parents, and headed for the door.

CHAPTER 12

Carmella had proven to be stronger willed than she appeared. For a moment, The Don wondered if he was losing power over the town. He had not walked the streets in many months because his focus was on punishing Rosario. Perhaps it was time to remind everyone why they adored him.

For decades, Don Salvatore cultivated the town's love. His recipe for manipulating them was easy; he gave them what they could not provide themselves. He hosted lavish festivals in the heart of town at a circular opening called the Piazza di' Ropollo. In the center of the piazza stood a multi-tiered, ornate fountain commissioned by The Don's great-great-grandfather. From it, strings of lights were laced to the buildings and back. Clinging to the periphery were over a hundred tables decorated with fresh flowers. Each family received a loaf of bread braided into rings to symbolize the town's people's unbreakable bond. To tantalize the taste buds, a dozen serving tables boasted a mountainous, mouthwatering feast. Aromatic steam rippled from spicy meats and savory dishes, fresh fruit slices were arranged in the shape of a giant flower, and colorful cookies were stacked to resemble the Piazza's historic fountain. All the tables filled with food connected to a central table with a grand, nine-tier cake. The citizens mingled and danced under the twinkling starlight, drinking barrel after barrel of the best wine until the early morning hours. The extravagance nurtured their adoration for him. However, in the children's pliable minds, he planted a seed that produced an undying love.

In the crowded Piazza, he stood before all of Brusnengo.

"Bring me the children! Come to me, my little ones, my precious sons and daughters! Sit at your Godfather's feet." Don Salvatore waved the children to all join him. "Now sit, sit. We have important business to discuss, si?"

They gathered in mass before him in udder enchantment, each sitting on bent knees in the cobblestone street, eyes wide in anticipation.

"Ahh! Look how you have grown! Like Weeds. Hahaha! Such beautiful smiles, sent from the heavens, warm my old heart. I am so blessed to be part of God's generosity of love. Love that he sends to this earth through you, through your beautiful smiles," Don Salvatore said, wiping his tears with a silk handkerchief. "Forgive your Godfather's emotions. I am merely moved by God's glory."

The dozens of small eyes gleamed up at him. They knew what was to come next, so they waited patiently for the tender emotions of their Saint Nicholas to pass.

"Now, now. Enough of my nonsense." He cleared his throat before removing a small bag. One by one, he pulled a coin from the sack and lovingly said, "This one, you may buy whatever you want. But you must save this one for the future!" He held up the third coin. "This one is by far the most important, for it is the one you give to God in gratitude for life's blessings. Capisce?"

Don Salvatore paused, holding the last coin between his thumb and finger. Golden sunlight reflected off the shiny surface, dappling light across the wide-eyed children.

"Good. Now, Nicholas, you are first. My, you have grown! Such a strong young man!"

Each child, whom he called by name, received three coins. He completed the ritual with a firm handshake for the boys and a gentle kiss on the back of each girl's hand.

In their youth, the fond memories of their generous Godfather were forever imprinted in their minds. In adulthood, these memories created conflicted souls. No one could fully commit to the tales of Don Salvatore's wrath, greed, and murder. All they remembered was his generosity, that he cared about their future, and that he was a man of God. It was a perfect illusion and purchased at a small price.

Don Salvatore pulled up to the gate. Beyond the ornate iron was the villa his deceased older brother, Victor, would have inherited. As he drove around the three-tier marble fountain, the sun danced across the hood of the shiny black Alfa Romeo, Freccia d'Oro.

The Don remembered visiting his grandparents at this stately abode. He was a wide-eyed child in awe of the ornately trimmed shrubs sprouting from beds of bright rainbow-colored flora. The manicured lawn was a vibrant green blanket that sprawled from the regal stone edifice to the neatly tucked edges of the gravel drive.

Many believed he maintained the four-story stone masterpiece as a holy shroud to Victor. Even though that held some truth, Don Salvatore's purpose was more to honor the glory of his strong forefathers.

When Victor's orphaned son, Giorgio, reappeared, it was proper for the young man to live in the majestic estate. Because of Giorgio's strife, Don Salvatore would ensure the young man had everything he ever desired. At least, that was his thinking before encountering Angelina. Things would change when she produced a more legitimate heir.

He pounded on the massive door, impatient to see Giorgio. Since the murders, his nephew had been bedridden. The mystery behind his injuries added to the growing stack of questions. The Don despised being the one blinded to reality. He *would* have the answers to his queries, and those who hindered his quest would suffer from his wrath.

A scarlet rose hung from the expansive bush near the entrance. The aroma filled the air when a little bluebird landed on the thin branch. Its tiny feet clung to the bouncing perch, easily missing the bloodthirsty thorns. The Don reached out as if to catch the bird, his massive hand twice the size of the winged creature. In fear, the bird squawked as it took flight, barely escaping the net that threatened to seize it. The branch sprung from the release of the bird's weight, waving the bloom up and down. Don Salvatore ignored the intended prisoner and snatched the tender rose from the vine. He inhaled the sweetness. His mind flashed a picture of the day before when he had Angelina pressed against the table. The soft petals grazed his lips just as his hand had glinted across her thigh. Even the memory of her made his cock tingle in anticipation of the succulent victory.

He eyed the crumpled red rose. It was as Angelina should be, helpless in his palm. She would have been placed in such a state earlier that morning; however, her absence at the vineyard thwarted The Don's plan. A snarl curled his lips as he slowly crushed the flower in his plump hand.

"I *will* have you!" He growled. "And my revenge!"

The heavy mahogany door creaked open, exposing the massive entry. Looking to the right, Don Salvatore gazed up the curved stairwell that led to the bedrooms. He contemplated shoving Constance aside so he could race up the steps. However, he noticed Catalina standing at the top, peering over the ornate metal railing.

She clamped her fingers on the black metal, and her knuckles blanched a shade whiter than her face when Don Salvatore locked eyes with her. She feared him, but The Don found her ability to hide most of her terror endearing.

Catalina put on a grand show of resilience, strength, and poise. Although she played the role well, Catalina was not as tough as she pretended. In reality, she was an innocent baby kitten with tiny claws and vicious teeth. Catalina would hiss and spit when tested, but her lack of confidence proved her inadequate in battle. She could leave a scratch that would draw blood, but in the end, she retreated to a dark space, shivering in fear, hoping her enemy would leave her alone.

"Buongiorno, mia Principessa!" Don Salvatore chirped as he flourished his hat and extended a slight bow.

"Come stai, Zio?"

Catalina returned the countenance of his salutation, though the unannounced visit obviously made her anxious.

"Sto bene! How is Giorgio this beautiful morning?"

"Resting. Do you bring word on who is responsible for the attack on my family?" Catalina asked as she began her elegant descent down the sweeping staircase.

Don Salvatore admired her beauty and regal stature. She carried herself like royalty and always maintained a certain level of decorum equal to any regent. Though Angelina was more beautiful, Catalina was the better choice for Giorgio. Catalina could be controlled. Angelina needed to be tamed, and he looked forward to becoming her trainer, whip and all.

"These things take time, Princepessa." Don Salvatore insisted as he began moving up the steps toward her. "But do not come down. It is early, and you probably left your breakfast tray untouched. Please return to your comforts. You have endured much stress. You should be resting, too."

His age did not prevent him from ascending quickly. He was upon Catalina before she could decline his compassion. Linking his arm in Catalina's, The Don guided her back up the steps, gently stroking her hand as a show of comfort.

"Carmella, please bring up some coffee and sweet rolls. I, myself, have yet to have breakfast." Don Salvatore commanded before turning his attention back to Catalina. "There is so much to do without my nephew. I had to leave early this morning to resolve some business issues."

Adding to his performance, he removed the handkerchief from his pocket and sighed deeply as he wiped his brow.

"I will be glad to have Giorgio back. These old bones cannot do as they used to."

Noticing Catalina's tense form and look of concern, Don Salvatore paused their progress up the steps.

"What is wrong? You look pale."

"You said, Carmella."

"You are mistaken."

The Don puffed his chest to elicit her fear and suppress the flush of anger rising to his cheeks. He did not like making mistakes but despised being corrected even more.

"Why would I call Constance Carmella? Hmm?"

She glanced away, and he knew his tone was harsher than he intended. This visit was to get answers. Being overly aggressive would cause Catalina to be emotional, thus ending his quest before it started.

"You look thin, Principessa. Have you not been eating?" He asked softly to soothe his frightened kitten. "Perhaps I should stay for a few days and ensure you eat and rest. After all, you could be carrying my great-nephew!"

"That is not necessary. I am perfectly fine. Constance and I manage quite well. Your finding the person responsible for my family's attack will provide me the most comfort."

He placed a kiss on the back of her hand.

"Forgive me, Principessa. I did not mean to offend you. My gentle nature wanes when I have little sleep. The days have been long. My nights are plagued with troubling thoughts. Last night, I could not sleep from the pain your situation causes my heart. I worry about you. And your sister."

He allowed Catalina to take the final two steps on her own, permitting him the opportunity to have some fun. Narrowing his eyes, Don Salvatore cast an evil glare at Constance's dazed form. It was hard to contain his amusement when the maid darted out of sight.

"Thank you for your concern. However, my sister and I..."

Ignoring her comment, Don Salvatore spoke over Catalina, preventing her from finishing her sentence. Stroking her hand gently as they walked down the hallway, The Don calmly explained the grounds for his worry.

"You are far better off than your sister, as you have a wonderful husband to provide for all your needs *and* desires. Angelina. Well, what a shame your father could not secure her a husband. And since he cannot do his duty, it came to me during my prayer time that I should intervene."

He felt her pull away, but he firmly held her hand captive.

Be calm, my little pussy-cat. I am merely planting a seed.

Catalina tried to free herself again. He refused to release her. *Easy, or I will plant my seed in you and your sister.*

As if she could hear his words of warning, Catalina relaxed her arm. A wiry grin curled his lips, and his eyes danced with delight at his submissive little kitten.

"It would be on his behalf, of course." The Don continued his false plea in a caring tone. "In fact, it falls to *my* duty because of you, Principessa. Your beauty has bound us together. We are a family. How it would break my heart to see your charming sister abandoned." He confessed as he tapped his fist to his chest. "We must be practical with things since it is not known if Rosario will ever be able to return. Why, just the other day, I heard people talking about him as if he were already gone. The words pierced my heart, and I found myself weak from grief at the idea! I immediately corrected them, but even my authority can only go so far. Perhaps, if I were to visit your father, he and I could discuss suitable arrangements for your sister. Then I could easily squelch the plague of lies festering in our streets."

"That is very kind of you, Zio. But Angelina will fare well on her own," Catalina quivered. "Besides, Papa will return before long. He and Mamma are merely grieving, that is all. In fact, Papa instructed Angelina and me to continue to run the business in their absence."

Catalina's attempt to manipulate was adorable, so he allowed her to continue expressing her delusion of safety.

"Papa was a wise man who taught his sons and daughters how to run the vineyard from start to finish. Sadly, Angelina and I are the only ones who know Papa's *secret* recipe."

Trying to suppress his wicked grin. He pounced on her words. "*Was?*"

Catalina raised her eyebrow in confusion.

"You said, *was*. If your father is no longer alive, the vineyard will pass to Angelina and you."

Before she could correct him about her father's mortality, he implanted the crux of his message.

"Well, more directly to *your* husband. Since Angelina has no one, she would be, well." The Don glanced up and rubbed his chin before connecting an intense glare with his timid little kitten. "She would be *impoverished*. That is *if* Giorgio ever became...Hmmm, how should I say?" His hand returned to his grey stubbled chin. "Irritated isn't the word. But you know what I am trying to say, eh?" He could barely contain his joy when the blood drained from Catalina's cheeks. "Ahh! I can see we understand each other perfectly!"

Don Salvatore gently raised her hand and applied a kiss while he savored the devastation that swarmed her mind. When he was sure she understood, he opened the door to her room and gestured for her to enter first.

"Zio, I miss spoke. My Papa *is* a wise man."

It was a useless attempt, and her eyes confirmed his victory. He was enjoying his game of mental torture and had no intention of stopping.

"When was the last time you and your sister had a respite? The two of you should go on holiday to someplace special. Someplace you could rest and regain your strength. It will be my treat! I will spare no expense for my two lovely nieces. You will see. It will be as if you died and went to heaven!"

Catalina's energy and composure slowly seeped from her pores as The Don verbally beat her into submission. As his puppet, Catalina would do as she was told or suffer.

"That is kind of you, but"

"No, buts! I insist! Why don't you have Constance fix the four of us dinner tonight. We will discuss the best place to visit. While you are gone, I shall move in. To the lower apartment, of course. My knees could not withstand so many steps every day. Our bodies do not stay young forever!"

"Four?"

"Si, you, Giorgio, Angelina, and myself. It will be good for you... for *us* to make happy memories in the wake of all the sadness. I will not take no for an answer! Think of it as a command from *your* father...well...foster father."

He allowed his devilish grin to emerge. The trap was set. All he needed now was to lock the gate on her eternal prison.

"While at the vineyard, I will ask if she can free herself from her work," Catalina agonized as her trembling hands, begging for support, groped at the spine of the sofa.

Watching his prey squirm, The Don unconsciously licked his lips. His visit to see his little kitten proved far more pleasurable than his call to the vineyard. Although he could have had fun with the old hag had he not been interrupted.

His fingers tap-danced across the back of the settee, mimicking the merry tune of his voice.

"You should visit your parents. Invite them to dinner. I long to give them my support in their tragic loss. Better yet, tell me where they are, and I will go myself?"

He let his suppressed smile peek out. Don Salvatore enjoyed how each torturous word squeezed out every ounce of his little kitten's strength.

"Did you wish to see Giorgio?" Catalina muttered.

"Later. Let my nephew rest. You and I shall enjoy some time together first. Forgive me, but until now, I had not realized what lovely company you are. Giorgio has told me so, and now I see what he sees in you."

Walking around her quarters, Don Salvatore's eyes wandered around the elegant space. He admired the decor and was ready to express his admiration for her exceptional taste when a smell tinged his nose. The damp, musty air was fused with the odor of charred fabric and smoke. It repulsed him, and he regretted his forced intrusion.

"What is that revolting smell?" The Don asked, holding his hand over his nose.

Catalina flushed, and he noticed her eyes take up a liar's dance of fright.

"I stumbled over a chair. It landed close to the fire and quickly began smoldering!"

His brow arched higher when she nervously rubbed her hands against her skirt. She was lying, but why?

Curiosity blended with anger; another question needed to be answered. However, the Don's interrogation was halted by Constance's appearance with a heavy silver tray at the door. He contemplated asking Constance what had happened but tucked the question away for another time.

"Put it outside on the balcony, please," Catalina said.

Constance's presence spurred Catalina's nearly instant transformation from terrified prey to the gracious hostess. For a brief second, The Don saw a bond between soldiers beaten down into their trenches and shackled together in fear. He had never noticed the women's special connection before. He wondered if he had missed it out of lack of interest or if a recent catalyst stimulated the tie.

"Si, Signora."

"Have you ever seen the view from here?" Catalina asked sweetly as she offered him the lead.

Abandoning all etiquette, The Don stepped out first, grateful for the opportunity to escape the dreadful stench.

"Not since your husband so graciously added such a lavish balcony. It was quite expensive, you know. But what is money if you cannot buy your wife a bit of happiness!"

A lull of grey hung from the sky, winning the war over the morning sun with battlements of gloomy clouds and an army of damp, chilly air. The white blankets of winter threatened their approach each day with a gradual decrease in temperatures. The thought of an impending winter chilled his bones. He briskly rubbed his arms before settling in the chair across from Catalina. His mind was preoccupied with the unpleasant smell from within and the cooling climate. He lost the momentum of his attack. However, the sight of Constance's hand trembling as she poured the coffee and served them rekindled his aggression.

Catalina picked at her sweet roll for a moment before absently gazing past him. It was her usual performance before aimlessly dragging the conversation down a meandering path of unimportant tales. In an ethereal voice, she would speak of the perfectly manicured garden or how she enjoyed her breakfast here many mornings just to listen to the singing birds. Uninterested in such worthless conversations, he took control of the tête-à-tête with his questions. He would drag her down to his verbal dungeon, where he planned to torture her until she spewed the truth. But he needed to proceed gently at first.

The Don gently began his query. He asked about her health and that of her sister's, hoping she would divulge something of use. After what seemed several hours of fruitless questioning, though the sun's unchanged position contradicted his lack of fortitude, his last wisp of patience disappeared. It was time for truth or torture.

"I know you are lying." Don Salvatore growled.

His sudden change in tone made her body stiffen.

"What *really* happened to Giorgio?" He glared at her. "And do not tell me he was drunk. I am no fool!"

"Zio, I told you."

"Did you push him down the stairwell? Do not test me! I have no patience for lies! If he dies, you lose *everything*! All of this!" His voice bellowed, causing the birds nearby to flee to a safer perch.

"Zio, I... I did nothing wrong! You must..."

Catalina's stammering caused his lip to twitch in anger.

"It is you who *must*! Or you will lose everything! Everything! It will all disappear, and you will too!"

"He was drunk and..."

"Nonsense!"

Don Salvatore slammed his hand on the table and leaned in closer. He could smell the remnants of Catalina's sweet perfume wafting into the air with the cool breeze. The scent was enticing, but the terror in her eyes stimulated a more invigorating sense of unyielding power.

"I have seen him drunk. He has never *stumbled*, so why should I believe your tale? Hmm? Why?"

The Don searched her face for the truth, but all he could see was her eyes swimming in a lake of tears. She would crumble under such intensity, leaving him with no new information. He slowly leaned back, and softened his tone.

"Forgive me, Principessa, my sugars are low, and I come off harsher than I intend. But I cannot eat until I know the truth about my nephew. He is all I have in this world, and like a troubled father, I am concerned for my son."

The Don bowed his head, sighed, and remained quiet for a moment. In the silence, a few birds returned, but none landed on the rail as they did when Catalina sat outside.

"Come now, tell me. I will not be mad, I promise."

"He was drunk."

The repetition of the same answer gnawed at his nerves. Trying to contain the wrath boiling in his gut, Don Salvatore's hands clenched the arms of his chair.

"I swear it is the truth!"

"Lies! Lies! Lies!" Don Salvatore roared.

"It is the truth!" A deep voice replied.

A thump followed by an unusual scraping noise added to the eerie voice. As the form entered the light, Catalina gasped and clutched her chest. The Don jumped to his feet like a man not plagued with the stiff joints of age.

In unison, The Don and Catalina exclaimed, "*Giorgio?*"

CHAPTER 13

Catalina and Giorgio sipped their coffee and talked in the wake of Don Salvatore's visit.

"I am sorry he bothered you," Giorgio said.

"You went against him. He will punish you for it."

"Maybe."

"Why did you get out of bed? You could not have known he was here."

"When Constance brought my breakfast tray, her hands trembled violently. Only one person could upset her enough to dump scalding coffee on my lap."

"Are you okay?"

"Yes, she is cleaning up the mess. When she is done, I will leave you to your day. I am sure you have much to do."

"I do."

The couple did not speak again until Constance returned to fetch Giorgio. He gently kissed Catalina's forehead and whispered, 'I love you,' before limping back to his room.

Catalina drove to the vineyard in a half-conscious daze. The Don's threats made her want to hide in a dark corner for fear of saying the wrong thing. His existence was an authoritative magnet, pulling her self-confidence out of reach. She was foolish to speak to him. Even her strong-willed husband suffered from his uncle's iron fist.

Since her marriage to Giorgio, Catalina had only spent a few minutes alone with Don Salvatore. Usually, their encounters were long enough to exchange pleasantries. This time, though, she spent an agonizing hour under his gargoyle perch while his beady eyes scrutinized her every word. When he arrived unannounced, she should have followed her instinct, which urged her to stay locked in her bedroom.

Giorgio's grand entrance into her room startled her. However, his defense of her and his bold defiance against his uncle was far more perplexing. Giorgio always became the puppet in his uncle's presence, acting the part designed by Don Salvatore. Even though Giorgio played his role well, he was not immune to his uncle's mental and physical torture.

More than once, Giorgio came home with the marks of abuse for his disobedience. After these episodes, Giorgio would drink and find the bed of another woman. Catalina forgave his infidelity since he never kept the same woman for long. In her mind, it was his way of releasing his frustrations, and far better on another woman than herself.

His appearance on the balcony was the first time he was out of bed in a week. The day after Giorgio's fall, Dr. Mariano advised him to remain off his ankle if he wanted to keep his foot. Catalina was grateful for the order. She needed time to deal with her brother's funerals and sort out the truths from the lies. The good doctor also took the time to educate Catalina on the typical side effects of Giorgio's trauma.

"Do not be alarmed if he seems different to you. It is common for head injury patients. He tumbled quite far, si?"

"Si, from here to the main level."

"Surviving that fall is a miracle, but do not expect him to be healed instantly! He needs to stay in bed for at least two weeks! I will come by every day to see him. And *you*," Dr. Mariano stated with a raised brow.

"I appreciate the offer, but I am fine, Dr. Mariano." The doctor's brow remained raised before releasing a harrumph.

"As they *all* say. Nevertheless, I *will* see you tomorrow. Remember, Giorgio's mood can swing from good to bad in an instant. And leave his memory alone. It will return in time."

The sun was in full blaze at its peak in the sky by the time she turned onto the long gravel drive that led to her childhood home. It was a place of splendid memories laced with horror. Her body shivered as a chill trickled down her back. Catalina wanted to stroll through the vines, as her father did when his soul needed to heal. However, this haven did not hold the same heartwarming effect as it did before her brothers' deaths. Catalina swallowed the lump of sorrow encased in fear. Her brothers were dead, and they would not want this tranquil place to become a nightmare for her.

She parked the car and walked to the chicken coop. The memory of her father asking if she would take Giorgio's hand rushed back. It was the happiest day of her life. A 'yes' flew from her lips. For the first time, she was the prized beauty. Her entire life, she existed in Angelina's shadow. No man ever looked twice at Catalina after they met Angelina. To have a gorgeous, wealthy man from a prominent family vying for her affection, not Angelina's, was a dream. It would have been foolish to reject the offer, especially with a sparse quantity of eligible men in Brusnengo.

She unlocked the door to the coop, quickly ducking under the low hanging threshold and closing the door behind her to avoid any escapees. Catalina scattered handfuls of the grain in front of the chickens, watching them cackle with delight as they scurried to the food. When they had finished, they cocked their heads to beg her for more.

"Maybe later, little ones, after my walk."

The rooster grumbled and scratched the dirt while the hens squawked in disappointment.

"Now, now, Chum-Chum! You can wait until I return, just like Bella, Rosa, and MiMi!"

Catalina walked up the gravel hill, past the stone buildings where the wine was made. Part of her wanted to go inside, but it would only add to her pain. What made working in those buildings fun was with whom she worked. Catalina placed her hand on her heart to honor her brothers as she passed the ivy-covered walls.

"Cat?"

Catalina nearly jumped from her skin when Fernando appeared in the doorway of the far building. For a moment, his figure, shadowed by darkness, made her think her brother's apparition moved toward her.

"Nan!" Catalina replied in shock.

"I wasn't sure if I would see you today."

"I was not sure if I *wanted* to be seen."

"I'm sorry to bother you." Fernando lowered his head. "I will be around here if you need anything from me."

"No. No, Nan. I do not need to be *completely* alone. I needed fresh air away from interrogating eyes. If you have time, your company is quite welcome." Fernando gave her a bleak smile. "Are you the only family I have left?"

Given his dejected appearance, it was a question she did not need to ask. Yet, she had to confirm what she suspected.

He nodded and looked away.

"A painful revelation." She slipped her arm in his. "At least we have each other...and your parents."

"And yours."

"If they survive," Catalina replied. "They did not look well, and there is no way to know if either will speak again."

Fernando's chin dropped, and the tears of sadness clung to the lower lid of his eyes. He loved her parents as his own, even if he never called them Mamma and Papa.

They ambled in silence to the top of the hill where Rosario liked to stand. It was his place above the clouds, away from the distractions of the world.

"Papa solved many issues here." Catalina sighed.

Absently, her foot found a rock and rolled it around.

"He did that."

"Did what?"

"When your father came here to think, he would find a rock with his shoe and roll it around."

Catalina cocked her head and waited for an explanation.

"I would follow him up here and hide behind that tree over there, then crawl on my belly through the tall grass so he wouldn't know I was watching him. He amazed me. I don't know why, but I was always in awe of him."

"Do you really think he didn't know you were watching?"

Fernando relaxed his tense features and smiled.

"He knew everything. When to speak and when to listen. He could stand here for an hour or a day, then walk down that hill and say the exact right thing. I wish I were more like him. Maybe Angelina would have loved me."

Catalina squeezed his arm.

"You are perfect as you are, and he would say the same."

The sun broke free from behind a puffy cloud, illuminating Fernando's face. He had his father's thick hair and long forehead but his mother's nose and thin lips.

She etched every line, angle, and curve into her memory for eternity. It was a picture she wished she would have captured of her brothers. An unforgettable image to remain long after time erased their mark from earth. Since she did not think of engraving her brothers' features, Fernando's pensive gaze would be the image she stored for them as well.

A flock of birds soared in the sky before winding to the lower hills. Their glorious formation added an enchanting beauty to the land. The view was more peaceful than an empty church. This was her father's heaven, as her balcony was for her. She understood why he stood there for hours.

Perhaps I am my father's daughter. Catalina thought as her foot unconsciously found another rock.

"Can I see them?" Fernando asked, breaking the silence.

"I am not sure how safe that is."

Fernando's jaw clenched as his sadness shifted to anger.

"He will stop at nothing to find them, including killing you and your parents." She gently touched his tense forearm. "Do you really want to know, with the risk of The Don's wrath?"

"Yes."

She wondered if his tone stemmed from inner strength, deep sadness, or intense anger. Her father and sister would have quickly determined the source of Fernando's grief and rage. They possessed the finesse to help him understand his emotions. She did not inherit the gift and was no help to him.

She gripped his arm as firmly as a long-lost friend's hug.

"I will not put you in grave danger. I will tell you anything, but I cannot tell you about my parents until it is safe."

"Why do you not trust me?" Fernando's face flushed red under his furrowed brow, and the tears that threatened to fall receded. "After everything my family has done for you!"

"Are we nothing to you? Is my family a trio of pawns for the Berettas' to abuse as they wish?"

His fiery rage rattled her, putting her on the defensive.

"Do not displace your anger on me. I am not your enemy!"

"Are you sure?"

"You know what will happen if they kill my father!"

The deep sadness looming in his eyes quickly shifted to hatred. "You are treating me like your enemy!"

"Is that what you need to believe? Does it justify your pain? You hurt, deep inside, you hurt! But that is not reason enough to blame me!"

"Don't shut me out like a stranger. I'm family, *remember*."

Catalina reached out to touch his arm, but he pulled away. Her heart ached with sadness.

"I am sorry you feel alone. Search your heart, Nan. You know she didn't leave because she wanted to."

As he stared into the distance, his skin transformed from an angry youth to a tired, weathered man overrun by time and lost to the chasms of loneliness. He stood in a patch of sunlight, but a looming darkness enveloped him. Three steps away, she could feel the ominous weight pressing on his soul.

"Nan, she left to find help."

"I offered to help, but she refused!"

"She refused out of love."

He glared. The anger in his reddened eyes startled her.

"Now, who is believing what they need?"

"Fernando, if she did anything that caused you harm, it would kill her. You know she would never recover from that grief." She caught his arm before he turned away. "You know it's true. That is why it hurts so much." She let her words sink in before pressing further. "Think it through, Nan. Think!"

He yanked his arm free of her grip and stepped out of her reach. She wanted to comfort him but refrained, allowing him time to sift through his own turbulent thoughts.

Sometimes, silence is the best medicine. Catalina thought.

Remaining quiet with her soul urging her to confide in him was difficult. But his volatile emotions made him unfit for the role of a confidant. Like him, Catalina felt alone in a sea of uncertainty. Her only connection to anyone was the strings sewn into her flesh by the marionette—Don Salvatore. The show began when he threatened her and her sister's survival. A sharp pain struck her gut, a premonition of the agony his tugs would soon cause.

CHAPTER 14

Maximus did not expect this trip to be anything more than a long, uncomfortable flight to New York in a military cargo plane. He believed expectations were a futile occupation of the brain that interfered with reality. Holding such illusions inevitably ended in disappointment.

"Boss, you sure about this?" Freddy's blue eyes widened.

Maximus found the uneasy expression comical.

"Why? You nervous?"

Maximus slipped his arms into the safety harness, clicked the buckle, and effortlessly synched the strap. Freddy, grumbling insults, fumbled with the contraption for several minutes. Maximus released an audible chuckle. Freddy had never flown and would have preferred to keep it that way.

As they taxied down the runway, Maximus glanced at his wingman. Freddy's enormous hands covered his ears. A futile attempt to muffle the roaring engines of the C-130. He glared across the plane's beastly belly. A deadly expression, burning a hole in the opposite wall of the fuselage.

"Planes have come a long way since the Wright Brothers!"

Freddy, less than amused, glared at Maximus.

Once in the air, Freddy's stress abated, allowing Maximus to return to the matter at hand. It was insanity to continue the microscopic analysis of his brief encounter with Rosario. Yet, Maximus continued his mental plunge into the past, replaying their meeting in Alessandria, Italy. A vivid memory of the fresh pastries and the aroma of his coffee brought the moment back to life.

It was easy to assume his business arrangement with Rosario triggered The Don. Yet, how would a plan so newly conceived cause this outrageous attack? There was an element missing, and he was determined to find it.

Maximus continued to examine every detail, resisting the heavy blanket of exhaustion. The past forty-eight hours had been hell. But the next few days were guaranteed to be worse. If Maximus were going to survive, he would need to be sharp. Reluctantly, he paused his rumination, leaned back, and closed his eyes. The aircraft's gentle rocking motion helped lull him into a much-needed slumber. Though sleep came fast, his dreams were filled with turbulent memories.

"Hurry up, Maxie!"

"Wait! I almost have it."

"Mamma won't let you keep it!" Olivia said.

Maximus gazed up at his sister with a flicker of orneriness. "She doesn't have to know."

"Fine, you win." She giggled, tousling his thick black hair

Lifting the hem of her skirt, Olivia joined the hunt to capture the tiny lizard. She loved her brother and would do anything to make him smile. She wasn't the only girl to have such desires. Maximus's smooth olive skin and dark eyes radiated a charm that effortlessly melted the opposite sex. Their mother said he was born with the gift of enchanting women. She was his first victim; Olivia claimed to be second.

From the moment Maximus entered the world, Olivia, at the tender age of four, claimed the handsome babe as her own. When her father showed Olivia her new brother, she quickly snatched him into her arms and showered him with kisses. Every day, Olivia happily tended to her precious brother's needs. She helped feed and rock him, taught him his colors and shapes, and read to him each night.

Being showered with the constant love from his sister, Maximus grew to adore her. Her dazzling onyx eyes, smooth caramel skin, pomegranate-red lips, and radiant smile attracted men, especially as she developed her feminine features. For Maximus, however, her loveliness ran to the core of her soul. One did not have to guess if Olivia loved you because she would stop at nothing to ensure your happiness.

"Get it, Maxie!"

Maximus lunged forward. His long arm extended quickly, and his fingers stretched out to pluck the little creature from the rocky trail. Dust plumed, then rapidly faded away to reveal a little tail that squirmed in his grasp.

"You got it! You got it!" Olivia praised. "I didn't think you caught him, but I should know better; you are relentless."

She embraced her brother before making eye contact.

"Promise me something, Maxie. Promise you will never give up on your dreams. Not for me, for Mamma, not even for Papa. You have rare gifts that should not be squandered." Olivia's giant onyx globes glistened as they danced in their sockets. "Will you promise me?"

Smiling, Maximus nodded.

"Anything for you, Livy!"

Olivia tucked her long black hair behind her ear and gazed down at the wiggling prize.

"Do you want to hold him?"

"Not particularly." She grimaced at the thought. "Come on, we will be late for supper."

Olivia picked up his books and dusted off his pants.

"I will shake the dust from them so Mamma won't notice."

Maximus smiled. "Do you think Sam is a good name?"

"I think it is getting late, and we need to hurry home before it gets too dark to see," Olivia said, pointing to the setting sun. "You can name our little friend later."

The glowing ball settled on the horizon, casting golden shades of yellow, accented with orange and purple, onto the few remaining puffy clouds that lingered above.

Maximus's gaze followed the morphing clouds as they shifted from one magnificent form to another. A dragon's long neck faded into a hooked staff before rolling into a fierce cobra's head. His pace slowed as he pointed to the sky to tell his sister of the shapes he saw in the distance.

"Maximus, you must run!" Olivia whispered.

She never said Maximus. He was Maxie to her and *only* her. Maximus turned to look behind him, but Olivia shoved his face forward. Her pace quickened, making him move faster. He wanted to see what or who made his sister run.

"Don't look back, Maximus, just run!"

"I am not leaving you."

"I will be right behind you. Now run! Please!"

Maximus locked his eyes forward, expanded his stride, and increased the speed of his gait to a full run. The rocky path required his focused attention, especially in the fading light. Large rocks jetted up from the tan soil. Each footstep caused a new cloud of dust. Usually, he controlled his foot's fall so the dust didn't agitate his sister's lungs. What usually took minutes to cross was accomplished in seconds. When he reached the top of the ridge that overlooked his home, he did not pause as he often did to admire the majestic view. Instead, he moved down the hillside, his agile legs maneuvering around the occasional obstacles protruding from the ground. The trail was narrow and pockmarked with large boulders and scraggly brush.

Halfway down the hill, he realized his sister was not behind him. He turned to peer through the dwindling cloud of dust hanging over the empty winding track. Frozen in fear, he tried to ignore the horror his imagination conjured.

She was right behind me; I know she was! He thought.

Maximus's heart pounded inside his chest when a desperate scream pierced the air. Instinctively, Maximus's body responded, unleashing the powerful stride.

"Let me go!" Olivia screamed.

The light had nearly vanished from the sky when Maximus reached the top of the hill. He saw three figures wrestling with his sister's little frame in the growing darkness. One struck her face, hurdling her body into the air. She landed with a loud thud. Like a rabid dog, another black demon ripped away her fabric flesh.

"That's some fine goods." The man unfastened his pants.

"Olivia! No!"

The plane jostled, pulling Maximus from his torrid sleep.

"You alright, Boss?"

Maximus did not respond. Had he a drink, he would slam it, hoping to find his nerves at the bottom of the glass.

The plane dipped into another pocket of turbulence, turning both of their stomachs. Maximus looked at his watch with dismay. They still had another hour before they landed.

"Boss, you said this was a one-time thing, right?"

CHAPTER 15

The shifting landscape drew her closer to the window. She had never seen such a magnificent view. The train slowly climbed to a higher altitude. The tall, thin trees standing like centurions along the tracks slowly transformed into small green blades before melting into the abyss. The expanding world was beautiful and terrifying all at once.

Angelina rested her head against the cold glass. Watching the trees become smaller and smaller pulled at her heart. In the universe of her childhood, she, too, stood tall, strong, and splendid. Yet, the further the train whisked her from Brusnengo, the more her life became an insignificant speck on an enormous planet.

You have the wisdom of an old soul, Principessa. Rosario told Angelina.

Her father taught her many things about life and making wine. However, he did not prepare her for life outside her hometown. In the shadow of the world's vastness, Angelina had to accept the sum total of all her talents equaled a single drop of water in the ocean.

"You are right, Papa. I have the wisdom of an old soul. The old soul of a powerless hermit!" Angelina muttered. "What do I do now, Papa?"

Angelina sifted through two decades of her father's pearls of wisdom, hoping to find one to help her. Solutions raced around her head, yet none seemed to solve the problem, only postpone the inevitable. It was foolish to be corralled in a space that ultimately helped the monsters hunting them. It was another poor choice. Her pseudo-self-confidence and her father's helpful words crumbled into a heap beneath her feet. There was no escape from a tragic end.

"Now what?" Francesca's shrilled with fear.

Damn it! Stop wallowing in self-pity! Think of something, anything! Angelina banged her head on the glass.

"Angelina? What are you going to do now?"

"*We!* What are *we* to do? I do not know...not give up!"

"I hope your brain conjures something more inspiring."

Angelina disregarded her friend's comment and peered into the hallway. Thankfully, the corridor was empty.

"Come on, we have to hurry before he comes back."

"Hurry to...? Have you not noticed we are caged hens?"

"We are getting off the train. If you want to survive, less talking and more moving. Grab your bag. Hurry!"

"He knows *your* name! Did you tell him your name?"

"No! I don't know." Angelina pinched the bridge of her nose. "No, I did not tell him."

Angelina tried to focus on their escape, but Francesca's worthless questions interfered with her thought process.

"Who is he?"

"I said, *I–do—not—know!*"

The tension threatened to extinguish the oxygen from the small space. Angelina was as impatient as Francesca, but agitation wouldn't solve their problems. They needed to move, but Francesca, in her blabbering, was right. To where? Even though the train had reached the other side of the mountain, they were still a long way up.

They could jump from the cabin window. The heavy snow might break their fall, but even that seemed risky. Most likely, one, if not both, would break a leg in the jump. Angelina looked past the hem of her skirt at her exposed legs, then at Francesca's attire. Coatless, wearing high heels and a dress, neither were clothed for the extreme cold or the terrain. The train's minimal descent, the thickness of snow, and the types of trees confirmed it would be a long, perilous journey to an unknown town in Don Salvatore's territory.

"Why did you let him trap us?" Francesca demanded.

It took a few seconds before Francesca's words penetrated her thoughts. Furious, Angelina grabbed her arm.

"What did you just say?"

"Why did *you* let him—?"

Angelina's brows arched high, she pointed at her chest.

"*Me? Me?* You think this is *my* fault? You jumped on this train all on your own. Remember?"

"I know, but—"

Angelina stepped closer to Francesca. She was only an inch taller, or at least her heels were enough to give her the appearance of more height, making her glare more ominous.

"I thought you were dead! Dead! Do you hear me! They were laughing at me! All of them! I was alone. *Again!*"

Angelina's eyes burned with tears of anger and distress. She tried to contain them, but a tear escaped.

"I am sorry, I didn't..."

Francesca reached to comfort her, but Angelina blocked the compassionate gesture.

"You passed out! That's all. Passed out! What the hell was I supposed to do?" Angelina dried her tears with a handkerchief. "You were in no condition to help decide!"

The admonishment made Francesca lower her chin.

"I know we are trapped." Angelina continued to rant. "At least they are not batting us about like a cat with its catch!"

Angelina, needing air, stepped to the window. The cabin walls loomed as if the room was shrinking. Her soft gloves felt constricting, and her scarf threatened to strangle her. Soon, they would not need to worry about the assailants outside the cabin because the walls would squish them.

Tugging at her scarf, her face went pale when the thud of heavy footsteps and the loud voice drew closer. Wide-eyed, Angelina looked at Francesca for confirmation of what she was hearing. Francesca nodded. It was Bruno's feet and Antonio bickering.

"Quick, put your bag out of sight!" Angelina pointed to the interior wall. "Try to stay in the shadow so they can't see you."

The rough grumble of the assassin's voices stopped as they peered into each unlit, empty cabin.

"Anything?" Antonio asked Bruno.

"No. You?"

"Keep looking. They gotta be in one of them."

Angelina's heart raced. She wondered if she could hit them over the head and escape while they regained their balance.

"Damn it!" Antonio looked into their cabin. "Where the fuck did he put them?" He slammed his hand against the door to their hiding place.

"Not in this one." Bruno grunted.

"Come on, maybe they are in the next car."

Francesca released an audible sigh. Angelina wagged her finger. She wasn't convinced they were in the clear. They needed to wait several minutes before opening the door.

The train pitched sharply to the side, then jerked back, unsettling the passengers and their baggage. The movement tossed Francesca into the middle of the cabin floor. Angelina's body slammed against the wall with a loud thud.

"Bruno!" Antonio shouted. "Get 'em!"

Angelina jumped down to protect Francesca from the oncoming attack. Neither could breathe. Curled in a ball, their bodies trembled. Several thumps echoed into their space. Bracing for the attack, the women huddled together. After five or six blows, their cabin door did not open. Francesca's confused expression reinforced Angelina's thought they were not seen.

Angelina motioned for Francesca to slip out of sight while she placed her ear on the wall. Muffled by the roar of the wind racing past and the chug-chug of the train, Angelina could barely make out what was said between the rhythmic thump.

"God damn it!"

Thump.

"Bruno!"

Thump.

"Get!"

Thump.

"Fuck!"

Thump.

"Off Me!"

Angelina knew Francesca heard the same thing when they both giggled in unison.

"You fucking ox! Wake the fuck up!" Antonio shouted.

"I say, what the devil is going on out here?" A man's high-pitched voice demanded.

"Mind your business, Ol' man!"

"I shall not! Is this man injured?"

"No! We like to snuggle in the hallway together!" Antonio barked.

"No need to be snarky, ol' chap!"

Grunts from Antonio and the stranger were followed by a loud thump from Bruno colliding with the floor. It was tempting to peek out the window and watch the hilarious satire. But Bruno's moan as he returned to consciousness chased away Angelina's curiosity. She would have to imagine Bruno, with as much grace as a frightened elephant in a small compartment, fumbling back to a fully upright position.

"Well done, ol'chap! You might get that lump checked. Looks a bit wonky."

Bruno growled.

"Right-o, Right-o. I shall be off then. A fella knows where he is not welcomed."

Bruno's elbow rammed into the wall that Angelina was leaning against. A bulge of splintered wood protruded into their cabin, allowing small rays of light to shine on her skirt. Her heart leaped back into her throat.

"You're a fucking idiot!" Antonio bitched. "Don't those giant feet do anything but take up space? Ya think a guy your size could keep on his fucking feet."

Angelina was afraid to breathe. She remained frozen, staring at the tiny spots of light on her skirt until Antonio's griping faded into the distance. When his voice was no longer audible, Angelina sighed.

"That was close!" Francesca whispered.

Angelina nodded.

The close call lasted long enough for the topography outside the window to change. The white winter ground had transformed back into the dull shade of the evergreen trees. The slope of the land was less steep, and the tree trunks were now visible statues holding their branches high above the ground.

"We have to leave this cabin before we reach the station!"

Francesca grabbed her bag, huddling behind Angelina as she looked down the hallway.

"It's clear, come on."

Swallowing the lump in her throat, Angelina slowly opened the cabin door. Hunched over, they moved quickly and quietly toward the next car, looking over their shoulders frequently.

Angelina's toes pressed the inside of her shoes as the train barreled down the mountainside. She did not care for fancy shoes. At that moment, she wished she would have worn her work boots. Maybe in them, her toes would not feel like squished grapes.

When they reached the end of the aisle, Francesca asked. "Why are we walking hunched over?"

The comment was enough to break the tension. Angelina could only imagine what other passengers would think of two women sneaking around the train. Their attire was neither fancy nor high quality, adding to their appearance of poverty. A stranger could easily assume they had stolen something. They straightened their backs and their skirts. For a dash of sophistication, they lifted their chins.

Peeking through the window to the next car was not a show of self-confidence. Even though they were moving in the opposite direction as Bruno and Antonio, Angelina was still afraid of running into the conductor.

Angelina looked through the window into the next car. Her shoulders relaxed when she saw their path was clear.

As she turned the handle, Francesca's hand clamped tight on Angelina's shoulder. Angelina heard Bruno's voice before she could tell her companion to release the death grip. Panic filled her body, and she flung the door open only to find the conductor walking towards them.

"Now what?" Francesca asked.

Angelina wanted to snap at her friend for always asking the same damn question in a moment of intense trouble. But this was not the time to squabble over nonsense.

"We can take the conductor." Angelina tried to sound confident, but her voice wavered.

Francesca's eyebrow arched in disagreement.

"What?" Angelina argued. "We have a better chance against one than two. Besides, we know what they want!"

"Yes, but he is bigger than two!"

"I would rather take my chances with him!" Angelina motioned toward the conductor.

Francesca's expression of doubt didn't change until she heard the thump of Bruno's feet. The rapidly closing distance ignited them to press forward toward the conductor, but they had waited too long. Two steps through the threshold of the next car loomed the barrel-chested beast. The look on his face was terrifying. His beady eyes danced under the bill of his official hat, and his face grew redder with each breath. He shifted his body to the side to accommodate his broad shoulders as he passed through the doorway. He was an arm's length away when Angelina realized how large her opponent was, compounding her fear.

The light bounced off something metal, catching her attention. Gripped in the conductor's massive hand was a long wrench. Instinct caused the women to run, but they didn't get far.

"Well, I knew we would meet again." Antonio flashed his wicked smile. He placed his hands on her shoulders, gripping them tightly.

"Bruno, what do ya say we ensure our lovely ladies don't escape us again."

The sound of the whistle and the screech of the metal wheels grinding against the tracks muted his next words. Like a domino reaction, the locks of the private doors responded to the sound of the next stop. It was enough of a distraction for Angelina to pull away. A door swung open behind her, creating a minor wall between her and the conductor. A young man glanced at Angelina before turning to find the help he needed.

"Oh! Thank God you are here!" the young man cried as he stepped out of his cabin. His face was pale, and his speech frantic. "My wife! She needs a doctor! The baby..."

The conductor looked at Angelina, then the man. The choice added to his frustration. His badge vibrated from the rumble of an inaudible growl. She held her breath, waiting, hoping he would choose the woman in labor over her.

"Please hurry!" The frantic father pleaded.

The dart of the conductor's eyes posed the question of *life or death?* Angelina pleaded with his mind, *please choose life!*

He raised his bushy eyebrow, and his jaw worked at the answer. The conductor's barrel chest rose and fell twice more before committing to his decision. Slowly, he picked up one giant foot, then the other, as he advanced toward his target. Angelina released the stranglehold on her lungs when the conductor entered the private cabin to assist the man's wife.

She heard Francesca gasp, then a loud thud. It took her a moment to grasp the reality of what was happening. She understood when Bruno dropped to the floor next to Antonio's limp form. Transfixed on who stood behind Francesca, Angelina could not move. The familiar smile wasn't an apparition; it was real!

"Come on!"

Francesca hesitated.

"It's safe, come on!" Angelina reassured her friend as she grabbed her wrist.

Exiting the railcar, they heard a scream echo down the corridor.

"I guess they found your friends." Her angel teased.

"In case you couldn't tell, they were *not* our friends!" Angelina quipped.

"Lose your bags or grip them tightly. We need to put some distance between us if we are going to lose them. Be ready to run when I tell you."

Francesca, stunned, clinched her satchel. Angelina thought about tossing hers. She hesitated, then remembered her papers and all the money she possessed was inside it.

A few passengers stood to exit the train, making the path congested. But a few sweet apologies cleared the aisle. Looking over the edge of the car, the wind whipped their hair, threatening to steal Angelina's and Francesca's hats.

"Get ready."

"Are you sure about this?" Angelina asked

The smile from her angel was enough to reassure her.

"Now!"

The train barely jerked to a stop when they jumped onto the platform. Francesca landed and cried out in pain. She had stumbled on her heels, nearly turning her ankle. Frustrated, she slipped her shoes off and sprinted to catch up.

Quickly, the three wove in and out of the sea of passengers milling about, waiting to board the train. Young lovers embraced for one more kiss, and mothers wept into their handkerchiefs as their sons anxiously climbed aboard.

The never-ending maze of people flowed into Turin's crowded streets as they dashed down alleys and raced through shopping districts. Though tempted, Angelina resisted the urge to glance over her shoulder to see if they had lost their enemies.

"Wait!" Francesca gasped. "Stop! Damn it! Stop!"

Angelina turned to find her friend supporting her winded body against the golden stone wall. Francesca's silk stockings were shredded, and her feet bloodied from the continuous pounding against the rough cobblestone streets.

"Are you okay?"

"No! We have been running forever."

"We need to run and not stop until we are safe!" Angelina demanded, barely winded.

"Why aren't you out of breath?" Francesca asked.

"Your feet are bleeding," Angelina said, ignoring the question. "We need to get some bandages and get out of sight before they find us."

"*They* did not see us." Francesca gasped for air.

"Are you sure?"

"Si!"

"They slipped onto the train *without* being noticed."

"Because you are terrible at sneaking around!"

"Me? They followed *you* on the train!"

Francesca, lungs less deprived, stood to defend her point.

"I have been running from them for a long time. Besides, I know because I have been looking over my shoulder while the two of you ran like maniacs."

With a Cheshire grin, Angelina's angel leaned on the wall.

"You enjoying yourself?" Angelina asked.

"I am always up for a good catfight!"

"Ha!" Francesca huffed. "Do you know where we are?"

Angelina opened her mouth to answer, but Francesca held a hand up in her direction.

"You don't! I know you don't because we are headed toward the train station. Is that what your friend here has in mind? Run fast only to end up where we started!"

"I..." Angelina stammered

"Do you have a plan? Are looks the only thing you are good at? Wait. I know! You are good at being stupid, too?"

His short, dark hair glistened in the sunlight. Sweat trailed down his temples as he rested against the caramel stone wall. Folding his long arms across his muscular chest, he smiled.

"I thought not!" Francesca looked at Angelina. "Tell me who this directionally challenged idiot is, and I will take us to a place where we can sleep tonight."

Angelina's explanation was interrupted by the thundering sound of Bruno's giant feet.

"There they are!" Antonio shouted from the alley.

Antonio's lean, muscular form was unaffected by the short jaunt. Bruno barreled forward with the grace of a bull. His lungs, heaving, attempted to keep up with his exertion.

"Move your fat ass!"

"Now, who is the idiot?" the young man asked. "Come on!" He headed down another alley.

"This way!"

Francesca grabbed his arm and led them into a courtyard just off the alley. A woman tending her laundry looked up in shock, but they were gone before she could scold them.

Winding around small buildings that contained homes and quaint shops, Francesca lost the two brutes that followed them. Through alleys and over bridges, her quick dashes in and out of homes left her companions confused. A small price to pay to no longer be followed.

The narrow alley opened into a wide cobbled avenue flanked by a variety of multistory buildings. At a brisk pace, Francesca walked down the street. Her hand lightly touched the fountains made of green, cast-iron bulls affixed to a stone slab. She stopped at the third fountain and counted four stones to her left, three down, and two diagonally to the right. She removed a brick and squeezed her hand into the hole. She retrieved a small object and slipped it into her pocket.

At a slightly slower pace, Francesca continued to walk in silence. Frequently, she looked over her shoulder. Her hand continued to land on the stone fountains as they passed rows of buildings and smaller alleyways. She stopped, patted the bull's head on the fountain, and fixed her gaze on something in the distance. Stepping back, she counted the windows of the building opposite her.

"There!" she pointed to a window on the third floor.

White curtains billowed in the breeze of the open window. It was peaceful and inviting, like a dance of angel's wings, luring them to safety. The flick of fabric in the wind, beautiful architecture, water cascading in a fountain, and the smell of fresh bread teased Angelina's senses. It was difficult to resist the temptation of letting down her guard to enjoy the world around her.

Francesca scurried down a side alley to a red door. While Angelina continued to be entranced by the wispy movement of the white fabric. The entire space seemed peaceful. Even the people who frequented the streets appeared to be without worry. It was a feeling much like she had when she stood amongst the vines back home.

Pulling herself from the dreamlike state, Angelina looked up and down the street for the men who hunted them. Families wandered hand in hand, exuding love and happiness. Two men about the same height walked in unison. The one on the left's arms moved with the vigor of a symphonic conductor as he led the conversation. His companion had his hands stuffed in his pockets, nodding his head as he listened. Bicycles careened their way through the sparse crowd. In the distance, she heard the chime of a chapel bell tolling the hour.

Francesca prodded her to keep moving. "Let's go!"

With each step toward the top, Angelina felt the impact of her trek. Her feet were sore, her back ached from running in inappropriate shoes, and her head was pounding. To add to her list of ailments, she was thirsty and would not turn down food. Francesca walked to a door at the top of the stairwell and inserted the key from her pocket.

"Come on!" Francesca mumbled, trying to turn the key.

"Let me." The young man said. "Some of these old locks require a little finesse."

Francesca's face scrunched. She wanted to make a snide comment but stopped when she made eye contact with him.

Angelina looked on in compassion. Francesca found it exceedingly difficult to trust men, especially since the two thugs chasing them killed her husband. Alberto possessed all the qualities she ever desired in a man, loving, gentle, and giving. Even though Alberto's jokes were a little dry, he made Francesca laugh every day. Now, his beautiful light was gone. She only hoped her son, Alberto Jr., would be like his father.

Effortlessly, the lock clicked. The young man grinned and opened the door. Inside was a small living room, sparsely decorated with simple furnishings and two small paintings on the wall. The white curtain in the open window whipped in the wind. A thick layer of dust covered the small table near the end of the sofa. Angelina pulled her finger across the top, leaving a squiggly pattern. Despite its unique charm, the apartment seemed to be abandoned.

Francesca rummaged through the cabinets of the small kitchen in search of food. Angelina doubted she would find anything a rat had not already dined on.

"Bona fortuna! Wine and bread!" Francesca smiled in victory. "I knew you wouldn't let me down, Erica."

"Who is Erica?" Angelina asked.

"Oh, no! You tell me who *he* is first!"

Angelina's eyes danced. She wrapped her arm in his and smiled. "Then you better open that wine."

CHAPTER 16

The flight to New York was bumpy. Although it was an uncomfortable ordeal, Maximus enjoyed watching Freddy being unnerved by the plane's constant rattle and stomach-lurching drops in altitude. The pleasant distraction ceased shortly after the plane landed. His feet firmly on the ground, Freddy's stalwart personality returned and Maximus's jovial spirit faded back to his natural pensive nature.

On the tarmac, a beautiful burgundy Cadillac Fleetwood limousine awaited them. Both men silently admired the car's elegant curves and the plush beige interior as they strolled down opposite sides of the vehicle.

A small, round, wooden table in the middle of the floor hailed from the plush carpet like a solitary statue. Six sharp-cut crystal glasses circled the outer edge. In the center was a silver ice bucket and a decanter of dark fluid.

Maximus could tell it was a temptation for Freddy. If he was honest with himself, he could use a drink, too. He was impressed with Freddy's adherence to their culture's code. Being mindful of his rank, Freddy would not partake in a drink alone or without Maximus's order.

"We both deserve a drink after that flight," Maximus said.

Freddy filled the first glass with four cubes and a long pour. Maximus accepted the drink and waited for Freddy to repeat the task.

"Salute!"

The glasses met, emitting the ringing sound of an ethereal angel's song. Freddy raised an eyebrow in appreciation.

"Nice."

After the traditional formalities were honored, Maximus leaned back into his seat. Freddy followed suit. The tick-tick-tick of Maximus's watch took command of the silence. The sound dripped against Maximus's ears like a leaky faucet. It was a reminder that his time was limited.

The ice danced gently as Maximus swirled the deep caramel-colored liquor. Watching the darker shades engulf the lighter in a never-ending war was spellbinding. His mind connected the nature of the bourbon to that of humankind. The evils of a man devouring the souls of the innocent without conscious thought. The blackest soul lapping up the purity with the bliss of a cat dining on warm milk.

Maximus had witnessed this brutality in his life, by others' orders, and by his own cruel retaliation. The guilt an ordinary man would feel after effortlessly dispatching a life only plagued his gut the first time his fist collided with flesh.

When his blow landed on his prey, guilt flashed through his core. But the remorse quickly converted to a deep hunger for more. The sting of guilt came and went from the second his fist collided with his opponent to the moment his arm drew back, elbow bent, cocked for another blow. The next second, a reverberation from the succeeding impact of two solid objects waved up from Maximus's clenched hand through his arm. From there, all his mind wanted was more speed, more force, more blood spewing from his target. The feel of a man's jaw shattering from the power of his fist and teeth launching into the air in a trail of blood-stained spit was exhilarating.

Maximus enjoyed destroying what he loathed. He liked, perhaps even loved it. The nimble feet of guilt tap-dancing with glee merely added to the charm of the moment. For him, it was not interminable guilt; it was pure joy. An unrivaled pleasure that quenched his raging thirst for revenge and justice against another darker, blacker evil. In Maximus's mind, he was not the devil in the dance of destruction. He was the angel of mercy, acting for the benefit of the innocent.

Don Salvatore did more than bludgeon the face of a man. His attack extinguished a man's legacy. He plucked the fruit and pulled the vine, root and all, from the soil, exposing the tender parts before hacking it into nothingness. It was the act of a meticulously malevolent being that possessed no humanity, not even in the atoms of his cells. Such a baneful existence stirred a chill that rippled across Maximus's spine.

The car cruised past the buildings that lined the street like a maze of dominoes. Maximus's gaze followed the ever-changing landscape, but he did not see the images before him, only the ones his mind played with a maddening repetition. The handsome faces of Rosario's sons glared like the blinding summer sun. Knowing that he would never shake their hands, kindle a brotherly bond, or express his admiration for their father pained him.

The booze in Maximus's empty stomach turned to bile at the thought of Rosario. Maximus *had* plans of his own, but Don Salvatore's actions forced him to make new ones. Maximus felt the thirst of the devil's dance grow. He would serve justice for Rosario, as well as for his own interests.

He remained immersed in his thoughts until the car stopped at the hotel entrance. They would make themselves comfortable here while waiting for Peter to join them.

Maximus pulled up the collar of his coat before he stepped out of the car. The deafening noise of the city assailed his ears while his eyes registered every detail of his surroundings.

The wind whipped down the sidewalk, ushering in the news of the impending snowstorm with damp, cold daggers across his cheeks. It was Mother Nature's brisk slap. A warning that seasons, like time, halted for no one.

The constant reminders that he lacked control over every step of the mission grated on Maximus's nerves. He was forced to engage by Don Salvatore's actions. He was forced to rely on Peter's help. He was forced to rush halfway around the world to protect the lives of people he had never met. He was forced to race against the harsh temper of the weather. These uncontrollable aspects hurled him into chaos, and chaos beckoned errors. The culmination of pressure felt like the threat of a giant crushing his neck under its massive shoe.

He nodded to the doorman whose red wool coat, lined with brass buttons and gold brocade, hung in perfect form to the man's torso. His black trousers, pressed with a heavy starch, fell to a precise length, covering the laces of his shiny black shoes. The doorman's ashen face held an expressionless gaze, frozen by the many years of exposure to the extreme cold. The man was fit for royal duty except for the wayward crease leaning toward his left leg's outer thigh.

"Good Afternoon, Sir," The doorman stated in a naturally deep, smooth tone. "Welcome to the Belmont."

In the window's reflection, Maximus observed Freddy and the bellboy. The boy's red woolen coat lacked the gold brocade. His trousers were scuffed with patches of grey dust from his legs brushing the car's bumper as he removed the heavy luggage. Unlike his elder compadre, the boy allowed his lips to curl into a charming smile, and his rosy-cheeked head bobbed up and down as he listened to Freddy's instructions.

Maximus took in the ornate woodwork that stretched into an arching bend in the domed ceiling of the lobby. The golden-yellow plaster walls enhanced the rich mocha color of the wood. Long, red carpet edged with gold trim stretched across meandering veins of the black-and-white marble floor. Like a runway, patrons subconsciously followed the lines as they walked across the rugs. They only turned when another carmine trail jetted out in a new direction.

"Get us a couple rooms." Maximus nodded to Freddy.

Maximus continued to observe his surroundings while Freddy sauntered toward the front desk. Maximus admired the unique décor. It was not to his liking, but it was placed with precision. Everyone had their preferred style, which he respected as long as it held order.

In a high-back chair, a man reading the Washington Post casually sipped from a gold-edged cup. Another man dressed in a striking dark suit paced in the space separating the two square living rooms of furniture. He stopped to look at his pocket watch at the end of each run, then resumed his march.

A petite woman in a form-fitting yellow dress attempted to catch Maximus's eye by deliberately walking close to him. Her long golden-brown hair fell in delicate ringlets across her shoulders, the tips of the curls framing her cleavage. The gentle sway of her hips and long legs added to her beauty. She was, exteriorly, desirable. Most men would easily bend to such a catch, only seeing her outer shell. He, however, saw the makings of a mantrap. Maximus did not make eye contact with her, nor did he smile and tip his hat. As she passed by, out of what she assumed was Maximus's field of vision, she cast a disgusted look toward him and muttered her distaste. Her reaction confirmed his suspicion of her repulsive character.

Her disappointment faded quickly when the man who arrived after Maximus tipped his hat and smiled. She gave a coy giggle in reply. Maximus did not need to turn around to witness the exchange. It was typical for both sexes.

The woman batted her thick eyelashes and gave the man an enchanting smile. It was her nonverbal attempt to lure him into her web, to which the man, with his own dubious plan, would willingly be caught. The man was a fool, for he had not seen the woman walk past two other men who did not exude a level of suitable wealth. Both men smiled, tipped their hats, and offered her a cheerful greeting, to which she gave a look of disdain. Seconds later, she attempted to lure Maximus. Upon his lack of interest, she preyed upon the next well-dressed man like a lioness on the prowl.

"Men chase skirts. Women chase wallets." Maximus mumbled.

"Ehh...Not all," Freddy said. "We are on the twenty-second floor. Made sure our rooms were door to door."

Maximus nodded his head in approval.

They made their way to the elevator, where the young bellhop waited as patiently as a teenage boy could. Maximus identified with the young man. He felt the uncontrollable bounce of each task waiting to be executed.

He watched the bell boy's leg twitch impatiently and wondered what future activity made him wiggle and fidget. He couldn't be much over fifteen. A smile pressed into Maximus's mind; that was when most boys experienced the pleasures of a woman's body.

Maximus had his first experience earlier than most with a young woman six years his senior. He lied about his age, which was easy to believe. He was always mature in manners and in his looks. At fourteen, he shaved daily. Around sixteen, his dark shadow re-emerged by midday, forcing him to shave a second time or give in to the persistent growth.

She was beautiful, with soft skin, hazel eyes, and a full budding figure. Her firm breasts, long legs, and the gentle curve that flowed from the small of her back over her tight ass drove Maximus swiftly to the finish line. He wondered if she noticed how rapidly she made him cum, or if his instant recovery held her attention. To her, he was an experienced young man in his twenties, not a fourteen-year-old boy relishing the pleasures of sex for the first time.

The young man opened the door of the first room. He placed a bag of luggage on the bed and pulled the curtains before removing Maximus's coat. He repeated the tasks for Freddy in the room directly across the hall.

"You need anything, Boss?" Freddy asked when he returned to Maximus's room.

Maximus stared out the window with his back to Freddy. His silence was the answer. Freddy handed the young man a twenty.

"Thank you, Sir... Sirs!"

"Would you like to earn another twenty?" Maximus asked, his gaze still fixed on the view from the window.

"Yes, Sir!"

Turning around to address the young man, Maximus paused long enough for his glare to make the boy squirm.

"What is your name?"

"Joey. Well, it's Joseph, but you can call me Joey. That's what my friends call me."

"Does the hotel have a restaurant, Joseph?" Maximus asked.

The young man flinched at Maximus's use of his proper name. Steadying himself, Joseph rubbed his hands together for a moment before replying, but his voice squeaked. Maximus waited quietly for the boy to recover and try again.

"Yes, Sir. We have room service, too," Joseph replied with less of a squeak.

"We need reservations for this evening. Would you arrange that for me?"

"The front desk can connect you." Joseph began but promptly stopped under Freddy's disapproving glare. "But... Um... it would be a pleasure to take care of that for you, Sir."

Maximus let Joseph fidget before giving an appreciative smile to relax the boy's apprehension.

"Seven p.m.," Maximus said, giving Freddy a curt nod. "A table for three."

Peeling another twenty off the thick bale of cash, Freddy added, "Make sure our table is secluded. We like to eat, *undisturbed*."

Staring at Freddy's wad of cash, his eyes wide in anticipation, Joseph nodded.

"Thank you, Joseph," Maximus said with a brisk finality.

Smiling brightly, Joseph pocketed his tip and scurried away like a mouse stealing the cheese.

Maximus sat in the wingback chair, returning to his pensive gaze out the window while Freddy took up the seat across from him. Freddy tried to make his enormous frame comfortable, but the fancy curves and narrow opening cut into his sides. After his fifth attempt to squeeze into the chair, he moved to the sofa, casting a snarly glare at his wooden nemesis. Instantly, his body relaxed in the openness, and he released a soft sigh.

Maximus nodded at the square-edged bottle on the oval table between them. Freddy didn't hesitate to repeat the task he happily and frequently engaged in.

"You want me to call for some ice?"

Maximus shook his head, still not making eye contact. They repeated the ritual as they had done in the car, but the glasses only clanked this time.

"Guess we all can't be perfect!" Freddy said as he examined the cheaply made glass. "Blah! This ain't kerosene. But it ain't fine scotch either."

Maximus smiled, slammed his drink, then handed his glass back to Freddy to refill. Freddy poured them each another drink. This time, Freddy did not relax back. Instead, he patiently sat, hunched forward with his elbows on his knees while rolling the glass between his palms.

Maximus felt Freddy's blank stare on his cheek, like the sun peering through the window. It was not an act of questioning but a way of showing he was ready for whatever next might be.

"Have you recovered from the flight?" Maximus asked.

"Freddy gave Maximus a blank stare.

"Sure."

"Good. We will be on another plane tomorrow."

Freddy's glare intensified, and his face hardened with a distaste for the idea. He slammed the remaining whiskey and winced while he evaluated the glass in his hand before responding.

"Whatever you want, Boss."

Maximus tried to savor his drink. After the fine bourbon, the cheap whiskey went down hard, leaving a harsh aftermath. He stood to look out the window. A different view usually shifted Maximus's perspective on a subject. Perhaps the view would change the liquor's bite.

The room, high above the street, gave them a broad view of the busy activity below. In the dwindling daylight, men and women hustled down the sidewalk. In their frenzied progress, the pathetic tiny figures looked like fire ants hurrying for shelter from the impending storm.

"I couldn't live like this," Maximus mumbled.

Freddy stood, topped off Maximus's drink, and joined him in his inspection of hell.

"Like what?"

"Look at them. They move frantically, all of them." Maximus took a nip of the bitter liquor. "So many people. Too damn many."

"Don't go to Chicago. The noise alone will grate your nerves," Freddy said. "But Kansas City isn't exactly quiet, either."

"Oh, my friend, it is not as bad as this."

Maximus fell quiet again, and Freddy followed suit. The only sound was the muffled noise of the city below and the persistent tick-tick-tick of his watch.

The sun started its closing dance of radiance on the horizon, casting brilliant purples and reds across the sky. The glorious view resembled the one from his quiet office back home and settled his irritated nerves.

"You haven't asked why?" Maximus stated, breaking the silence.

"Don't need to. You sent for me; that told me all I needed to know."

"Few have your loyalty."

"I know. Like I said earlier, not everyone can be perfect."

Maximus chuckled, "They definitely broke the mold after you."

The blazing sunset that held their eyes captive hindered their vision even after they settled back into their chairs.

"You want another douse of kerosene?" Freddy asked.

Maximus waved away the offer.

"What did you think of Peter the first time you met him?"

"Seemed like a stand-up guy."

Matching the beat of his watch, Maximus tapped his gold pinky ring against his glass.

"Not sure he shares your level of loyalty."

"He has never let you down before. No need to think differently now."

Maximus slammed his whiskey and clenched his jaw.

"People change. Our last interaction was pretty heated."

"So, you sayin' in my absence, you pissed on a few lifelines? I knew you'd miss me."

"Yes, you were missed, Freddy. But this issue started brewing many years ago. Unfortunately, it fractured more than my affiliation with him."

"Everyone has a hot button: one to piss 'em off and one to bait 'em. Pete's gotta have something you can offer. If you need him as much as you think."

Maximus released a slow, pensive sigh and shrugged.

Freddy leaned back in his chair, put his feet on the coffee table, and flashed a devilish grin.

"Don't worry, Boss. If he doesn't give up what ya need, I'll use one of my effective negotiating techniques. Doubt I'll need to. If there is anybody who knows when to sacrifice a pawn or a horse to win, it's you!"

"This time, I may have to sacrifice something far more valuable."

"Must be one hell of a plane, Boss."

"Regrettably, we need more than a plane."

Over the next hour, Maximus told Freddy the details, even the promise he broke to Rosario. Such admission would be a sign of weakness to anyone else, but to Freddy, it merely added to Maximus's humaneness. They discussed every aspect of the mission. As usual, and further proof of why Maximus hired him, Freddy added additional strategies to refine the plan and formulate an alternate.

"When do we leave?"

"That will depend on whether Peter will agree."

"Will he supply what we need?"

"For now, only the plane. I prefer you to handle the more *sensitive* items." Maximus glanced at his watch before moving back to the window. His mind divided into two trails of thought, one ever mindful of Freddy awaiting his dismissal, the other down the well-worn path of his memory.

"We have an hour before we meet Peter."

"I will be ready, Boss."

Maximus absently raised his hand in dismissal, then softly returned it to his pocket. He had sixty minutes to decide whether to sacrifice a prized mare for what he needed. Everything had a price, but not everything was worth the cost.

CHAPTER 17

A plume of dust erupted from the table when Francesca plopped down two bottles of wine. In jest, she rubbed her chin while scrutinizing the labels.

"Well, we have options. Red or Red?"

Francesca wrinkled her nose and looked at both labels again. With a shrug, she grabbed one bottle and tried to open it, but her trembling hands could not manage the corkscrew.

"Need some help?" Angelina snickered. "I can show you."

Francesca folded her arms. "Just open the damn thing!"

"Does your friend have any glasses, or shall we play pass the bottle?"

Francesca rolled her eyes and growled under her breath, but Angelina did not hear it. The feel of the glass bottle in her hand summoned her full attention.

Angelina's mind slipped into the past as her long, thin fingers wrapped around the neck of the bottle. Gripping it tightly with her left hand, her right turned time back with each evolution of the corkscrew. Her nose drew in the musty scent conjured by her memory, and her senses happily drifted back to the cold, damp stone cellar at Beretta Vineyards. Like the last rays of the sunset, the present moment slipped away. In seconds, she was back home.

On each cellar wall, a pillar candle emitted a yellow glow that danced around the small space with the grace of angels performing an unwitnessed ballet. Her father stood at the round table, preparing the wine bottle to serve his customers.

As a little girl, Angelina would secretly follow her father as he led the customers around the vineyard. From time to time, Rosario would notice her trying to be his invisible shadow. He told her he did not mind her watching, but she needed to make sure her presence did not distract the customers.

At the end of each tour, Rosario led the clients to the cellar to taste the wine. This part was her favorite, and she never missed it. Cautiously, Angelina pressed her body against the cold stone wall that curved down to the cavernous room. She was five steps from the bottom, far enough away to remain unseen but close enough to watch her father. She memorized every action, every word, and every gesture. Her deepest desire was to perform the ritual under his approving eyes.

"Papa, when can I open the wine for the customers?"

"Principessa, do not rush your childhood." Rosario cupped her pouting chin, connecting one pair of dark brown eyes with the other. "I know you want to help. One day, you will, but first, you must be taller than a bottle of wine on top of the table."

"Promettere?"

"Si, io prometto."

Always true to his word, Rosario began her training two years later. Angelina's first attempt ended in a broken bottle, for which she profusely apologized to her father.

"Words are not an apology. Actions are!" Furrowing his brow, Rosario crossed his arms. "Try again."

Angelina's hands trembled as she stared at the second bottle. Her family did not have a lot of money, only wine. Every bottle sold provided the means to purchase food for the growing family or a much-needed pair of shoes. The destruction of such a valuable commodity deserved sufficient punishment, and she braced for a beating that never came.

Physical violence was not the way of her father. He believed in empowering the mind. Regardless, Angelina still feared a lashing for her clumsiness, a fear cultivated by the nuns' reprimands at her school.

Her second attempt did not break the bottle, but it spoiled the wine. She did not tap the screw correctly, causing the cork to crumble. Not wanting to see the disappointment in his eyes, she hesitated to look at him.

"Bella!" He stepped within arm's length of her. Angelina! Look at me."

She sniffed back the trail of snot running to the end of her nose, then wiped away the tears before looking up.

"Your tears are for what?"

"I am sorry, Papa."

"Sorry? Do your tears mend the cork?" He nodded toward the useless bottle of wine.

She shook her head.

"Then why cry? It mends nothing. Tears change nothing. So why do you cry and waste your energy on uselessness?"

The word 'because' lingered on the edge of her tongue. 'Because' was not the reason nor the answer; another lesson taught by her father.

Rosario waited patiently, his dark eyes examining her every move. This form of interrogation seemed cruel, but later, she learned it was not a harsh form of scrutiny. Her father possessed an infinite amount of patience. His silence was not to unnerve her. It was to provide her mind with an open path to expand and discover the trueness of self.

"I do not want to disappoint you, Papa, and..." She sniffled again. "And I made us lose money."

His deep, hearty chuckle echoed in the small chamber.

"Ah, my little angel. You do not disappoint me. You fear for nothing."

Rosario wrapped his arms around her, holding her close to his chest for a moment. Stepping back from her, Rosario placed his hands on her shoulders.

"Look in my eyes. If you ever think you should fear me or that you will disappoint me, remember one thing." He hailed his pointer finger, wagging it back and forth. "For this one thing shall release you from the shackles created by your mind. I shall never set you up for failure. Never! It is my job to teach you. In fact, I have so much that God has given me to share that I will live as long as Moses!"

Laughing at his own joke, Rosario gave her another hug.

Angelina engraved the warm embrace into her memory, the smell of his shirt, the strength of his arms, and the calm, lubb-dub, lubb-dub of his heart. In times of despair, Angelina slipped back to this moment, this mental sanctuary, to restore her inner peace.

"Thank you, Papa," She hugged him tightly. "I love you."

"I love you too, Principessa."

When he stepped away from her, she felt the sadness of a child being pulled from her mother's womb. The stillness of the peaceful utopia slipped away as effortlessly as a droplet of water rolling off a grape leaf. The trail of existence was left, yet the fullness of its presence was gone.

She kept her eyes closed, wishing for that warmth to return, but it did not. When she opened her eyes, Rosario plucked an object from the rack and threw it. A bottle crashed against the wall, splattering into a mess of glass and wine. Angelina's jaw dropped. She could not believe he had thrown an expensive bottle of wine, destroying it and the monetary reward it would provide. Rosario smiled with the fervor of a young man about to win the race against a lifelong adversary.

Rosario kneeled down to meet Angelina at eye level.

"That wine was not wasted. It taught you something, and to learn is never a waste."

"But the money, Papa! Mamma is pregnant. We cannot afford to lose the money."

"You are thinking with the mind of someone who lives in lack. God created so many resources for us. How can we box our minds in with walls? Things are replaceable. Money comes and goes." He brushed a wayward strand of hair from her cheek. "If you think you will not have enough, then you will not." Rosario gently ushered her back to the tasting table. "Now, let's try again."

On her third try, her trembling hands performed the task correctly.

"Bravissima, Principessa! I knew you could do it!"

Opening wine bottles became a game to her. She honed her skill at every dinner so that when the day came to entertain the customers, she could perform the ritual precisely like her father. She was sixteen when she started being a part of selling wine. By seventeen, she engaged the customers while her father walked along, adding bits of information Angelina omitted. Now, she talked with the customers while her father happily became her shadow.

Her mind lost in the past, Angelina poured enough wine into her glass to twirl. As she lifted it to view the colors, her impatient friend snatched the bottle.

"Yes, I would love a full glass." Francesca tapped her foot.

The abrupt motion yanked Angelina from her blissful daydream. Before she could reply, Francesca grumbled.

"It's open, stop your...whatever," Francesca said, shooing away the unwanted commotion. "Tell me who he is, or should I just let him explain while you play vintner?"

"Sorry, it's a habit," Daized Angelina shook her head, reeling her mind back from the distant past.

"Well, enough...habiting and more jabbering!" Francesca snapped, waving away the nuisance.

Angelina sent a loving hug through her soft hand as she embraced the rough callouses of his. It felt like a decade had passed since their last time together. But that longing stemmed from the stress caused by recent events and her heart missing home. In the fading light, she noticed a few new strands of grey. He had earned them, and she was surely cultivating her own.

"Francesca," Her voice faltered for a moment. She cleared her throat and tried again. "This is my brother."

An avalanche of shock tumbled down her friend's face, and her hand grasped her heart.

"What? They were— "

"Murdered? Yes. Well, I thought as much." Angelina took a sip of wine. "When Giorgio held a knife to Mamma's throat..."

The strong clamp of tension in her brother's hand halted Angelina's explanation.

"I thought Marcus was..." Holding the wine glass, her hand trembled violently. Her other hand tried to steady the glass but failed."How did...I don't...?"

Angelina's eyebrow raised as she scrutinized Francesca.

A pink blush fused into Francesca's formerly pale cheeks, and her eyes darted back and forth. Lacking the ability to complete a sentence, Francesca closed her mouth except to frequently take gulps from her glass.

Angelina logged the oddity of her friend's behavior but did not linger on it. Her brother's distress was far more critical than the antics of a disconcerted woman.

Marcus's powerful grip threatened to crush the glass. A rush of red flushed his face, and his boiling blood pulsed through the throbbing veins of his temples.

Angelina gripped his arm, sending a flood of compassion from her wounded heart to his. She apologized, but he halted her with a wave of his hand.

Marcus sipped his wine before asking, "And this is?"

"My friend, Francesca."

The newly met strangers awkwardly stretched out their hands, missing the other's attempt by seconds. To end the uncomfortable exchange, Marcus nodded his head politely.

"It is nice to meet you...Miss Francesca?"

Francesca's cheeks warmed from pink to red, and flashed a timid smile. "Yes, it is. I mean...um...nice to meet *you*."

Flustered, Francesca stared into her glass, only looking up when she needed to replenish her wine.

The mutual affection between the two strangers relieved Angelina's tension. Francesca's odd behavior stemmed from a schoolgirl crush, while Marcus's angst stemmed from more than the family tragedy. Francesca's beauty undoubtedly captured the hearts of many men, and he appeared to have been caught in the same alluring net.

More at ease, Angelina added more wine to everyone's glass before sitting down, only to stand up a few minutes later to open the second bottle of wine. The trio had much to discuss, but the only time anyone opened their mouth was to consume their libation.

Angelina was the only one not entirely entranced by her drink. She watched her two companions drift through the voids of their own thoughts, occasionally refreshing their unused tongues. The silent abyss reminded her of when the customers would sample the wine. They thought, and she watched them, looking for anything to strategically help her decide what to say next.

"Get the customer tipsy, and they will tell you what you need to hear," Rosario explained to his daughter. *"Get them drunk, and they will only remember how bad they felt the next day."*

Angelina slowed her drinking to keep her mind sharp. At some point, the giant elephant in the room would have to be addressed. There were many questions to be answered. At the rate they were drinking, she would be the only one lucid enough to talk.

Francesca drained her glass and sighed as she examined her empty wine glass. Disappointed, she looked around the room, her eyes avoiding Marcus.

"We need more wine." Francesca popped out of her chair.

Rummaging through every cabinet, Francesca grumbled. Unsuccessful in the kitchen, she searched the furniture in the living room.

Shaking her head, Angelina asked, "What are you doing?"

"Looking."

"For wine...under the sofa cushions?"

Francesca ignored Angelina and continued her hunt. Concerned with her friend's more than odd behavior, Angelina monitored her more closely.

"Buona Fortuna!" Francesca up two bottles she retrieved from a small wooden cabinet near the balcony. Looking at the labels she mumbled, "Erica, there are other wines than red." Plopping into her chair, she looked at Angelina. "I'm very thirsty, so you probably better open both of them!"

"Are you *trying* to get drunk?"

"Nope." She held her chin up. "I'm gonna *succeed* at it!"

Francesca picked up the second bottle and drained the remaining wine into her glass, allowing the last drops to rejoin their companions. Promptly, in a single swig, she emptied her drink again and slid it across the table.

"More, please!" Francesca requested in a child-like voice.

"It's your head in the morning," Angelina said.

"Yep!" She raised the newly filled glass. "Gratzi!"

Angelina offered Marcus more wine, but he held his hand over his glass. He rubbed the back of his neck, before looking up. His tired eyes spoke of his pain yet begged for forgiveness.

"Where do we begin?"

"Does it matter?" Angelina sunk into her chair.

Marcus shrugged his shoulders.

"Blub-blub...Swirly...Swirly!" Francesca twirled the glass.

He shook his head. "Start with the blonde elephant."

"We met in the convent."

"Convent? You? *Her?*" His eyes widened. "A convent?"

Angelina considered telling Marcus everything, including the pretext of the Salvatore's vendetta. She had not shared that with anyone, and for good reasons. Yet, Angelina hesitated to tell her brother anything because of Marcus's alleged part in the tale.

"She was hurt. The nuns and I helped her heal!" Francesca slurred in a jubilant voice. "We were sisters. Get it, '*sisters.*' Hee-hee! 'Siss-ters'! Lolly-lolly-la!"

"It looks like she succeeded." Chuckling, Angelina shook her head.

"Pretty much!"

"Francesca, perhaps you should lie down."

Francesca's head agreed with a wobbly nod, but her tongue felt differently.

"I fine! Keep talking. We have sooo much to...um!" Francesca peered into her half-empty glass and frowned. "Wine, please! My glass is empty."

"Sis-ter." Angelina mocked. "You still have half a glass."

Francesca slammed the wine in one gulp and smiled.

"Nope! See, it's all gone!"

"You are gonna hate yourself tomorrow."

"Hate is such a strong word! But! I don't have to wait till tomorrow! I already do!" Francesca looked into her empty glass. With a frown, she sighed. "Sad...sad. Empty glass to match my empty soul. I made a mistake. Well, *you* made a mistake." Francesca pointed at Angelina. "I made a mistake, and you made a mistake. But who cares, right? No one is perfect! I am sure not a perfect mother! Why did I leave my baby? I miss him. Do you think he misses me?"

"Francesca, you should lie down for a little while."

Francesca moaned before allowing her body to slump forward. Her head hit the table with a loud thump.

"Not exactly what I meant."

"Ehh! It's not so bad. Well, not until you wake up!"

"You know from experience?"

Marcus grinned and plucked Francesca out of the chair.

"Actually, I am a bit of an expert in the matter!"

Smiling, Angelina watched Marcus delicately maneuver around the furniture with the limp form draped across his arms. It brought back memories of him carrying her to bed when she had fallen asleep on the sofa. Marcus would gently lay Angelina in bed, tuck the blankets around her and kiss her forehead before wishing her sweet dreams.

When he returned, Angelina had a dreamy, far-off look.

"What are you smiling about?"

"Pretty, isn't she?"

"Nice try. Answer my question."

Angelina crossed her arms to affirm her intentions, eliciting a mildly frustrated look from her brother.

"She is a little drunk for my taste." He shrugged.

"Wow, I thought you had a bit of fondness for her. Perhaps I am losing my gift to read people."

"I doubt that, Sis. You are the grand master in that field."

Marcus relaxed in his chair and smiled with admiration.

"How much do you know?"

He leaned against the table for support and stared into nothingness for a minute. Shaking his head, he released a sorrowful sigh.

"I was there."

"Where?"

"The funeral." A tear found its way down his cheek.

"No!" Angelina leaned away. "You couldn't! I would have seen you! Everyone would have seen you!"

Marcus stared at his glass and mumbled. "I am sorry."

"That is impossible!" Angelina stammered, ignoring the apology. "I would have recognized you. You are *my* brother! *I* would have recognized my brother!"

"You were not supposed to see me."

"You hid? Where? In the grapevines? Why?"

"In a manner of speaking, yes, I hid, but not in the vines. As to the *why*? You know it was the way it had to be."

Angelina suppressed the urge to scream at the top of her lungs and frantically whirl her arms, pounding punch after punch on his body. She wanted to leave bruises that healed slowly, like the ones she collected because of his absence.

"None of it would have happened." Trembling with anger, she shook her head. "I suffered because you did not protect me!"

"I am sorry, Lina."

"Sorry, is a word. It does nothing to fix what has happened!" Angelina teetered on losing control. "You have no idea what agony I suffered because you hid like a coward!"

Overwhelmed with emotions, Angelina dropped her head into her hands; she needed to hide from all of it.

The gentle breeze flipping the curtain with intermittent crisp pops filled the uncomfortable silence. Though the air flowed freely into the apartment, their lungs did not devour the night air. Pain and misery held a firm grip on their chests.

One of them had to break the eerie tomb of anguish. Marcus was not entirely to blame, so Angelina pulled back her emotions. She gently placed her hand on his forearm. He reflexively tensed. The abrupt response stirred the memory of Sofia's words about men and war.

"Soldiers must suppress all feelings of empathy, compassion, and love to survive the brutality of battle. Your father was the same way when he returned from the Great War." Sofia explained with a tenderness only she could give. *"Our love is a beacon, showing them the way back home. It is our duty to help them fight the demons spawned by war. They fight their enemies on the battlefield and in their sleep. We fight to pull them from the grasps of hell...back to the nurturing solitude of home."*

Angelina could hear the calmness of her mother's voice urging her to say comforting words. But in a low, somber tone, Marcus spoke first.

"I am sorry I stayed hidden from you." He held up a hand to silence her. "This is difficult enough. So just listen."

Marcus's tone was edged with an angry harshness that quickly silenced her; it was unlike him. Afraid of what he was about to say, Angelina's hand retreated to her lap.

"I wanted to come to see you. To tell you I was okay..." His head hung low. "Nothing should have stopped me, most especially the words of others."

The heavy burden slouched his shoulders and crumbled the damn containing his emotions. Tears streamed down, and he looked into her eyes for the first time in hours.

"I am truly sorry, Angelina." His jaw tensed.

She opened her mouth to speak, but he slammed his hand against the table. The thunderous boom echoed the torment festering in his soul, scaring any words back into her throat.

"Damn it! I was a coward. I spent years fighting on the battlefield, killing the enemy, marching through blazing heat, going days without food and shelter. I could muster the strength and courage to trudge on in the harshest conditions the land could throw at me. Yet, I faltered at the words describing Don Salvatore's destruction to our family."

Angelina hesitantly reached out. When he did not move away, she gently squeezed his arm.

"Marcus, it was the right choice."

"To abandon you? Letting that monster chain you to his side, growling his commands! Your body was rigid. I—could—see..." Sobbing, he pounded his fist against his chest. "I—could—see—*it!* You struggled to appear unaffected. Your eye's flitting from one table of guests to the next. That night, you were the brave soldier, fearless in the face of the enemy. Like a coward, I hid in the shadows instead of fighting to protect you. I could not even muster the courage to fight alongside you. I am your brother! It is my duty to protect you." His anger grew, and the veins in his temples pulsed. "It—is—my—duty! I failed you! Papa would be disappointed in me...and he *should* be."

"Marcus, stop! Please!"

His face turned red as the anger consumed him.

"I heard what he said to you!"

Angelina's face went pale. The memory of the devil's tongue, salivating, and the sound of his wicked voice sent a shiver up her spine.

Marcus slammed his white-knuckled fist against the table, this time harder than the last. The force sent two empty wine bottles into a wobbling frenzy before toppling over. Marcus ignored them, but Angelina grabbed them before they could crash to the floor.

"I should have cut his throat right then!"

"Marcus, where were you?"

Angelina's head was spinning, her mouth was dry, and her heart raced. How could she have missed her own brother? How could Don Salvatore miss him?

"I failed you. I failed our family!" Marcus shouted. "Papa will never forgive me!"

"Marcus, are you sure no one recognized you?"

"Did you?"

Angelina bowed her head.

"I served you wine."

Scrunching her brow, she shook her head in disbelief.

"You asked him, *do you prefer white or red?*"

Angelina's eyes widened. She covered her mouth, suppressing a gasp as she recalled the precise moment. Instantly, an icy chill nipped at her vertebra. Marcus repeated her exact words to The Don. It was a simple question asked to buy her time to think. With a flick of her hand, she summoned the unidentified waiter to bring a tray of wine.

"When I offered you the wine, I tried to make eye contact, but you were lost. You were as tense as I have ever seen you. Anyone, much less a man, to paralyze *you* had to be a master at manipulation. His obvious control made my blood boil."

Angelina replayed the funeral reception. Even now, she could feel the iron chain pulling on her neck. The power Don Salvatore had over her with just his hand placed lightly on the small of her back was shocking. He was the puppeteer, and she was his puppet.

"Lina, I tried to make eye contact, but you were transfixed on the far table."

"I...I did not want him to know who was important to me." Tears filled her eyes. "I was afraid he would kill them too!"

After a long silence, Angelina returned from her distant gaze. She dried her face and drained her glass. Marcus promptly refilled it, acknowledging the need to wash away that night.

Questions filled her mind. She did not want to open the iron box that contained the harsh memories. But she had no choice.

The answers to her questions required her to break open that which was created to survive.

"Angelina, I have to know the truth. You must tell me what happened? Why? Why did he massacre our family?"

Giorgio's greedy gaze, illuminated by the firelight, flashed before her eyes. The hiss of Giorgio's tongue as he explained the reason for the attack echoed in her mind, but the heinous actions that came after made her body stiffen. Angelina contemplated confessing what happened in Catalina's room that night. But she was uncertain of Marcus's reaction. He might blame her or accuse her of jealousy as Catalina did. She couldn't bear losing his support.

She shook her head, unable to explain anything to him.

"I'm sorry," Marcus said, wrapping her in his arms.

As she sobbed, Marcus gently rocked her as he did when she was a little girl. The fluid sway was a calming magic spell that conjured loving memories of him protecting her from her other brothers. Anton pulled her hair and hid her doll high up in a tree and other out-of-reach places. Ricardo put bugs in her bed, filled her shoes with mud, and tickled her until she vomited. Rosario and Sofia's reprimands for Anton and Ricardo's abuse did nothing to stop them. They learned they would get away with it if Mamma and Papa didn't see. Eventually, Marcus figured out their game and came to her defense. Ricardo and Anton learned torturing Angelina would earn them an ass-whooping from Marcus.

Angelina felt a teardrop land on her head. She sat up and looked at him. His complexion was pale, and dark circles loomed under his eyes. For the first time, Angelina noticed how thin he had become over the years in the military.

"So much has happened, Marcus. All I can tell you is Don Salvatore ordered our brothers to be killed." Swallowing hard, Angelina chose her next words carefully. "He ordered Giorgio to kill Mamma and Papa after they watched him murder our..." Her voice faded away. She couldn't say it.

"Where was Ricardo?"

"They grabbed him while he was out on delivery. I had a nightmare and went for a walk before sunrise and saw them toss him into the river."

The memory of Ricardo's body floating down the river, slowly emerging from the thick morning fog, made her stomach lurch. Angelina shook away the vision, but other disturbing images took their place.

"Lina?" Marcus pressed her.

"Huh? Um...After they left, Papa was still alive, as was Mamma, though she would not speak."

Marcus gave Angelina a moment to collect herself before he pressed her for more information. Reluctantly, she acquiesced, sharing remnants of the events. She could not bring herself to share every detail, especially the part about her encounter with Giorgio at Catalina's home.

The hours passed with brief exchanges of the past few days. Marcus gave Angelina intermittent breaks in her account with details he knew or with some much-needed silence. The task was daunting and drained what little energy they had left.

After satisfying Marcus's inquiries, she braved to ask the question she wanted to ask the moment she spotted him on the train.

"How did you...?"

Marcus's puffy eyes sparkled.

"Escape? Don Salvatore isn't as smart as he thinks he is. A few weeks ago, a recruit was sent to our unit. That in itself was peculiar."

"I don't understand?"

"The war was over. Why would they send a new soldier when several were going home every day? Those of us who had been together since Sicily thought it odd, so we watched him. He was completely unfamiliar with military ways. He couldn't make a bunk or pack his gear, and his shooting was terrible!" Marcus chuckled. "Man! He really was a terrible shot! Worse than Fernando, if you can believe it possible!"

Marcus was enjoying telling the tale. The amusement in his voice spurred a quiet giggle from Angelina.

"My friend, Almafa, overheard this arrogant idiot bragging about his orders from Don Salvatore. The coward was going to slit my throat while I slept! How Don Salvatore came up with this half-wit, I don't know."

Marcus offered Angelina more wine, but she declined. He filled his glass, then wetted his palate before resuming his story. He spoke as though he was spinning a tale about an exciting adventure.

"I suppose I owe the idiot my gratitude. Had he not been so bold, I would be dead!"

Angelina stiffened at Marcus's lightheartedness. Sensing her uneasiness, he cleared his throat and tempered his tone. However, he quickly shifted back to a level of happy boasting.

"Once we knew when he was planning to attack, we formed a counter plan. We tossed around the idea of having a dummy with a bag of blood, but a bloody bunk wouldn't fix everything. There had to be a dead body to throw Don Salvatore off my trail. So, we put a prisoner in my bunk that night! It was a perfectly simple solution!"

Smiling, Marcus swigged his wine to give his sister time to praise his brilliance. His anticipatory grin did not urge a compliment from Angelina. Instead, she winced at his brazen disregard for murder.

"He was to be executed. We did him a favor, believe me." He leaned closer, but she refused to make eye contact. He snarled and slammed his wine. "I did what I had to, Sis!"

He was a kind soul and would do nothing intentionally to harm anyone. At least, that was the case before he went to war. Angelina resisted the mindset of placing Marcus in the same category as a heartless killer like Giorgio and Don Salvatore, but murder was murder.

"You believe me, don't you?" He crossed his arms.

Angelina hesitated. The lines on his forehead deepened. The boyish need for her to believe him tugged at her heart. Yet, condoning a sin disregarded her moral compass. Unable to answer honestly, she shifted the conversation slightly.

"What happened to this soldier?"

"The prisoner?" Narrowing his eyes, his tone grew colder.

"No. your...assassin."

"We made him send a telegram back to The Don, as instructed. The next day, we found him dead."

"Who killed him?"

His jaw set tightly, he shrugged. "All I know is he died."

The Don, having his own man killed, or worse, her brother being the murderer, stunned Angelina. Marcus's dismissive response left her no opportunity to press for more details.

Marcus tossed the empty bottles into the metal bin. The sound of glass on glass reverberating around the room dwindled into nothingness, much like their conversation.

As he moved to the window, she wondered if he lied about the soldier's death to save her from the harsh truth. It would be honorable, yet she did not want him to keep secrets.

A lie for a lie. She thought, joining him at the window.

"It won't be long before dawn," Marcus said.

The cobblestone street that had bustled with life only hours ago had shifted dramatically. Now, its only inhabitants were the pigeons cooing on their perch and the wind gently carrying yesterday's post from one side of the walkway to the other. The tranquility of nothingness entranced them. The empty street strummed her heartstrings. It was as peaceful as the vineyard on a crisp autumn evening.

"We should get some sleep," Marcus said. "I don't think staying here more than one night is wise."

Gazing out the portal to the world, Angelina nodded absently. The thin, white curtain gently whipped in the cool breeze. The scalloped, eyelet lace across the bottom of the curtain reminded her of the ones her father gave Sofia for her birthday. She could still see Rosario standing on a ladder, hanging them for his excited bride. As always, her Papa gave her mother exactly what she desired. Angelina's heart sank. Catalina said Giorgio did the same for her. It was endearing to think of her parents in a fairytale romance, but accepting her sister lived one was difficult. Perhaps she was jealous.

Marcus wrapped his arm around her, and she relaxed her head against his shoulder.

"I am so glad you are alive."

"Me too, sis. Me too."

CHAPTER 18

Through the slightly open door, Catalina could see her mother's limp form blankly staring into the catacombs of a childless motherhood. The motionless form's pale, sallow face did not emit the radiant glow of a once vibrant mother. Black matted hair lacked the usual luster of silky onyx cascading in soft curls. Dry, cracked lips were void of the natural pomegranate hue. A dank grey tone starkly contrasted the typical charming aura of beauty and grace. Yet, there, in a prison without walls, sat the woman who pushed Catalina into this world.

Catalina's trembling hand tentatively pressed the door open. The hinges groaned in defiance, foretelling the harshness of the separate universe that lay beyond.

The path leading to this point was an art museum. Every few feet, a masterpiece displayed its brilliant strokes of aged colors. Statues chiseled into life by the hands of prominent artists. Vases laced with the delicate touch of a fine brush herald atop pillars to emphasize their glorified existence.

She would have enjoyed examining every detail but did not stop to admire the relics. Her mind barely registered the extensive collection. Stepping into her mother's room, Catalina realized the significant difference between the two spaces. The transition from marble tunnels to the depressing cell was as contrasting as a sunny day to a moonless night.

The barren walls framed the dull room like beaten slaves forced to stand sentry, without expression, for eternity. To the left, a small, unremarkable bowl with a matching pitcher sat on a battered dresser. No mirror or scenic painting hung in the room, only a simple crucifix peering down at Sofia from its perch on the wall.

The sin of vanity pulsating from Catalina's attire. Her silk gloves, purse, hat, and shoes matched her dress's dull, green fabric. Emerald earrings swayed, and the matching bracelet slid freely on her wrist. The guilt of her luxurious life crushed her chest. She struggled internally for a moment before wiping away her tears. Catalina pressed past the threshold of perceived sin. She was here to see her mother, not repent.

She placed Sofia's arm on her lap. As she unraveled the bloodstained bandages, she braced for the smell of rotting flesh or deeply seeded infection. To her relief, none came.

She could not look into her mother's eyes while she worked. It was the only way she could keep the tears that burned her lashes at bay. On previous visits, Catalina gazed into the empty orbs. It was not what she saw but what she did not see that unleashed her emotions. In Sofia's thinning face sat two dark portals to a space void of love, light, and joy.

"I do not blame you for not wanting to see Mamma," Catalina whispered as she finished wrapping Sofia's hand. "Angelina told me about the horror you were made to watch."

She continued to talk aloud as she tended to her mother's wounds. Her gut told her not to expect a response, but she hoped anyway. She longed for Sofia's sweet parables, which seemed far from the subject yet addressed the point. Catalina *needed* her mother's advice now more than ever. The desolate silence remained the only response to Catalina's mindless jabber. Yet, she rambled on while removing the bandages, exposing the raw and jagged strips of dying flesh.

The blade was applied to Sofia's throat in several short slices but was not deep enough to reach her jugular vein. The lacerated tissue already formed a broad, ropey scar that would be a reminder of the tragedy endured by one of the town's most loving of mothers.

Catalina tucked the end of the gauze inside the previous layer before assessing the quality of her work. With no other wounds to attend, Catalina couldn't avoid the ghostly look on her mother's sallow face.

The weight of a thousand pounds of sadness pulled at the corners of Sofia's colorless lips. The bruises accentuating her milky white complexion painted a tragic scene. In seconds, Catalina's emotions bubbled to the surface. Unable to hold back, her soft whimpers swelled into whaling sobs. She allowed her tense form to collapse onto her mother's legs.

"Mamma, Angelina blames me for our brothers' deaths. She thinks marrying Giorgio opened the door for the attack. She even said Giorgio attacked you. I know it is not true because he was out of town with Mario. Besides, he would not hurt our family. Oh, Mamma! Was I wrong to marry the man I love?" Sobbing, she collapsed into her mother's lap. "Is it really all my fault?"

"It is not, so stop your blubbering!" A deep, commanding voice bellowed into the small space. "Did your hand hold the blade that cut her skin? No! So do not martyr yourself. Remove yourself from that bed! Immediately!"

With the automatic response of a soldier to his general, Catalina rose from the bed.

"Now clean yourself up! You can do your sniveling someplace else!" Mother Concetta snapped. "Hurry, I have pressing matters to attend to, and your sister is one of them!"

"Si, Mother Superior."

She resisted the urge to give a short curtsy to the authoritative presence. Instead, she kept her back straight, slightly bent her knees, and extended her arm to pluck her purse from the bed. The nun's abrupt about-face told Catalina she poorly hid her awkwardness or the nun did not care about her emotional state. Most likely, it was the latter.

"Your sister left this." With the finesse of a magician, Mother Concetta freed her hands from her robe, revealing a letter stuffed up her sleeve. "She snuck in like a ghost and left as quickly! She took another woman with her. Of all things, a young mother who has abandoned her child to our care. Does she think we are here to raise the children of the reckless? What is the meaning of this foolishness?" The nun impatiently tapped her shoe. "Well? Confess!"

The nun was two inches taller, and her girth nearly doubled Catalina's. Even though black fabric commonly gave a slimming effect, this woman's holy attire did not appear to flatter her figure. Instead, it enhanced the older woman's appearance as an ominous dark cloud of intimidation.

An image of The Don and Mother Concetta facing off popped into Catalina's head. She giggled inwardly. She consciously suppressed her amusement as she had done in the years under the nun's tutelage. Yet, Mother Concetta's intuitiveness registered the wayward childish thought. With an arched brow, the nun barked another command, flushing any desire Catalina had to smile.

"Be quick about it, child!"

Catalina switched her focus from her vision of the comedic confrontation to the note the nun waved about. The elegant swirls creating each letter were Angelina's handwriting.

"This *is* from your sister, Si?"

Catalina nodded.

"Do you know why Angelina took the woman?"

She shook her head, but her flashy earrings swaying made Catalina squelch her emphatic response.

The Nun's brow arched, her patience quickly thinning. "Do you know what she is planning?"

Catalina hesitated to respond. She did not want to lie, but she also did not want to reveal anything that could jeopardize her parents' safety. As she contemplated an answer, Catalina replayed her last conversation with Angelina.

"I am not like you, Lina." Catalina stared at her lap.

"Staying is too dangerous! He may kill either of us!"

"And the world outside of Brusnengo is a pussycat?" Catalina looked up, her brow furrowed. "I cannot leave, Lina, I cannot! And I will not! You blame Giorgio, but I know things you do not."

"You cannot believe anything he says! He is a liar, Cat! For your safety, come with me, please!"

"Not everything is as it seems." Catalina's lips tightened.

"I saw Giorgio murder our brothers!"

She stood to meet her sister's glare. "That is impossible! It may be hard to accept, but you do not know everything! Everyone knows The Don is the greedy murderer!"

"And you married his nephew!"

"No one crosses Don Salvatore because of his power." Turning away, Catalina feigned deafness. "He attacked our family because our vineyard is profitable. Papa was well on his way to being rich, making this attack inevitable. If Papa dies, The Don will need us to keep the vineyard going."

"And will kill us when it suits him!"

"Not me! I am family." She turned, her hands landing on her hips.

"By marriage!"

"Precisely! Giorgio *is* my protection!"

It was a bitter conversation void of empathy and love. The pain from their deviation in views was a poisoned burr, working deep into the flesh of her heart. As always, nothing could make Angelina understand Catalina's situation. They were bound by blood, yet divided by circumstances of life.

Her hand trembling, she accepted the letter. She opened her purse, but the Nun's prying glare meant she was to read it now. The perfect impression made by their grandmother's signet ring sent a twinge of jealousy to her heart.

You have always been the favorite. Catalina thought. Sighing, she snapped the red rose seal in half.

> *Dearest Catalina,*
>
> *Forgive me, Sorella, for not accepting the same path as you. Your choice to stay in the wolf's den pains my heart, just as my leaving frightens you. Nevertheless, I must seek retribution for our family. To stay would require I become Don Salvatore's slave, and that is a role I refuse to fill.*
>
> *You love your husband and will protect him as a dutiful wife. For that, I understand your inability to believe the facts. As your sister, I will always love you unconditionally, even if you cannot allow yourself to accept the truth. You will do what you must to survive. Papa always said one must make their own choices, for they are the only soul to endure the consequences. I pray we are stronger than the trials we face and the decisions we endeavor to make.*
>
> *Until we are together again,*
> *Love Always,*
> *Angelina*

"Well?" Mother Concetta stomped her foot.

"I do not know. Angelina's letter says nothing of her plans. Nor anything about another woman."

Catalina restrained her anger. The letter said nothing except that Angelina was right and all-knowing once again. Therefore, Catalina was the stupid little sister.

"Do not lie to me, child! I know when you are lying. You make the same face you made when you were a little girl!"

Catalina rubbed her neck. She had done nothing wrong, yet her head dangled from the chopping block.

"Tell me what the letter said! When will they return?"

"Who left her child?"

Mother Concetta paused for a moment, her eyebrow twitching while she scrutinized Catalina.

"Francesca, the cobbler's wife. Do you know of her?"

Catalina shook her head, making a spattering of dancing light shimmer on the walls and the nun's black dress. Instinctively, her hands moved to stop the motion, but it was too late. The display of wealth and vanity was done. Grabbing the earrings would only bring more unwanted attention.

Mother Concetta scrutinized her target. "I see by the continued blank expression you were unaware."

"Thank you for understanding."

Before Catalina could finish her appreciation, the nun began a new storm of gruffness. Mother Concetta placed a hand on her hip and used the other to wag a finger in Catalina's face.

"Do you have no respect for the lives of others? Each time you and your sister come here, you jeopardize the safety of all who are protecting your parents. Do you have ill will for us? For your parents? I agreed to take them in because of your father's charity over the years. You and your husband, however, have not been as generous."

"A matter I wanted to address after my visit." Catalina lied.

She felt a twinge of guilt and the need to repent a second time. Mother Concetta's ominous form looming over her did not help. Her childhood fear of the nun's black dress being an earthly black hole engulfing the innocent children sent a shudder down Catalina's spine.

"I cannot give you much money." Catalina stammered. "Because of the need to keep this location a secret. I did, however, wish to offer you my emerald bracelet as a promise to pay." Catalina paused, hoping to appease the woman.

"Pure vanity! There is no place in God's house for vanity!"

Catalina wanted to drag the nun, preferably by the ear, into the hallway and point to the art that lined the path.

"Then, perhaps the two cases of wine in my car would show a gesture of good faith?"

The nun continued her gaze of displeasure, prompting Catalina to increase her donation.

"And twenty thousand Lira."

"Your charity is always welcomed and appreciated."

Her hand out, the nun impatiently waited for Catalina to dig into her purse.

"Ah, here is my 'mad' money," Catalina joked. "I spend it when my husband upsets me."

The nun, not amused, tapped her foot.

Catalina removed twenty-thousand lire from her wallet and placed it on the nun's palm. Mother Concetta looked into the wallet and raised her eyebrow. The displeasure was emphasized with a huff. Catalina sighed and placed another bill on the nun's palm, but it did not stop the disapproving glare. Under the duress, she repeated the action. The nun ceased her torturous stare when Catalina had one lonely bill in her wallet.

Next time, if there is a next time, I will remember to bring less money. Catalina grumbled to herself.

Satisfied with her fleecing, the nun folded the small stack of money and slipped her hand back under her smock.

"Perhaps next time you feel the need to depart with your 'mad money,' you will give it to a cause more worthy than your vanity." Mother Concetta gave a harrumph. "I will have the sisters carry the wine in for you. I wouldn't want that lovely green dress to be smudged."

The nun's condescending comment made Catalina eager to return home and change. To ease her guilt, she imagined ripping the bobbing earrings from her lobes to repent.

"Are you finished?"

A confused stare melted across Catalina's face.

"With your mother?" The nun nodded in Sofia's direction.

"Um...yes. Mamma is healing...on the outside."

"Then say your goodbyes. I do not have all day."

She returned to her mother's bedside. As she leaned over, the nun's intrusive gaze burned a hole into Catalina's spine.

"I love you, Mamma," Catalina said loud enough for the looming ears to hear. "Please, come back to me. I need you!"

Catalina's last words quivered with emotion, and she felt a fresh flood of tears surface. Instead of collapsing onto Sofia's lap and unburdening her heart, Catalina pressed a loving kiss to her mother's brow. It was the same gesture Sofia gave Catalina at night as she tucked her into bed.

"I understand," Mother Concetta said, her voice much softer. "You want to see them, but it is not wise nor safe."

Catalina opened her mouth to speak, but she was silenced by a simple wave of the nun's hand. As if all the nun's tenderness was spent in seven words, Mother Concetta's voice returned to its original gruffness.

"Do not expect much of a recovery from *either* parent. They have been through much. It is a miracle they are still breathing. If it is God's will, they will live. Make your visit short, and do not return until I send for you."

Before she could argue, Mother Superior vanished down the next corridor, leaving Catalina outside her father's room.

"And you thought Angelina moved like a ghost! She must have learned it from the best!" Catalina mumbled.

No matter how hard it hurt, the nun was right. Visiting her parents put too many lives in danger. They had a long recovery ahead, but Catalina believed they would mend quickly, unlike Mother Concetta. She *had* to believe it.

Rosario's room held the same dank presence as Sofia's. Everything looked old and worn, including her father. His torso was raised by several pillows, and his knees were slightly bolstered. The swooping shape of the blanket looked like a mountain range covered in snow. His head sunk deep between two white clouds that stretched out from his ears. His flesh lacked the slight rose hue of life, allowing him to blend like a chameleon with the colorless slate around him.

This tranquil scene made Catalina's heart stop. Nearly every detail was the same as her grandmother lying on her deathbed, only hours after her soul fled her ailing body.

"Papa?"

Catalina took several steps closer to her father's bedside and called him again. The sting of her tears pressed against her lashes. She sniffled, wiped away the impending gush, and drew a deep breath. He would not want her to be upset.

"What is wrong, Principessa? Dry your tears so I may see the beautiful face God gave you." Catalina heard in her head.

She sat on his bed, plucked his icy hand from the snow-white blanket. Her green dress seemed to glow against the colorless backdrop.

"I will fight back my tears, Papa. But you must fight against the darkness that has consumed you!"

His response was the same as her mother's, cold, lost, and lifeless. Catalina prayed for a miracle. If one parent rose from their catatonic state, babbling with parables and strategies to aid her, she would praise God's goodness.

"Oh, Papa. I am so lost. Even your favorite spot could not give me the enlightenment as it so often gave you." With a chuckle, she added. "Is there a magic word or a stone that needs to be moved to open the channels?"

"That's my girl."

Her father's nonexistent voice in her head eased her sadness, just like it did every time she faced an issue.

"You always preferred a light-hearted conversation," Catalina said with a smile. "Well, if I cannot get a conversation out of you, perhaps we should examine your wounds. Are you healing faster than Mamma, or does she have you beat by two bushels of grapes?"

The bluish-purple contusion on his face was a dark yellow. The inflammation near his broken leg had decreased.

"Those appear to be doing well." She stated professionally. "Now, let's see that stab wound."

She peeled back his blankets and lifted his shirt to reveal the large bloodstained patch. She felt the bandage.

"Oh, no, Papa!" She felt his forehead. He had a fever and not a slight one. "Don't move, Papa! I am going to get help!"

Racing out the door, Catalina ran down the corridor. Her temper was raging like her father's fever. She wondered if she could keep her fire hot while making demands of a woman she had feared her entire life. Determined, she forged down the hall, her green heels clicking against the marble floor.

"If you want my wine and my money, you better keep my father alive!"

When she rounded the last corner, she came upon a scene that shook her core. An icy chill replaced her fire. Catalina was outmatched.

CHAPTER 19

The sun's rays performed their last dance on the horizon as the day came to a close. The weakening beams of light tap-danced on a cluster of windows to Maximus's left. Invisible stagehands pulled the ropes, drawing in the thick, violet curtain at a snail's pace across the stage. The performers in that evening's show would take their twinkling bows in the blackened sky, but he would not see them all. The glare of the city's lights would hide the stars, allowing only those who dwelled outside the noisy metropolis a glimpse of the stellar nobility. It was a familiar show, one he ruminated over every evening. However, most nights, his mind was not performing mental gymnastics over utter chaos.

The quiet stillness of his hotel room was pierced by the blaring sounds of his world. A delicate chime came from his left pocket as his fingers pensively fondled the coins. The ice in his dwindling drink cracked and popped like a whip in his right ear while the endless tick of the metronome marked each passing second. Four-wheeled bullfrogs croaked and moaned in the muffled distance. The culmination of the noises inflamed the tension that hardened his shoulders. Maximus's mind yearned for silence, real silence. A place where his surroundings could not linger in the front row of every thought.

He shook away the sounds and persistent thoughts to freshen up. He pressed a warm washcloth against his face. The soothing heat felt good against his skin. He stretched his neck left to right, urging the tension to release. Unsuccessful, Maximus stepped into the shower.

Hot water danced on Maximus's chest, washing away the frothy white bubbles that clung to his black hair. In a liquid avalanche, the water rolled over his firm pecs and down his rippled abs. The undulating waves of steam flowed up in rolling curls of vapor, reminding Maximus of Angelina's flowing locks of silky black hair. Her dark eyes, smooth skin, and enchanting smile lured him into a web of desire.

Lost in a vision of Angelina, Maximus stepped under the cascading rain. Closing his eyes, he allowed no other thoughts to disturb his vision of her. She was his Venus, and he longed to be her Mars. Maximus would willingly fight her war if only to win her affection.

Maximus grabbed the door handle at the exact moment Freddy knocked. They exchanged a wordless, cryptic message that outsiders would see as a meaningless glance. The silence continued until they were seated in a booth at the back of the restaurant. From their table, they could see the skyline of the city. Freddy peered out from the top floor and shivered.

"Don't like heights?"

"Not particularly."

Big, burly Freddy *did* have an Achilles' heel, Maximus thought. Out of habit, he mentally tucked that information away. To know a man's weakness was powerful. He had known Freddy for nearly two decades yet recalled no vulnerability. Even though Freddy was a friend, it would be absurd to think Freddy could never turn against him. It was human nature and foolish to think otherwise. Anyone could betray you. Some would do it without hesitation, others needed to see red *or* green. Blood and money are two things that could make you or break you. A lesson he learned at sixteen from his mentor, Johnny.

To Maximus, Johnny was a man who liked to laugh and ride hot and fast. Johnny's business and personal relationship with the O'Hara twins was proof of Johnny's proclivity.

Paul and Patty O'Hara were inseparable twin brothers who ran a small bar on the West side of town. At its inception, the place was a family run business that catered to the Irish population, as it had done since the early 1900s when the O'Hara family migrated to Kansas City.

As did other cultures, the Irish and Italians carved out their own area of the growing river city. It was an unwritten division that was felt by all. No kind liked the other much and always found a reason, fictitious or not, to create chaos with an attack.

Johnny B, a young Italian upstart, befriended the brothers around the time of prohibition. The walls of race became rubble and eventually eroded to dust in the wind. Patty and Paul found a brother from a different culture, and Johnny felt the same.

During prohibition, Johnny helped the O'Hara family transition their bar into an Irish restaurant on the street level. In the basement, they ran a distillery and distribution center for bootlegging. During this time, all three became silently wealthy. The O'Hara brothers taught Johnny how to appear as the poorest, rich man by hiding all the signs of a high roller.

Johnny adopted an underprivileged man's appearance by abandoning his culture's silk suits, shiny shoes, and gold chains. He wore an old hat with holes in the brim, tattered pants, and simple shirts purchased from the thrift store. To complete the look, he never shined his shoes and kept his beard to a rough stubble. Johnny was rich. He was rich enough to dress like his Italian family but spent his money differently. Besides purchasing land on the outskirts of Kansas City, Johnny ate out frequently. Threw massive parties where the booze ran like the Missouri River, deep and wide. It was evident if you were paying attention, but most people didn't put forth the effort to look beyond the facade. No one wanted to see another getting ahead, especially when they were struggling to survive.

It was a good run for the three, but it did not last. The brothers enticed Johnny into a drinking contest at one of Johnny's backyard festivals. Both cultures held their liquor well, but the Irish constitution was more compatible with hard liquor. The brothers changed the recipe a little before brewing a new jug of their famous 'fire-n-the-hole' whiskey. It went down strong and came out just as harsh. Patty and Paul tested their new brew on Johnny. It made him go blind for a week and shit blood for two. When Johnny regained his vision, he could see the town was still laughing at him. It was hard enough to only hear the chuckling for seven days. To see the laughter in people's eyes was infuriating. His ass and pride were rubbed raw.

Johnny wanted to seek revenge in a way they wouldn't forget. They had broken a brother code with him, so he would break the brother code they held with each other. It was a simple plan that would devastate the entire family.

Patty's wife, Bridget, always had an eye for Johnny. A year before the O'Hara brothers played their prank on Johnny, she made sure he knew it.

During one of their many drink-a-thons, Patty passed out at about nine, with Paul following quickly after. Johnny drank wine that night, avoiding the O'Hara brew. He stayed to help Bridget clean up after the party dwindled to the two brothers in the living room, trying to out snore the other.

Bridget asked him to help her tuck her son and nephew in, which he did without hesitation. She closed the children's door, grabbed Johnny's hand, and led him into her bedroom. Before he could blink, Bridget had her clothes off and her tongue down his throat. Johnny didn't refuse. She started it, after all. Not to mention her perky tits and big nipples looked even better out of her dress. He let her unbutton his pants and work her way down his hairy chest with her mouth. She wanted him, and he was ready to take one for the team.

Without her boobs in his face, his eyes wandered half in a daze of ecstasy around the room. On the dresser, he saw a picture of Patty, Bridget, and their son. He felt Patty's dark, disapproving stare and something else. He couldn't pin it right then, but it was strong enough to make his nuts crawl up and dick go limp.

The next day, what ended the potential ride of his life was clear. The three peering faces resembled the holy family sorrowfully gazing at him for breaking a consecrated law. The piercing gaze from the six sacred eyes in that picture haunted him. So did her tits. He did what any good Catholic boy would; he went to confession *once*. For the next three hundred and some days, he used the vision of her creamy-white boobs in the shower.

It took about two months for the laughter from the O'Hara brother's prank to fade into a distant memory. Once it had,

Johnny started his plan. It began with banging Bridget harder, longer, and better than Patty, or so she said.

Johnny knocked up two broads and probably more. He was confident he could do the same with Bridget, especially since their interludes became a daily practice. In less than a year, Bridget would pop out a dark haired, dark eyed baby that looked nothing like its older, green-eyed, redheaded brother.

In the meantime, while his bun roasted in the oven, he went about making more chaos. Johnny became chummy with an Italian friend who was the son of the local Don. In a short period, the Don magically had more booze and money than usual. Meanwhile, the O'Hara brothers clamored about the loss of dough. The pinch on their wallet and the uptick in highjacked trucks made them jumpy. Adding to their distress, Johnny watched, waited, and fed false information to each brother.

In less than six months, Patty and Paul suspected the other was the enemy. Johnny slid to the back of the room and kept his nose clean unless he was busy making Bridget moan. Even pregnant, she still could turn him on. Didn't hurt that she could do some amazing things with her tongue.

Patty was light on cash and felt the pinch with the impending birth of a second child. Paul didn't believe his brother was broke because Patty had to be skimming. In Paul's mind, he was the one in poverty, and Patty should give *him* money.

The upheaval allowed Johnny to step in as a concerned 'brother.' In the last phase of Johnny's revenge, he brokered a deal between his Italian friend and his Irish 'brothers.' To seal the deal, they all had drinks and smokes while Bridget pushed out what was believed to be Patty's second son.

Two weeks later, Patty committed suicide, and Paul was found washed up on the riverbank. Johnny was flush with dough, had a son, and the hottest piece of ass in town.

"Ya live by the sword." Johnny would preach to Maximus. "Ya gonna die by it. That's in the bible or something. Either way, those are words to live by."

Maximus often thought back to his days with Johnny. Johnny treated Maximus like a son. The two years together were wildly fun but crammed full of lessons. Johnny always asked Maximus if he had gained the wisdom from the latest falderal.

Three months after the O'Hara brother's deaths, Johnny deteriorated. He was drunk from sunrise to sundown and every minute in between. He learned why Irish husbands drank hard booze. To forget they were married to fiery, redheaded daughters of hell.

"Never get mixed up with a redhead, ya hear me, Max?"

Johnny took a swig from his bottle whenever he thought of a redheaded demon. Well before noon, he would polish off a fifth of whiskey.

"They are right, crazy bitches, Max. Scary crazy! Marry yer own kind, hear me? A dark-haired, brown-eyed beauty who can cook a good meal. If a crazy redhead doesn't scare ya, the Irish food should, 'cause it is just as harsh as their women." He washed the words down with another gulp before he grunted the question. "Max, do ya hear me?"

"Yes." Maximus replied.

Johnny had fallen in love with Bridget, and Maximus believed she loved him too, at least for a little while. When Patty committed suicide, Bridget was convinced she and Johnny had committed so many sins God would never forgive them.

Maximus was leaving for college at the end of that summer. The impending loss sucked more of the life out of Johnny. Bridget hated him, the O'Hara family hated him, he hated himself, and he believed humanity did, too. In his world of drunken abhorrence, the darkness bubbled up around him, intensifying his loneliness.

The last night before Maximus left town, Johnny sat down with him. It was the only time Maximus could remember him being sober.

"I am proud of ya, Max." Johnny began his somber speech. "I am real proud. Yer Pops is gotta be proud, too. And yer Mamma, never forget ya Mamma. She pushed ya into this world."

"And she can push me out." Maximus completed his friend's saying.

With a waned smile, Johnny nodded, "Ya, that, too."

"They are gonna teach ya all kinds of fancy things up there. But remember, just because they have money doesn't mean they are different from those who don't. It's human nature to think ya are different or better." Johnny preached as he played with the unopened bottle of whiskey. "We are cannibals. We don't dine on the flesh but on the souls of men. It doesn't matter if ya be the same *kind* or different. Once ya taste another man's soul, ya will crave the taste *forever*. Forever, Max...until ya die... Max, do ya hear me?"

Johnny twirled the bottle on the concrete stoop, his eyes hypnotized by the spinning golden liquid.

"What did ya learn from the O'Hara boys?" Johnny asked, staring into nothingness.

Maximus waited to answer. What he wanted to say would make Johnny laugh. Johnny's tone told him he wanted the real answer, the profound, introspective answer. Not some goofy retort.

"Well?" Johnny pressed, looking up at him.

His eyes were dark blobs in the middle of a red ocean, and his skin was more yellow than olive.

"Don't trust the Irish."

"Ain't that the truth!" Johnny chuckled. His broad smile made the black whiskers along his cheek protrude like spikes on a cactus. "Ha! Ain't it." He shook his head. "I appreciate yer attempt to humor me. Ya know that wasn't what I was asking. But it is a good point."

"Couldn't help it." Maximus patted him on the back. "The truth is, and more to your point, don't trust *anyone*."

"That is true, but ya knew that just from life. What did the *O'Hara* brothers teach ya?"

Maximus gave him an inquisitive look.

"This ain't the stuff they gonna teach ya at Harvard, Max. They won't teach ya to read between the lines. College is a good education, but don't let yer mind stop at the end of the sentence."

Johnny pulled the cork from his bottle and stared at it but did not take a swig.

"I made a mistake, Max. I screwed up a really good thing, all out of revenge. They humiliated me, and I wanted them to pay a heavy price to appease my pride. All the cards on the table, everyone was holding a winning hand, and one match burned it all down."

Johnny put the bottle to his mouth, stopped, then pulled it away. He was teaching Max. His mind needed to be sharp.

"Ya are right, don't trust anyone. However, the real lesson from them is everyone has a weakness. Mine was pride. It made me snap in two in a hot second. Those two parts of me spun off in search of revenge and money. My revenge ruined a beautiful family and money, well." This time he took a swig from the bottle. "Hell, money ruined us all." He put the cork back in the bottle's mouth. "And this shit. Booze. The devil's elixir. A temptress in a bottle. Fuck, this shit is as bad as a redheaded bitch! Feels good goin' down. Then she punches ya in the gut, kicks yer nuts, and hits ya over the head so hard ya wake up in the morning praying, *God, please turn off the lights!*"

In two gulps, Johnny hammered the rest of the bottle.

"The O'Hara brothers had their weaknesses, too. It wasn't just me. We all have them. Know what yers is so no one can use it against ya, including yerself, Max. Including yerself."

Johnny went quiet while his eyes watched a movie only he could see. His gaze drilled past the beauty of the day. In respect, Maximus remained silent, allowing Johnny time to process the visions projected by his mind.

In the silence, Maximus admired Mother Nature's display. The air danced on the leaves, and the crickets sang in the waning daylight. After a while, Maximus returned to his catatonic friend and examined his features. It was the most peaceful Maximus had ever seen Johnny. Maximus etched the details of Johnny's face, hands, and the tone of his voice into the stone of his memory. Something inside of him told him this was his last lesson from Johnny. It was. Three days after he arrived at Harvard, he received a letter from Johnny.

"Don't fuck up the good things, Max. It is the sword that will kill ya."

In the next day's paper, Maximus read Johnny went on his last joy ride off the Liberty Bend Bridge and into the Missouri River.

A petite waitress with reddish-brown hair, fair skin, and a contagious smile walked toward the table. The movement pulled Maximus back from his memory.

"One Macallan Scotch for Mr. Handsome. We are all out of 25, but I figure you can suffer through a 30," the waitress teased.

"I'll do my best," Maximus nodded in appreciation.

"For Mr. Muscles, one Van Winkle - neat," the waitress said with a flirtatious wink.

Maximus raised his glass, "Thank you, Ms. Lori B."

"Call me Lori. The other Lori ain't workin' here no more."

With a smile of appreciation, the gentlemen raised their glassed to toast Lori B.

"You boys are gonna make me blush!" Lori beamed. "I'll be over here if you need me."

Maximus stared at his drink. The caramel brown liquid looked like the stuff in Johnny's bottle that day. With a mental salute to his old friend, Maximus took a swig. When he looked up, he saw Peter Berg approaching his table.

CHAPTER 20

Marcus allowed Angelina a few more minutes to rumble through her thoughts before interrupting her.

"Sis, you need to get some rest. Trust me, day two of a battle is just as exhausting as day one."

Angelina nodded again. With a sigh, she laid on the sofa. Once she was comfortable, Marcus draped a blanket over her.

"I will be in that chair if you need anything, okay?"

"Thank you, Marcus."

He leaned over and kissed her forehead. "Sogni d'oro, Sorella."

"Marcus? How did you know I was on the train?"

A mischievous grin emerged on his face.

"I thought you would never ask!" Marcus chuckled. "The night of the funerals, after everyone had left, you and Carlos sat on the bench under the cherry blossom tree. He heard a movement in the vines."

"That was you?" Angelina sat up.

"I was under your nose the whole time, Sis." Marcus's grin broadened. "Honestly, I'm surprised you didn't notice me! You were not yourself, so I kept close in case you needed rescuing, and here I am, your hero!"

Pleased with himself, Marcus plopped his shoes on the shabby wooden coffee table and folded his hands across his abdomen. Even though the chair and pseudo-footstool did not appear comfortable, he instantly fell into a deep sleep. He was a soldier, sleeping when time allowed, yet ready to jump to his feet and fight. It was another heart-wrenching reminder that he experienced many difficult days in the military.

Angelina watched his chest rise and fall. She said a silent prayer, thanking God that he still drew breath. The rhythmic flow of air in and out of his lungs became a soothing metronome, lulling her off to sleep.

The first face she saw in her dream was Rosario's. With open arms, he smiled at Angelina.

"Papa! I have missed you!"

"I have never left, Principessa." Rosario embraced her.

"You can speak!" Breaking the hug, she examined him.

"What are you looking for, Principessa?"

"You were hurt. I saw him stab you, Papa!"

"Once again, Principessa, you have allowed your imagination to get the best of you!"

"No, Papa, it was real! He murdered my brothers!"

"If that is so, why are they standing behind you?"

Angelina's confused expression transformed into shock when she saw four men walking down the hill, just as they would do every evening after a long day of work. Ricardo plucked RJ up and set him on his shoulders while Anton and Fernando carried on a conversation.

"You are alive!" Angelina ran to embrace her brothers but halted when her sister called from inside the chicken coop.

"You lied to me!"

"What? No, Cat! It was not a lie. I would not lie to you!"

"You could not stand my happiness, so you lied!"

"No, Cat. I want you to be happy!"

"Then why did you destroy our family?"

"It was not me!"

Grabbing his abdomen, Rosario moaned. The color in his cheeks faded. His smile was replaced with a grimace of pain.

"After everything I have done for you, Angelina! Why, Principessa, why?" Rosario groaned, reaching out with one blood-soaked hand.

"You left him to die, Lina. You left us all here to die."

"No, I went to get help. Marcus is alive! I brought him home to save us."

"His existence is a dagger in my soul!" Rosario growled in anger. "Marcus is not my son!"

Angelina stood three feet away from her father's crumbling form in shock. She reached out to catch him, but he fell through her arms.

"Do not look so surprised, Lina. You knew he was not our brother. Mamma told me. Did she not tell you, Lina?"

"Cat, that is not true!"

"I do not tell lies," Sophia emerged from the vines. "I hid him, but you brought him home. Now, he is dead."

"He is alive, Mamma!"

Rosario cried out in pain. Angelina knelt beside him and wrapped her arms around him. His body was hot to the touch. The smell of burning flesh made her gag.

"Papa! What is happening to you?"

"I must burn in hell for your sins."

"Papa!"

Screaming in agony, Rosario's flesh bubbled. Dozens of small black spots, ringed in a fiery red, expanded into large gaping holes that exposed his muscles. Grey smoke billowed from his dark eyes and gaping mouth while his organs melted into a pool of black tar around Angelina's feet.

"You could have saved him." Catalina pointed at Angelina. "If you would have kept Marcus a secret. Mamma and Papa would still be alive! We *all* would be alive if not for you."

Angelina looked up at her sister to ask how she died, but Catalina's appearance was explanation enough.

"See what your jealousy did!"

Catalina's hands held her abdomen where a growing dark patch spread across her dress, and blood splattered on the ground between her feet. A sharp pain pierced Angelina's gut, making her double over, writhing in agony. Her body collapsed onto the blood-soaked ground at Catalina's feet. Angelina tried to break free, but every attempt strengthened her bond with the dirt.

In the distance, a pair of shiny black dress shoes slowly moved closer to Angelina. Muddy tendrils held her face to the ground, preventing her from looking up at the man's face.

"Someone help me! Please help me!" Angelina sobbed.

"I vill help, if you come with me," The Conductor smirked.

"No! No! Please don't take me to him!"

"He is good man?"

"He murdered my family!"

"No! It vas you. Admit ze sins and be free!"

The shiny shoes stopped inches from Angelina's face.

"How is My Little Dove?" A voice from behind her asked.

"Get away from me. Get away from my family!"

"Why would I leave *my* family? To leave. To abandon family is a sin. But, My Little Dove, you know all about sin, don't you?" Don Salvatore cackled.

The ground beneath Angelina melted, and she felt her body slowly being engulfed by small granules of sand.

"Admit ze sins! Now!" The Conductor growled.

The black shoes morphed into Catalina's battered and bruised face.

"Oh, Cat! Did he hurt you again?"

"You hurt me. Why can you not be happy for me?"

Sobbing, Angelina reached out to caress her sister's swollen face.

"I am sorry, Cat. I never meant for this to hurt you."

"Time creates unhealable wounds, Lina," Catalina said in a distant voice as her image disappeared.

Angelina reached out for her sister's fading image, but it vanished.

"No!"

Angelina pawed at the dirt, trying to bring Catalina back, but all she retrieved was a small gold cufflink.

"Lina? Angelina?" Marcus's hands tightly clamped on her arms. Marcus shook Angelina until her eyes blinked open. "Lina? You are okay. It was a dream."

Frantic, she searched her blanket. "Where did it go?"

"Where did what go? Lina, stop it was a dream?"

"I need it!"

Marcus shook Angelina's shoulders again. "Look at me, Lina! Angelina! Look—at—me!"

Angelina looked up at Marcus, and their dark eyes locked together. She sucked in air as if she had just emerged from the bottom of a deep lake. Her heart thundered. She lunged into her brother's arms and embraced him tightly.

"I got ya, Sis. I got ya. You are okay." Marcus stroked her hair. "It was just a dream."

"Oh, Marcus, it was more than a dream."

"Do you want to tell me about it?"

Francesca, standing behind Marcus, had a ghastly stare that silenced Angelina. Her dream must have been worse than it seemed.

"Don't move, Sis. I will get you some water."

"I will draw you a bath."

"We don't have the time for that." Marcus abruptly raised his hand, stopping her. "If you want to clean up, I suggest you do it quickly. We need to keep moving. I will use the kitchen sink so you two can have privacy in the bath."

"How noble of you." Francesca snapped. "No one knows we are here. This is the safest place to stay."

Ignoring Francesca, Marcus helped his sister up.

"Come on, Angelina." Francesca scrunched her nose in rebuke of Marcus's rudeness. "We need to change. We do not want our appearance to mislead people. Some might think we have no place to stay!"

Still dazed, Angelina numbly walked to the bedroom.

"Are you okay?" The vinegar was gone from her tone.

"It was just a bad dream, that's all."

"Seemed like more than that to me!"

"I have always had troubling dreams, even as a child. It is nothing."

Francesca stopped rummaging through the closet to look at Angelina. Truly concerned, she asked, "Are you sure?"

"Yes. It is from stress, that's all."

"Plenty of that to go around." She removed a dark grey dress. "This should fit you. The shower is in there."

Angelina hesitated. "He didn't mean to upset you. He is just protective."

Francesca stopped sifting through the closet. Her head lowered, and she sighed. "Trusting men is difficult for me."

"You can trust him." Angelina placed a hand on her friend's shoulder and gently squeezed.

Francesca straightened her spine. She pulled out a blue and a green dress to examine.

"The hot water doesn't last long."

Understanding her friend's pain, Angelina squeezed her shoulder once more.

"The blue one matches your eyes."

Two caterpillars breaking free from a cocoon, Angelina and Francesca emerged from the bedroom. The morning rays dancing on Francesca's curls reflected a golden glow that held Marcus's gaze for longer than a glance.

Francesca avoided his eyes and, in a tempered tone, said, "Marcus, there are several clean shirts in the closet. My friend will not mind if you take one."

He gave her a nod of appreciation before disappearing into the adjoining room.

"We need to eat something." Francesca picked up her purse. "There is a caffé close. Maybe a five-minute walk. I will be back before he is finished."

"No! Wait for Marcus."

Francesca looked confused. "I know this town well."

"He is a man and a soldier. It will not take him long."

Avoiding further debate, Angelina stepped closer to the window to watch the morning come to life. It was a beautiful morning. To her left, the sun painted beautiful hues of pink and yellow across the skyline. It was a softly glowing backdrop for the endless rows of buildings divided by narrow cobblestone paths.

A horn honked to her right, drawing her attention. A slow-moving mule and cart blocked the way of an idling car. The driver leaned out of his window, cursing profanities between the obsessive blares of the horn.

Beyond the ruckus, at the end of the street, was a four-story building damaged by the war. Rubble cascaded down the sides, exposing the inside of several apartments. One end of a grand dining room table jetted up from the fallen debris. Several stories up from there were four perfectly hung pictures in a room with no flooring. Above that apartment was the frame of a shattered mirror dangling above two chairs divided by a small table. The grand corner apartment on the top floor was obliterated. The few walls remaining were partial barriers cut with jagged edges and scorched black by the fire.

The car and mule's dispute resolved. Now, the area was covered with men and women swarming around, leaving one building before flitting to another. An unseen trolley's bell jingled. A few moments later, dozens of men dressed in neatly pressed suits filled the streets.

A tall man with broad shoulders tipped his black Fedora hat to a young woman. The gesture made her flush, tucking her chin so he could only see the top of her felt beret. Another gentleman allowed the woman to cross his path as he gave her a slight bow.

The normality of life next to such drastic destruction was unnerving to Angelina. She had seen nothing like this and hoped she never would again.

"Welcome to Turin," Francesca said, stepping beside Angelina. "It was beautiful once."

"Is all of Italy like this?"

"Not *all*," Marcus replied, joining the ladies in surveilling the world outside. "Unfortunately, I have seen much worse."

"So much violence for what purpose?" Angelina looked on in sadness.

"It's always about money, Sis."

"And power." Francesca wiped away a stray tear.

"Sorry to break up this party, but we should get moving." Marcus quickly gathered up their things.

"We can not go home!" Angelina placed a hand on his arm.

"Of course, we are going back to Brusnengo! Your brother is alive! Don Salvatore has no control anymore!"

"We will go home, but not yet." Angelina suppressed her fear of making another poor choice. "There is something we must do first."

Before Angelina could explain, the grind of metal against metal came from the apartment's front door.

"Shh!" Marcus whispered, holding one finger to his lips.

Angelina and Marcus looked at Francesca for an explanation of who was unlocking the door, but it was too late. The door flung open. Terrified, Francesca released a loud scream and fainted.

CHAPTER 21

Catalina jumped out of sight and pressed her body against the cold stone wall.

"Dear God! Why is he here?" Catalina's fingers fidgeted with the handle of her purse as she peered around the corner. She strained to hear the conversation, but the voices were garbled echoes off the marble. She retreated back to the stone wall, clenching her purse handle. "Damn it!"

"Do you need something?" A little girl asked, tugging at Catalina's sleeve.

Catalina covered her mouth to muffle her scream.

"I am sorry, Signora. I did not mean to frighten you."

"Then, why did you?" Catalina pursed her lips.

"I saw you run from your papa's room. You stopped so quickly, I thought you were lost." The girl said, swishing her skirt. "It took me a year to learn my way around."

To quiet the young girl's excited voice, Catalina put a finger over her lips. "Softer."

The girl shook her head in understanding.

"I even know about the old passageways. No one has used them for a long time."

"Oh, really?"

Her eyes twinkling, she leaned closer. "I bet Mother Concetta doesn't even know about them!"

"Mother Concetta is resourceful and clever."

"You will not tell on me, will you?" Margaret pleaded.

"No. No. You don't have to worry about that, not from me," Catalina smiled. "I was your age once, and Mother Concetta is the same now as she was then. Only a little older."

The girl giggled.

"What is your name?"

"Margaret."

"Can you help me, Margaret?"

The little girl dropped her chin. "Mother Concettas says I don't do anything right."

With a finger, Catalina raised the girl's head and looked directly into her eyes. "I believe you can do this job."

Margaret swallowed hard and wiped back the puddle of tears in her eyes.

"That's better. You know my father is here recovering."

"And your mother, too."

"Yes, and my mother. That man talking with Mother Concetta wants to kill them."

Gasping, Margaret stepped back. Catalina pulled her closer, reminding her to be quiet.

"My father's wound is infected. He is running a high fever and needs medicine, or he will die. I need you to get a doctor."

Shaking her head, Margaret moved further away from Catalina. "I can't do that..."

"Yes, you must!" She squatted, meeting the girls terrified eyes. "Please, Margaret. He will die."

She wilted. "I can't." The youthful mind, bounced from shame to excitement. "Sister Juliann will. She is nice to me."

Catalina's shoulders relaxed. "Can we go find her?"

Margaret nodded.

"Good." Catalina took a few steps back down the hallway, but Margaret's small hand stopped her.

"We have to go that way."

A rock sunk in Catalina's gut. Her green dress seemed to glow next to the white walls. Even if she could sneak across the hall, Mother Concetta and her guest would notice the streak of green racing past.

"I can't go that way. He will see me."

"Ok. I will go." Quite pleased with herself for doing something right, her body bounced with happiness. "Go to your papa's room. I will bring her to you."

Catalina cupped the girls chin then hugged her tightly. The girl returned the embrace. A smile radiated from Margaret's bright face before skipping away.

Before turning back to her Papa's room, Catalina confirmed Mother Concetta's guest's identity.

"Why is Mario here?"

CHAPTER 22

Marcus dashed to Francesca's aid, catching her before her head connected with the floor. The commendable feat was worthy of applause, but Angelina's attention was held by the towering figure looming in the doorway.

"You are quite the elusive little woman, aren't you?"

"Stay where you are!" Marcus squared his shoulders.

A burst of bellowing laughter reverberated around them. It was a familiar, haunting echo that chilled Angelina's core.

"What are you going to do to a man like me?"

The thunderous thud-thud of his enormous feet against the wooden floorboards intensified his taunting words.

"How did you find us?" Angelina gasped as she moved behind the chair her brother used for a bed.

"It was easy, and...this is not my first job." The Conductor paused in the middle of the room to inspect the space. With a humph, he stretched his massive form and yawned. "Do you have any coffee?"

"No." Angelina's stomach growled. She would follow the man for no other reason than a desire for coffee.

"Hmm... I figured as much."

"Your accent?" Angelina turned pale at the revelation.

"Like I said, it is not my first job."

Marcus and Angelina exchanged worried looks.

"Job?" Marcus asked, but the Conductor ignored him.

"Well, wake up that fragile creature. We have a long way to go, and I'd rather not encounter those two idiots who sat across from you on the train."

"I would rather die than be Don Salvatore's whore!" Angelina spat at the man's feet.

A flicker of amusement danced in the Conductor's eyes.

"That is good to hear. You are far too beautiful for that mongrel." The Conductor glanced out the window. Popping his knuckles, he released a quiet growl. "Get your things. We need to leave."

"We are not going anywhere." Marcus held his sister back.

"If you want to live, you will."

"Live, huh? Great trust building skills. Nothing about you screams, come with me and live!" Marcus narrowed his gaze.

Angelina placed a hand on her brother's arm.

"You said, *job*, what is it you do?" Angelina, exuding calmness, stepped closer to the Conductor.

"The answer is not one you want to know. I am sure you have more questions. I will entertain them over coffee...and food. I didn't get this size by accident!"

"Why did you help me on the train?" Angelina's gentle, sweet voice halted him in the doorway.

The Conductor turned his head, exposing a devilish grin.

"Because that was what my Boss hired me to do."

"Who is your boss?" Marcus demanded.

It was another question that was ignored. The doorway was empty, and the Conductor, gleefully whistling, was halfway down the stairs.

"Did he fail charm school or what?" Marcus rolled his eyes. "Sis, did he really help you on the train?"

"In a way, yes. He knows my name too. My *full* name."

"Probably saw it on your bag." He shrugged the coincidence away. "That is what conductors do."

"He never touched my bag, and I don't think being a conductor is his real job!"

"Well, Sis," He ran his hand through his hair. "You read people better than anyone I know. If you think he is someone to trust, then I will not argue."

Slowly sitting up, Francesca moaned.

"Easy. You are alright." Marcus said in a tender voice.

When her eyes met his, she scurried to her feet. Taking several steps back, she gathered her balance before speaking.

"What happened?"

"You fainted." Marcus held his hands out to catch her if she passed out again.

"Today is good, kids. Now is even better!" The Conductor hollered up the stairwell.

"Well, Sis?"

"What do we have to lose?"

"We have a lot to lose...like maybe our lives!" Francesca stamped her foot.

Angelina shrugged and headed out the door. Francesca threw her hands in the air.

"Did you hear me? Our *lives,* for starters!"

"Ladies! Don't forget you have me to protect you!"

"Fantastic! I feel safer already." Francesca sneered at Marcus. "Angelina, wait!"

"He was sent to help us," Angelina said, popping her head back into the apartment.

"Are you kidding me? I thought you were the smart one!"

The exterior door at the bottom of the stairs banged shut, spurring Angelina to not engage in the argument Francesca was creating. She flashed her friend a half-smile and a shrug before running down the steps. Francesca slammed the apartment door shut, making Angelina and Marcus jump.

"What was I thinking." Francesca griped as she stormed down the steps. "Was I even thinking?"

As the trio raced to catch up with the Conductor, Francesca continued to bicker between huffs and grunts.

The Conductor moved quickly down the alley before taking a hard right onto a wide cobblestone street. Occasionally, he would slow his pace to glance about before barreling forward or tucking down a narrow backstreet.

Angelina admired the unique lines and images etched into the façades of each building. The filigree spilling down from stone arches, stone crests adorning the rooftops, mythical creatures hugging the façade, and Cherub's outstretched hands' yearning for the heavens were works of art. Focused on the architecture, Angelina stumbled on the uneven stones of the sidewalk. Marcus slipped his arm into hers.

"You might keep your eyes forward, Sis."

"It is so beautiful!"

"This part is." Marcus replied.

Angelina glanced up at him.

"Remember the decimated building we could see from the apartment?"

Angelina nodded

"I think he is taking us around those buildings. I imagine to keep us, well, you and Francesca from seeing the destruction."

"I don't have a weak stomach."

"No, but you have a heart. To see the decimation of hundreds of families' homes is soul-crushing."

An image of the rubble at the end of the street stirred the pain in her heart. Marcus made a valid point. Those families lost their homes *and* loved ones.

At least I still have a home. She thought. A tear escaped her lashes.

Lost in her vault of sadness, Angelina did not notice Marcus's step quicken. His gentle guidance through the crowd shifted to a jostling hustle. She looked up. The gap between them and The Conductor had grown significantly.

"Why is he moving so damn fast?" Marcus gritted his teeth. "Ladies, we have to walk faster."

They careened their way through the crowded walkway like passengers late for a train.

Panting and annoyed, Francesca shouted. "Where did he go? How can we lose a guy that big?"

"He took a right up there." Angelina pointed toward the street. "Unless he started a hard run after turning the corner, we should be close to catching up."

"We better! These shoes only have one gear, and it isn't *fast*!"

In sync, Marcus and Angelina released a loud chuckle.

"That wasn't meant to be funny!"

When they turned the corner, The Conductor was at the bottom of the hill. He bowed to a lady and entered a building.

"Finally!" Francesca grimaced and slowed her pace. "Go ahead, I'm done running!"

Marcus tapped Angelina's arm to slow their pace.

"Sis, do you know who he works for?"

"Not with certainty."

"What does that mean?"

"It means I am uncertain!"

"What are you hiding?" Marcus's eyes narrowed.

"I'm not *hiding* anything!"

His hand clamped tighter on Angelina's arm.

"Stop squeezing my arm! You are hurting me!"

"Good morning," a young lady chirped, breaking the brewing squabble. "Your friend is waiting inside."

Marcus's lips tightened. He reluctantly released her arm. His agitation was obvious, but Angelina did not care. She told the truth about the conductor. She was not certain...about anything anymore.

"Go ahead. I will wait for Francesca."

"There is no hurry. We can wait for her," the lady said kindly. "Ah, is that her? The one grimacing with each step."

Francesca hobbled the final few feet to where her companions waited.

"Signorina, there is a good shoe store three doors down if you wish to be released from your prison sentence."

Francesca gave the lady a half-hearted smile.

"Suit yourself!" the lady quipped. "This way."

The trio followed the lady as she weaved between the tables in the first room of the caffé. She opened a door and ushered them into a narrow hallway that led to a set of stairs. At the top, they walked past two closed doors. She opened the third door to a small room with one table. Opposite the door, The Conductor stood to greet the trio as if they were special guests attending a formal event.

"Thank you, Alessandra." The Conductor smiled his appreciation. "Please, come, sit. Sit. We shall fill our bellies with some coffee, savories, and my favorite sweets." He patted his abdomen, emphasizing his love of sugary treats. "Given our limited time, I took the liberty of ordering for us."

The Conductor pulled back a chair for Angelina while Marcus did the same for Francesca. Marcus opened his mouth to speak, but the Conductor halted him with a menacing look.

"First, Signorina Beretta, let me offer my condolences on your three brothers. I am relieved to see one survived the attack. However, you are still in great danger."

Angelina's jaw dropped open. "How did you know he...?"

The Conductor laughed, and a grin pressed against his plump cheeks. "As I said on the train, I know more about you than you could imagine. That is why I was hired for this job."

"Who hired you?" Marcus's jaw clenched.

The Conductor, staring at the closed door, held up his hand. The abrupt movement instantly silenced everyone. Angelina exchanged concerned looks with her companions. A moment later, the fear in her gut took flight when the handle slowly turned, and the door opened.

"Ahh! Look now, Alessandra and her sister Anna bring us food from heaven! The espresso's aroma is heavenly to my senses, *sei un angelo bellissimo!*"

The young girl's cheeks flushed slightly at the compliment.

"Grazie," Angelina said to Anna as the charming lady placed the small cup in front of her.

"Is there anything else I may get you?" Alessandra asked.

"No, thank you," Angelina smiled.

Angelina glanced at the other three in the party, each with their mouth full of food. The conversation was reduced to silverware clinking against the porcelain plates, followed by gentle sips of a hot liquid.

When she entered the caffè, Angelina's stomach reminded her she had nothing to eat the day before. Unlike her ravenous companions, Angelina refused to inhale her food like a wild animal. With an air of sophistication, she sipped her coffee for a few minutes before starting her inquisition.

"What happened to your accent?"

"One of my specialties is the ability to blend in. In my line of work, we must be able to be seen but not seen."

For his non-answer, Angelina gave him a placid smile.

"All of you must have many questions. I do not mean to deter your query, as it may have appeared. Especially to you, Signore. Do you use Beretta as your sir name?"

The question silenced the clink-clink around the table.

"Yes, what else would it be?" Angelina scoffed. "I thought you knew *everything* about me."

The Conductor, ignoring Angelina, stood to extend his hand to Marcus.

"I am Gerhard Dümmel. It is a pleasure to meet you."

"Why do you know everything about my sister?"

"In my business, I am paid for my skills, one of which is gathering intelligence."

"Then, why question my last name?"

"It is good to know the minds of everyone in your traveling party. Frau Francesca is from my country and has lived here for nearly seven years. She is the most skeptical of your group but for good reasons."

At the mention of her name, Francesca stopped eating.

"I must extend my apologies for the brevity of our time in Turin. It is a beautiful city with so much to see, as you well know, Frau Francesca. However, we must not linger long at any one location. To do so places the surrounding people in grave danger. Besides, Signorina Angelina, you have somewhere to be, and I am never late with a delivery."

"What do you mean?" Angelina's eyes widened.

"If you could finish your breakfast quickly." Gerhard lassoed the air with his pointer finger. "We have a long journey ahead. Now, if you will excuse me, I have a bit of personal business to attend to before we leave."

Gerhard dabbed his napkin to the corners of his lips before leaving the table. Angelina looked at his empty plate. In minutes, Gerhard consumed several cookies, two sweet rolls, and his espresso. She had yet to finish her coffee or her pastry. Defiantly, she savored her hot drink, occasionally dipping her biscotti into the warm liquid.

"Sis, you better slam the rest of that."

"He hasn't answered our questions, Marcus. We only followed him this far for him to tell us what *we* want to know." Angelina leaned back and sipped her coffee.

"I am not too fond of him either, but he has a point."

"A point?" Francesca snorted derisively. "He hasn't talked long enough to have a point!"

"Precisely." Angelina agreed. "We go nowhere until he tells us who he works for and where we are going?"

Their squabble was interrupted when Gerhard returned to the table with two white paper sacks and a childish grin.

"I thought we might enjoy some sweets along the way. I could eat a dozen of these little yellow cookies," Gerhard beamed and popped one into his mouth. "Since I have never met a sweet I didn't like, I bought a variety."

"Tell us who you work for and why he wants to help us?" Marcus leaned back and crossed his arms.

"Ah, the first I can answer. As to the second, that is for him to say. As I said, I work for him. I do as I am told, nothing more." Gerhard dug in the bag for another cookie. "My boss was born near here, but his family moved to America when he was about ten."

"Signore Fiori is your boss?" Angelina asked.

"Ahh! I was told you were a clever lady!"

"A man at my brother's funeral gave me this letter from Signore Fiori." Angelina pulled the note from her purse. "But I do not understand why he wants to help me, or if he can!"

Marcus stiffened and tapped his foot. Fully aware of his displeasure, Angelina ignored him. At that moment, while Gerhard's attention was split between her questions and the bag of cookies, she needed to discover all she could.

"My boss is very resourceful. If he says he will help, then that is what he will do. I can say I have never worked for a man truer to his word." Gerhard popped another cookie into his mouth. "You will meet him soon enough, and I have no doubt that you will feel the same."

"Who is this Signore Fiori? Why is he so interested in us." Marcus's patience for the conductor was gone, and he was none too happy Angelina kept information from him.

"The protective brother, I see. Good!" Gerhard patted Marcus's shoulder. "I like to see such fire in a young man! But, given your commander's remarks, it is no surprise."

"If you work for Signore Fiori, you must know what he intends to do." Angelina scooted forward in her seat.

"As I said, that is for my boss to discuss. I am here for one reason." Gerhard gestured toward the door. "Shall we!"

Gerhard handed the waitress several bills folded together and whispered something into her ear. A look of surprise washed over the young lady's face as she stared down at the money. Before she could question the substantial amount, Gerhard told her the extra was because of her beauty. Instantly, the young lady's cheeks flushed pink, and her smile broadened with appreciation.

Outside the caffé, Gerhard puffed his chest and took in the warm morning sun. He patted his gut and sighed.

"Now that he has had a treat, we can begin our journey!" Gerhard, falling in step with Angelina, spoke to her with a father's tenderness. "It must be difficult not knowing all you desire. I know it would frustrate me to be in your position."

"Then tell me why Signore Fiori..."

Gerhard held a finger up to his lips. "No names."

Shocked by his harsh tone, Angelina paused her response until the logic of his comment took root. She nodded obediently.

"Be patient. My boss is exceedingly resourceful. More so than I, and I am considered the best in Europe. He will take care of you."

"Why did you ask about Marcus's last name?"

Gerhard cocked his eyebrow. "Do you truly not know?" His eyes widened. "Ah! By your expression, I see you *do*."

Angelina shook her head.

"I see. Then it is not for me to tell."

Gerhard fell silent and quickened his pace. His long strides forced Angelina to hasten her steps to keep up.

"You are not from Italy?"

He shook his head and peered down the street.

"Then how did your boss find you?"

"We have been acquainted for many years."

"Have you worked for him before?"

He nodded absently.

"Doing what?"

"That is not an answer for your ears."

"I am not a child!" Angelina's hand landed on her hip.

"No, you are not. But satisfying your curiosity is not my priority." Gerhard stopped walking and glared at Angelina. "Getting you out of this city is. Had you remained at the vineyard, I would have greeted you properly and escorted you to your destination. Your impatience led us into this mess. Now, I must fix it!"

They continued their zig-zag path down alleyways and side streets, with the occasional jaunts along the busy thoroughfares. On the crowded avenues, Gerhard's head swiveled frequently. Angelina followed his gaze; however, her height did not lend her the same vantage point as his.

After his last harsh comment, Angelina hesitated to ask another question. Finally, her curiosity won, and she broke her silence.

"What are you looking for?"

"Your previous traveling companions."

"From the station? No one could have followed us!"

"No one?" Gerhard grinned. "Are you sure about that?"

Angelina grimaced.

"Ah! There she is!" Gerhard beamed. "Wait here."

"Who?"

Her question was fruitless. Gerhard, nearly skipping, was already across the street. He disappeared into the smallest of three buildings.

Angelina took advantage of the moment of solitude to examine more of the surrounding sights. The war untouched Many nearby structures; however, their façade was stripped of any brightness. Scattered among the dank survivors were buildings grandly repaired, sparkling with crisp colors of fresh paint that seemed to glow next to the worn, chipped neighboring façade.

From the apartment above, a pianist was playing an elaborate arrangement. The beautiful notes spilled into the air, carrying beats of tranquility flowing in a peaceful waterfall. Lost in the soothing notes, Angelina did not notice Francesca next to her.

"I'm going into that boutique." Francesca pointed to the next building. "I promise not to take long."

"We will wait here for you." Marcus smiled warmly.

When Francesca was out of sight. He pulled Angelina inches from his red face. "We need to talk!"

"Ouch!"

"Why didn't you tell me about the letter?"

"It is hard to remember every detail!"

"A letter is an unforgettable detail. Especially one you have in your pocket!"

"It was in my purse, not my pocket."

"A technicality. What else have you not told me?"

Gerhard's reappearance prevented her from responding.

"You will enjoy this, my friend!" Gerhard said as he placed his hand on Marcus's shoulder.

With a big grin, Gerhard dangled a key in front of Marcus's face before guiding him toward a burgundy automobile. The sleek lines, long front end, and spacious interior were breathtaking.

"It is gorgeous!" Angelina's eyes reflected the car's beauty.

"This is an Alfa Remao!" Marcus slowly walked around the car, taking in every elegant curve.

"Ah! You know your cars!"

"I have dreamed of owning this car! When I signed on to the military, I saw a picture of one. It was the same burgundy color. Talk about love at first sight." Marcus bounced his brows. "She is even more beautiful in person!"

"So beautiful, you need to tickle her curves, ehh?"

Grinning, Marcus nodded.

Francesca reappeared, two inches shorter, in a new pair of shoes and joined them in their admiration of the stunning vehicle. Beaming with pride, Gerhard stood aside and savored the universal appreciation of his impeccable taste.

A consummate gentleman, Gerhard, opened the door. He offered his hand to assist the ladies into the car, flashing each a charming smile. Once they were settled, Gerhard removed a booklet from his jacket's breast pocket and waved it to catch Marcus's attention.

"Marcus, look at this map with me."

Gerhard smoothed the map over the hood and whispered to Marcus before tracing his finger across the page.

"Angelina." Francesca tapped her shoulder. "Angelina!"

Angelina brushed her away. Gerhard and Marcus were speaking quietly, too quietly for Angelina's curiosity.

"Are you really going to allow him to take us somewhere?"

"Shh!" Angelina snapped.

Placing his hand on Marcus's shoulder, Gerhard mumbled something. Angelina flinched when she saw her brother's eyes widen and his face run pale.

"Then I shall drop behind you. You know the way from there," Gerhard added at an audible level.

After Marcus gave him a nod, Gerhard walked back to address Angelina.

"This is a gift from my boss."

Shocked and confused, Angelina awkwardly accepted it.

"As is this." Gerhard cupped Angelina's hand gently and kissed the back of it. He was a chivalrous knight extending a greeting on behalf of his king. "I can see why he will spare no expense for you. If your family is even half as enchanting as you, his determination is not unwarranted."

Angelina's cheeks flushed. "Thank you."

"Your brother knows where we are to go."

"I thought you were to keep us safe?"

"I am. Two vehicles are merely a precaution. In my line of work, having a plan 'B' in play can be quite handy," Gerhard said with a wink. "Until we meet again, Auf Wiedersehen!"

Angelina absently played with the package, slowly spinning it in several directions as they drove out of town.

"Well," Marcus prompted.

"Huh?" Angelina shook away her dazed thoughts.

"Are you going to open it?"

From the backseat, Francesca stretched her arm over to block Angelina.

"No! Don't! What if it is a bomb?"

Angelina and Marcus flashed an incredulous glare at her.

"Why would you say that?" Angelina scowled.

"You can't tell me I am the only one to think it."

"It did cross my mind." Marcus shrugged.

"He is too nice, Francesca. There is no way he would harm us. Besides, he knows Signore Fiori!"

"Does he?"

"What does that mean." Angelina's brow furrowed.

"Gerhard, if that is his actual name, never said his boss was Signore Fiori!"

"Yes, he did!"

"No, Angelina. *YOU* asked him, but he did not say *yes*. He only stated how *clever* you are!"

"She is right, Sis!" Marcus grimaced. "Gerhard never said Fiori, only you. He always referred to *his boss*!"

"That is not true! Both of you are wrong!"

"Face it, he works for The Don!" Francesca flopped back in her seat and mumbled. "How far does his tendrils reach?"

"Then why did he protect us from Antonio and Bruno?"

"Did he? Or did Marcus thwart all of their plans?"

"Sis, she makes a good point."

"You are on her side?"

"I am on the side of being alive! I don't think that excludes one *side* or the other, Lina."

"It would explain why he is not riding with us!"

Angelina stared at the package. The idea it was a bomb wrenched her gut. Reviewing every exchange with Gerhard, she searched for the evidence needed to prove Francesca's theory was wrong.

"Lina, Francesca is right. I don't think you should open it."

"How can it be a bomb? It is not ticking!"

Marcus chuckled.

"Sis, not all bombs *tick*. There are many types of explosives. Some require a simple trigger to set them off. Opening the box could be enough to make it explode."

"You should throw it out the window, Angelina!"

"I disagree with both of you! Gerhard is who he says he is. In my gut, I know it! And this...this is a gift, *not* a bomb!"

"Well, your gut can go boom without me! If you are going to open that, let me out!"

"Suit yourself, Francesca. You will see, the only thing that lights up as we drive away will be our taillights!"

"Marcus, pull over!" Francesca demanded.

"Francesca, that is not wise, especially after what Gerhard told me."

CHAPTER 23

"Hello, Peter." Maximus gave his old friend an overly wide smile and extended a hand toward a chair across from him.

"Maximus." Hatred seeped from Peter's voice.

"I ordered you a drink." Maximus motioned to the waitress. "Still a bourbon man?"

"This will be a short meeting." Peter waved off the waitress. "There is no need for her to bring the lavish spread you undoubtedly ordered. I will not stay long enough to enjoy the generous hospitality of a kind soul such as yourself."

"Buying an old friend a drink isn't against the law."

Maximus motioned again for Peter to sit.

"You are right. Miss, I will take a water, please...no ice." Defiantly, Peter sat down. "How have you been, Freddy? They treat you alright in there?"

Freddy kept his elbows on the table, one hand clenched and the other holding his drink. He nodded to Peter, then sat back to observe the upcoming match.

"Always a man of eloquent silence." Peter snorted. "So, what is so urgent?"

"Relax." Maximus held up his hands. "You are too tense?"

Peter arched a brow at Maximus.

"Peter, I know our last exchange was less than pleasant."

"Really? Less than pleasant? Go fuck yourself, Maximus!"

Maximus firmly gripped his glass. "Do not overstep."

"Me? Now, why would I, your friend, ever....overstep? It wouldn't be in response to your actions? No, not you. You are the good guy...at least you believe you are."

"Do you really want to air your dirty laundry here?"

"Why not? You never gave me a straight answer."

"*No* is as straight as it gets!"

"Fine. Then give me the meandering, bullshit story of why your answer was a flat *no*! Even better, let's get Freddy and the waitress's opinions on the matter. You might learn something about yourself."

Maximus released a slow, steady sigh while he twirled his drink between his fingers. It reminded him of Johnny spinning the bottle of whiskey.

"What do you want, Peter?"

"I believe it was you who asked for a favor. So don't waste my time any longer. What is your big emergency, and what must I do to get off your list of abusable vendors?"

Freddy leaned forward, making Peter shift in his chair.

"I need a plane."

"You had to ask that in person?" Peter nervously glanced at the ominous giant on his left.

"Tomorrow."

"Sure, I will snap my fingers, and you will have a plane." Peter shook his head in disbelief. "I work for the government, not a magician."

"You get done what you want." Maximus straightened his cuffs, his diamond pinkie ring spraying a hundred shimmering shapes around him. "We may need a ride back the same day or the next."

"Wow, you sure ask a lot of a guy. All I get is a glass of water."

"He offered you a drink." Freddy growled. "*You* refused."

Peter squared his shoulders. "Aren't you supposed to be rehabilitating in Chicago, away from the uncivilized Italian culture? Looks like Judge Jack's orders once again didn't stick to the slippery Fiori."

Maximus gave Freddy a nod to stay put.

"Peter. I don't like what has happened to our friendship."

"Fuck you."

"Things should have gone differently, but I cannot change the past. What's done is done."

"Is that your way of apologizing?"

"If it is, will it make you less of an ass?"

Maximus shook his head. He drew a breath and cognitively shifted his attitude to a friendly tone.

"I don't want us to be enemies, Peter."

"Then you shouldn't have thrown me out of your house."

"You went behind my back." Maximus's temper escalated.

"Behind *your* back? She is a grown woman. I think she can choose the man she loves. But then, what does Maximilianus Fiori know about love?" Pausing, he looked into Maximus's eyes. Peter's lips curled into a devilish grin. "Wait! Have you found your true love, Max? Is that why you need a plane?"

Maximus gripped his glass. He envisioned grabbing Peter's hair and repeatedly banging his thick skull against the table. It was a soothing thought but not a productive one.

"Peter, I think you need to cool down, or this will not go the way either of us desires."

"You are right, Maximus. Except this is going to go exactly the way *I* want it. This time, I will turn my back on *you*." Peter stood to leave. "How did you say it to me, *this is an act of brotherly love?*"

Maximus grabbed Peter's hand. Squeezing tightly, he began racking Peter's knuckles against each other. Adding to the pain, Maximus turned Peter's wrist enough to cause his thumb to bend backward.

"Sit. Down." Maximus bared his teeth.

Peter tried to hold the pain in, but a small squeak chirped from his throat. It was loud enough to cause other patrons to turn around for a look at the commotion.

"I will break your thumb, then each finger, one by one. Sit—Down!" The veins in Maximu's temples throbbed.

Peter sat down, and Maximus released his grip.

"Now, let's try this again...Like adults."

Nodding, Peter sat quietly and nursed his hand.

"Peter, we have been business partners for a long time and friends even longer."

"I was not your partner."

"Okay. You *facilitated* my business with the government. Because I executed my part, there are certain rewards for, shall we say, *services rendered?*" Maximus, leaning closer, held Peter's gaze, and he asked his companion. "Freddy, do you think the American people would trust a government that lied to them about their involvement with Italy *before* they changed sides? The war may be over, but the wound is still fresh."

"Please. We lie to people every day." Peter shook his head, unimpressed by the threat.

"Peter, I am going to explain my proposal, and I expect you to take the generosity that comes with it."

"I will pass on any of *your generosity*. The last time I accepted it, I found my face on your sidewalk!"

Maximus drummed his fingers on the table. He wanted to strangle Peter, but that would not get him on a plane.

Quietly, Maximus groaned. "Do you still love my sister?"

Peter opened his mouth to give a smart-ass remark but promptly closed it. His loss of wit was the confirmation Maximus needed. Olivia was still Peter's weakness, which would bring him to his knees.

Olivia was still in love with Peter. Frequently, she reminded Maximus of his interference in her happiness. The anniversary of tossing Peter out was filled with harsh words and broken dishes. He allowed her the tirade and the repetitive slaps to his cheek. He could have fixed the situation, as his sister frequently reminded him. He promised he would. However, Maximus hoped Peter would move on, saving him the trouble of explaining why it was an unsuitable match. They were wounded, mindless animals lashing out in their world. In a mental state such as that, neither would see reason, no matter how convincing. Nonetheless, it was true he destroyed their love affair, so he bore the abuse.

"I will never stop loving Olivia!" Peter's voice quivered.

The card was played, and Maximus was honor-bound to follow through. He was unsure if he would ever be prepared for the consequences of reuniting the two lovebirds. But that did not matter at the moment. He would deal with each fallen tree in his path *when* it was before him. Right now, a redwood engraved with the Beretta name was before him.

"As I said before, I would have preferred things to go differently at our last meeting." Maximus spoke in a soft but commanding tone. "This time, however, things will go exactly as I tell you."

CHAPTER 24

Carlos gently opened the door and peered into the dark space. He lowered his head and sighed.

"I thought I would find you in here. Sleeping in Angelina's bed and hiding in her room will not bring her back."

Fernando, hunched forward, ignored his father. He focused on stabbing the corner of Angelina's letter into his palm, imagining it was a knife piercing his skin. This habitual tap-tap of the note had become his pensive masochism that pained his heart, not his hand.

Carlos sat beside Fernando and looked over his son's shoulder. "What is that?"

"A letter."

"From?"

Fernando gave his father an unenthusiastic glare.

"Son, we can play the game of questions and smart-ass replies all night. It will not be the first time for us."

"What do you want me to say?" Fernando rubbed his eyes and sniffled.

"It is not what *I* want you to say. It is what *you* need to express to be released from your self-imposed prison."

"Have you been taking notes from Rosario?"

"In three decades, one melds the good qualities of others into your own persona."

Fernando rolled his eyes and returned to jabbing his palm with the blunted corners.

Carlos placed his hand on his son's shoulder. "Do you want me to talk or listen?"

"Neither."

"What does the letter say?"

"I don't know, haven't opened it yet,"

"Then you have a strong will. If your mother left me a note, I would tear down walls to get to it."

"Sure you would. But Mamma is your wife, not someone pretending to return your love." Fernando gritted his teeth.

"Pretend? Why do you say that?"

"She kissed me because she didn't want to marry Giorgio."

"But she did not. In fact, she was never engaged to him."

"Because she pretended to be engaged to me."

"To my recollection, She only wears the ring that made the impression in that wax. When did you give her a ring?"

"I haven't."

"Ah, so she was not the only one pretending then."

"Lina shoved me away when I could have helped her!"

"Like you are doing to everyone around you since she left."

Fernando glared at his father. The fire of anger melded his fears and sadness into tears of acid pooling around his eyes.

"It is not the same!" Fernando growled.

"She is angry and afraid. You are angry and afraid."

"Afraid of what?"

"Angelina fears that which she has no control over." Carlos wrapped his arm around his son. "You fear her leaving you behind, something *you* have no control over."

"My love should have been enough to make her stay."

"From your eyes."

"They are the only two I have!"

Carlos rose from the bed, shaking his head.

"Then you don't truly love her."

"I love her! You know how much I love her! Everyone knows. Everyone but *her*!"

Carlos ran his hand through his dark locks. He could not solve Fernando's problem. It was a prison of despair created by him, for him alone.

"Breakfast should be ready soon. Come down prepared to get to work. We have a load to deliver."

Never making eye contact with Fernando, Carlos gently closed the door to Angelina's room. The hinges whispered a squeak, and the click of the latch filled the room for a second. It was the last note to an opera filled with tragedy.

Fernando looked at the letter with blunted corners, contemplating his options. His father filled Rosario's shoes well, but Fernando still did not know how to heal his pain.

"There are no words to fix this. None!" Fernando growled. "I love Angelina, but the fact is *she* does not love me... Err! After everything I have done for her!"

Fernando resisted the urge to crumble the letter in his palm. The red wax rose stared up at him, pleading for his mercy.

Carmella's voice echoed from the kitchen below. He was being summoned for breakfast. Being late to a meal she had spent long hours creating was an insult. Out of respect, Fernando made a point to never keep her waiting.

He tossed the letter onto the bed, then ran his hand across the crumpled fabric where he and his father sat. With a few tugs, the comforter was returned to the original elegance created by Angelina.

Fernando turned to leave the room, but the red wax seal on the note seemed to glow on the white bedspread. He snatched the letter off the bed and flipped it over to break the seal. His finger traced the impression of the wax. No matter how mad he was, Fernando loved the author and could not destroy the seal. Slowly, he slid his thumb under the flap and softly popped the wax from the paper.

Gently pulling the note out of the envelope, Angelina's perfume touched Fernando's nose. The sweet aroma begged him to hold the letter close and breathe deeply, savoring her essence. As he inhaled, the scent embraced him with the tenderness of a hug.

Fernando's hand trembled as he unfolded the note, exposing Angelina's elegant script. The sight brought tears to his eyes and intensified his longing for her.

A gentle knock on the door. Fernando wiped away his tears and looked up.

"Son?"

Carlos peeked into Angelina's room. He saw Fernando's red eyes, rosy cheeks, and the open letter in his son's quivering hands.

"Take your time, Son. Your mother will understand."

Fernando nodded in appreciation. He pushed past his fears and read the letter.

My Dearest Fernando,

As I write this, I know you lay awake in the room down the hall. I can feel the worry you hold for me and our future. Your love is a gift that I will always treasure.

I regret not speaking the words that frequently lingered on my tongue yet never passed my lips. Nan, I love you. I have and always will.

After all that has happened, you deserve better than me. I dare not tell you of the darkness that has soiled me, for I fear the look of disgust in your eyes. For your safety and that of your parents, please let go of your love for me.

Even though the temptation will be great, please do not keep this letter. He will punish you in ways you cannot imagine. He is the devil that walks on earth.

Lovingly,
Angelina

Angelina keeping secrets wounded Fernando, but her thinking anything could destroy his love for her hurt the most.

Fernando slumped into the chair by the small writing desk and reread Angelina's words. Striking a match, Fernando allowed the dancing red and orange colors to lick the corner of the parchment. He agreed with Angelina. Destroying the message was wise, yet Fernando pulled it away from the flame. The match burned close to his fingers, but he ignored the heat. His mind was enraptured with the three words he wanted to fall from her lips. To hear them would be a moment to remember. But now, in her elegant handwriting, he had them for an eternity.

CHAPTER 25

"Peter, I am not asking for a luxury liner. Just get me on a fucking plane!" Maximus shouted, gripping the phone.

Peter held his response as if contemplating the terms, but Maximus knew all too well the stall was to agitate him.

Transatlantic transportation ran continually during the war. Therefore, adding two people to the list of passengers did not raise eyebrows. With the war over, a top federal agent sending two men across the Atlantic required finesse. To complicate things, Peter insisted the trip remain a secret and free of any connection back to him.

"Fine, Peter! No trace back to you. When do we leave?"

"Tomorrow is the best I can do."

"What time will the car pick us up?"

"There will be no car, not here, not from me. You asked for a plane, and that you will get."

Maximus pinched the bridge of his nose. "Fine, I will get a cab."

"If one will take you that far. Since you are a man flush with cash, maybe you should buy a new car! Either way, it is a long drive," Peter said with sadistic pleasure.

"The airport is ten miles away."

"You are not flying out of this airport. Better get your start now if you want to make your flight. I think Fort Jackson is at least twelve hours from here. Maybe more." Peter's glee came through as clear as his words.

Peter hung up, flaring Maximus's temper to a new level. Stretching his neck from side to side, he snarled at the receiver.

"You want to marry my sister, and you treat me like this! If she didn't love you, I would kill you myself!"

Maximus regretted not setting a standard for the trip. It allowed Peter to make sure it was pure hell by arranging for the plane to pick them up at Fort Jackson's old concourse. Inside the airbase's dilapidated building, Maximus paced, his shoes leaving an impression on the grimy floor. Strips of faded wallpaper with jagged edges curled off the crumbling plaster walls. The sour odor from a rotting animal carcass in the bathroom burned his nostrils. Everywhere he looked, something singed Maximus's fried nerves. The only solution to cleaning the place was a gallon of gasoline and a match.

"The smell! Jesus! When was the last time they used this place? At the start of the Great War?" Maximus held his nose.

"The prison's shitter, the morning after ham and beans, smelled better than this!" Freddy said, covering his face.

The long drive from New York put Maximus and Freddy's tempers on a short leash. Though the smell was unbearable, they kept their cool while waiting outside. Their freedom from the toxic air was cut short when gusts of wind pummeled them with gritty dust.

"Please tell me the plane is in better condition than this shit hole!" Freddy's eyes were watering, and he suppressed the reflex to gag. "Is this really the best Peter could do?"

"This is exactly how Peter operates. He has a grudge and knows exactly how to push my buttons. Not sure which pisses me off more, this hell hole or the fact we had to drive all night to get here!"

"Not exactly the way to your sister's heart."

"Ha! Olivia probably instructed him to fuck with me. She hates just as hard as she loves."

"Don't all women?"

A middle-aged man appeared at the end of the room. The man's posture, eyes forward, and chin level reflected years of military experience. His gate was more of a swagger than a march. Coming to an abrupt halt, heels snapping to attention, the airman nodded politely.

"Sir, my name is Captain Larry Welch. I understand you need a lift across the pond." Larry extended his hand.

"That is correct," Maximus replied with a firm shake.

"I hate to bear bad news." Welch's stalwart composure gave the sense that giving any news, good or bad, did not affect his mood. "We cannot fly until the storm passes."

Clinching his jaw, Maximus arched his eyebrow. "You have got to be kidding me. We are grounded for how long?"

"What storm?" Freddy asked.

"That one."

Maximus and Freddy followed the pilot's finger. Out of the dirty windows, a large black cloud stretching the length of the horizon blotted out the sun. A flash of light glimmered in the mountainous puffs, adding to its ominous appearance.

"Fuck me. Did Peter and Mother Nature ban together?" Maximus grumbled, running his hand through his hair. "Freddy, Call Figgy."

"Anything you want me to tell him?"

"Let's see if you can get him on the phone. He is probably polishing that damn car."

While Freddy dialed, Maximus pressed the pilot.

"The storm looks a few miles out. When my friend finishes on the phone, we can get off the ground before it gets here."

"It is gaining strength, sir."

"Looks twenty minutes out. We have time."

Larry jetted out his chin, feigning he was impressed. "Oh! You a pilot, too?"

Catching the intentional mocking, Maximus's nostrils flared. He wanted to clobber him until he was unconscious.

"Didn't think so. Better let me call the shots. Make yourself comfortable! Do not worry, I won't leave without you!"

"Any chance you are wrong, Captain?"

"Sir, I have lived here my entire life. When Mother Nature gets a pinecone up her ass, we wait. Trust me, you do not want to fly into those clouds. They make for a rocky ride."

"How much?"

"Sir?"

"Money. Everyone has a price."

"Sir, you do not understand. Flying in these conditions is a death sentence!"

"I thought you flyboys were made of steel."

"That would be the marines. They get off on staring death in the face while giving God the bird. We *flyboys,* as you call us, are the brains, not the brawn. You want to fly in this shit, go ahead, but you will do it without me and my plane."

Larry's condescending tone was gasoline on Maximus's already raging temper. Maximus squared toes with the pilot, his fist clenched and face blazing red. Larry did not flinch. Just as Maximus opened his mouth to berate the pilot, Freddy shouted across the room.

"Boss!"

"This conversation is not over." Maximus audibly growled.

Unmoved, the pilot shrugged. "No problem, Sir." Larry pulled a comb from his pocket and used the dingy window as a mirror. "I got all day to talk."

Maximus ignored the snide comment and joined Freddy.

"I got Figgy, but your Pops is shouting something. I can't make out a thing because of the shitty connection."

Maximus nodded at Freddy to give him the receiver.

"Figgy put him on the phone."

"Youse want to speak to your Pops?"

"Yes."

"Whose Tess?"

"God damn it, Figgy! Put Vito on!"

Figgy had many unpleasant habits, one of which was never covering the phone when he spoke or, in this case, yelled. Maximus cringed at the blaring noise assaulting his eardrum.

"Mr. Fiori, it's Maximus. Says he wants to talk to you."

Maximus clenched his teeth as he listened to the crackling conversation.

"Where is he?" Vito roared. "Is Rosario dead?"

"He ain'ts said."

"A Fiori never breaks a promise! If Rosario is dead, Maximilianus is dead to me. Dead! Tell him. Dead!"

"Boss, youse hear dat?"

"I heard him." Maximus shook his head. "Jesus Christ, This day keeps getting better!"

"What's youse want me to tell him?"

"I don't have time for games, Figgy. Tell him whatever you need, then go to my office and close the door. I will call you back in five."

"Sure thing, Boss. I got it."

Maximus slammed the receiver on the hook and groaned.

"Pops wouldn't shut up?" Freddy asked.

"He never does, especially when he is angry."

"You dead to him...again?"

Maximus ran his hand through his hair, exposing the throbbing vein in his temple.

"Easy Boss! You are gonna stroke out on me."

"When has anything in my life been easy?"

"Ignore him. In three days, you will be like Jesus and resurrect from the dead; you always do."

"The idea of staying dead is more appealing."

"That don't sound like you, Boss." Freddy leaned over to examine Maximus.

"Ever get tired. Tired of every fucking idiot."

"In prison...every...day. But nothing a few months in solitary confinement couldn't fix."

"I swim in a sea of them. Everybody wants something. Give me, give me, give me. And my family is worse! My mother cries out of fear I will be murdered. My father is like the wind. He likes this, doesn't that; nothing pleases him. Getting a private audience with the Pope is more likely to happen than Pops admitting you did something right. Even sweet Olivia busts my balls. She was not like that when we were young. Now, she punishes me for everything that doesn't go her way. I swear to God, Freddy. If I could disappear for a few months." He tilted his shaking head back. "They'd find me, though. Clever, resourceful bastards that find their way into my pocket, into my business. They can't take care of themselves! They look to me to feed, protect, carry, and placate their fragile souls. Every fucking one of them! Fuck! It just gets old."

"Ain't that the price you pay for wearing the crown?"

"Don't push my fucking buttons. Not today, Freddy. It won't go well for you!"

With both hands up, Freddy took two steps back and gave Maximus a slight tip of his head.

"Where the fuck you going? Call Figgy back. Find out if your cousin called with an update. And tell Figgy to keep Peter away from Olivia. Nobody gets what they want until this job is done!"

Maximus removed his jacket and loosened his tie as he paced in front of the panel of tall windows. The wind whistled through the deteriorating rubber seals, and the torrential rain kicked in. Minutes from the first drops dappling the window, the rain shifted to a pounding force against the glass. A small stream of water grew in width and speed across the floor to the lowest point in the room, creating a puddle of murky water on the dirty tile.

Spinning on his heels, Maximus marched back to Freddy.

"And tell Figgy to tell my mother to pray this Goddamn storm away!"

CHAPTER 26

Marcus's recount of Gerhard's warning fed the cancerous disease of fear gnawing at her soul. Life, like her dreams, had transformed into a nightmare.

"Gerhard said the two men sitting across from you on the train are still tracking us. What do you know about them?"

"Impossible!" A tension gripped Angelina's shoulders.

"A blind dog could find us!" Francesca's sarcasm was tinged with fear. "We should have stayed in the apartment."

"No, Francesca. Gerhard said he caused a distraction to get us out of the apartment before they arrived."

Angelina shifted to glare at Francesca in the backseat. "Safe? Really? Who is being naïve now, Francesca?"

"Marcus, did Gerhard give you proof, or is this another one of his verbal manipulations of the truth?"

Marcus shrugged.

"It appears *you* are the naïve one, Angelina!"

Gripping the wheel, his knuckles turned white, and he released a low moan.

"Two bickering women. No wonder I joined the military." Marcus shook his head. "Look, Gerhard planned to take Angelina to the drop zone in this car, but you and I were not part of the equation. Neither was Don Salvatore's henchmen. Gerhard taking a second vehicle is a form of protection; it is a logical strategy!" Marcus held his hand up, silencing their rebukes. "That is enough on the matter. We have a long drive ahead. We may need to drive in shifts, so get some rest. I will drive as long as I can."

The car was a cavern of silence, allowing Angelina to admire the view. The moonlit towns faded in and out of view. Rolling acres of farmland abutted the white peaked mountains stretching high into the night sky, yearning to touch the stars. Moonbeams sprinkled thousands of shimmering diamonds across the surface of the lakes and rivers. It was an endless display of God's beautiful creations.

Half of her heart enjoyed the adventure, while the other felt the weight of empathy. After passing through the third town destroyed by the war, Angelina, as she had done in Turin, discounted her personal pain. Her tragedy was nothing compared to the dwellers of these cities. They lived every day in terror, in a never-ending cycle of stress. The fear of the next bombing raid or the enemy confiscating everything was a veritable hell. They lost homes, jobs, family, and money. Angelina's emotional pain would fade with time. These people, however, would need more than just time. Their deep wounds transcended mere death.

The morning sun was well into its glory the morning they arrived outside Cherbourg, France. The deep sound of a ship's foghorn bellowed as it approached the port. On the horizon, three tall, black smokestacks billowed columns of darkness into the crystal blue sky.

Wide-eyed, Angelina soaked in as many details of the bustling city. She had never seen the Atlantic Ocean, much less a busy seaport. From their hillside perch, the pattern of buildings that lined the many crisscrossing streets created a kaleidoscope of details. It was a far different world than the rolling hills of vines back home.

"This is the place." Marcus pointed.

"It seems so...so..."

"Big?" Marcus chuckled as he parked the car alongside the road. "You should get out more!"

Angelina grimaced, but his smile was contagious.

The war decimated Cherbourg, France, but the citizens did not let the ominous weight of the past hold them down. Her residence's communal healing hands were transforming segments of the crumbled structures back into a beautiful oceanside port. To see the transition was to watch an artist pull the beauty of life from the tragedy of death.

"What are we supposed to do?" Angelina asked.

"Wait here."

"Do you think it will work?" Francesca posed.

He shrugged. "We won't be alive to know the difference."

His reply was humorous, but no one felt much like laughing. The truth of the statement was all too real.

"There are a few cookies left. Anyone want breakfast?"

Angelina held the bag up. Francesca shook her head, but Marcus quickly snatched a couple cookies.

"In the military, I learned you eat when there is food and rest when you can. It may be a long time before you get the chance again."

It was a bleak philosophy but one laden with logic, enough to convince Francesca to accept several cookies.

"Coffee would be nice." Angelina stared at her cookie longingly. Subconsciously, she wished she could transform the sweet nugget into the soul-soothing dark liquid she loved.

"Hot, black gold!" Marcus relaxed back, melting into his seat. "None of that brownish muddy water! Rich, dark deliciousness."

"Mmm, Mamma's espresso. She made the best!"

Oblivious to Francesca's bubbling impatience, Marcus and Angelina mused over fond memories.

"Could you please stop talking about food! And stop acting like that box isn't dangerous!"

"How shall we pass the time?" Angelina cocked her head, looking back at Francesca.

"How about getting out of this car and stretching our legs? Better yet, we go into town and get some food!"

"I could use a stretch." Marcus perked up. "Gerhard should be here soon. Food will have to wait."

Marcus helped Francesca out of the car. A wild, pinned-up mare, she took long, quick strides away from him. The wind whipped her hair, adding to the things she grumbled about.

"What's the matter, Sis?" He leaned against the car.

Angelina glanced over to see if Francesca was close, but her long legs had quickly put her out of earshot. "She wasn't like this when I met her."

"I think I make her nervous. What you said about her experience with Don Salvatore's thugs, I am not surprised."

She leaned against the car next to her brother. Staring into nothingness, she reviewed her recent decisions.

"Marcus, do you trust Gerhard?"

"I don't know, Sis." He wrapped his arm around her shoulder, giving her a firm squeeze.

The siblings watched the town of Cherbourg come to life. Large engines roared as the heavy equipment moved piles of rubble to a location on the outskirts of town. Small sparks of light flickered and fell from blowtorches several stories high above the shell of a ship. The repetitive clank-clank of sledgehammers driving spikes deep into metal echoed in every direction. It was a mesmerizing symphony of sounds and activity.

"Are you ready, Sis?" Marcus nodded toward the oncoming car. "He is here."

In a black Alfa Remao, Gerhard abruptly stopped behind them, sending a plume of dust into the air.

"Stay here!" Angelina grabbed the package from the front seat and strode to Gerhard's vehicle. She hopped in before he had a chance to get out.

"Don't move!" Angelina commanded.

Gerhard cocked his head. "What is the matter?"

Scrutinizing his every reaction and movement, she held the box in the air. "This!"

Gerhard flinched, but his tension was fleeting. His eyes, except for the dark bags of exhaustion, were normal. His skin color was pale, and his breathing slightly accelerated. For a man who drove nonstop, Gerhard appeared as he should, exhausted. If he was fearful, he was very good at his job, or too tired to show it.

"Why did you not open ze box?"

Angelina noticed his slight slip to his homeland's dialect. It was his only sign of nervousness.

"Who is your boss?"

"I told you his name." He shook his head, confused. "Why so agitated?"

"I will ask the questions. You get to answer them!"

Gerhard relaxed his shoulders, leaned back against the driver's seat, and sighed his resignation.

"Tell me your boss's name!"

He released a hearty laugh that faded into a yawn.

"I do not understand women. My wife, she is wonderful woman, but like you, she is strong-headed. Sometimes, I think she picks a fight just to fight! Why does she do this?" He shrugged. "Why do ze want to fight against me? Ahh! But you are to ask ze questions. I am to answer, and I shall. Once you put that box down."

Angelina's face went slack and pale.

"Is it a bomb?"

"Nice...and...easy, Frau."

Tears welled in Angelina's eyes. She fought to keep them contained, but two escaped as she slowly placed the box on the seat between them.

"Good. Good, Frau."

Angelina's gaze remained on the box, willing it to transform from a bomb to a gift.

"Angelina!" Marcus cried out as he lunged toward the car.

Her brother's panicked voice made her heart race, but not as much as the terror in his eyes. Angelina followed the imaginary line from Marcus's finger to Gerhard. Caught by both of them, Gerhard froze with his hand inside his suit coat.

"Lina! He has a gun!"

CHAPTER 27

"Si. I will tell her," Constance replied as she left Giorgio's room.

Her trembling hands struggled to hold the heavy silver tray as she used her backside to open the wooden door.

"Remember what we agreed, Constance." Giorgio cocked his brow.

"I pledge my soul to her wellbeing, Signore."

Once free of his direct gaze, Constance leaned against the closed door to catch her breath.

"Forgive me, Lord, I know not what I am doing," Constance muttered. "Save all I love from the devil's teeth, for surely, if I fail, he will devour those dearest to me."

The thump-thump sound of Giorgio approaching prompted Constance to scurry out of sight. Giorgio's door flung open as she tucked into the servant's corridor.

"Are you supposed to be up, or are you disobeying Dr. Mariano again?" Catalina asked, slightly winded from her quick ascent up the stairs.

"I thought I heard a car door." Giorgio stepped into the hallway, greeting his bride with a wide smile. "The doctor was here an hour ago. She released me from my bedded prison!"

"Where is Constance?"

"Around the corner, listening."

A muffled gasp and the clank of china echoed down the hall, eliciting a quiet giggle from Catalina.

"You have the most beautiful smile. It is what captured my heart." Giorgio's smile softened to one of adoration.

Catalina dipped her head and unpinned her hat. She ran her fingers through her long dark curls, fluffing them into a presentable formation.

Giorgio was inches away before the hand in her hair returned to her side. His cane crashed against the floor, and his right arm scooped Catalina into a lover's embrace.

"I love you." He whispered, his lips nearly grazing hers.

She was surprised by his quick advancement. Her mouth opened to comment on his agility, but Giorgio pressed his lips against hers. For a moment, she resisted, but his hard, muscular body against her stirred a powerful lust.

Part of her wanted to refuse his passion, but her tumultuous life was a desert of sadness. Her wounds were dry, expansive cracks begging Mother Nature to send a soothing rain to replete the loveless drought. A drought stemming from Angelina's poisonous words and Giorgio's adultery. Yet, Cat loved and desired Giorgio despite his transgressions. The smell of his cologne, the warmth of his embrace, and his lips tenderly yet urgently kissing her melted away Catalina's hesitation. She absorbed every molecule of love and hoped the utopian moment would last forever.

Her hands reflexively roamed across his back. His muscles flexed under his soft cotton shirt, exciting her. It was the same uncontrollable desire she experienced during their first kiss. She would have allowed him to take her long before their wedding night, but Giorgio never did. It was another reason Catalina ignored her sister's accusations. Angelina did not know the *real* Giorgio. He was a different man when alone with Catalina.

Two days after the official announcement of their engagement, Giorgio and Catalina walked alone through the rows of vines. Giorgio smiled and laughed at Catalina's excitement. She wanted to show him everything. All the places and stories that made Catalina who she was at that moment. Twirling around him, hand in hand, Catalina led Giorgio around the vineyard. The last stop on her tour was where Catalina frequently imagined her dreamy future.

Catalina tucked her chin. "As a little girl, I was always shadowed by Angelina's presence. No man, except you, paid any attention to me once they met Angelina. So, I would dream about the man I would marry. I wanted my love story to be like

Cinderella's. Instead of a shoe, I would enchant him with a bottle of my family's wine at his birthday gala. When he tasted the wine, he would proclaim it the best. From then on, the prince craved the wine to wet his lips. His men hunted for the winemaker's daughter. They found me at my favorite spot on top of this boulder by the stream. With all haste, they rushed to their prince, sharing the grand news. The Prince...almost as handsome as you." Smiling, she batted her lashes, soaking in his attractive features. "The Prince rode to the vineyard to meet the enchantress."

She looked up at him, lost in his aura of charm and beauty.

He held his hands out, waiting for the rest of the tale.

Catalina blushed and looked away.

"He found my beauty intoxicating, my lips more desirable than the wine, my eyes captivating. He professed my personality completed his quest for the perfect bride. I would be forever known as Princess Catalina and live happily ever after." Still unable to meet his gaze, she added. "I have never shared my fantasy with anyone."

He grabbed her face and stared into her eyes.

"You will *never* be a princess!"

She flinched at his harsh words. Biting back her tears, she tried to free herself from his grasp. "Why would you say such mean things to me! I opened my heart to you."

Putting his finger on her lips, he hushed her.

"You will never be a princess," Giorgio repeated, his face only inches from hers. "Because you will be my *queen!*"

Under the robin-blue sky, the sun transformed the babbling stream into a river of dazzling diamonds. The crickets and springtime frogs harmoniously sang a love song while the breeze danced with the leaves to the sweet melody.

Giorgio gazed passionately into her eyes. Her body, hot with lust, pressed against the cold, smooth edges of the bolder. His warm hand found the small of her back, drawing her closer to him. Her heart pounded with anticipation of her first kiss.

Catalina's body ached for him with an intensity she had never known. As he pressed his body against hers, she could feel his throbbing passion. Catalina had never seen a naked man, so her mind imagined what his pants concealed, making her desire him even more.

They held a lover's gaze for what seemed like an eternity until he leaned in, pressing his soft lips to hers. The world went silent, and time had no control over their lives.

The sun descended in the sky before they broke from their passionate tryst. That night in bed, her lips were still tingling from his kisses. She exhaled deeply, releasing with it the idea of her fairy tale. Giorgio was not her prince; he was a king, *her* King. And she would not be a mere princess. She would be *his* Queen forever more.

He stole her heart with their first kiss. However, the memory of his naked body next to hers on their first night together bonded their souls. Giorgio exceeded her dreams in every way. He was giving, compassionate, thoughtful, and loving. Yet, their equally ravenous passion for each other bound them even closer. In Giorgio's arms, Catalina's dreams and needs were fulfilled.

Even now, after the funerals, Angelina's accusations, and Giorgio's miscreant behavior, Catalina's desire for him had not waned. His caressing hands soothed Catalina's battered soul. Butterflies whirled around her heart when he whisked her off the ground and carried her to his bed.

"But, your cane!" Catalina reached for it.

"I think I can handle *next* well enough without it."

He gently laid her on his bed and resumed his passionate pursuit. Catalina unbuttoned his shirt, and he peeled it off, his lips never leaving hers.

Shoes, pants, shirts, and undergarments flew from the mattress until the two lovers were warm flesh against warm flesh. There were no words, only moans of pleasure as the lovers melted together. Time did not exist, just their passion.

Giorgio, winded from their exertion, pulled Catalina close, wrapping his arm around her. She nuzzled in and rested her head on his shoulder.

"Trapped in this room for days has opened my eyes," Giorgio said in a soft, far-off whisper. "Lying in bed, staring at the curtains, I realized two things..."

Catalina felt her body tense in his embrace. Was this when reality crushed her fantasy?

"I need you."

In a reflexive motion, she snapped her head away from his chest to look at his face. She wanted to see his dark pupils dance with the lie, but his eyes were entranced in a dreamy wonder. The broad lines across his brow had softened, and his face, though pale, glowed like an honest man at peace. She fought the urge to ask about his other epiphany. After a long pause, her curiosity won.

"And?"

Giorgio stared into her eyes with a fiery intensity. Catalina felt the world shift. Suddenly, her life became a rock on a ledge during an earthquake.

"You said you realized two things."

Giorgio revealed a wicked grin.

"I *know* your secret!"

CHAPTER 28

Angelina reached for the door handle, but Gerhard grabbed her wrist, holding tight.

"Stay!"

"You lied to me!" Angelina screamed. "I believed you!"

"Are you more upset about a lie or your belief in a lie?"

Angelina ripped her wrist free of Gerhard's massive hand.

"Tell him to stay where he is." He glanced towards Marcus.

Angelina held her hand up, stopping Marcus in his tracks. Rubbing her wrist, she returned her attention to Gerhard.

"Now. I think we should talk. Hmm?" Gerhard removed the gun from his jacket and rested it on his thigh.

"Are you going to kill me?"

"You are asking ze wrong questions, Signorina Beretta. I was told you were clever, but you do not ask ze questions of a clever girl. Why is that?"

Angelina's eyes darted from the gun to the box to Marcus and back to Gerhard. Stressed wrenched her stomach. She consciously had to talk her body out of vomiting.

"Who hired you?"

"Ahh! A better question." A subtle smirk thinned his lips. "One, I will answer. Although you had ze answer since Turin." He relaxed back, his fingers gently tapping the gun. "Why did you not open ze box?"

"Because it is a bomb."

"I thought we had formed some trust." He released an exaggerated sigh. "Perhaps not. Trust is ze most important part of any relationship. My first job was with ze man who hired me to find you. He and I had never met. How can you trust what you do not know? Of course, it was less about knowing him and more about ze money. I was poor and needed ze money. But how could I know ze fee would be paid if I did ze job? You can learn much by meeting someone face to face. Especially when reading people comes naturally. Much like you a moment ago. You assessed my eyes, my breathing, my skin, yes?"

It was more of a rhetorical question, but Angelina responded with a nod, anyway.

"See. It is so easy if you know what to look for. Your brother, he is very protective. With all that has happened to your family, I understand. But...I think he was protective long before. Frau Francesca trusts no one because of her husband's death. Has she told you what she thinks of her husband now?"

"Francesca loved him deeply. She still does."

"Yes, she loves him, but she hates him too. Alberto had secrets. Now, his secrets are monsters she must fight. Even worse, Frau questions ze validity of his love. I am surprised she has let you in so easily. A woman can lie as easy as a man."

"Enough chit-chat. You are jabbering to avoid answering my question. What you think of me, my brother, or my friend, is irrelevant. Tell me, *who* hired you to find me?"

"Frau is a frail woman since giving birth." Gerhard continued, ignoring Angelina's demand. "Very unusual for a German. We are a hardy breed. She has ze coloring of a German, but I think ze frame of a Swed. Life, though, is ze biggest influence on a person, much more than lineage. Do you think? No struggle makes for a weak mind. Yet you are different. Your life has been good, with minimal stimuli to induce a cunning mindset, yet you are clever. To say ze box is a bomb is ingenious. Who would assume such a small box could be dangerous?" Arching his brow, he tapped a finger to his chin. "But it is not you who thinks it is a bomb."

Unconsciously, Angelina glanced toward Francesca. Delighted, Gerhard's smile broadened.

"Ahh! Thank you. Do not feel you betrayed her. She is who I suspected already. I am curious how she convinced you?"

"She claimed it was a bomb."

"And you believed. So simple. If I claimed Frau was a spy, would you believe me?"

"No!" Angelina glanced at Francesca. "A spy for who?"

"Ah, ze seed is planted. Now, you will wonder if Francesca is or isn't a spy. You will even retrace ze steps that led to your friendship. Doubting her allegiance seems wrong, but then is one week long enough to know someone? A person's past forges their present. Do you know Frau's past?"

Angelina glanced at Francesca again, this time making eye contact. Gerhard's accusation worked, and Francesca's guilty expression gave it merit.

"She cannot hear us, yet she knows ze doubt I sew. Does that give you concern?" Gerhard asked but did not give Angelina time to respond. "How powerful one simple rumor can be. How easy it breeds ze chaos. I do not feel guilty for expanding your mind. Planting ze seed of distrust is ze same game she plays against me."

"Is she a spy for Don Salvatore?"

Her sudden leap to conclusions made Gerhard grin.

"Ah!..See! I did not say Don Salvatore, but your mind connected ze two." He shook his head and wagged a finger. "Tsk-tsk." His grin broadened. "One rumor is soo powerful!"

Angelina's face blanched. Gerhard was proving even more manipulative than Don Salvatore. She knew little about both men but learned so much in one conversation with each.

"Good. Etch ze lesson into your mind. It will help you much along your journey." Gerhard slipped his gun back into his holster and reached for the door. "You have many miles and many more lessons if you wish to beat your monsters."

She hung her head low. Gerhard was right. She was not as smart, clever, and experienced as her adversaries. The revelation was demoralizing.

"Come. Since Frau is ze skeptic, she should open ze box."

"No!"

Gerhard's brow raised, surprised at her staunch reply.

"She is a mother."

"And?"

"Whether or not she is a spy, the child is innocent and deserves to live a life with his mother."

"You do not wish to prove her wrong?"

"I do not wish to make an orphan if she is right."

"Clever *and* compassionate. Admirable traits."

Angelina reached for the box, but Gerhard placed his hand on it, blocking her.

"I will open it."

"What?"

"I know it is not a bomb. But to prove myself to you, I will open it...*alone.*"

Angelina grappled with the intent of his actions. Her eyes darted from the box to the three souls lingering on the ledge of death. It was her choice, all hers this time. Her hand trembling, Angelina opened the car door and hesitantly climbed out.

"Lina?"

Holding her hand up, Angelina shook her head. Marcus stopped and glanced at Gerhard, then back to his sister.

"Angelina, he is a liar!" Francesca wrung her hands.

"You do not know what he said to me, but you accuse him of falseness! Do you have a guilty conscience?"

"Sis, what did he say?"

Angelina's inquisitive gaze lingered on Francesca before looking at her brother. Still processing Gerhard's *lesson*, Angelina remained silent. *One rumor is so powerful!* The words replayed several times until a revelation took hold.

"Gerhard will open the box to prove his allegiance."

"Who is his boss?" Francesca's voice wavered.

Angelina refused to make eye contact. Standing beside her brother, she watched Gerhard. Ten days ago, Angelina would not have watched the gruesome display of Gerhard's body being obliterated. After witnessing death in the vilest form, the thought of seeing another man die seemed trivial.

She clasped her brother's hand and looked to him for reassurance. His eyes were filled with trust. At that moment, he trusted her judgment more than she did. Angelina swallowed hard and nodded to Gerhard to open the box.

"Does it get easier to watch a man die?" Angelina asked.

Marcus shook his head.

Angelina held her breath. What happened next would determine the man's fate and the validity of Francesca's allegiance.

Gerhard removed something from his back pocket before picking up the box. Angelina glanced at Marcus.

"Probably a pocketknife," He said with a reassuring nod.

Angelina's shoulders relaxed a little. Wrapping his arm around her, Marcus drew her in close.

"Sis, I don't think it is a bomb."

"Neither do I, but not everything is always as it seems."

"True."

Angelina and Marcus fell silent as they watched Gerhard's movements closely.

"How do we know he is opening the box and not something else?" Francesca tugged at her skirt.

"We don't! But then, we never know everything, do we?"

Francesca's face went pale from Angelina's harshness.

"Easy, Sis. She is trying to be helpful." Marcus mumbled.

"Is she?"

"She is not a spy if that is what you are thinking."

Angelina looked at Marcus wide-eyed.

"He said she is a spy, but Sis, I can assure you, she is not."

"How..."

"They teach soldiers to do more than shoot guns."

"Are you certain?" Angelina asked.

"Positive! They teach us to march and make a perfect bed."

Angelina snickered. She appreciated the humor.

Gerhard looked up with a broad grin and a twinkle of excitement in his eyes as he waved the box's contents at Angelina.

"Oh, thank God!" Angelina's knee buckled for a moment.

The trio exchanged looks of relief.

"I believe you have a note to read, Signorina!" Grinning, Gerhard climbed out of the car. "And a gift for ze trip."

Timidly, she accepted the box's contents. "Thank you."

Angelina turned away from the intense gazes of her travel companions. She tucked a strand of hair behind her ear before examining the Western Union Telegram sent three days prior. It was addressed to Signorina Angelina Beretta. Though short and to the point, it was all she needed to conclude who sent Gerhard.

Angelina folded the telegram and turned her attention to the small manila envelope.

"Oh, Dear God!" Her eyes widened.

Instantly, Marcus moved closer, as did Francesca.

"What is the matter, Lina?"

Her hands trembling, she showed Marcus the contents of the envelope.

"Generous!" Marcus whistled and pulled out a thick stack of crisp bills. Shaking his head, he fanned them with his thumb. "*Very* generous! Wow, Sis! Who is your benefactor?"

Angelina avoided his gaze and handed him the telegram.

```
Angelina,
   To know you are protected by one
of  the  finest  men  calms  the
brewing  storm  in  my  mind.  With
him,  you  are  safe  from  the  evils
of the world.
   Until we meet, M.F.
```

"Fiori?" Marcus posed.

"Maximus Fiori." Angelina's eyes twinkled.

"I don't know whether to like him or distrust him."

Angelina arched her eyebrow.

"Lina, that is a lot of money. A lot to have *and* to give. How did he make this money?"

"He is an American. Aren't they all rich?"

Impatient, Francesca moved the final few feet closer to join the conversation.

"Money does not convince me and shouldn't convince you either. For the record, I still think this is a trap!"

"Does that sound like a trap?" Angelina asked, handing Francesca the telegram.

"Anyone can create a telegram!"

Angelina moaned and rolled her eyes.

"Francesca, I understand why you do not trust people! But you trusted me, why? Why was it so easy for you to trust me?"

Tears pooled under Francesca's eyes, but she turned away before any fell. Angelina reached to comfort her. Gently, Marcus held his sister back.

"Let it play." Marcus mouthed to his sister.

It was difficult advice to swallow, but Angelina recognized its wisdom and returned to Marcus's side.

"Because of what happened." Francesca's voice cracked.

The sincerity in Francesca's declaration pierced Angelina's heart. Their friendship developed because of similar tragedies. Both lost loved ones by Don Salvatore's order. Understanding the basis of their bond and how cruel her words must have seemed drained the life from Angelina.

One rumor is so powerful! Replayed in Angelina's mind. She glanced at Gerhard. He was leaning against the shiny black car, grinning like a proud father.

"I understand now," She said, shaking her head slowly. "A tough but good lesson."

"Good! Class dismissed." Gerhard gave a short nod. "Signorina, you have a boat to catch!"

"A boat? To where?"

"Not any boat. That boat!"

Angelina followed Gerhard's finger to the bustling harbor. Some vessels were heading out to sea while dozens slowly progressed to the port. Their sizes were as vast as the number, and their purpose was the same. Boats with nets strewn high, billowing white sails attached to masts, cargo ships, ferries, and several large passenger ships puttered about. The busy lives on the vessels were impervious to the onlookers watching in amazement.

"Ze one with ze tall black stacks is ze ship you will board. She is ze RMS Queen Mary, ze fastest and most elegant luxury liner. She and her sister, ze RMS Queen Elizabeth, travel from here to New York every week."

"We are supposed to meet him in America?"

"My instructions were to get *you* to ze pier and buy *your* ticket," Gerhard replied.

"What about Marcus and Francesca?"

"My orders did not include any traveling companions."

"Which is for the best," Marcus added.

"What?" Angelina and Francesca blurted in unison.

"My resurrection should not be public knowledge yet."

"Are you crazy?" Francesca stomped her foot. "She is not traveling alone! We have no proof he is who he says!"

"I believe him," Angelina said, but Francesca ignored her.

"Your sister's safety takes priority over hiding your existence! Besides, this Fiori guy doesn't know either of us." Francesca tugged at her skirt. "We will stay...at a distance. We will only come out if she needs us."

"All good points, Frau, even ze distrust in me." Gerhard nodded his appreciation for her skepticism. "No one knows you are alive, Marcus. Keeping this secret can be helpful, but watching over your sister would be wise, too."

"Lina, do you want me to come with you or return home?"

Angelina looked at each of her traveling companions, searching for any reason to change her answer. In each pair of eyes she saw a level of trust in her decision making abilities. It bolstered her confidence. In less than two weeks, the sum total of her self-esteem was obliterated. Seeing the faith in their eyes was water for a dying man in the desert.

"There is nothing for you to do at home. Not now, at least. If you return, your identity may not be concealed for long. Papa told me, it is better to leave so you can regain your wits and live to fight another day."

"Then it is settled," Marcus confirmed.

"Gerhard, is this enough money to buy them passage?"

Gerhard's laughter shook his belly. "More than enough!"

With his hand open, Gerhard offered to distribute the money. Angelina smiled in gratitude. She had purchased nothing other than groceries or clothing until a few days ago. The one-way train ticket to leave Brusnengo was as far out of the realm of spending money as she had ever gone.

"It will be best if we do not move as a single party. Marcus, please put Angelina's bag in ze trunk. At two, I will take Angelina to ze pier. That should give you long enough to get on board."

Angelina gave her brother a long hug.

"Do you trust Gerhard?" Marcus whispered.

"Yes."

"Remember what you would say to me when Ricardo was picking on you when we were kids?"

Angelina giggled. "Help me!"

Laughing, Marcus shook his head.

"No, mordere il lupo."

"I can't believe you remembered that!"

Marcus tilted his head. "You said it enough!"

"I guess I did." Angelina's smile turned mournful. She missed her other brothers. Even the torturous Ricardo.

Marcus lifted her chin. "If you need me..."

"Bite the wolf!"

Marcus smiled and nodded his head. They embraced in a long, loving hug. A hug that impressed the strength and longevity of their love for each other. If it were their last hug, it would be one to stand the tests of time.

In unison, they said, "Love you."

"Take care of my brother." Angelina hugged Francesca. "He is one-of-a-kind!"

"I am more worried about you!"

"Gerhard will protect me."

The life drained from Francesca's face. She cupped Angelina's chin and sighed.

"They will never stop hunting us, Angelina. They are rabid wolves, more cunning than you can imagine."

"You have been able to shake them for two years. I don't plan on breaking your streak." Angelina smiled.

"We should get moving." Gerhard tapped Angelina's shoulder. "I will wait a few minutes so we do not enter town together."

Marcus shook Gerhard's hand. Before he got in the car, he looked at Angelina. "See you, Sis."

Angelina smiled. "Only when I see you."

.

CHAPTER 29

Catalina posed her question again. "What secret?"

The words scratched the back of her throat, leaving a raw, burning sensation in their wake.

"I will give you one chance to confess on your own."

Her life had crumbled since the night of her brothers' deaths. Confessing the truth meant the past few hours of bliss would transform her life back into chaos. She needed the safe haven of love. She rolled to her side, avoiding his intimidating glare and the darkness it could extract from her.

My husband will not beat it out of me. If you are not the same mind... Catalina recalled telling Constance.

"I have nothing to confess!"

Giorgio pinned her beneath him.

"Don't make me pull it from you!"

Catalina squirmed out from under him and untangled herself from the silky sheet. She moved out of his reach. Putting distance between them was her only shield.

"There is nothing to *pull* from me!" Catalina avoided his eyes. "Because I have no secret!"

Giorgio's temper intensified, and he moved to pursue her. The sheet was wrapped around his cast, holding him hostage. His growl of frustration quickly shifted to a cry of agony.

"Dammit, Woman!" Writhing in pain, he clutched his leg.

"Me! Me! Why is anything my fault? I do nothing but eat, sleep, and move for your pleasure. Everything I do is out of love for you. You, however, take, take, take! *I* should ask *you* why! *Why* are *my* desires the last on your list?"

"*Really*? You think you are the last on the list? Your lack of appreciation is intolerable! Look in your rooms! Your jewelry box is overflowing! Your closet is crammed full! You live in the largest villa! And the balcony cost a small fortune!"

Giorgio attempted to free himself, sparking another wave of shooting pain. Wailing, he collapsed onto the pillow.

"You deserve the pain! I have nothing to confess, but you do. You sick bastard! How could you?" A swell of emotions gushed out in tears. "How could you do it?"

Giorgio demanded she return to him, but she waved him away. His pain was too intense to fight. He fell silent, leaving the crackling fire and her sobs to fill the air.

She wrapped her trembling body in a blanket and collapsed into the gold brocade chair by the fire. The frigid air nipped at her skin, sending goosebumps across her body. She moved to the fire and gently placed another log in the pit of hungry yellow tongues. In moments, it was engulfed by the fire. As the glow expanded, so did the heat, enveloping her like a hug. The dancing flames lured her into a trance, slowly pulling her back to the night of the brutal massacre.

Angelina's accusations were harsh, but what followed that night burned Catalina's stomach. She gripped the fire stoker, stabbing the vision of Giorgio and Angelina together.

"Catalina!" Giorgio attempted to get her attention again. "Cat, this is not how I..."

The words, *how I,* made her snap. Her anger burning hotter than the fire, she stormed toward the bed.

"In my room! How could you? That is *my* space. *Mine*! You gave that space to me. Now it is soiled, soiled by you!"

Giorgio braced for her assault. "What the hell are you talking about?"

"Do not *what* me! You know what you did! With her, of all people *her*!"

Catalina smacked his cast to punctuate her point.

Giorgio yelped, "My leg!"

"Your ass! How could you! With my sister! In *my* room? On the night I learned my brothers were dead? As if being a drunk and a philanderer wasn't enough! I tolerated your behavior out of love, and this is how you repay me!"

"No. No! Cat, I didn't. I wouldn't do that to you!"

"Apparently, you would!" Catalina raised her arm to deliver another wallop.

"Wait!" Giorgio pleaded. "I don't remember! My memory is a blur. Please, I can't think. My head is throbbing!"

"A headache. How convenient!" She held her hand up like a viper, ready to strike. "Too bad! Confess!"

"I...I remember Angelina telling us about your brothers. Then, I left so you could have time alone."

Her eyes narrowed.

"I...remember lying in bed, but I thought of you. The thought of us...like we were a few minutes ago... You know how I get when I drink."

"Oh, I know! All the *girls* at Mario's hotel know, too!"

"Please. I thought it was you! I swear!"

"Liar!" She whacked his leg.

"Dammit, Woman! Have you no heart!"

"I did. You broke it!"

Raising her arm, she moved to the head of the bed.

"Don't..."

"If I wanted to hurt you, I would hit your leg again!" Catalina sneered before pulling the cord to summon Constance. "Constance helped pull your drunk ass off of Angelina. She will set the record straight!"

Giorgio pulled the sheet over his private area and relaxed his head on the pillow.

"Oh please, she has seen you naked." Catalina scoffed. "Practically *everyone* in town has!"

"Fine!" Giorgio whipped the sheet off his lower body with a flip of his wrist.

"Oh, for Christ's sake. Just because she *has* seen it doesn't mean she *wants* to see it again!"

Giorgio growled and flipped the sheet back.

"Get over yourself!" Catalina rolled her eyes. Slipping on her plush green robe, she hissed. "You pushed me to my limit! Now, you will see what happens when you betray me!"

A gentle knock on the door interrupted Catalina's threat, but not the anger seeping from her pores.

"Come!"

"Signora," Constance said, bowing her head.

"Tell him!"

"Signora?"

"Tell him what he did to my sister!"

Constance bowed her head and rubbed her palms against her apron. "He was having...well...he was..."

"Fucking...Say it, Constance, he was?"

"Si, he was...with your sister, Signora."

"And!"

"I heard him call your name in passion, Signora."

Catalina gave Giorgio a grin of satisfaction.

"See!"

It took a moment for the maid's words to sink in. The smile on Giorgio's smug face made her knees buckle.

"What? You said he called out Angelina's name?"

"No, Signora, *your* name."

"Why did you tell me to hit him over the head?"

"Because it was not you."

"No! No! That can't be true. If I knew Giorgio was saying *my* name, we wouldn't have thrown him down the stairs!"

Constance's hand flew up to cover her gaping mouth.

"You did what?" Giorgio demanded.

"You want a confession?" Her hands landed on her hips. "Yes! WE threw you down the stairs! Are you happy?"

"I could have died from that fall!"

Catalina's eyes narrowed. "And I *wanted* you to die! You bastard! You were on top of my sister! Enjoying every second of it, too! So yes! Yes! I wanted you to die! Anybody but *her*!"

"Signora, I am sorry. I should have told you. But you were so upset! I am sorry, Signora. I couldn't bear to tell you any of what I saw or heard. To see you cry."

"Any? What else did you not tell me?"

Rubbing her palms against her apron, the maid took three steps back. "Signora, you are a happy couple, so in love!"

"Constance!" Catalina's rage launched her toward the terrified maid.

"A noise woke me. You know I sleep lightly and..."

"Yes, yes. I know. What else did you see, Constance?"

"When I entered the hallway, your door was open. I saw Angelina stoking the fire. I did not think you would want your guest cold, so I went to help her. But I stopped at the door when I heard her talking to someone." The maid, rubbing her apron, stared at her shoes. "Signora, what she said put me in shock. I should have stopped it...but...I couldn't move!"

"What did she say?" Catalina's eyes lasered on the maid.

"She...she..." Constance looked up, her eyes floating in pools of sadness. "Angelina begged your husband to take her. Signora *she* seduced him. He was drunk and said your name, so Angelina told him she was you. She tricked him, Signora."

The maid trembled, and tears streaked down her face.

"No. Angelina is a power-hungry bitch, but she would never betray me like that!"

"Signora, I swear on my dead mother's grave." Constance drew a cross over her body. "May she rest in peace."

Catalina clutched her robe as her tough façade crumbled into a heap of uncontrollable sobs. Her entire body quaked with each wail of sadness.

"Constance, bring my bride to me. I will hold her while you draw her a bath," Giorgio instructed with his arms wide.

"Si, Signore."

With her trembling body in his arms, Giorgio covered Catalina with the heavy bedspread.

"I am sorry, Giorgio. I am sorry." Catalina blubbered. "This was not supposed to happen. It was not part of our plan!" Catalina buried her head into his chest.

"It is okay, My love. I have you."

The lub-dub of his heart and the gentle caress down her back brought peace to her troubled world.

"Shh-shh, everything will all be okay. It is over. We know our enemy, my love. She can't take what we have. None of this changes our plans. Okay?"

She nodded and dried away her tears. Giorgio said what she needed to hear. Once again, he loved her the way no one ever did. She loved him, filling the void of love in his life. They were two broken hearts made whole together.

His muscular peck flexing with every tender stroke made her body tingle. Catalina trailed her hand down his body. His arousal was irresistible. Every fiber of her soul craved him. She needed him, and he needed her. She threw the blanket off and straddled him.

"My love, maybe we should wait." He glanced at the door.

"Can you make it that long?" She snickered. "You can make her watch." A grin curled her lip. "If you last that long!"

"That is one thing I love about you!"

"What is that, Love?" Catalina rocked her hips slowly.

"You do know how to satisfy me."

She slid off her robe. "What are we going to do to her?"

"Constance?"

She snarled and drove her hips down hard. "My sister!"

"What do *you* want to do to her?"

"I want her to pay!"

"Tell me how, and I will make her pay?"

A gentle knock stopped Catalina's response.

"Come in." Giorgio hollered.

As Constance opened the door, Catalina glanced over her shoulder, making eye contact with the maid.

"Oh! I am sorry, Signora!"

Constance covered her eyes and turned to leave.

"Stay!" Giorgio barked.

"Signore?"

Catalina smiled and whispered. "Yell at her."

"Are you ignorant? What does *stay* mean?" He roared.

Catalina's grin broadened. Giorgio's physical strength was arousing, but his power over others stirred her passion.

"Signore, no. I cannot stay. It is not right!"

"Come here. Constance!" Catalina shouted.

The maid stood frozen in the doorway, terrified of the harsh tone that came from her kind mistress.

"I told you to come here!" Catalina glared over her shoulder. "*Now!*"

Constance hesitantly moved closer to the bedside. She stayed outside of arms-length and averted her eyes.

"Look at us!" Catalina hissed. "Watch us!"

Two feet away from the bed, with her head bowed, Constance's body trembled as she sobbed.

"Please, Signora. I am sorry. I promise never to lie again! Please do not be like this! It is not you!"

Catalina sneered at her groveling maid and mocked her.

"*Not you!* If you knew me at all, you would not have lied! Do you know what I do to people who lie to me?"

"No, Signora."

"When they bring Angelina back, I will show you. For now, watch us! Don't look away, Constance!" Catalina growled. "Watch the happy couple, *so in love!*"

Giorgio chuckled, enjoying his bride's dominance.

"Show her, Giorgio. Show her how I like it! There will be no more secrets in my house!"

With a broad grin, Giorgio smacked his bride's face.

"More!" Catalina cried out. "Show her why I have bruises!"

Giorgio abided with two more slaps, busting her lip. A wicked laughter spewed from Catalina. Sweat dripping from her brow, she smiled at her lover. She locked eyes with Constance and wiped the blood from her cheek.

"Now you know what makes the happy couple a *perfect* match. From now on, there will be no more secrets!" Grinning, she licked the blood off her finger.

The horrified look on Constance's face made Catalina's grin widen. Satisfied in more than one way, a malevolent Catalina slipped on Giorgio's shirt. She nuzzled her nose into the white fabric, drawing her lover's scent. As she strolled toward the door, Catalina pointed to her clothes strewn around the room.

"Pick up my clothes!"

Slightly winded but thoroughly pleased, Giorgio stopped his wife with a question.

"Did you really mean to kill me?"

She stopped for a moment, then looked back at him. Her cold gaze turned icy when she arched her brow.

"Yes. *You*, too, would be wise to remember my temper has limits!"

The door slammed behind Catalina, making Constance jump. The weeping maid hurriedly grabbed all the clothing.

"You did well." Giorgio grinned at the maid.

Sniffing back her tears, Constance bowed her head.

"I did as I was told."

"Yes, you did. As soon as I am able, I will uphold my end of the bargain."

CHAPTER 30

"Park here." Francesca pointed to an empty spot. "We can walk the next three blocks to the pier."

"It has been a pleasure to drive you! You are the most beautiful thing I have ever seen!" Marcus whispered.

Francesca fidgeted with the strap of her purse.

"Thank you. I am sorry I have been so unbearable. You are unlike anyone I have ever met, even my dear Alberto."

His mouth gaping, his face flushed red. "I...was...um."

When Francesca looked up, Marcus turned away.

"Oh, no! I am so embarrassed!"

"Not as much as I am." Marcus cleared his throat. "I mean, it fits for you, too."

"But...you were talking to the car."

Beat red, Marcus looked up and shook his head.

They sat in silence for a moment, unable to look at the other. Francesca's quiet giggling broke the awkward tension and spurred Marcus to chuckle. A volley of laughter lobbed back and forth until both were in tears.

Francesca blotted her eyes and regained her composure.

"Thank you, I needed a good laugh!"

"I think we both did!"

Leaning his head back, Marcus soaked in the car's beauty, this time keeping his admiration to himself.

"Do you smell that?" Francesca asked.

Jolting upright, Marcus exclaimed, "Yes, I do! Come on!"

"Should we get our bags?" Francesca asked.

"I'll come back for them. This way!"

"How do you know where it is coming from?"

"My stomach will not lead you astray, I promise!"

Around the corner, a sign gently swaying in the morning breeze creaked above the door.

La pâtisserie de Carl et Doreen

Francesca stopped Marcus from opening the door.

"What's wrong?"

"Do you speak French?"

"Yep! I'm fluent in Finger-French."

"I've never heard of Finger-French. What is it?"

"This!" Marcus replied, holding up his pointer finger. "I point to what I want. They put it on a plate. I eat it!"

Grinning, Francesca shook her head.

"Perhaps I should do the talking!"

"Great! Then you can translate while I point!"

A bell jingled as Marcus opened the door. A white-haired lady stood behind a glass front case with trays of tarts, quiche, pastel macarons, buttery croissants, and chou à la crème. With a pleasant smile, the woman greeted them.

Francesca spoke with the woman. The elegant syllables rolled off her tongue. Marcus looked up from the delicate pastries lined in perfect rows.

"Beautiful!" He whispered.

"Me or the pastries?" Francesca winked.

His smile broadened. "Oui!"

Marcus's 'yes' in French brightened Doreen's smile, almost as much as the childlike grin plastered to his face.

Three years after the last shot was fired, Cherbourg was still scarred. At the end of the road, a single building stood unscathed between two piles of bricks. In contrast, a line of repaired buildings was directly across from his seat. Each freshly painted structure had several floors of apartments above a shop. Sparkling in the morning sun, crystal clear windows provided a dazzling display of the treasures inside each store. Though a similar design as in Turin, the façade echoed the exquisite taste of the French people.

A couple emerged from a woman's clothing store. The man cheerfully carried the packages while she chattered. Her mouth only stopped when she peered in the next window.

"What are you looking at?" Francesca asked.

"The buildings. They are beautiful."

"Is everything you see beautiful?"

"After years of death and seeing hundreds of towns obliterated into heaps of rubble. Green fields with planes riddled with holes, crippled tanks abandoned on the roadside, and the skeleton of charred homes with garments flapping on the clothesline are haunting. So, yes, everything not tainted by the scars of war *is* beautiful."

"Merci," Marcus said to Doreen as she served their food.

"Oui, Merci." After Doreen walked away, Francesca asked, "You said you did not speak French?"

"I like to think I am full of surprises!"

More relaxed, the pair continued their lighthearted conversation through the meal and on their way to the pier.

Near the ticket booth, Francesca excused herself to use the restroom. Marcus sat on a nearby bench with their luggage and watched the people milling about. Couple after couple passed by, each expressing their own version of adoration. One woman snuggled her man's arm, another batted her eyelashes and giggled. The third couple's felicity stung Marcus's heart the most.

In the middle of the walkway, a young soldier, poised on his left knee, opened a small black box. Elated, the woman squealed in delight as he slipped the ring onto her finger. As they embraced in a passionate kiss, onlookers applauded.

The display of love reminded Marcus of his loneliness. His adult years were spent in the sewage of death and destruction. The only love he knew was through the pictures and letters of boasting comrades. In the beginning, hearing about others' relationships did not bother him. Marcus had no interest in shackling a war bride with anxiety. Her mind forever wondering if her love still drew breath. And if he did, would he return mentally or physically damaged?

But his view changed late in his second tour. Marcus met the woman who freed Cupid's arrow from his bow. Of all her fine qualities, her smile imprisoned his soul. Over the next two years, Marcus plotted out every detail of next, including how and where he would propose. Marcus reached into his breast pocket and stroked the picture of his soulmate.

"That could have been us, my love."

CHAPTER 31

Gerhard and Angelina approached the pier shortly after the majestic ocean liner docked. Gazing at the kaleidoscope of colors, activities, and people, Angelina took in the entire experience, mentally noting all the exciting details.

The smoke billowing from the three black stacks dwindled while passengers trickled down the gangway. A hundred feet to the right of the exiting voyagers stood the next group of anxious travelers gathering near the ticketing stand. A cluster of women in vibrant dresses with coordinating hats, shoes, and gloves chatted away, oblivious to their surroundings. Their male companions shouted orders at young men who scurried to attend to every need. The gentleman slipped a folded bill into the boy's jacket pocket when their luggage was cared for.

"Not a bad way to make money," Angelina muttered.

"As long as no one lies."

"Why would you say that?"

"See that cluster of people? They are the upper class. What matters to them is *all* that matters! See the young man gathering bags from the man wearing a blue suit. If anything is missing, the boy will be forced to pay for the lost items."

"If he steals something, he should return it."

"Several years before the war, a young man was charged with thievery. His sentence was death, as the item he stole was quite valuable. The boy, of course, claimed innocence, but his voice was never heard. An aristocrat claimed the boy robbed him, and that was enough evidence to convict the lad. On the morning of the boy's execution, a young woman appeared at the jail, claiming the boy did not steal the jewels, and she had proof. It took six hours for her to reach the man who could stay the execution. By that time, it was too late."

"Too late?"

"The boy's life was already taken."

"That is awful!"

"Not as terrible as the accuser being the actual thief."

"Why would anyone steal their own jewels?" Angelina stopped and looked up at Gerhard in confusion.

"Most jewels are insured against theft. Blaming the boy allowed the man to claim the insurance money."

"Why didn't he just sell them?"

"In a way, he did. He used the jewels as payment for a gambling debt. The man spun the tale when his wife discovered the stones were gone."

"She believed him?"

Gerhard shrugged.

"Now you understand why I say *if*."

"You knew the boy, didn't you?"

"Yes, he was my brother."

Angelina squeezed his forearm in sympathy. He nodded in appreciation.

Staring in disgust, Angelina watched the cluster of wealthy passengers happily conversing. The sun made the spray of brightly colored dresses and hats glow. For every elaborately decorated woman, a man in a stately suit was tipping his hat toward the next affluent couple.

"Do not let my brother's story sway you into thinking all wealthy people are crooked." Gerhard patted her forearm.

The scowl on Angelina's face tightened.

"I know three rich men. All three would sell someone else out just for fun."

"Three?"

"Don Salvatore, his nephew Giorgio, and Giorgio's foster father."

"Ah! A devil, a pawn, and a fool."

A deep voice shouting in French drew Angelina's attention back toward the far end of the ship. On the bow, a man leaning against the railing gave two thumbs up in response. The crane's engine sputtered, and the screeching metal cable with a giant silver hook drew taut. Slowly, bands of thick rope creaked and groaned as they formed a massive net around a stack of crates.

"What is that for?"

"They are loading cargo onto the ship."

"Will all that fit inside the boat?"

"The *ship*. Yes. She is larger than you think."

Mesmerized, Angelina watched the men made of pure sinew work in the blazing sun. Their massive muscles flexed, and veins protruded from their temples as they hoisted luggage, crates, and sacks onto more nets.

Angelina nudged Gerhard and gestured toward the small café across the street. "Do we have time?"

"Yes. Boarding has not started yet."

Angelina slipped her hand into Gerhard's proffered arm and crossed the narrow street to Nora's Café.

A pretty lady with long blonde hair and a charming smile greeted them as they approached the door.

"Bonjour, je m'appelle *Rachelle*. Table pour deux?"

"S'il vous plaît," Gerhard smiled.

Angelina's eyes widened at Gerhard's instant vocal transformation.

"Is there an end to your talents?"

"I hope not." Gerhard chuckled. "But - probably."

Since they exited the car, Gerhard's attention was divided between Angelina and the surrounding activity. Now, seated at a table near the street, Gerhard's attention drifted farther from her. His warm, jovial nature faded, revealing harshness that shocked Angelina.

"Have you been here before?"

"I have been to many places."

The sting of his bitter tone lingered until the waitress brought them lunch. Though the food revived his sweet nature, Angelina refrained from attempting to start another conversation. Instead, she focused on migrating her food from one side of her plate to the other until Marcus came into view.

"There is Francesca and..."

Gerhard waved for her to stop.

"Do not use their names. The less the world knows, the safer everyone is. Do not even acknowledge their existence."

With a sigh, Angelina nodded.

"My apologies, Signorina. I do not mean to be harsh with you. Being stationary with so many people is a risk I cannot take lightly. I must think like a soldier, not a gentleman."

Gerhard's explanation was delivered with sincerity, yet he remained distracted. Not even the food on his plate or the fork shoveling it into his mouth received more than a glance.

"I understand."

Her plate, colorfully filled with carrots, beets, and vibrant greens, made Angelina's stomach lurch. The hunger she experienced an hour before was replaced with a thousand butterflies swooshing inside her gut.

"What am I doing here?" Angelina mumbled. "I should be home, saving my family, not chasing the unknown."

She migrated a carrot across her plate. Marcus's comment about a soldier eating when the opportunity arose echoed in Angelina's ear. She gulped back the bile that tickled her throat. Even in the best of circumstances, Angelina could not devour food like Gerhard, but she needed to consume something. She stabbed the carrot and shoved it into her mouth, ignoring the desire to examine the bite. The flavor was bland and unappealing. Determined, she silently repeated, *just chew.*

"The fish is fresh," Gerhard said, his eyes never lingering in one spot long.

The half-hearted attempt at being attentive did little to soothe Angelina. His eyes continued harvesting information from the roving crowd, and every sentence dripped off his tongue like a daydream.

"Have you ever seen France?"

"No. I have never left Brusnengo... I mean, I have never left my home."

His gaze still focused behind her, Gerhard released an approving smile.

"You should come back when the pain has been buried and her majestic charm fully restored. She is..."

Gerhard's voice deepened, and his eyebrow arched when he locked on something. Angelina turned to see who he had lassoed in his vision, but he shifted his attention back to her.

"What are you looking at?"

"She is quite a lovely country."

Frustrated by his ping-pong attention, Angelina's voice turned sour.

"Why am I getting on the ship?"

"You know why."

"Am I *expected* to go to America? Does he think my family has the luxury of *weeks*?"

"I cannot answer that question for your safety and mine."

"Yes, you *can*, but you *won't*."

"I was hired to get you on the ship, nothing more."

"Gerhard, look at me! I won't board until you answer me!"

Gerhard stabbed the last chunk of potato but did not eat it. He clenched the fork, and locked eyes with Angelina.

"Your toughness is charming, but as you said, your family does not have the luxury of time. So, you will board *if* you wish to protect those you love."

Angelina's cheeks flushed pink, and tears welled in her eyes. She held his gaze, contemplating pointing out his rudeness. It was a battle unworthy of her time or energy. In an hour, she would be headed for the unknown and would never see Gerhard again. There was no gain in fighting, so she returned her attention to her food.

The fresh bread was richly flavored with herbs, pairing nicely with the dry, red wine, as did the platter of fresh cheese and fruit.

Gerhard picked up his wineglass and leaned back. "Signorina, you are a clever woman with volatile emotions. Learn to control your agitation. Think with your mind, not your heart."

His tone, tempo of speech, and caring expression were that of a loving parent. In the worn tracks across Gerhard's brow and the darkening shadows under his eyes, Angelina recognized a father's concern for a daughter.

"Can a man in his line of work have a family and keep them safe?" Angelina contemplated.

"You wonder if I'm a father?" Gerhard said with an admiring grin.

Angelina's pupils widened. "Yes! How did you know."

Gerhard wiped his mouth, pausing momentarily before looking into Angelina's eyes.

"It is an art, one you are well versed in. I watched you struggle over losing your brothers when their deaths should fuel the drive for victory. Life dealt you a few bad cards but not a bad hand. Discard what does not serve you. The choice is your's alone. Only you know what serves you best!"

"Why are you telling me this?"

"If my daughter were in your position, I hope someone would tell her what I could not."

Angelina bit at her lip. Gerhard felt for his daughter as Rosario did for her. A void opened in her chest, exposing her homesickness. She missed the happiness only a home provided, even if it was shrouded in darkness.

"My boss is only one of many cards you hold. Until you take the time to hear his offer, you will not know if he can help you. Listen with an open mind, then decide."

A tear rolled down her cheek. Many times in the past week, she longed to hear her father's guidance. Yet Rosario remained silent. At that moment, Gerhard fulfilled her need for fatherly advice, bolstering her confidence.

"I don't know what to say."

"For now, listen and only say what is needed, nothing more. Too many details muddy the water, blinding everyone, including you, from the truth. I believe recent events have proven this for you, yes?"

Angelina nodded.

"Good. Now, it is time to go."

Gerhard stood and offered Angelina his hand.

"Thank you."

CHAPTER 32

Freddy ran his hand through his damp hair, exposing the contrasting colors on either side of his hairline.

Black and white. Maximus thought. *If all of life followed that simple divide.*

His compadre's nervousness was contagious, but Maximus kept his symptoms hidden. Time was ticking by, and they were still a long way from saving Rosario's daughters. Even if his master plan worked, other details needed attention. Removing Don Salvatore from his throne was at the top.

"How much longer until we land?" Maximus hollered.

The pilot did not move.

"Peter's need to be anonymous is bullshit! He planned every single delay, including this piece of shit pilot!"

"Was Peter always a prick, Boss?"

"No. he was a good guy with almost all the right qualities."

"Why block him from Olivia?"

"I had my reason. Still do." Maximus looked out the window. The world below seemed a million miles away. *The ground is closer than I am to protecting Rosario's daughters.* He thought, running his hand through his hair.

The pilot pulled off his headset and shouted over his shoulder. "Buckle up, boys! Things are about to get bumpy!"

Maximus and Freddy exchanged unenthusiastic glances.

"The bullshit never ends. I'd give my left nut for the rest of this mission to go as planned." Maximus grumbled.

"With all due respect, Boss, I'll keep my nuts. Both of 'em."

CHAPTER 33

Don Salvatore danced around his courtyard with an imaginary partner. Each bliss-filled step grinding the seeds beneath his shoes, robbing the pigeons of their feast. In his joy, he didn't care if he destroyed his most loyal subject's dinner. Soon, he would no longer look to the filthy birds for entertainment.

That morning, his maid, Amalea, delivered his coffee to the courtyard as she did every morning. She had made him his favorite sweet roll, and the coffee was piping hot. It was not the hot food nor the unseasonably warm temperature that perked his mood. He could enjoy hot coffee and his pastry filled with sweetened ricotta any day. The telegram tucked under his plate brought him to this level of elation.

```
Mole worked.
Dove flying into the cage.
```

The message sent a jolt of jubilation through him. Springing from his chair like a man in his twenties, Don Salvatore twirled his maid like a ballerina as he hummed a bubbly tune. Amalea's resistance added to his merriment, so he forced her to dance back and forth across the middle of the courtyard. When he became slightly winded, Don Salvatore released the frightened girl, and she sprinted back inside the villa.

"Ha! I do enjoy terrifying her. Even if I must hunt her down when I need something. No matter. Soon, My Little Dove will be here to do my bidding!"

CHAPTER 34

Angelina and Gerhard waited in line to board the ship for hours. Pointing to structures, Gerhard explained their uses. Though the conversation helped pass the time, its real purpose allowed Gerhard to monitor the area.

"Here is your passage ticket. You are in first class. My boss *always* travels in luxury, and so do his guests. I can promise you will want for nothing while aboard."

"That is generous, thank you."

"No need to thank me. I did not pay for it."

Gerhard looked up, evaluating their progress. His jaw tensed, and he growled.

"What is it? Is something wrong?" Angelina asked, straining her head.

He grunted under his breath and glanced back toward the ship before looking at Angelina.

"One more bit of advice. The world is full of sharks. If you do not trust someone, there is a reason. Discover why your gut has suspicions. You may uncover a truth about them or yourself. My boss and I have a special arrangement, one that is far different from the one he seeks with you."

"Why is he interested in helping my family?"

"As I have said before, that is a question for him, not me."

Angelina nodded. She hugged him, partly in gratitude, yet mostly to remember what it felt like to be hugged by a father. However, Gerhard pulled away.

"There is something you deserve to know before you get on board," Gerhard confessed, shattering the tender moment.

A chill washed over Angelina's skin when she saw the coldness in Gerhard's bright blue eyes and the scowl of deep lines across his brow.

"Why are you looking at me like that?"

Gerhard leaned close and whispered in her ear. Each word he spoke urged the acid bubbling in her stomach to erupt. Yet, it was his last three words that made her stumble.

The blood draining from her cheeks, Angelina grabbed her stomach. "I think I am going to be sick."

"Do not allow your emotions to show." Gerhard helped her regain her footing. "There is a price for everything. You are next. Show that man your ticket. Once you are onboard, a steward will take you to your room."

Gerhard grabbed her chin. A menacing sternness washed over Gerhard's face. He no longer appeared as a father-figure, but an angry Oger barking orders.

"Remember!"

With a gulp, Angelina nodded.

"Good. Now, compose yourself and do exactly as I told you! *Exactly!*"

As Gerhard walked away, an icy wind cut through the line of passengers. Angelina's body registered the air's significant drop in temperature. Her hand trembled as she showed her passage ticket. Outwardly, one would surmise her tremors were symptoms of the bitter cold, but the true cause was the chilling way Gerhard ended their friendship. With a nod, the man helped her up the step, then pointed toward the line of passengers waiting to board.

"Thank you," Angelina mumbled to the steward.

The line moved at a snail's pace, giving Angelina too much time to ruminate over her situation, including the daunting trek up the unstable walkway.

"Dear God, that is a long way up!" Angelina gulped.

The bodies pitching left to right, the towering height, and the demonic, dark water lapping below intensified Angelina's growing desire to run to the rail and expel her lunch. Others complained about the wait, but none more than the man standing behind her. His grumbling started low, but his impatience won over, and he shouted, "Get moving!"

The ringing in Angelina's ears added to her growing list of discomforts. The man pushed Angelina aside and shoved his way up the line. A roar of disgust rumbled up the steps as the man bullishly moved other passengers out of his way. The commotion intensified the gangway's sway, causing a young man, about twelve, to vomit over the rail. Another roar of disgust cascaded down the steps, but Angelina ignored it. She was seconds away from echoing the young boy's actions.

Angelina stepped out of line and filled her lungs with air. Her left hand cradled her stomach while her right clinched the rail. She looked for a focal point. Ten yards away, she saw Gerhard staring at her. He had no smile for her, and she did not have one for him. The line moved again, momentarily breaking their locked eyes. When Angelina looked back, Gerhard waved. Before she was engulfed by the surge of passengers eager to board, she asked an important question that had eluded her.

"Gerhard, what does he look like?"

A mischievous grin curled one side of Gerhard's lips, plumping his cheek.

"I do not know. I have never met him!"

CHAPTER 35

"Giorgio, this is Margaret," Catalina said. "Say hello, Margaret."

Giorgio peered over his newspaper and arched his brow.

The girl tucked her chin and gave a small curtsey.

"She is a child!"

Planting her hands on her hips, Catalina scowled at him.

"Fourteen is not a child! I could do every job at the vineyard by fourteen! Well, except drive."

"Where did you find her?"

"I cannot do everything myself." Catalina removed the paper from his hands.

"You don't. Constance is *your* maid, Tommaso cares for the grounds, and Pierro cooks every meal. Tell me again why you need more help?"

"Margaret, dear, the kitchen is through there. Have Pierro fix you something to eat. If you see a crabby old woman, her name is Constance. You can tell her why you are here."

Once the girl was clear of earshot, Catalina sat in the chair opposite Giorgio. Reclining back, she sighed.

"Knowing this time would come, I started looking for a young girl months ago. Constance is no spring chicken."

"Then fire Constance!"

Catalina rolled her eyes and continued to ramble.

"What she does, she does well. She cannot take on this task, or any new one for that matter. I must run the vineyard, now. There is only so much of me to go around, you know. I asked a nun at church if they had anyone suitable for the job. I was told weeks ago, but I had no time to meet the girl between harvest, the funerals, and...*you.*"

Sitting up, Catalina looked toward the kitchen to see if anyone was lurking.

"The other day, I decided a long drive would improve my mood. While I was out, I stopped by the convent to meet the girl. Strangely, Mario was there. He was walking around with Mother Concetta, talking like old friends! I thought it odd, and when he made that stone-faced woman laugh, I was completely shocked! Did you know he visited her?"

"Yes. Unless Mario is on business, he visits the convent every week."

"If he feels guilty about the high-class brothel in his hotels, he should visit a priest, not a nun!"

"The key part is *if* he felt guilty. He doesn't."

She scooted to the edge of her seat. "So they are *friends*?"

"At one time, they were more than friends."

Catalina gasped. "I don't believe it! Not a word. There is no way that callous old hag could love, much less *be* loved!"

"Ask him." Giorgio picked up his paper.

"If he loved her, why did she become a nun?"

"It was a short-term affair. Mario was married and refused to leave his wife, so Concetta left him."

"What was she like before she became a nun?"

Giorgio lowered his paper and sighed. "I don't know! The affair happened a year or two before Mario took me in."

"Did Mario ever talk about her?"

"Not until a few years after his wife died. But Concetta had been a nun for a long time by then."

"Well, true or not, had I known, I wouldn't have wasted the trip! He could have met the girl for me!"

"My father picks women for specific talents, not the type of worker you want."

Giggling, Catalina leaned back in her chair.

"A good point. No matter, I am so happy, my love!" Catalina stared dreamily at the ceiling. "With Angelina gone, life is...well...*wonderful*! I hope your Zio's men never find her, and she stays away forever!"

"Sorry, my love. Zio received a telegram."

"Oh?"

"He refused to tell me anything more than his 'Little Dove' was flying right into his trap!"

"Little Dove? Yuck! What a disgusting thought."

"It plays in our favor."

"How so?"

"*If* she makes it back alive, she will be shackled in my Zio's villa. He will make her his sex slave. I promise you, she will be too busy to bother you! It will be like she is in another country."

"I would prefer she moved away permanently. But I suppose it would be fun to watch her squirm in Zio's grubby hands." Catalina smiled at the vision of Angelina in shackles, beaten, and suffering from The Don's wrath. "Are you sure Angelina won't bewitch him?"

"Hopefully, long enough for my plan to take root."

"I suppose her distracting Zio would be useful. But do not allow her to sink her claws too deep. She is a devilish bitch!"

With a giggle, Catalina hopped out of the chair and kneeled by him. Batting her eyelashes, she looked at Giorgio.

"Do you think Margaret is a suitable choice?"

"That depends. Are you going to let me fuck her?"

Catalina slipped her hand under Giorgio's groin and squeezed.

"You touch her, and I will do more than throw you down the steps!"

"Easy! Easy! It was a joke!"

Rolling her eyes, Catalina stood and moved toward the roaring fire. Giorgio grabbed her hand and pulled her into his lap. He brushed away the strands of hair obstructing her eyes and gently cupped her cheek.

"Us. Our lives. Our future is all that matters to me. On our wedding day, we vowed more than *to have and to hold*. We vowed to get revenge for all the atrocities we have suffered under the hands of those who thought we were nothing!"

CHAPTER 36

Angelina gripped the rope and hesitantly began her ascent up the gangway. The sloshing water lapping against the hull of the boat compounded her uneasiness. There was no need to become fearless in the face of heights at the vineyard; nothing was built to this height, much less grew this tall.

You are not at home, so suck it up and move. Angelina silently prodded herself.

"First time, mademoiselle?" A gentleman asked.

Keeping her focus on the next step, she nodded.

"It only appears to be a long way. We will reach the top faster than you think. May I offer you my hand?"

Without hesitation, Angelina clamped her sweaty hand onto his. If he were covered in oozing puss-filled sores, Angelina didn't care. She welcomed the man's kindness.

"You have quite a grip!" Angelina tried to release her hand, but he did not let go. "It is merely an observation."

The gentleman remained at her side, occasionally adding a comforting remark to ease her anxiety.

"A snail on ice could move faster." He chuckled. "It rarely takes this long to board. Mark my word, mademoiselle, decadence awaits you! And some things are worth the wait!"

Angelina's voice quivered. "If you say so."

The exuberant laughter and chatter from the main deck grew louder with every step. Curious, Angelina snuck a peek. She sighed with gratitude. The trek was nearly over.

"Here we are. One last step." He gently guided her. "Don't worry about the sway of the vessel. Best if you just hop over. I will be here to catch you."

Engulfed by fear of the murky abyss below, Angelina had not even given the man a smile of appreciation. Yet, he patiently waited for her to jump from the precarious perch.

I will thank him...when I am on the ship. She thought.

Angelina fixed her eyes on her landing area, ready to make her leap. The impatient crowd behind her pushed her off the gangway and into the gentleman's arms. Angelina gasped, filling her lungs with his musky cologne. His warm embrace and alluring scent overpowered her desire to recoil into a more lady-like posture, but the man did not mind.

A sudden burst of music interrupted the embrace. Cymbals crashing and a tuba bellowing a cheerful beat seized everyone's attention. Angelina turned to see the chipper ensemble, but her eyes were blinded by the blazing midday sun. The bright light burned small glowing circles into her retinas. She blinked several times, struggling to regain her vision. A fresh wave of passengers, drunk from excitement, rudely rushed in, separating her from the gentleman.

"Signore? Wait! Signore, please!" Angelina shouted. "Stop! Let me by!" She jabbed her elbow into a large woman. "Move, you giant green blob!"

The low bouncing notes from the tuba overpowered her voice. Wave upon wave, people surged into the overly crowded space, enveloping her in the chaos.

Her cry to the faceless gentleman was lost in the surrounding noise, as were her pleas for space. Balancing on her tippy-toes, Angelina stretched up to see over the growing crowd. If she could not thank him now, she would find him later, a task that required she know him by more than his stylish black shoes and sensual cologne.

In the sea of flesh, people took turns pressing against Angelina, some muscular, while others were rolls of squishy fat. The disregard for personal space and body odor mixed with different colognes and perfumes made her gag.

A bright yellow feathered hat moved, obscuring her view. Angelina spat the feathers from her lips. She attempted to regain her line of sight by balancing on her tippy toes and craning over the yellow plume.

"Where are you?" Angelina asked.

"Here!" A tight grip bit down on her upper arm. She snapped around but was blinded by the sun.

CHAPTER 37

"Bruno, there she is!" Antonio shouted. "I have you now, *Little Dove*!"

Bruno's massive form sprinted past a middle-aged couple admiring the view from the observation deck. Once clear of them, Bruno lengthened his stride, darting around a maze of lounge chairs. Hurdling over clusters of luggage, Antonio kept pace with him.

Antonio pushed a tall man in a grey suit. "Out of my way!"

"Hey! Watch it!" The man adjusted his jacket and huffed.

Antonio did not care about ruffling feathers. His target was within eyesight. They continued to plow through the crowd, inciting other cries of reproach. Bruno pushed a woman, catching the attention of a steward. Antonio's mind registered his partner's situation but did not veer from his course. He nimbly maneuvered over and around the obstacles. Lengthening his stride, he lunged over a man's briefcase and shoved a steward. The boy's pillbox hat tumbled to the ground. Antonio glanced back and cackled.

Three women wearing elaborate bonnets and matching dresses moved, obstructing his view of Angelina. A slight adjustment allowed Antonio to swerve around them. The quickly shifting obstacle course continued to alter his path. A large woman in a green dress blocked him, but a quick twirl put him back on target. Another surge of passengers flooded the space as the band's gleeful beat drew their attention. An overweight woman in a buttercup-yellow dress craned her neck to glimpse the musicians.

"Get the fuck out of my way!"

Oblivious to the surrounding space, the woman did not hear him. The excitement on the left side of the lido deck was far more important than the surrounding people. Antonio reached his hands up to shove the giant glob of blazing yellow out of his way. Before he could, Bruno, who had circumvented the steward, cued Antonio to move to the right. Two steps to the side, Antonio's adrenaline rocketed. He had a clear path to his prey. Invigorated, he quickened his gait to close the ten-foot gap between them.

"Perfect. *Little Dove* is blinded by the sun," Antonio licked his lips. "She won't even know who grabbed her!"

Adrenaline coursed through his veins when the smell of Angelina's perfume tickled his nose. With a grin of satisfaction, he stretched his arm out.

"Come here, *Little Dove!*"

CHAPTER 38

"Unhand me!"

Angelina yanked her arm back, but the grip did not budge. Her vision compromised by the blazing sun, she craned her neck to see who had latched onto her, but another swift tug pulled her off balance.

"Ouch!" she screamed.

The bub-bub of the tuba accenting the beat of the drum smothered her words, and the gleeful travelers entranced by the band's music ignored her. Another sharp tug pulled her deeper into the crowd. She struggled, but she was not strong enough to win her freedom.

Impatient, Angelina's assailant growled. "Move!"

"Unhand me!" Angelina twisted her arm, but the grip clamped tighter.

"No!"

The sea of brightly colored dresses, glaring sun, and exuberant music intensified Angelina's confusion. With a yank, she was pulled through a set of doors and hurdled into a lobby. The spectacle drew looks of astonishment and cries of reproach.

"Now I say!" a large man shouted, followed by another man raising his fist to punctuate his warning, "Watch it!"

Witnessing the ghastly behavior, the women turned their heads to hide from the horror of Angelina's situation. Their purposeful ignorance quickly shifted to a large woman fainting. Encircling the heap of powder blue material and dazzling diamonds, the aristocrats forgot Angelina's strife.

As she was dragged down the stairwell, Angelina heard the shouts of "Oh my God!" and "Call a doctor!"

"You aren't *worth* their time. You may be pretty, but here you have to be rich to mean anything."

With no aid, Angelina turned to her instincts for survival. She noted the brass handrails, plush carpet, and polished wood-paneled walls as she twirled past. None of these details were unique and would not guide her later. At the base of the first set of stairs, her luck changed. A brightly colored painting of a boat sailing across a placid sea hung on the wall. She logged the billowing white sails into her memory. She stumbled down the next flight of steps. An alabaster statue of a creepy-eyed man in a corner of the landing greeted her. A statue of a sea maiden with long flowing hair occupied the other corner. The oddity of the pair, more than each statue's unique features, captured Angelina's attention.

She was yanked to the left at the bottom of the third flight of steps, then a sharp right into a hallway. The momentum flung her free of her assailant. With a thud, she slammed against the polished wood paneling. Angelina regained her balance and stared into the eyes of her aggressor.

CHAPTER 39

His triumphant cackle shifted to a growl. His fingertips grazed the sleeve of Angelina's dress. As he made his final move, so did someone else. The hand that landed on Angelina's beat his by a second. He growled again when the faceless usurper yanked his prey in a different direction.

Infuriated, Antonio tucked his head like a ram to push through the multiplying number of passengers. Several men in double-breasted suits and a gaggle of women adorned in sparkling rivers of jewels expressed their ghastly displeasure for his rudeness. A tall, slender blonde draped on her well-dressed counterpart's arm sneered with contempt at Antonio's disheveled appearance.

"Fuck off, bitch!" Antonio snapped.

The snooty passengers added to his fiery rage, but the usurper was the gasoline fueling his wrath. Plowing through the crowd, Angelina's assailant pulled her through a set of doors, removing her from Antonio's field of vision.

"Mother-fucker!" Antonio howled.

"Antonio, over here!" Bruno stood near the doors where Angelina passed through.

"About time your fucking height did us some good!"

Inside the lobby, a large woman released a high-pitched squeal, grasped her gaudy diamond necklace, and collapsed into a heap of light blue fabric. The turmoil stirred a unified gasp that echoed around the lobby. Within seconds, the small crowd doubled, all pining for a view of the scandal.

Struggling to keep his eye on Angelina, Antonio shoved his way through the mass of passengers.

"I saw her at the pier." A man grumbled to his friend. "She was quite the handful. Moody and bossy, a terrible combination."

"She needs a wallop for her behavior!" The friend retorted.

"Shameful!" A lady added. Aghast, she placed her white silk handkerchief to her nose. "An utter disgrace!"

"Which way did they go?" Antonio barked at the woman.

His abruptness made the woman's eyes fill with terror. She retreated further behind her silk handkerchief. Stepping back, she opened her mouth to reprimand him for his lack of decorum, but Antonio interrupted her.

"That woman is my sister! Please!"

Timidly raising her hand, she pointed toward the stairwell.

"Thanks!" He raced down the stairs, chuckling. "Too easy. Did you reply out of fright, or did you believe me?" A smile thinned his lips. "I'll go with fright."

At the bottom of the stairs, Antonio glanced left and right. A sharp cry to his left answered his silent question.

Antonio slowly peered down the hallway. Angelina argued for her freedom. He could easily ambush them, but curiosity stopped him. He wanted to know more about this usurper.

"Now, *Little Dove*, tell me who this mother-fucker is!"

CHAPTER 40

Her aggressor clamped down on her bicep, hitting the crippling nerve within. Angelina's legs buckled, and he loosened his hold.

"You are hurting me!" Angelina huffed. "Let me go!"

Angelina yanked her arm from his grip and rubbed her throbbing appendage. Her bruised arm was not her only injury. The embarrassment of being drug through a crowd and down the stairwell left a dreadful bruise on her ego.

"What did that man want?"

"No, I have no other injuries except the bruise your grip left on my arm and the embarrassment of being handled like a wayward child. Thank you for your concern, dear brother!"

"Those people don't care about you!"

"Apparently, neither do you!" She adjusted her dress. Like the past few minutes, it was utter chaos.

"Are you a raving lunatic? Who the hell was that man?"

"Which man?" She pointed toward the lido deck. "You just drug me past a hundred people!"

"That man?"

"Half of those people are men!"

"You have no clue, do you?" Her shrug infuriated him. "Exactly!"

"*Exactly what*?"

"You don't know who that man was or his allegiance!" Marcus reached up to grab her other arm, but she shoved him away. "Lina! You are not safe. *We* are not safe!"

"I am keenly aware of the dangers around me!"

"Are you? Then why were you holding hands with a stranger?"

An elderly couple walking down the hall stopped abruptly. The woman clenched her purse close to her chest, and the man wrapped a protective arm around her. Terrified, they scurried out of sight.

"The man who helped me up that wobbling thing? What did you want me to do, dear brother? I was nervous and alone! He was merely acting like a gentleman, which is more than I can say about you right now!"

"I can hear you all the way down here!" Francesca shouted out of a cabin halfway down the corridor. "If I can hear you, I am sure everyone can!"

Marcus and Angelina exchanged defiant glances.

"Fine! You want a gentleman." Marcus held out his hand. "After you."

Angelina released a low growl of frustration.

"I am not a child!"

"Then don't act like one!"

CHAPTER 41

"Who took her?" Bruno asked, stomping to his partner.

Antonio glared at Bruno's feet, silently reprimanding him for his oafish behavior.

"I'm a big guy, it's what we do."

Antonio held a finger to his lips and nodded for Bruno to keep out of sight.

"A guy my size can't melt into the wall and disappear!"

"You are an ignafuck!" Antonio mouthed.

Bruno was not the only one about to blow his cover. An older couple walking down the hallway approached in trepidation. Antonio flashed his knife, encouraging them to go on their way. Frightened, they scurried on past without saying a word.

Once clear of all distractions, Antonio and Bruno listened to the squabble between Angelina and her assailant.

"Did she..." Bruno asked, but Antonio silenced him.

"Shh! Listen."

"Brother?" Antonio whispered with his brow arched. "How is that possible?"

"Does it matter?" Bruno griped.

Antonio released a low, raspy growl. "The Don doesn't enjoy being lied to. So, of course, it fucking matters!"

Bruno gave an apathetic shrug.

"Come on. Perhaps we can rid ourselves of all three problems. Maybe then Don Salvatore will be more appreciative of our services."

Antonio and Bruno rounded the corner to catch their prey off guard.

"Where are they?" Bruno asked, looking up and down the hall. "You said they were right here."

Antonio's agitation bubbled. "Dammit, Bruno! Is there no oxygen up there? If you don't see them, that means...?

Bruno shrugged.

"They went through one of these cabin doors, you ignafuck!" Antonio growled. "Your idiocy is beyond reason."

"What the hell does that mean?"

"Means shut the fuck up! Make yourself useful for once!"

Antonio rubbed his temples. All the excitement and pleasure of hunting his prey was now a laborious endeavor made more tedious by Bruno's stupidity.

"Now what?" Bruno grunted.

"Are you that much of a fucktard! Try each door!"

Bruno's ape-size paw tested each door handle. "Locked."

"If they are locked, then bust them open! They ain't gonna come out to play with the evil Oger just because he knocked!"

The apathy in Bruno's voice and persistent repetition of the same word intensified Antonio's rage.

"Where are my smokes?" Antonio grumbled, patting his jacket. "Ah! The medicine to cure all my woes."

The red tip scraping across the abrasive surface instantly burst into an orange and yellow flame. Antonio paused to savor the single wisp of smoke. In two short drags, the sizzling tobacco eased his stress. Relaxing his head back, the trail of grey flowed from his nostrils.

"Now, if I could burn flesh," Antonio mumbled, releasing another stream of smoke into the air.

He finished his last draw on his cigarette and held the burning butt between his thumb and forefinger. He exhaled slowly. An evil grin formed as the smoke rolled across his lips.

"Bruno, wait! I have an idea."

CHAPTER 42

Sitting at the head of the long marble table, Don Salvatore shouted for his maid to bring him food.

"Where is my dinner, wench?"

Amelia was already two steps into the dining hall when The Don demanded his meal.

"Here it is, Signore."

"About time. Is it still hot? You know how I despise cold food!"

"Si, Signore. Very hot."

"It better not be too hot!"

"Only hot, Signore. Like you like."

Don Salvatore tucked his napkin into his collar, then picked up his knife and fork. Holding them vertical, his fat fingers wrapped tightly around the utensils, he fidgeted impatiently.

"Hurry up, woman!"

Her hands trembling, Amalea placed a platter of braised pork chops, a bowl of risotto, and a plate of polenta on the table. Don Salvatore wiggled in his chair while Amalea filled his plate. Ravenous, he barely gave her hand enough time to leave the proximity before stabbing at the food. Careful not to become part of the meal, Amalea took two steps back to fill his wineglass,

His mouth full, Don Salvatore smacked his food to a cheerful beat while contemplating Angelina's needs.

"Clean the room next to mine. Make it spotless! I want fragrant flowers, silk sheets, and fresh fruits. Make the space fit for a queen!"

"Si, Signore."

"Send one of the yard apes to Bergamo, have him select the finest silk robe. Better yet, *you* go! Somethings cannot be trusted to an ignorant man."

"Domani, Signore?"

"Of course, tomorrow, you idiot! Where does Antonio find you people?" He held the glass out for Amalea to refill. "Take enough money to buy her a complete wardrobe. Everything she needs. Only silk. Lots of silk to flow over her curves."

The Don's hands flowed through the air, drawing Angelina's shape. His eyes danced as the imaginary figure posed for him.

"*Red* silk to flow over My Little Dove's curves. Oh! And lace. *Black* lace! Si, sheer, black lace."

Lost in his fantasy, Don Salvatore absently stabbed at a chunk of meat but missed. Displeased that his dream was interrupted, he snarled at the runaway piece of pork before spearing it. Victorious over the skirmish, The Don narrowed his eyes and pointed the skewered meat at Amalea.

"Choose wisely! Unless you enjoy being beaten'!"

His lips curling, Don Salvatore contemplated a naked Angelina whipping a naked Amalea.

"Signore? What size does she wear?"

"Blast it, bitch! Refill my glass and my plate, then be gone! Or I will start your beating here, with your face smashed against the table and my cock up your ass!"

CHAPTER 43

The small space was suffocating, especially with her brother's neurotic pacing back and forth across a ten-foot span. The click, click, click of his heel against the floor followed the metronome of a four-four time. On the fourth beat, his foot slapped the floor harder than the rest. He ran his hand through his dark locks as he performed a quick pivot and a sharp glare at his sister before repeating the process.

"We should move to my cabin. It is first class and probably roomier than this place."

"Already an aristocrat?" Marcus snapped. "We were lucky to even get on board. This was the last cabin available!"

"I am not insulting your accommodations. Merely offering an alternative."

The room size and her brother's temper were part of Angelina's inner turmoil. The phrase, *do exactly as I told you,* played on an endless loop, stirring her anxiety. The longer Angelina sat in this room, the farther she was from following Gerhard's instructions. Staying in this cabin put them all in more danger.

"This isn't first class, but at least we have a window bigger than a dinner plate," Marcus growled. "What would you have done if we couldn't get on board? This guy could be a madman or a pawn for Don Salvatore!"

"Fiori knows Papa. Even Carlos knows who he is! Besides, isn't it a little late to be concerned? If you were worried, you should have said so when we were outside town!"

Marcus slammed his fist against the wall, leaving a small dent in the thin veneer surface.

"Well, being locked in the belly of this beast gives me a bad feeling." Marcus grumbled. "We are stuck on this ship. If this Fiori cat can't help us, we have sentenced Catalina to over two weeks without help!"

"A little late for that conclusion." Francesca put a hand on her hip. "I believe I told both of you this was a bad idea!"

"Until we talk with him, we won't know!"

"And when *do* we meet him?" Marcus's anxiety flushed his face. "Is he on the ship? Did Gerhard *specifically* say he was on *this* ship? What does he look like?"

Angelina plopped onto the corner of the small bunk. The bed was hard, and the brown blanket felt like steel wool. The unpolished wooden floor was a stark difference from the main deck. The shabby accommodations were reminders she was not following Gerhard's orders.

She rested her head in her hands. Recalling the gentleman's comment about the splendid accommodations, she rolled her eyes.

"So this is decadence?"

"Lina? What does he look like?"

"Huh? I don't know!" She looked away and mumbled, "Gerhard has never met him."

"What was that? Lina, please tell me I heard you wrong?"

A rumbling sound reverberating through the floor startled Angelina. She popped up, bumping into a startled Francesca.

"What was *that*?" Francesca's voice cracked.

Before anyone could answer, the ship shifted under their feet, and a haunting bellow from the foghorn cried out three times. An eruption of cheers from the upper deck pulled Angelina closer to the window. As the space between the ship and the pier expanded, blue streamers and red confetti littered the water.

With her nose tipped high, Francesca sniffed the air.

"Do you smell that?"

Looking around the room for the source of the pungent odor, Marcus and Angelina began sniffing, too.

"Yuck! Dead fish." Angelina gagged.

"No, not fish. I smell smoke!" Francesca's pale complexion turned chalky white.

"You mean the smokestacks?" Angelina offered.

"She is right." Marcus held up his hand.

Marcus's agreement melted a sliver of her aggression.

"See, Francesca, we are fine!"

"No, Lina, *she's* right! There is a fire somewhere on the ship!" He sniffed again. "Stay here! I will find out what is going on."

"But I don't smell anything."

The door whooshed open and wafted the burning stench into the room. Angelina's stomach lurched.

"Stay here!" Francesca took up pacing. "There is a fire, and we are supposed to stay in the belly of this beast! We can't stay here. I can't stay here!"

Francesca's voice echoed her terror. Staying meant she would suffer the same horrid end as her husband. A fact that was not lost on Angelina.

"He will be right back. We need to wait for him."

"No! It is not safe. We have to leave!"

"Francesca, we will not die."

Francesca's pace quickened. "Yes, we will!"

Angelina grabbed her hand, stopping her nervous pacing. "Give him five minutes. If he isn't back, we leave. Okay?"

Francesca squeezed Angelina's hand and nodded.

Several minutes after Marcus left the cabin, the roar from the engines stopped, leaving a momentary void of noise. A haunting groan from the belly of the ship pierced the silence. In its wake came an eruption of panic on the main deck.

Angelina dropped Francesca's hand and looked out the window. She gasped in horror as the bodies zoomed past, screaming until they were silenced by the water.

"I am not staying here!"

As Francesca's hand turned the knob, a fist hammered the door, making her scurry back to Angelina's side.

"Fire! Everyone out!" The raspy voice yelled at their door.

The sounds of passengers screaming and the echo of a fist beating on every door intensified Angelina's fear.

"Where is Marcus?" Angelina whispered.

"We can't wait. We have to go. Now!"

Francesca raced to the door, flinging it open without hesitation.

"Well, well. We meet again," Antonio sneered.

Francesca screamed louder than Angelina, but neither permeated the raging chaos of the entire ship.

"Finally, I will finish what I started with the two of you. You have been far more trouble than you are worth. So, before we all die in this Fire, I will take what you owe me!"

Antonio licked his lips and slowly stepped closer to Angelina, his eyes maniacally undressing her. Francesca lunged at him. She unleashed her wrath in a barrage of blows against Antonio's chest.

"You murdered my Alberto!"

Her attempt to hurt Antonio was pathetic and spurred a guttural, wicked peal of laughter from him.

"So feisty, Francesca. To know you think so much of me really warms my heart! Adorable! Truly adorable. It is touching and, under other circumstances, might stir some compassion. No one likes to be second, I know. But sweet, Francesca, someone has to be. Today, that is you!" Grabbing one of her wrists, Antonio twisted Francesca's arm until she wailed in pain. "Believe me when I say I would really enjoy taming you. And normally, I would go for the blond first, but I think Angelina may be a little feistier cat in the sack than you!" Antonio cackled.

"Here's your *cat*?"

Francesca's hand streaked across Antonio's face. Her nails were tiny daggers drawing red lines on his right cheek. The surge of pain spurred a blistering fury in Antonio. With one sweeping blow, his arm sent Francesca flying across the room. She crashed into the wall and yelped.

Angelina raced to help Francesca. A glint of light grabbed her attention. In Antonio's left hand was a six-inch blade dripping with blood. Angelina looked at the limp form on the floor but saw no blood pooling under her friend. Not yet.

The Grim Reaper's black fingers crept across the ceiling, inching into the cabin, replacing the oxygen with suffocating darkness. The room was growing darker by the second, hindering Angelina's vision. She glanced in every direction for Antonio, but he disappeared in the thickening smoke.

To her right, a shadow caught her eye. As she turned to follow the figure, Angelina noticed a dark splat on the wall above Francesca. Under her friend was a growing pool of blood. Angelina gasped. A rush of smoke filled her lungs, sending her into a violent spasm of coughs. As she stumbled toward her friend, the shadowed figure moved again. She tried to focus, but the lights flickered twice and then went black, leaving her disoriented. Angelina took two wobbly steps to the left. A surge of Antonio's sour breath wafted up to her nose. She swallowed hard. Her movement put her closer to the enemy.

Antonio cackled with glee as he pressed his body flush with hers. Angelina looked away, but his hand quickly snatched her chin, forcing her to look at him.

In Brusnengo, the children were told wild tales about seeing the flames of hell in Antonio's eyes. They were nothing more than scary stories to frighten children. However, as she stared into his black orbs, Angelina understood the frightening tales were true. Tears fell from her burning eyes. This time, there was no escaping his torture.

Antonio's eyes never blinked, and his lungs did not resist the smoke. This hell was his heaven. He would gladly die in the blaze if it meant he would go while assaulting her. He slipped his hand around her waist and smiled, exposing his yellowed teeth. He held their bodies firmly together and nuzzled his face into her neck. His sour breath filled her nose.

"Mmm, you are sweet!" Antonio purred. "I bet you are tasty as well. Shall we see how sweet you are, Little Dove?"

An intense pain ripped through her neck as he sunk his teeth into her flesh. Angelina wailed in agony and rammed her knee into his groin. Antonio, cupping his nuts, stumbled, cursing Angelina's name with every step. She grabbed her neck. The slippery fluid against her palm made her ill.

Don't pass out, Angelina. she thought.

Angelina's hand scurried across the small night table, searching for something to stem the bleeding. Her fingers landed on a pillow. She ripped off the pillowcase and pressed it against her gaping wound. Her warm blood saturated the fabric. Angelina felt her pulse thundering under her hand. She struggled to stay conscious, but the vision of Antonio's disgusting, yellowed teeth tearing off a chunk of flesh made her legs buckle, sending Angelina into a downward spiral.

Antonio stopped her fall. His hand clamped on her throat, crushing her windpipe. Effortlessly, he picked her up and slammed her against the wall.

"You bitch! I don't give a shit if Don Salvatore wants you alive! You have proven yourself to be a cunt. Cunts die! Do you hear me, cunt? And I am going to enjoy killing you."

Squirming, Angelina tried to free herself, but each wiggle encouraged his hand to clamp tighter. Her body weak from oxygen deprivation, Angelina's resistance lessened, as did his grip. She sucked in enough air to beg for mercy.

"No! Please!"

His right hand clamped tighter on her throat while his left pressed the point of the blade against her skin.

"No? Ha! You deserve to die, you vile little cunt!"

"Not as vile as you!" A faceless voice bellowed.

Angelina tried to see who entered the cabin, but Antonio's grip prevented her head from moving.

"Get the fuck out!" Antonio growled. "This ain't your business."

"Help!" Angelina squeaked.

"Unfortunately for you, this *is* my business!"

Antonio cackled. "For me? Ha, you barkin' at the wrong dog! Hey, Bruno? Take out this piece of shit!"

"Bruno appears to be a little busy."

Still holding Angelina hostage, Antonio's grip loosened enough for a new rush of warmth to flow down her neck. A swift kick to his side might free her, but she did not have the strength. Her vision blurred, and Angelina's tense body relaxed under Antonio's destructive hold.

"Who the fuck do you think you are?"

"A powerful adversary."

"No, you are a dead man!" Antonio barked.

Antonio released Angelina, and she slumped into a heap on the floor. She heard the huffs and blows from the fight concealed by the blackening air.

Angelina struggled to remain alert, but the blood loss and lack of oxygen drew her farther away from consciousness. The thick smoke gripped Angelina's lungs, sending her into a coughing fit. Her body slowly slid to the floor. As she reached out for stability, her hand grazed the sole of Francesca's foot.

"Francesca! Francesca, please! Don't die! Please!" Tears streamed down Angelina's cheeks as she placed her trembling hand on Francesca's neck. "Please, God, don't take another life from me. Please!" Readjusting her hand, Angelina found a thin thread of a pulse. "You're alive! Oh, thank God, you are alive!"

Another coughing spasm consumed Angelina, and she collapsed into the growing pool of Francesca's blood. The warmth was oddly soothing and comforting, urging Angelina's body to relax into oblivion.

In the distance, miles away from her consciousness, Angelina heard the two men fighting. The sounds of fists connecting with flesh and cracking bones were as prevalent of noise as the groan of pain caused by the blow.

The feet danced close to Angelina, stirring her back to consciousness. She struggled to see the two men battling in the thick smoke. Her heart fluttered. Marcus came back. Her brother was fighting Antonio. It was enough to give her the will to live and to help.

Marcus slightly overpowered Antonio, but not the only one landing hard punches. Both were formidable fighters, trading strings of powerful blows.

Angelina sat up, and her lungs seized again, this time more violently. The layer of smoke was pressing closer to the floor; they had to get out before the fire trapped them. They did not have time to wait for Marcus to win. Angelina needed to help but was too weak to trade punches. A clink-clink grabbed Angelina's attention.

"The knife!" she murmured.

The shoe tapped the blade, making it clink again; it was close. Angelina reached in that direction, floating her hand above the floor, feeling for the knife.

"Where is it? Come on, it has to be close!"

On all fours, Angelina moved deeper into the cabin. Her hand scurried across the floor like a mouse, avoiding the paws of a cat. She reached into the dark abyss and quickly retreated when a set of feet trampled past. Angelina's hand planted in a pool of blood and slid out from under her. She crashed against the floor, knocking the wind out of her. Her eyes grew heavy as consciousness tiptoed away.

The thundering feet approached her head, vibrating the wooden plank under her cheek. Inches away from her, a shoe slapped the ground, splattering blood across Angelina's face, jolting her awake. Angelina rolled out of the way. Her shoe touched the blade's handle, surging her motivation. She stretched out her fingers and gently tickled the leather-wrapped hilt.

"There you are!" Angelina stretched.

One finger at a time, she pressed the weapon to prevent it from slipping away, but her blood-soaked hand made the task difficult. Angelina extended her torso as far as she could. She placed her pointer finger on the handle, but it was not enough.

"Come on!"

With all the strength she had left, Angelina stretched further. This time, it was just enough for her middle finger to hold the handle in place. Delicately, she placed her pointer finger back on the hilt.

"Now, I have you!"

The handle was firmly in her palm, and relief spilled over Angelina. Though her triumph was exhilarating, the activity drained her.

The men continued to fight, dancing close to Angelina's outstretched arm, but they, too, were losing strength. Both coughing forcefully, they stopped fighting for a second. Angelina looked up and saw Antonio's devilish glare. As she retreated, his black leather shoe stomped on her hand, crushing her fingers. She wailed from the pain.

Angelina withdrew her throbbing hand and huddled against the wall by Francesca. Through the grey smoke, Angelina gasped when Antonio, locking eyes with her and chuckling, reached down to grab the knife. The pause for arrogance gave Marcus time to kick Antonio's abdomen. Out of the blackness, a hand wrapped around Antonio's throat, pulling him back into the unknown.

Angelina quickly reached out to find the knife. Her fingers frantically wandered around the wooden floor. She could feel the fire's heat raging on the deck below them. It was now or never; they had to escape.

"Damn it!" Angelina cursed.

The exertion sent her lungs into another round of spasms. She braced her body on her right hand, but the lack of oxygen was too much. She fell limp against the floor, gasping for air. A sharp pain stabbed at her chest. When she moved, the blood-soaked knife clanked under her.

Before Angelina could admire the weapon, a loud thud startled her. A foot away, under the thick layer of smoke, Angelina tried to see whose body collided with the floor. In seconds, the victor straddled his victim. His face, covered in soot, added to his menacing stature. He locked eyes with Angelina. In his dark orbs, she saw a ravenous lust for glory muddled with an untamable rage.

"You are not Marcus!"

Slowly returning to consciousness, Antonio moaned, startling Angelina. She drew away, but another, louder groan from the ship spurred her into action. Both hands wrapped around the hilt, she drove the knife into Antonio's body. The sensation of flesh tearing and the warmth of his blood on her hand made her gag. It was justice to inflict pain or even death on her enemy. Yet, she did not feel righteousness. Instead, she felt a sea of guilt engulfing her as she collapsed.

Two muscular arms gently lifted her off the ground and carried her out of the cabin. She reached back toward Francesca and mumbled her name. Hopeless, Angelina's tears flowed as she struggled to remain conscious. In her blurred vision, Angelina watched as the stranger carried her down the hallway, leaving behind her friend and her enemy.

CHAPTER 44

Disoriented, Marcus pulled himself up from the floor. His hearing, muffled by the roaring silence, aided the spinning world he fought to escape. Every movement hurt. His ribs were sore if not broken, as were his knuckles. But the worst pain came from his throbbing head. He touched the growing lump, and a sharp bolt of pain brought a rush of burning tears to his eyes.

"Argh! Son of a bitch!"

Blinking away the pain, he grabbed the brass rail and pulled himself up. The smoke was thick, almost suffocating. Instantly, his lungs added a thunderous harmony to the choir of torture. The violent spasm of coughs forced him back to his knees.

"Get your shit together, soldier!" Marcus's mind barely overruled the body's desire to give up. "You ain't dead. Yet!"

Down the hall, the devil's golden, undulating tongues etched in red and black lapped at the ceiling and dribbled down the walls. The fire savored every inch, slowly creeping forward. Unholy growls roared from the belly of the beast. The Grim Reaper's long black fingers searched the ceiling for another morsel to devour. The ominous force slowly crawling toward Marcus spurred him to get his ass moving.

The thick smoke decreased the visibility, making it difficult to know which way led back to the room. One wrong turn could prevent him from rescuing his sister and Francesca and trap him in the furnace of flames.

Before he was confronted by Bruno, Marcus remembered reaching the top of the nearby staircase. Retracing his steps back to the cabin, the sight of cleaner air around the stairwell gave him hope.

"Please be okay." Marcus prayed.

When he reached the lower deck, he recognized an armless statue. It was a poor rendition of the original, at least he hoped. The proportion of eyes to mouth and bust to shoulders were disturbingly off. He had planned to mock the figure during the trip to lighten everyone's mood, including his own fowl attitude. Instead, the eyes from their superior position mocked Marcus.

"Please, God, let them be okay!"

Frustration and guilt urged him to hurry. Approaching the bottom of the staircase, the smoke thickened. His lungs revolted again, sending him into another round of powerful coughs. Each plea for oxygen threatened his consciousness, making the journey endless. Allowing his body to collapse would be easy, but his sister's life pushed him.

One floor below, the hand of the Grim Reaper, exacting his power over life, claimed the souls of passengers trapped by the inferno. Their cries of misery pierced the air and pulled at his heart. The souls entombed in hell were lost, and Marcus prayed his sister was not suffering the same fate.

Marcus moved down the long hallway that led to their room. The rippling, hungry blaze at the opposite end taunted him. The fire crept toward him, yet Marcus fought to win the race to the cabin. Long black fingers tickled the ceiling above the doorway as he approached the room.

"Oh, no!" Marcus cried. "No, no, no!"

In the grey haze, he could see a dainty, pale hand lying across the threshold. His heart pounded in his chest, and his lungs heaved against the smoke. The heat became more intense with each step, adding to his enemy's army.

"You have fought stronger adversaries!" Marcus hissed. "This is no hotter than Sicily in mid-summer!"

It was a lie, but he needed to believe in something—anything to keep him moving. Approaching the door to their cabin, fear coursed through his veins, and the phrase 'you are too late, soldier' echoed in his head.

His knees gave way when he saw the pool of blood around Francesca. Crouched below the thick smoke, Marcus raced to her side. She was pale, more so than usual.

"Oh dear, God, No!" He felt her neck. "Come on, come on!"

A moan from deeper in the cabin startled him. Peering through the darkness, Marcus saw a body.

"Angelina?"

On his knees, he crawled into the cabin, but a frail hand touched his wrist.

"Don't!" Francesca mumbled.

"But Angelina?"

"Gone," Francesca muttered.

Tears stung his eyes. Shaking his head, he repressed his emotions. He didn't want to believe it. Angelina wasn't gone, only injured. As he moved to aid his sister, Francesca tightened her grip. Her eyes pleading for him to stay.

Memories from the battlefield plagued his heart. It was the law of war. Sometimes, a soldier had to leave brothers behind to save one. It was a tough decision he made too many times. Even though his comrades were brothers, Marcus never had to choose between a sibling and a companion. All factors weighed, including his physical condition. He could only save one from the burning flames. Once again, Marcus had to choose who would live and who would die.

Marcus stared at the thick smoke inside the cabin. His heart pleading for a sign of life or anything that could determine his next move.

"Angelina?" Marcus called out. "Angelina?"

Francesca's hand squeezed harder for a moment, but her strength faded. Much like the battlefield, he ran out of time.

"Damn it!" He growled.

He gave one last look inside the cabin and sighed. Marcus cradled Francesca's frail form in his arms.

"I got you. Hang on to me. I will get us out of here." She was thin, too thin. But he appreciated her frame as he barely had the energy to carry himself, much less that of another. "When we get back home, I am going to feed you the biggest bowl of pasta!" Marcus whispered.

Francesca smiled at him, then nuzzled her head into his chest. The affectionate caress intensified his desire to save her from the ensuing inferno.

"Damn, is it me, or is this hallway longer?" He muttered.

His humor made Francesca smile. The fuel it brought him quickly vanished. The ship collided with something. The hard pitch slammed him against the wall.

"Arrhhh! Son of a... Arrhhh!"

Francesca stirred in his arms, adding to his pain. He swallowed the chorus of agony from every body part. Her weight, his wounds, and the new trauma from the collision with the wall beckoned him to stop moving.

"Probably a barge sent to put out the fire." He grunted each word. He struggled to maintain consciousness.

Francesca reached her arm up and wiped the tears from his cheeks, her eyes twinkling with gratitude for his exertion. They were two blue jewels conferring love.

He blinked away the tears as he gazed into the cool blueness. It was not Francesca's eyes he saw, but that of his love. The woman he longed to make his bride. Marcus smiled. He was given another chance to save what he failed to save six months ago.

I won't fail you again, Katherine! I promise! Marcus vowed in silence.

Muffling his internal agony, Marcus pushed his body up and regained his footing. The memory of the love of his life fueled each painful step forward. In the shadows of the smoke, a figure approached.

"Oh, thank God, they sent crews to extract us." He sighed.

His jaw dropped, and his shoulders tensed when the figure emerged from the black veil.

"Fuck me!"

Francesca jumped, and her movement sent a flash of pain through his side. It was enough pressure to finish breaking the rib Bruno kicked repeatedly. Marcus tried to re-balance himself, but the pain was too much.

"Leave the bitch!" Bruno growled. "And I will let you pass."

Francesca's scream pierced Marcus's ears.

"Don't you ever die?" Marcus growled.

A voice behind him said, "I can say the same for you."

Marcus turned around. Antonio limped toward him. Bits and pieces of the situation were illuminated. Francesca had stopped him from mistaking Antonio for Angelina.

"Where is Angelina?" Marcus mumbled.

His heart sunk at the thought of her body lying in wait for the flaming demon to engulf her. He shook his head free of the horrible image. He had to focus on facts, not if's.

His body was plagued with pain, but he was a soldier. A warrior who could not be trapped. The guarded steps of his attackers allowed Marcus to review tactical scenarios.

Antonio limped forward, spitting blood every few feet. His symptoms finalized Marcus's plan. Now, he must wait until the right moment.

"Patience is my sword." He mumbled. "If I fail, Valhalla awaits."

"In fact, I have already attended *your* funeral. Your picture...displayed next to your brothers. A poor likeness...by the way." Antonio taunted. "The church...filled... with flowers and tears. Very touching...to those who gave a damn. Rest in peace, Marcus, knowing I will tell your sister exactly how you *really* died." Antonio flashed a wicked smile. "She will want to correct the date on your tombstone. Wouldn't... want false tales...about the eldest son of the pious Sofia Beretta."

"Do not interrupt your enemy while he is making a mistake." Marcus whispered the wise words of Napolean.

Marcus patiently waited, allowing his enemies to exhaust themselves with unnecessary speech and forced movements. Antonio's lungs convulsed, halting his step to expel the blood hindering his breathing. Red oozed from his lips like a dog foaming at the mouth. Marcus smiled. The exertion drained Antonio's energy and the color from his face.

Time was Marcus's ally and his foe. As an ally, every second Antonio remained standing and coughing gave Marcus the edge of strength, albeit by a small margin. In war, everything counted, and the slightest advantage could shift the outcome. Marcus would use all that he had to achieve the upper hand. Yet, his strength meant nothing, with time racing to destroy him. The raging fire and Bruno's advancement made time Marcus's enemy. His plan required Antonio to reach him before the giant oa. That is if the flames and smoke didn't consume them all.

The boat shifted again, flinging Antonio to the floor. Marcus internally cheered. That fall added to his favor, but his good luck was matched with bad. Bruno's ominous figure seemed unaffected by the jolt. At this pace, Bruno would be upon him long before Antonio. Marcus had already lost a fight with Bruno. A fact every breath sharply reminded him. He searched for anything to help him defeat the giant.

"Damn it!" Marcus murmured.

Marcus's eyes ping-ponged back and forth, gauging the distance between him and his assassins. Bruno's long stride continued to work against Marcus.

"God, a little divine intervention! Please!" Marcus prayed, resting his head against the wall.

A loud pop echoed around them. Marcus searched the walls and ceiling for the cause but saw nothing. It was not the same groans from the ship's belly. The noise came from the hallway, yet nothing appeared to cause the sound.

"What the fuck?" Bruno stared at his feet.

A long, thin crack in the wood ran between Bruno's feet. Marcus could barely contain his excitement. His inner child screamed *Hallelujah!* He prayed the crack would expand.

The ship released another haunting groan. Another loud pop echoed around them. Marcus's eyes widened, but not as much as Bruno's. The crack spread, splitting the wooden floor beneath Bruno's feet.

"What the fuck!" Bruno repeated, backing away.

"Now, I know how Mose felt!" Marcus shook his head.

He flung Francesca over his left shoulder. Dropping his right shoulder, he plowed into Antonio. Antonio landed with a thud and spewed a string of cuss words.

The commotion pulled Bruno back to the chase. His enormous feet slammed against the floor.

Antonio stretched his arm out. "Bruno! You fucking idiot! You are going to kill us both! Damn it! Stop, you ignafuck!"

Marcus ignored the consternation. He focused his energy on finding an unlocked cabin and breathing. He struggled to maintain his footing as he wobbled down the hallway.

"What the...?" A warm fluid trickled down his arm. "One of many, soldier." He told himself. "You will die of oxygen deprivation before bleeding to death."

The first two doors were locked. The third burned him.

"Dammit! That's hot!" He growled, shaking away the pain.

Francesca stirred.

"Can you walk?" He asked, setting her down.

"Use my sweater."

He removed her sweater, and she collapsed. Marcus hoisted her back onto his shoulder. He wrapped his hand in the thinly knitted blue fabric and tested the door again.

"Locked, damn it! No time to waste, soldier. Think!" He looked for their cabin. It was four doors away.

A loud pop followed by a haunting wail grabbed Marcus's attention. The floor opened like the Red Sea beneath Bruno. His torso wedged in the gap. He pawed the floor, screaming.

"My legs! They are burning! Help me!"

His begging turned to blood-curdling cries of misery. Out of self-preservation, Anntonio did not reach out to Bruno.

"You're the dumb fuck who caused the fucking crack!" Antonio growled, scooting away. "You are a fucking idiot!"

"Help me! Please!"

Francesca slid down Marcus's torso to watch Bruno's end.

"Don't look!" Marcus said, covering her eyes.

"No! It is justice for him to die from what he used to kill."

"Yes." He tried to turn her away. "The comfort of justice can't erase the horror of a graphic death. Some sights cannot be unseen."

"Yes, but it will be *his* screams I hear in my nightmares, not my Alberto's," Francesca replied, pulling his hand away.

Bruno's voice shrilled as the flame's golden tongues excitedly licked his soot-stained shirt. Red-edged circles rapidly expanded into black splotches. Flesh bubbled on his face, and his eyes bulged. His hair caught fire in a flash, sending the acrid smell into the air. His mouth opened and closed as his plea for help became a gurgling noise. The fire's crimson teeth devoured him.

"We have to go!"

Marcus met little resistance after Francesca saw Bruno's form encapsulated in flames. He hoisted Francesca onto his shoulder. Both grunted in pain, but the thought of being engulfed by fire was more than enough motivation to leave.

Their pause to witness Bruno's end fed the fire with more than a soul. It moved with a purpose, a living force hungry to consume. The heat intensified, stinging Marcus' exposed skin. The raging fire could explode, instantly engulfing them. Marcus pushed the thought away. He wasn't giving up.

Closing the ten-foot gap to the doorway, the fire sprinted to the finish line, sending a small surge forward. The golden legs danced in a taunting victory dance in the open threshold. Every instinct in Marcus told him to turn back, to find another way out that didn't include the unbearable heat.

"You are a warrior. Face your enemy!" He growled.

Marcus ignored the blazing heat and his internal pleas to fall back. The fire roared at his arrogant approach. In the last few feet of his approach, it surged again. He did not heed the infernal warning. The fire spit flames at him as he darted into the room. He slammed the door. The fire squealed and popped outside, barking its fury for Marcus's small victory.

Marcus's eyes needed time to adjust to the darkness. He did not have that luxury. His memory would guide him to the window.

"Don't fall over. Let me get the sheet, then sit on the bed."

He yanked the bedding off the flimsy mattress and separated the sheet from the blanket. Unlike all his other tasks that day, the thin white fabric easily tore.

"Help me wrap this around your wound."

Marcus held the end of the long strip of fabric to Francesca's side. He wrapped the material snugly around her torso, apologizing after every whimper she made.

"It should feel tight, but not too tight. You okay?"

She nodded and collapsed back on the corner of the bed.

"Good. Don't give up on me. I will get us out of here!" His voice trailed off. "If I can break the window."

Marcus blindly felt for the chair in the far corner. A clink-clink stopped his movement. He squatted down below the thick smoke to see what treasure his foot had found.

A grin curled his lips. "Well, hello! You might work!"

Under the toe of his right foot was a bloody knife. His hand firmly gripped the hilt. He slammed it against the window. Each impact sent an intense pain throughout his torso.

"Come—on—break!"

A spasm of coughs forced him to stop. Hunched over, he struggled to regain his breath. Every ounce of his body revolted against him. The thick smoke burned his eyes, and the lump on his head throbbed. Their escape was hopeless.

Outside the door, the raging fire roared, and the ship groaned. Death knocked; time was up. They would suffer the same fate as Bruno. The memory of singed hair and the horrific squeals of misery emitted from the giant shook Marcus to the core. He did not want to die like Bruno.

"A warrior fights until his last breath. You still draw air!"

He growled and turned the sharp bites from his ribcage into mental lashes from a whip. He would fight on and earn a warrior's victory.

It took five more slams before the window shattered. The sea air rushed into the room, replacing the toxic smoke. It was refreshing, even if it smelled like dead fish.

"I hope you can swim." Marcus held out his hand.

"I...can't!"

"You will today!" He helped her to the window. "Kick your legs and move your arms. Don't stop. I am right behind you!"

The afternoon sun illuminated Francesca. Her battered form told the story of the tragedy. The black soot made her pale complexion ghostly. Blood matted and tinged her blonde hair. Her blue eyes danced in terror from the past and the prospect of jumping into the angry water below. They were far from safe. To jump out of a ship into a busy harbor was as dangerous as the burning vessel.

The synchronized rhythm of their breathing drew their bodies closer, intensifying Marcus's desire to embrace her. His thumb wiped away the tears cascading down her cheek. Beyond the terror, the beautiful blue gems urged him to kiss her. He gently stroked his thumb across her soft lips. She smiled, and the chaos surrounding them dissolved. His heart urged him to seize the one and only chance. They would likely die in the tumultuous water below. Marcus leaned closer, her breath warm against his lips. He closed the gap, their lips touching ever so slightly. A passing boat's blaring horn startled them. The tender moment was lost, they separated.

"You must jump." His abruptness made her smile vanish like a shooting star. "I will be right behind you. I promise."

"I can't swim!"

The door handle rattled. They exchanged terrified looks.

"Jump!" Marcus shouted. "Now!"

She shook her head.

"Please forgive me, Francesca."

"For what?"

"Kick." Marcus pushed her out the window. "Kick!"

Francesca plunged into the waves. The bile in Marcus's gut rose higher with each passing second that she didn't emerge.

"Kick, damn it! Kick!"

The doorknob rattled again. Marcus glanced at the door and back to the agitated water below. Still no Francesca. The cabin door flung open. In the doorway, half his body covered in flames, Antonio flashed a maniacal smile. He lunged, grabbing Marcus's ankle with a hand encased in fire. The connection created a bridge for the tiny flames to hop onto Marcus's grey slacks.

"Die, you evil bastard! Die in the fiery hell you love."

Marcus tried to free his leg, but Antonio held firm and released a demonic cackle. Marcus cringed. He slammed his free foot into Antonio's chest. The last thing Marcus heard before plummeting into the water was another eerie cry from Antonio.

On his way down, Marcus scanned the water for Francesca. But a large wave swelled and consumed him before he could discern her location.

Marcus resurfaced and scanned the waves. He shouted her name in every direction. The rapidly rising and falling water made visibility no farther than the crest of the adjoining wave. Time was crucial. A one-word lesson, *kick*, would not keep her afloat long.

The wave crested, revealing her head, a bobber being tugged by a catfish. Francesca was seconds from drowning.

Marcus kicked his muscular legs as hard as he could, closing the gap. An arms-length away, she dipped under the water. In a last surge of energy, Marcus dove down, wrapping his arm around her. They re-emerged, both hungrily sucking in the air. Marcus rolled to his back with Francesca close to his chest and headed for the shoreline.

"I got ya. We are gonna be alright."

Francesca stopped him and pointed at the broken window.

"Marcus, is that...?"

In the window stood Antonio, his body engulfed in flames. He stretched out his arm and extended a finger encased in a golden blaze. His demonic lungs howled.

"I will get you, cunt!"

Marcus and Francesca, motionless, watched Antonio commit himself to the water. The waves ebbed and flowed, sloshing against the hull of the boat. As they waited for their enemy to reemerge, Marcus and Francesca silently prayed he would drown.

"Do you think he is alive?"

"A devil never dies."

CHAPTER 45

The Don read the front page of the post. The main headline perpetuated his felicity.

Massive Fire on Ocean-liner bound for New York.

"That is my boy!" He rejoiced. "Antonio, my ferocious firefly. You do live up to the title of 'Demoni di Fuoco'!"

He read the article several times, savoring every detail. Eighty dead, hundreds injured, and the ship must be dry-docked for a complete overhaul. Sources were unsure of *how* the fire started. Some affluent passengers claimed the fire was a calculated heist to steal over a million dollars in jewels.

Don Salvatore did not need to speculate on how or even who caused the fire but was curious about the stolen jewels.

Sitting under the magnolia tree, The Don sprinkled a handful of fresh grain on the ground. One lonely pigeon swooped down to feast on the tiny seeds. Looking at his feathered friend, he started a one-sided conversation.

"My boy was busy! What fun is a heist if you don't get something to line your pocket! Hmm? Shall we give him all the jewels for a job well done?" The pigeon tilted its head and cooed before returning to its meal. "You greedy little ball of feathers! No wonder we get along so well."

Don Salvatore cackled and leaned back into his chair. "You make a good point, my friend. I will take my cut of the prize. One shouldn't disregard precedent. That would be foolish."

He grabbed another handful of grain and pensively poured the grains from one hand to the other. The soft shuffle of seeds drew the bird's attention. It eyed his master briefly before continuing to feast on the scattered grain.

"Besides, My Little Dove will need something to wear! She can't be naked all the time." His boisterous laughter sent his feathered friend into flight.

He strolled under the magnolia tree branches toward the three-tiered fountain at the end of the stone path. The cooing doves, trickling water, and rustling of leaves blended into a symphonic chorus. A perfect melody for The Don to enjoy while dreaming of Angelina's supple body.

"Ah, My Little Dove, you are a beautiful jewel, and I will enjoy every facet and sparkle. The more you please me, the more I shall give you. It will be a simple arrangement." Don Salvatore mused as he picked a silky leaf from the tree. "You have opened my eyes, My Little Dove. I can see why my nephew craves the fruit from the Beretta tree. Greed and lust, however, are sins of the flesh. As his only parental influence, it is my responsibility to impress the gravity of his actions. Your sister despises your natural gifts, but she must learn her place. When you give birth to my son, you will wear the crown which your sister so desperately desires. Giorgio shall realize he is merely a puppet, a pawn in a game of kings. The spoiled brat will understand his life is only a means to an end, and his end shall be meaningless."

Continuing to play his mental chess game, Don Salvatore strolled into his bedroom that adjoined the courtyard. It was time to inspect his dove's future cage.

Don Salvatore unlocked the door between his room and Angelina's. Twirling the only key on the leather string, he inspected the space. His eyes combed every inch of the room, looking for any missed detail.

The fragrant flowers lured him to the table under the window. The sunlight danced around a small diamond-cut vase of a vibrant array of colorful flowers. He gently stroked the petals and admired the natural beauty. The rose's sweet scent and soft petals caressing his chin made his cock tingle.

Across the room, a clank of a metal bucket caught his attention. He had assumed he was alone, but the Don saw Amalea gathering her cleaning supplies in the shadows. He flashed her a devilish grin. She scurried out of sight, nearly dropping every item in her clutches.

"She is more skittish than the last maid." He laughed. "A pleasing attribute that will make her perfect for my fantasy!"

In the private sanctuary he created, Don Salvatore strutted around the room. As if they were guests at a party, he shared his plans for Angelina's first night with each piece of furniture. Gliding his hand across the silky beige sheets, The Don's cock pulsed with anticipation.

"No doubt, she will be hungry and need a hot bath. Antonio is good at some things, but being a gentleman, he is not. Perhaps I shall grant her one night to rest."

After another sensual stroke of the sheets, The Don made his way to the other window. He pulled back the heavy velour curtains and examined where the light would land in the early morning hours. He planned to watch her sleep while the sun danced across her soft olive skin, accenting the round curves of her hips. It was a tantalizing visual.

"Mmm... yes, even the thought of you is invigorating."

From the bowl of fruit, he snatched a plump lemon. Gently squeezing it with his chubby fingers, he shared his thoughts with the supple fruit. The fresh lemon scent tickled his nose. Holding it close, he inhaled.

"No doubt, Antonio will have treated her poorly. All for the best, for I will be sweet and kind...*at first*."

The Don clamped his hand around the lemon and squeezed. The juice oozed into his hands, and he lapped up the tart liquid. His mouth did not pucker from the sourness. He smiled and savored it.

"Will Angelina be a rose, soft and frail? Or a lemon, with radiant skin, an alluring scent, yet bitter inside? Oh, how I do hope you are tart, My Little Dove. It will make our time together so much more enjoyable!"

After he had eaten the flesh of the lemon, he discarded the mangled carcass with a dismissive flip over his shoulder.

Don Salvatore tied the leather strap with the key around his neck. Gently patting the key, he made his way down the stone stairwell to his private cellar. The musty smell was a harsh contrast to the fragrant flowers in Angelina's room. He lit a candelabra and peered in the crates.

"Shall we drink the *family* wine on your first night?"

Holding a bottle with Beretta written in an elegant script, he mocked Angelina. *"White or red?* Why, My Little Dove, I am not sure? With you as my glass, I can say which is better?"

The Don licked his lips, imagining Angelina naked, pouring wine onto her breasts while he lapped it off her skin.

"Hmm...yes. I think that will be the perfect way to taste the family wine. I have been told you are magnificent to watch when you serve customers a sampling. But you will no longer sample the wine, as your father taught you. I will teach you the *only* way the wine is to be presented to my customers or me! You will serve *me*, My Little Dove. You will be what I make you and nothing more!"

Don Salvatore poured a glass of red and hummed a cheery tune. He twirled the wine and sniffed it.

"Ah! A hint of...blah, blah, blah! See My Little Dove, you teach me to describe the wine. I will train you to be my slave!"

Don Salvatore pushed a tall Teak-wood cabinet by the stairwell to the left. His fingers lightly danced across the wall, stopping at a slightly raised stone. A plume of fine dust filled the air as he pulled the brick from its tomb. Slipping his fingers inside the space, he popped out a segment of the wall. He brushed away the dust, revealing a keyhole.

The Don removed two keys from his pocket and used the smaller one to unlock the two-foot-tall metal door. The hinges groaned, resisting the command to open. The metal edges grated against the rock, creating another cloud of dust. Don Salvatore took a long swig of wine before removing the heavy treasure chest made of cherry wood with black metal straps. The second key fit perfectly into the old padlock. With a little finesse, he persuaded the cylinder and pins to line up.

"Of course, you will be rewarded for your efforts!"

Plunging his fat hand into the box, he removed a handful of jewelry. He held up the strands of black pearls, a cascading diamond necklace with teardrop rubies, and a canary diamond ring. The dim lighting muted their radiant beauty.

"These will look lovely against your bare chest. After all, beauty deserves beauty!" He wetted his lips with wine and grinned. "My Little Dove, you *will* learn to enjoy your life here, for that I am certain."

CHAPTER 46

A sliver of sunlight pierced the darkness, illuminating Angelina's face. Her eyes flashed open but quickly closed. The beam of bright sunshine intensified her throbbing headache.

"Move! You are not a victim! You must move forward for our family's sake!" Angelina thought, but quickly mocked her reasoning. "Ha! Family; what is left of it?"

Every fiber of Angelina hurt, but none as much as her heart. Her choices led Francesca and Marcus to horrid ends.

One tear streamed down Angelina's cheek, followed by an unstoppable river of them. She choked back her sobs, but the restraint sent her into a coughing fit. Each convulsion burned her lungs and increased the pounding pressure in her head. When the spasms subsided, she rested her head on the soft pillow. The exertion drained what little energy she possessed.

A battle between Angelina's mind and body ensued. She needed to get up, find out where she was, but the pain from another tragic loss was overwhelming.

Rolling away from the window, Angelina snuggled under the heavy blanket. The weight was comforting, and the plush pillow felt good against her head. A whiff of gardenias filled her nose. Angelina's hair was wet from a shower she did not remember taking.

"I can forget a shower, but not the tragedies," she grumbled.

Her mind persisted in questioning *where am I*, but the pain in her heart kept her in bed. Her body had won, and she allowed her eyes to close again.

When she awoke, the sunlight had shifted, illuminating the far corner of the room. Her headache dulled; Angelina sat up to examine the décor. The sparse pattern of crimson flowers shimmering in the light from the crystal sconces, scenic oil paintings, crown molding, and thick, burgundy velour curtains provided a soothing background for the creamy beige furniture.

A warm rush of relief filled her core, and she smiled.

"Catalina."

Relaxing back on the pillow, Angelina's body soaked in the warmth and love. It was comforting to be back in Brusnengo, at her sister's villa. Soon, Catalina would enter the room and tend to Angelina's wounds while Constance poured them hot tea. The thought of the tender care filled Angelina with relief.

The fading sunlight filled the room with an amber glow, and the tick-tick of the clock counted the minutes as Angelina waited for her sister. Surprised by the lack of attentiveness, Angelina crawled out from under the warm sheets. The chilly air nipped at her skin. Every muscle resisted, urging her to stay in the soft bed. Her curiosity overruled her body's protests. Angelina took a couple steps. A wave of nausea forced her to sit on the edge of the bed. She clutched the blanket, willing her stomach to settle. She slowed her breathing and focused on the plush carpet beneath her bare feet. The wave of nausea subsided enough for her to stand. Slightly hunched, Angelina shuffled toward the chair by the window. She clutched each piece of furniture, fearing her wobbly legs would give way. The last two steps before collapsing into the chair lacked any gracefulness.

"Ouch, what the..."

As she pulled a gold box the size of a book out from under her hip, a rush of panic filled her chest, and her skin rippled with gooseflesh. Her mind was occupied with the décor, her heart consumed by guilt, and her body crying out in agony. Angelina missed one significant detail. She was naked.

She stumbled toward the bed. On her third step, her legs gave way. In a loud thud, her body collided with the hard floor, knocking the wind out of her lungs. A few feet away, the box tumbled, pausing for a second on its edge, giving Angelina a glimpse at some of the letters on the card.

For Angelina   My   ove

A strand of black pearls spilled out of the box. She was too busy filling the missing letters on the note to notice them.

"*For Angelina, My Little Dove.* How could you, Cat? How could you take me to Don Salvatore?"

Her cry of desperation turned into a convulsion of coughs. Fading from consciousness, Angelina heard footsteps approaching and someone calling her name. She willingly slipped into the abyss. There was nothing to live for now. Her sister had betrayed her.

CHAPTER 47

The night air bloomed with the smell of fresh gardenias, stirring Marcus's memories of home. But all the people who made home a comforting place were gone. There would be no elated expressions welcoming him back. No lavish meals that took all day to prepare. No family gatherings around a fire, laughing and drinking an entire case of wine before sunrise. The void of heartwarming events made the rolling land in front of him a piece of property lined with grapevines. It was no longer his family's legacy.

"Where are we?" Francesca asked.

"At the vineyard where I grew up," Marcus replied.

As the light breeze caressed the grass and tickled the small limbs overhead, Marcus closed his eyes and drew in the cool air. He tried to see his brothers' faces and his mother's smile, but those details were shrouded in black.

"My mother cried when I left for the military. I can see her wiping away the stream of tears with a black handkerchief. I remember feeling her body tremble as I gave her one last hug. Every detail of that day is vivid in my mind, but when I try to remember her smile, her face is hidden behind a black veil," Marcus confessed. "If I would have stayed like she wanted me too, none of this would have happened."

"You would have been dead too. Don Salvatore is vicious and greedy. Nothing could prevent him from attacking your family. Nothing. Not you or anyone else. This was not your fault, Marcus."

Weaving through the grapevines, they crept toward the entrance to the house. The kitchen light glowed brightly in the moonless night.

"Isn't it late for someone to be up?" Francesca whispered.

"It has been so long, and so much has changed. They should be asleep, but to be safe, we will walk close to the buildings." Marcus stretched out his hand. "I will guide you."

She hesitated. Marcus withdrew the offer with a nod of understanding. Before his hand reached his side, her thin fingers slipped into his palm. He glanced back and smiled.

"There are several rocks ahead. They are big enough to trip you but not large enough to see in the dark."

By the time they reached the last building at the top of the hill, the house lights were off, reducing their visibility. Moving out from the shadows, Marcus and Francesca walked the last hundred feet on the gravel path.

"We can rest in the cellar. If we are lucky, Angelina's food pantry will be full. It won't be a feast, but at least it will be something."

"How can you see anything?"

"You get used to it. Don't worry. There is a box of candles on this ledge. Even in daylight, the stairwell is difficult to maneuver."

The chilly air, gentle breeze, and near darkness reminded Marcus of the night he convinced a girl from school to go into the cellar. He intentionally chose a moonless night, hoping to intensify the girl's uneasiness. It worked too well. Before he could light the candle, she was running back to the house with tears rolling down her cheeks.

Suppressing a smirk, Marcus held the match to the wick. With a surge of light, the candle captured the flame, doubling its glow.

"Ahh! Much better."

Francesca tilted her head. "Are you laughing?"

"Yes. I will tell you why, but first, you need food, and I need a glass of wine."

"Who keeps food in a dungeon?"

"You'll see."

Holding out his hand, Marcus helped Francesca down the steps. The flame's yellow glow dancing in her golden hair gave her the radiance of an angel. She was thin and pale but captivating. Lost in her beauty, Marcus tuned out the rest of the world until a gun clicked behind his head.

"Turn around. Slowly."

It was a risky choice to return home. But Marcus believed he could remain hidden long enough to determine if he was more powerful as a ghost or a resurrected man. The barrel pressed to his skull, Marcus's options slipped away.

"Now!"

The hatred exuding from the voice startled Francesca. Wide-eyed in terror, she pressed her body against the cold stone wall and looked to Marcus for protection.

"Now, dammit!"

Marcus flinched, causing the gunmen to intensify the pressure of the cold steel against his head. Slowly turning around, he held the candle high, ready to use the flame and hot wax as a weapon.

"Marcus? Is that really you?" Fernando lowered the gun.

"Fernando?"

Marcus's hand trembled from a rush of emotions. His shock was quickly replaced with relief.

"Thank God you are alive!"

"It is good to be alive!"

Marcus handed Francesca the candle and embraced Fernando. Once for gratitude, a second out of joy.

"I thought... We thought..." Fernando's voice trailed off.

"Angelina told me what happened, at least most of it. I could tell she was holding something back."

Angelina's name transformed Fernando's expression to a boy mourning his lost dog. "You found her?"

"I followed Angelina onto the train."

Fernando craned his neck. "Where is she? Is she here?"

Marcus, shaking his head, avoided eye contact with Fernando. This was not the time to discuss Angelina's whereabouts, especially with the person who loved her more than any man could. Marcus wanted to ignore the question because the answers were complicated.

"Is she okay?"

"I don't know," Marcus confessed.

"What do you mean, you don't know? You left her? Where? Where did you leave her?"

"Nan. Let me explain..."

"After everything, *why* would you leave her?"

"Easy, Nan. Calm down." Marcus said, placing his hand on Fernando's shoulder. "Give me a minute to tell you what happened. We have been on the run for several days. In fact, from the moment we jumped off the train, we have been running. It was one damn mess after another."

Stepping inches away from Marcus's face, Fernando growled, "If she is hurt, I swear to God, I will kill you!"

"She is alive…" Marcus glanced at Francesca. "We think."

"THINK!"

"Nan. Keep your voice down. No one knows I am alive. We need to keep it that way."

Marcus paused to let the reality and the potential consequence of his presence sink into Fernando's thought process. It took a minute, but eventually, Fernando stepped back from Marcus.

"Nan, I will tell you all I know. For now, we need rest and food."

"Who is she?"

"This is Francesca. She is a friend of Angelina's."

Marcus stepped to the side to allow them to greet each other, but Fernando's raised eyebrow thwarted any niceties.

"If you are her friend, why have I never met you?"

"We can discuss specifics another time," Marcus interrupted. "She is hurt and needs rest."

"Fine!" Fernando snapped. "I will leave you alone."

"Nan, wait. Stay. Stay and have a glass of wine with me, please?"

Reluctantly, Fernando nodded.

Making their way down the stairs, the musty air became colder, and the sound of dripping water grew louder. Marcus lit a candle at the bottom of the steps and handed it to Fernando. The second flame's glow pressed the darkness back enough to see the outline of a table encircled by four iron-back chairs. Traveling in opposite directions, Marcus and Fernando lit the three-candle sconces centered on each wall. With each added flame, the darkness slowly crept back from the cozy space, revealing a dark wood buffet server, a matching double-door cabinet, and two tall wine racks separated enough to create a doorway into a veil of blackness.

After helping Francesca to a chair, Marcus disappeared into the rows of wine racks, his candle a floating orb marking his movements.

Eight-foot-tall, double-sided racks spaced four feet apart formed twenty-foot long hallways extending from both sides of the central aisle. Each rack was bolted to a square header at the top, creating a structurally sound space that felt like an underground wine library.

"Five, six, seven," Marcus said, counting each row. "Nine."

He turned right and held the candle up high to illuminate the labels.

"Ahh, here we are!"

Holding the candle close to the bottle, Marcus read the scripted letters on the label.

Beretta's 1925 Nebbiolo

"After narrowly escaping a burning ship and the devil's henchmen, I think we deserve a bottle of the best wine!"

Marcus stopped at the fifth row on his way back to the tasting table. Holding the candle close to the bottles, Marcus searched for the name '*Barbera.*'

"Might there still be some 1938s?" Marcus asked, clearing the dust with a swipe of his finger across each label. "1935, a decent year, but not my favorite. 1936. 1937. 1928, you are a bit out of place." He chuckled. "Ahh, here we are!"

Marcus returned with the wine. The table was dressed with a white tablecloth, a candle abra, and three wine glasses. Fernando carried a small wheel of cheese and a loaf of bread.

Fernando's agitation toward Francesca was palpable, but she was unaffected. Her pain held her attention enough to prevent her from noticing. The uncharacteristic attitude was unwarranted. Marcus did his best to shift the discourse to a more suitable temper.

"It looks like your father is honing his craft," Marcus said, pointing to the cheese.

"Yes, he enjoys it. Well, he did. RJ helped him with every step. Papa lost the desire to make it anymore. He said it brings back the memory of RJ's lifeless body." Fernando stared at the wheel, his jaw grinding. "This attack has been hard on my family, too."

Marcus placed his hand on Fernando's shoulder and gave him a gentle squeeze. "We will fix this, Nan. We will get everything back to normal."

Fernando shoved Marcus away, shaking his head in disbelief. Frustration and rage rattled Fernando's voice, and his hands punctuated every word as he unleashed his feelings.

"Normal? There is no normal! Not anymore. You came back from the dead, but your brothers, *our* brothers, are gone forever! I saw their lifeless forms." Fernando's voice cracked as he jabbed his finger into his chest. "I cleaned up their blood! Me! These hands... covered in blood... *my* best friend's blood! It took hours to scrub the floors. Hours, Marcus! Long hours that felt like an eternity!"

Marcus understood the gore of death. The horror of helplessly watching a grown man crying for his mother while cupping the stump of his leg. A brave soldier frantically crammed his intestines back into the gaping hole in his abdomen while Marcus cradled him. The faces of men slowly bleeding to death still haunted Marcus. Being alive among the dead forced one to ask the question; *why was he taken and I spared?* This consuming puzzle grew in strength each day, plaguing the mind and soul. It was the curse of living with an immortal mental trauma.

Fernando did not have a commander pushing him to the next town, the next fight fueled by vengeance. Nan had no place to unleash the anger forged by the enemy, unmercifully steeling kindred souls. Worst of all, no words would ever erase the harsh memories and volatile emotions left in the aftermath of a tragic death. Marcus's soul was tattooed with the curse, the burden of remaining alive among the dead. Now was not the time to bond over such misery.

"I am sorry, Nan. I didn't know."

"You didn't know because you hid like a coward!"

"Nan..."

"Do you know the hell Don Salvatore has put my family through since every one of you abandoned us? He hovers like a vulture, waiting for one of us to stumble. My family struggles every day to save *your* family's legacy. Why Marcus? Why? Why should we sacrifice our lives for your family? Why does Catalina refuse to tell me where your parents are? Why did Angelina leave? Dammit, Marcus! Why?"

"I don't know, Nan. Saying I am sorry doesn't ease your pain nor mine. No words will change the past, but fighting won't change it either."

Marcus extended his arm to encourage Fernando to sit. The offer was refused. Resolute, Marcus softened his facial features and extended his hand again.

"Please, Nan."

Fernando's bloodshot eyes glanced at the chair and back to Marcus. The chair was an apology. Nan accepting it was forgiveness. However, Fernando's trembling body and sallow complexion spoke louder than his hesitation. He was not ready to forgive.

"Angelina and I met two days after your brothers' were murdered," Francesca said with compassion. "Our friendship is a new affair. One that began in the ashes of sadness. I will tell you most of what I know. However, there are some details Angelina forbade me to share."

Francesca's soothing voice lured both men into their seats. Her words dripped from her tongue like the wax from the candles behind her.

While she spoke, Marcus poured three glasses of wine before slicing the cheese and bread into thick slices. Grateful for the time to remain quiet, Marcus leaned back in his chair and savored his glass of Nebbiolo. The subtle notes of cherry, fig, and rose accented with a hint of spice wrapped his soul in a warm blanket, soothing every ache and pain.

Francesca's energy lasted long enough for Marcus to enjoy a glass of the 1938 Barbera. The variety of berries laced with anise and herbs sent a wave of perky sweetness across his tongue. His last memory of the flavors seemed as distant as a past life, a *déjà vu* of once sipping his favorite wine.

"Nan, we have faced death more than once in the past several days. I have seen some terrible things, but nothing as horrifying as our last glance with the Grim Reaper."

As Marcus described their narrow escape from the ship and Antonio, he opened the third bottle of wine. After refilling Francesca's glass, he turned to fill Fernando's.

His brow furrowed, Nan held his hand over the glass. His drooping and bloodshot eyes told of Fernando's exhaustion, and the deep lines across his forehead expressed far more.

"I will toss some bedding out the upstairs window. If I leave out of the house again, my father will ask questions," Fernando informed as he stood from the table. "He comes down here every morning after feeding the chickens. If you intend to remain a ghost..."

"Thank you, Nan," Marcus stood to hug Fernando. "It is good to be home."

"This place is not the home you remember. The longer Don Salvatore rules over us, the farther we veer from our true nature. I have changed Marcus. We all have, but none more than Catalina."

"What is wrong with Cat?"

"That you will have to see for yourself."

CHAPTER 48

"Will she recover?"

"Most likely. However..." Dr. Lane replied.

"However, what?" Maximus snapped.

"She has been unconscious for several days, and I am the first doctor to examine her, correct?"

"What is your point?"

"She suffered trauma and stress prior to her current state, correct?"

Squaring his shoulders, Maximus's breathing slowed to a long, deliberate pace. Two hours ago, when Dr. Lane entered the house, Maximus explained the situation in detail and answered the doctor's questions. Reaffirming his original answers was a waste of time.

"Doc! You are trying my patience!"

"Yes, of course. Your patience is all that matters. Shall I factor that into my diagnosis?" The doctor asked with an arched brow.

"You are here as a medical professional. If I wanted a lecture, I'd call a priest!"

Packing the stethoscope back into a small black bag, the doctor released a harrumph before returning to face Maximus, eye to eye.

"I doubt a priest or a lecture could affect you. Nevertheless, do you want the truth, or shall I appease you like you require from everyone else?"

Narrowing his brow, Maximus stepped closer to the doctor. Twenty years senior and six inches shorter, Dr. Lane stepped toe to toe with Maximus, matching his glare.

The agitation shared between the two was an unusual event. Dr. Lane was a longtime friend of the Fiori family and highly respected. As an educated adult, Maximus considered the doctor an intellectual counterpart. Over the years, the pair shared many bottles of scotch as they pontificated on politics, societal changes, and literature.

"I see." Dr. Lane sneered. "She is in shock and needs to be monitored with round-the-clock care. If her life is important to you, I suggest we call for an ambulance to take her to St. Joseph Hospital."

"For how long?"

"I am a doctor, not a soothsayer! Had you obtained treatment for her several days ago, *before* you dragged her halfway around the world, she would not be this ill!"

Staring at Angelina, Maximus ran his hand through his hair. The doctor's words agitated Maximus. Not because of the tone they were spoken but because they were facts. Facts that pointed to Maximus's error.

"Boss, you want me to go with her?" Freddy asked.

"No!" Maximus snapped.

"Are you quite finished with your temper tantrum?" Dr. Lane barked. "I can take care of Angelina or not. You are the only one standing in the way of her recovery!"

"With all due respect, Doc, Mr. Fiori is..."

"Shut up, Freddy!" Maximus held up his hand. "Or I will add another patient to the doctor's list!"

"Ha! If there was medication to adjust attitudes, I would hand it out like candy at a parade!"

"I swear, Doc. One more snide joke from you, and I will disregard your connection with my family!"

Unmoved by Maximus's spout of superiority, Dr. Lane stood silent with one brow arched.

Maximus ran his hand through his hair again. Anger and guilt made reasoning a struggle. From the start of this mission, everything that could go wrong went wrong. Had they landed in France on time, they would have met Gerhard at Nora's café as planned, thus circumventing the entire catastrophe. As icing to the multi-tiered cake of disaster, Angelina remained in a deep sleep. His rational mind thought the rest would do her good, but after the third day, he realized that not getting her medical help was a grave mistake.

Twisting his neck back and forth, Maximus popped his neck before returning to Angelina's bedside. He picked up her hand and gently kissed the back of it.

"Dr. Lane, whatever you need, I will see you have it!" Maximus pledged in a civil tone.

"For starters, stop popping your neck unless you want to have a stroke! Outside of that, if I may use your phone, I will call for the ambulance. Fredrick, you can ride with her if you like, but you may feel like an elephant in a milk bottle."

"Freddy will follow in the car. I will ride in the ambulance with Angelina."

"Very well. It will take the ambulance at least thirty minutes to arrive. You can talk to her while you wait."

"Talk to... Angelina?" Maximus tilted his head, confused. Can she...*hear* me?"

"Yes. She is merely in a coma, like a deep state of sleep. Hearing a friendly voice can speed her recovery."

The redness in Maximus's cheeks drained away, making the dark circles under his eyes and three-day-old scruff a stark contrast to his pale complexion.

"What do I say?"

"If I were you, I would start with an apology!"

Speechless, Maximus nodded his head.

"I will show you to the phone, Dr. Lane," Freddy said, holding the door to Angelina's room open.

"Thank you, Fredrick."

Freddy led the doctor out of Angelina's room, leaving Maximus to gaze at the pale form entombed in white. Picking up her limp hand, Maximus gently kissed it again.

"Things were not supposed to happen this way. None of this tragedy was supposed to happen. I promised your father, and I am a man of my word. Those who hurt you will pay! I promise to deliver retribution for you, your brothers, and your parents! No man shall remain standing. I swear on my mother's soul."

"I would prefer you to leave my soul out of this," Philamena objected.

Maximus did not turn to look at his mother. Her comment was not spiteful. It was her way of lightening the mood.

"Do you think she will survive?"

"Dr. Lane is the best. Angelina will be safe and well cared for. Her recovery may be rocky, but she will come through this. You need to stop blaming yourself for Angelina's situation. Like Olivia, your hands did not inflict her wounds."

"I am man enough to own my faults, no matter how heavy the load becomes."

"Owning them is not the problem. Allowing them to continue to punish you solves nothing, cures nothing, and changes nothing. You are wise enough to know this, but why do you insist on cracking the whip against your own back?"

Maximus avoided his mother's eyes. Even if he accepted her logic, no comment or conversation could ever erase the day of Olivia's attack. As he stared at Angelina, a jagged blade carved into his soul, a notch alongside the one formed from his sister's tragedy. A permanent scar to memorialize the day Angelina nearly died in the ship's fire.

"You did the right thing bringing Angelina home. She is safer in America. That evil man cannot harm her here. Once Angelina has recovered, you can bring her sister to safety."

"She didn't like the gangway. It terrified her to be so high. She squeezed my hand so hard it nearly broke it." Maximus gently stroked the back of Angelina's hand. "I could have prevented this. We didn't have to get on the ship."

"As your mother, I insist you stop beating yourself up! She is here and safe. Focus on that and nothing else."

Philamena kissed and made the sign of the cross on Angelina's forehead before saying a brief prayer.

"Trova la tua forza Angelina."

After his mother left, Maximus sat on Angelina's bed and caressed her face with the back of his hand.

"Boss, the ambulance is at the front gate."

His eyes locked on Angelina, Maximus nodded.

"When she pulls through, you think she will understand?"

"My sister won't forgive me. Why should Angelina?"

CHAPTER 49

His face flushed and blood pressure elevated, Don Salvatore's temper bubbled to the brim. It had been several days since he read about the ship's fire, yet Antonio's whereabouts remained unknown. If an issue caused a delay, it was understandable as long as it was reported.

"Blast it! Where are you? I hear nothing from you for days. No telegram. No phone calls. Nothing! Nothing but crickets! Crickets! You fowl piece of shit, you will suffer for this insolence!" Don Salvatore barked, pacing Angelina's room.

Three days ago, every element of Angelina's quarters was perfect. The flowers were wilting, the fruit blemished, and the glistening sparkle from the freshly polished furniture faded. The room's luster had diminished, as did his patience and excitement. He walked around the room one last time, mentally noting what needed to be done. Don Salvatore grumbled the list to himself as he locked the door.

"I will cut his balls off if he defiles her." Don Salvatore stormed down the hall. "She is *mine*! No one is to touch her, no one! I will pluck her virtuous rosebud!"

After barking the list of duties to Amalea, The Don drove to the vineyard, grumbling the entire way.

"Even if he has not touched her, I will cut his nuts off with a dull blade! If you are not dead, Antonio, you soon will be!"

His gruffness continued with Carlos and Fernando while inspecting the vineyard. He grilled the father and son for information about the vintner trade. Neither provided the information he desired.

"Fine, you worthless ape! Give me the money from your deliveries." Don Salvatore held out his grubby hand.

Carlos pulled a white envelope from his pocket. The Don snatched it. With a grin, he removed the cash, discarding the worthless envelope into the wind. A quick fan of the thick stack of bills placated his soured attitude.

"Signore?" Carlos timidly held up his hand.

Stuffing the wad into his breast pocket, The Don ignored the man and waltzed to his car. Carlos's second attempt did nothing to stop Don Salvatore from leaving. The Don, merrily chuckling, slammed his foot on the accelerator, intentionally pummeling them with gravel.

Don Salvatore approached his home as the sun was setting. The warm, golden sunlight blanketed the villa and surrounding land. The soothing view brought a smile to his face, but not from the soft aura. His home appeared to be made of shiny gold ribbons, an epitaph of his tremendous wealth. Don Salvatore patted the wad of cash as he drove up the last hill to his fortress.

"A very *fruitful* day. Nothing to *wine* over." Don Salvatore chuckled as he rattled off several puns.

He slowed to a stop at the twelve-foot tall, black iron gate with gold-coated, sharp points at the end of each vertical iron bar. Elaborate horizontal scrolls created bands across the upper and lower third of the gate. The most prominent feature was a giant gold-plated *S* encircled by black laurel leaves edged with gold. The ominous entrance and tall stone walls were intimidating. The barrier was designed to keep intruders out and prisoners in.

As he drove the last one hundred yards to the villa, the tiny beige pea gravel crunching under the tires and the three dogs barking permeated inside the car. But Don Salvatore was only interested if Antonio had returned.

"Damn it! Where have you taken her?"

Storming inside, The Don continued to grumble his displeasure for Antonio's absence. The rhythmic slap of his shoes against the marble floor echoed around him, sealing him in an invisible bubble, an impermeable space for his wounds to fester.

Don Salvatore remained lost in his thoughts until a movement in the shadows snatched his attention. His heart racing, he removed a gun from his side holster and cocked it. The click stirred the movement again.

"Whose there? Speak or die!"

A moan resonated off the walls, and a foul stench assailed Don Salvatore's nose. After three cautious steps forward, he noticed the movement was a leg in spasm. He holstered his gun and covered his nose with a silk handkerchief. The Don kept his distance more out of repugnance than a precaution.

"Amalea!" The Don shouted. "Amalea, Dammit. Where are you?"

"I am right here, Signore."

Don Salvatore jumped when he saw the maid standing behind him.

"Blast it! Stop lurking and light that lamp!"

The flash of light from the match gave Don Salvatore a glimpse at the moaning creature. Shocked, he stepped back and covered his expression of horror.

Amalea carried the oil-lamp to The Don. When the light illuminated the space, she dropped the lamp and screamed. Prepared for his maid's reaction, Don Salvatore caught the oil-lamp in his left hand and the maid in his right. Once Amalea was steady on her feet, he instructed her to ring for the doctor. Wide-eyed and speechless, she nodded, then disappeared down the hall.

Kneeling down, The Don used the oil lamp to inspect the injured man propped against the wall. The pungent smell of infection, singed hair, and burned fabric made Don Salvatore gag. Covering his nose again, he held the light close to the disfigured creature. A yellowish-green puss oozing from the black crust covering half the man's face glistened in the warm glow.

"Antonio?"

His eye was swollen shut, his mouth frozen, and his lungs gurgling; Antonio moaned as he tried to sit up. But Don Salvatore urged him to stay put.

"Easy, my boy. Easy. We will get you a doctor. Just rest for now."

Gazing at Antonio, Don Salvatore wondered how the man was alive. His injuries alone should have killed him. Antonio's fierce resolve tickled Don Salvatore's pride.

"You limped your way across an entire country mostly dead, yet that fool-hearted Giorgio drinks himself into a little tumble down his steps and can't move for days. Weak, that is what he is! *You* are a warrior, an unstoppable Spartan. Survive, my boy, and I will reward you well!"

Don Salvatore placed the oil lamp a few feet away from the gravely injured form. He watched Antonio's chest struggle to rise and fall; even the shallow breaths were labored.

"My boy. My boy," Don Salvatore grinned.

He reached out to pat Antonio's leg, but the wet clothing reeked of dead fish, smoke, and vomit. The Don pulled his hand back and gazed over Antonio. The fluid bubbling in the dying man's lungs and the groans of agony seemed magnified in the silence. Disgusted, The Don quieted the noise the only way he knew how—by chatting.

"You wield fire like a Samurai wields a blade. Ha! It is ironic to succumb to your own weapon." The Don chuckled. "But think of the tales to be spun about the Demone di Fioco! Survive this, my boy, and you will be immortal in your enemy's eyes!" His nose grew more accustomed to the stench, allowing him to move in closer. "I am impressed by your drive. I see now why I have not heard from you. Now that you are home, where is she? Is she with Bruno?"

The Don waited a moment before repeating the question. After the third attempt, Don Salvatore's temper escalated.

"Dammitt. Where is she? Does Bruno have her? Say something! Nod your head if you can't speak!"

A raspy gurgle slowly crept up Antonio's throat. The Don leaned in close, eagerly rubbing his hands together. A bolt of excitement tickled his veins when Antonio opened his mouth to speak. But his thrilling rush was squelched when only bubbles passed Antonio's lips.

"Curse you, you piece of shit!"

Don Salvatore raised his hand to strike Antonio, but stopped. The thought of touching the oozing, repugnant carcass awaiting the Angel of Death made The Don gag.

Frustrated, he stood up to pace the floor, grumbling words of agitation. In his rant, a thought sent a shot of optimism to his mind. Hopeful that Bruno was in the villa with Angelina,

The Don searched his room, Angelina's room, the courtyard, and every room along the way. Ending the unfruitful hunt, he headed back to interrogate Antonio.

"Damn it! He will probably die before he tells me."

"Signore! Signore," Amalea scurried down the main hall. "The doctor, he is here. Do you wish to speak with him?"

"He doesn't need my permission to examine him! Tell him to do his job, then report to me!"

"Si signore. Where shall I send him?"

"The courtyard, dammit! Where I always go to think!"

In the chilly night air, the gentle breeze rustling the leaves and the cascading water in the fountain created a tranquil mood. It was a soothing melody that relaxed The Don into his chair. However, a few minutes later, the doctor appeared in the doorway, shattering his utopia.

Winded, the short, round man gripped his hat but held his tongue. Don Salvatore made the man wait several minutes before acknowledging his existence. It was a universal game he played with everyone. The Don found pleasure in dangling the weak above the fires of hell. To see his prey's eyes wide, cheeks pink, and brow beaded with sweat was satisfying.

"Well, doctor?"

"His injuries are fatal, Signore. Unless... I mean... even with proper care, his chances are minimal."

His brow arched, The Don slid to the edge of his seat.

"You want money, don't you? It is always money. You blood-sucking bastard."

"No, Signore. No. I... I cannot care for him..."

"Cannot or *will* not?"

The doctor gripped his hat tighter and danced on the imaginary hot stones beneath his feet.

"Um... cannot, Signore. That is... I cannot give him proper care *here*."

"What does that mean?"

The doctor gulped and took several steps backward.

"His wounds, Signore, are infected and require antibiotics, salve, and bandages. Bandages which need to be changed frequently and with great care. I do not have these things. He *might* recover at the hospital."

The Don, his eyes wild, sprung to his feet and charged toward the doctor. "No hospital! You will tend to him *here!*"

"But, Don Salvatore..."

"You will do as you are told, or your family will never find your remains!"

"But... Signore. I ..."

The doctor tried to inch away, but his foot caught the leg of a decorative table, causing the antique on top to wobble. Frantically, he embraced the vase before it crashed against the floor.

His prey distracted; Don Salvatore closed the gap between them. His nostrils flared with each exhale. Looming over him, The Don snarled at the trembling man. The doctor tried to retreat, but the wall behind him foiled his escape.

"I will do my best, Signore," the doctor surrendered.

Don Salvatore patted the doctor's shoulders, smoothed his lapels, and gently dusted off his jacket.

"Good. Good. That is all I ask," The Don said with a smile.

They exchanged smiles, The Don's broad and the doctor's timid. With a slight bow, the doctor wiggled free of the compressed space while mumbling 'thank you.'

"Where the hell do you think you are going?" Don Salvatore growled, flipping back to his ominous tone.

"I must fetch the supplies, Signore." Counting each item on his short, stubby fingers, he recited the list. "I need bandages, salve, antibiotics—"

"You are not going anywhere," The Don interrupted. Stretching out his arms, his voice bellowed. "This place, this entire villa, is where you will live. Or die!"

"He will die without..."

"Send a yard ape for supplies. You do not leave! Your fates are the same! If Antonio dies, so do *you!*"

CHAPTER 50

Fernando returned mid-morning with food for Marcus and Francesca. Squares of polenta, two apples, and a small plate with slices of Bresaola were crammed into a lunch pail.

"Fratelli Beretta, Bresaola Punta d'Anca. La qualitá é una tradizione di famiglia." Marcus grinned, quoting the company's motto. "Fine meat with a fine name, too bad there is no relation to our family!"

"I couldn't bring clothes or anything to wash with. Mamma would notice. Papa will take her to the market after lunch. Listen for the car to leave, then go inside."

"Where will you be?" Francesca asked.

"I have a delivery to make."

Fernando's voice matched the sadness he expressed on his face. Marcus recalled Fernando and Anton's first delivery. Neither had the strength to hoist dozens of crates of wine. Their lack of height made it difficult to reach the accelerator pedal while sitting back in the driver's seat. Despite their physical obstacles, the pair set out on the journey with bright eyes filled with excitement. At the end of the run, Fernando and Anton were exhausted but still smiling. After six months, their arms were stronger, and their legs were longer, reducing the comical aspect of the run. The pair made everything they did together fun. With Anton dead, Fernando lost more than a friend. The heart, humor, and spirit that matched his own was gone.

"I wish I could help."

Fernando interrupted him. "No. You were right last night. Only the three of us know you are alive."

"And Angelina." Francesca added.

Glaring at Francesca, Fernando stiffened.

"I'm not sure how, but we must kill the Don."

"I agree," Marcus replied.

Her eyes darting, Francesca wrapped her arms across her chest and rubbed away the chill.

"No, you can't! It is a death wish to even try." Francesca shuddered. "You will die! We all will die!"

"He is the one who hurt Angelina! He murdered my best friend, and he threatened my mother." Fernando towered over her. "I *will* kill him!"

Marcus was shocked. The aggression and anger oozing from Fernando was not the sweet, caring young man who loved Angelina. Fernando changed, and not for the better.

"Easy, Nan. I know you are angry. Don Salvatore has taken from all of us. I agree, he deserves a heinous death, but we must discuss how and when!"

"I bought a gun yesterday."

"I know, you held it to my head!" Marcus took a deep breath. "Nan. Promise you will not do anything stupid. There are risks. Discussing this puts our loved ones in danger. Think. Please, dear God! You must think this through."

"I have to go." Fernando turned to leave.

"Wait, Nan. Give me five more minutes. Please?"

Fernando's gaze cast down, he stopped with one foot on the first step. In his thoughtful silence, the trickling water echoed in the damp air. Fernando sighed. Shaking his head, he continued up the steps.

Marcus dashed to the stairs to plead once more.

"Nan, you are one of the gentlest souls God has ever made. It is why my sister loves you. Do not sacrifice who you are for this man. You stand to lose far more than The Don."

"Anger and revenge can change a person."

"Change is a choice, Nan. You can allow bitterness to make you something you are not, or you can remain your true self."

"Anton believed Angelina loved me, too. Before all of this chaos, I wanted to believe it. I convinced myself she loved me. When she left without discussing her plan. She couldn't even say goodbye. It made me question the idea."

"People's lives are at stake, my parents, your parents, my sisters, your life. What you desire is dangerous and, at a minimum, foolish. I have killed men, Nan. I know the mental pain that haunts the mind after ending another's life. Do not become what you despise. What Angelina cannot love."

Fernando returned to the bottom of the steps, his eyes floating in a pool of tears. Poking his chest, he voiced a fear.

"Every moment The Don draws breath, I feel a part of me slipping into darkness."

"As do I. But we cannot let that dictate our choices. Before starting a war with a powerful man, we must ensure the people we love are safe. That includes your parents and you!"

"He will kill her too," Fernando argued.

"Who? Who will kill whom?"

"Don Salvatore visits the vineyard almost every day. One day, he showed up with Catalina. He held her like a dog on a leash and demanded that she tell him everything about making wine. Cat held her head high. She played her part, but she is afraid of him. We all are. He threatens all of us. Before he left that day, he told me to get to work. If I didn't do my job right, he would slit Catalina's throat. We can't wait. We must kill him before he murders anyone else."

The root of Fernando's ferocious hunger to commit murder was clear. He was a caged animal tortured continuously by his keeper. It was a painful revelation and a red flag. Fernando was a weak link, a volatile team member who could act irrationally in the heat of battle.

"Putting anyone's life at risk is not an option. We must devise a plan." Marcus placed a hand on Fernando's shoulders. "A well thought out tactical strategy. Okay?"

Fernando gave a reluctant nod.

"That is a relief. I know how bad you shoot in daylight. I'm not going into The Don's house at night with you!"

Marcus's slight grin and humor conjured Fernando's smile. It was a minor victory. At that moment, he willingly accepted any positive result.

"Promise me you will work *with* me and not against me."

Fernando stared at Marcus for a moment, then said, "Only if you promise me one thing..."

"Yes, Nan. I promise he *will* pay for his crimes."

CHAPTER 51

Angelina's eyes flickered for a moment before opening.

"Welcome back," Dr. Lane smiled. "I thought you might wake today. How are you feeling?"

Groaning, Angelina pressed her body upright, but the doctor encouraged her to lie back.

"Easy, you have been unconscious for several days. You will be weak at first, but your strength will return in time. For now, just rest."

The doctor checked Angelina's I.V. bag and line. Before listening to her heart and lungs, the doctor warned Angelina that the stethoscope would be cold.

"Breathe. Again."

Dr. Lane scribbled on Angelina's chart for a moment. The scratch of the pen jetting across the page filled the silent space, adding to the dank white room.

"I need to ask you a few questions and perform some tests. Do you feel up to it?"

Her throat raw, Angelina nodded.

Dr. Lane placed the metal clipboard on the foot of the bed next to Angelina's leg and proceeded with the evaluation, briefly explaining each test. The information was helpful. However, the doctor's voice breaking the sterile silence soothed Angelina's anxiety the most.

"Open your eyes wide. Good. Keep your focus on my ear for a moment," Dr. Lane instructed, then shined a small penlight into Angelina's eyes, carefully watching her pupils. "Hmm. Can you squeeze your hand around my finger?" Angelina's firm response pleased the doctor. "Good. Very good. On the other hand? Good, good! Now, I need to ask you some questions. Do you think you can do that?"

"My..." The word scraped the back of Angelina's throat, making her wince. "Water, please?"

"Not too much," Dr. Lane cautioned. "Little sips."

Angelina held the small glass to her cracked lips and carefully allowed the cold liquid to moisten her parched tongue. The urge to gulp the water was difficult to resist, but swallowing stung the raw flesh at the back of Angelina's mouth.

"Easy!" Dr. Lane urged. Taking the glass away from Angelina, the doctor reassured her. "You can have more in a few minutes. Does it hurt to swallow?"

Angelina nodded.

"That will get better over the next couple of days."

"Thank you," Angelina croaked.

"Are you ready?"

Angelina's eyelids were heavy, her body ached, and her mouth was an arid cavern desperate for hydration. Her desire to drink created a magnetic lock between her eyes and the glass. She tried to break the internal fixation to look up at the doctor.

"What is your name?"

Unmoved by the doctor's voice, Angelina focused on the clear liquid she craved, mumbling her answer.

"Angelina."

"What day of the week is it?"

Angelina crinkled her brow. "Tuesday."

"Do you know where you are?"

"I am at the hospital." Angelina smiled.

"Clever." Dr. Lane chuckled. "Where is this hospital?"

The bond between Angelina's eyes and the glass instantly broke. Looking up at the doctor, she opened her mouth to answer, but no words came to mind. She looked out the window for a clue. She saw nothing. She only noticed the sun was put to rest, and the moon was only a sliver in the sky.

"I... I don't know."

"It is okay. You have been through a lot. Do you know who brought you to the hospital?"

A strong pull tightened the wordless noose around her neck, and the slight shade of pink in her cheeks vanished.

"You are safe, Angelina. No one here will hurt you. You are being watched by one of our city's finest officers, Sgt.

Stephens. Can you see him standing outside your door? No one will come in or out without his permission. He is an honest man and takes his job seriously."

The doctor handed her the glass of water and encouraged her to sip it. Angelina's hand trembled, nearly spilling the contents onto the white sheet. She was desperately thirsty, but now something more pressing held her attention.

"Do you know where you are, Angelina?"

With a blank stare, Angelina shook her head.

"You are in America. At St. Joseph's hospital in Kansas City, Missouri, to be exact."

Angelina's grip on the glass loosened, spilling water onto her lap. The cold water adhered the thin sheet to Angelina's thigh, but she did not notice it. Her eyes were focused on the doctor's round face. The questions Angelina wanted to ask quickly vanished from her mind before her tongue could speak them. In her head were incomplete thoughts looming behind a grey curtain of fear and insecurity.

"What is the last thing you remember?"

"I remember... I... I remember..."

Angelina rubbed her temples, willing the memories to surface in an orderly timeline. But visions of a raging fire, blankets of green, smudges of burgundy, and blue-green water swirled together.

"Everything... is blank."

"That is normal for the level of trauma you experienced. It is called amnesia; do you know what that is?"

Angelina nodded but replied, "No. What is it?"

"A loss of memory. It can be a permanent loss, but not always. You have been through quite an ordeal..."

"What happened?"

"I was not there, so I do not know." Patting Angelina's leg, Dr. Lane gave a wane smile. "For now, rest. This is a process. A delicate process that requires patience."

CHAPTER 52

Concern for his parents, Angelina's whereabouts, and revenge did not keep him awake. The muffled whimpering from the other side of the wine rack was what prevented his slumber.

Narrowly escaping the cloaked demon's clutches haunted Francesca's soul more than watching the Angel of Death devouring Bruno's life. Both were burned into Francesca's memory, permanently changing the way she viewed the world. Marcus sympathized with Francesca. His first dance with death happened years ago. Time soothed his tortured mind, but the repetition of seeing death numbed his soul.

"Seeing death is tragic," Rosario explained to Marcus the night before he left for the war. *"Being within a millimeter of your own death is mind-altering. You will never see the world the same again."*

At the time, Marcus shrugged off his father's words as a melodramatic exaggeration to keep his son home and appease his wife. Three months later, however, a near-death experience solidified the truth in Rosario's warning. The world did appear different. His perspective forever changed. His entire decision making process was altered.

Once Marcus and Francesca reached land after committing their lives to the ocean, she spoke of only one thing. She was a mother who needed to be with her son. Every mother needs to see, embrace, and hear the lub-dub of her child's heart. Without this soothing interaction, life becomes hopeless. Francesca's brush with death created an unquenchable desire to cradle her son and stroke his dark locks. She never wanted to leave his side.

Marcus watched for her to leave. There was no question of *if*, only *when*. Francesca would risk her life and everyone else's if only to see her son again.

Marcus listened to her footsteps and waited until she climbed the stairs before leaving his bunk. Dressed in black, he moved through the darkness like a ghost, lurking but never coming into full view. When the light from her candle faded up the stairwell, Marcus followed. He paused when Francesca glanced back. She did not see him, nor would she. Being invisible was a skill he had mastered in recent years.

She climbed into the car and carefully closed the door to keep from waking the family sleeping a hundred feet away.

"Impressive," Marcus mumbled. "An impressive fool!"

When she was halfway down the long gravel drive, Marcus turned the truck's key and gave the accelerator a gentle push. The engine gurgled and rumbled before settling into a soft purr. He coasted down the hill with the headlights off. He could roll past the ivory stucco house blindfolded. He watched in the rearview mirror for any signs of life. Each second unnoticed eased the tension in his shoulders.

Marcus maintained a reasonable distance between the two vehicles. She drove through town and past the rolling hillsides of vines illuminated by the waning moon. A few times, he did not follow her down the same road. He knew where she was headed once they went through town. Any slight detour from the primary route would still end in the same place. The narrow two-lane road passed the expansive land that surrounded the convent.

In the last thirty minutes of the two-hour drive, Marcus held a three-kilometer distance between the vehicles. His delayed arrival allowed Francesca to park and address the nun, keeping vigil at the front gate. Marcus crept the truck up the gravel drive and watched the women exchange pleasantries. After a brief hug, Francesca slightly bowed her gratitude before scurrying toward the east entrance. She melted into the darkness under the blooming olive trees that flanked the stone path. A sporadic white flash of her blouse between the tree trunks told Marcus where she was headed.

Marcus leaned back and grumbled about her idiocy.

"Foolish! Damn it! How did you elude The Don's henchmen for so long when you make stupid decisions?"

Watching her bound up the stairs, Marcus groaned. He was angry at her choice, yet his heart empathized with her.

"How can I fault you for something *my* mother would do?"

His eyes trailed across the stone facade, tracing the eves and arches that accented the multi-tiered building. The convent had been around for centuries. With help from generous donors, the nuns expanded and kept the abbey in excellent condition.

His mother was behind one of those walls, and he longed to be beside her. A small part of him wondered if knowing she still had a son living could ease her suffering and pull her from her catatonic state. It was difficult to be a kilometer away from his parents and not race to their bedside, hold their hand, and pray for their recovery.

"Papa suffered six broken ribs, internal bleeding, and a shattered jaw," Angelina explained as they drank wine in Turin. *"Mamma's face is badly bruised, and she has several cuts across her throat. But her mental condition is the worst of all of Mamma's injuries. Neither will speak, Marcus. They only sit lost in a horrid dream."*

Being unmercifully beaten was cruel. Forcing them to watch two of their sons brutally murdered was an act of war.

"Fernando may yearn for a murderous revenge, but a simple death is not enough." Marcus growled. "He will pay for his sins. In a way, Nan, that you can never imagine."

Marcus became lost in his thoughts as he played out several lethal scenarios, each more gruesome than the last. Visualizing his revenge brought him to the edge of satisfaction, a breath away from an intensely desired climax. Every retaliation was the seductress teasing him but never allowing the cataclysmic euphoria. Time ticked by, and his imagination blended with torrid sleep. His body twitched his part in the bloody acts of his dreams.

A golden beam of light pierced the blanket of trees surrounding the holy utopia. The chrome hood ornament reflected the light into his eyes, snapping him awake. He checked his watch. He rubbed his eyes and checked it again.

"Crap!" He looked where Francesca parked. "Crap!"

Marcus chastised himself for sleeping on the job. He missed Francesca's exit and, worse yet, had the truck away from the vineyard at dawn. Carlos and Fernando would be ready for work soon, and he was two hours away.

Daylight allowed Marcus to drive faster, albeit more reckless. Swerving in and out of his lane, he ran a car off the road. The pudgy driver leaned out the window, shouting obscenities, his arms punctuating his words. Marcus held his foot on the peddle. He did not give the man a second glance.

Marcus returned to the vineyard. He slowed the truck down to reduce the billowing dust spewing from the tires. Crossing the bridge, he could see the car Francesca had borrowed was in its original location.

"Thank God!" He sighed.

Marcus looked around for any life as the truck crept up the hill. The vineyard appeared dormant. The strangling grip around his chest relaxed.

His boot landed on the second step when a familiar voice seized him. Marcus slowly placed his feet on the ground.

"Where have you been?" Fernando roared.

"I had to make sure she was not followed, or worse."

"Or worse? Or worse? What the hell do you think 'or worse' is for *us*? You want my support and loyalty, but you jeopardize my family for a woman you barely know!"

"Nan, shh!" Marcus stepped closer. "I am still a ghost. Carlos doesn't know we took the truck or the car."

"No, you are a fool!" Fernando, puffing his chest, closed the gap between them. "If *anything* happens to my family, you will have two enemies!"

Marcus opened his mouth to speak, but Fernando turned on his heels and marched away. The coldness left by the abrupt departure seeped into Marcus's bones.

CHAPTER 53

Sitting in a metal chair next to the window, Angelina wrapped the wool blanket tighter around her shoulders. The golden sunlight, warm against her cheek, pulled her closer to the window, looking over the busy city.

The world below was loud and chaotic, but she closed her eyes, drew in a deep breath, and allowed the chaos to melt away. Only doves cooing and the occasional groaning wind pierced her utopia.

It had been three days since she woke. Three days of being fussed over by hospital staff. Three days of staring at blank white walls. Three days of trying to remember. The day before, the doctor expressed confidence in Angelina's memory returning, but Angelina disagreed.

"Dr. Lane, I feel like a part of me doesn't want to recall something. Is that strange?"

"Not strange at all. In fact, the form of amnesia I believe you have is a form of psychological protection."

"Inside of me." She pointed at her chest. "Aches when I try to remember."

"Did Maximus tell you how you came to be here?"

"That we were to meet and discuss my family's business."

"Is that all?" Dr. Lane questioned with a raised brow.

"He didn't want to create false memories, so he didn't give many details."

"Can you recall any part of this meeting?"

Angelina closed her eyes and rubbed her temples, pleading for any memory to emerge, but she saw nothing. Frustrated, she flopped back onto the pillow and sighed.

"Would you be willing to try something, Angelina? It may help you remember, maybe not everything, but a little would be nice, right?" Dr. Lane coaxed with a sincere smile.

Sitting up, Angelina pulled her knees to her chest. The possibility of remembering anything gave her hope.

"I will ask you a question. You respond without thinking of an answer. Tell me your first thought, okay?"

Her dark eyes locked on the doctor; Angelina nodded.

"Let's start simple. What month were you born in?"

"January."

"Good! January, what?"

"26th."

"Where do you live?"

"Brusnengo!" Acknowledging memories felt good.

"How many brothers do you have?"

"Four!"

"Are they older or younger than you?"

"Both!" Angelina's smile widened.

"Are they living or deceased?"

"That is a terrible thing to ask!"

"You didn't answer my question?"

Angelina resolutely crossed her arms.

"All right," Dr. Lane conceded. "What is the last thing you remember doing at home?"

Angelina paused. Her mind was a blank slate.

"Say your first thought, Angelina."

Closing her eyes, Angelina's fingers found the grooves of her temples. "Come on, remember."

"You are trying too hard. Relax. What is the last thing you remember doing at your family's vineyard?"

Angelina released her temples, opened her eyes, and gently laid back on her pillow. One by one, she relaxed each part of her body, starting with her legs. When the tension in her shoulders melted away, a memory gradually appeared.

"Papa and I dancing."

"Good. Why were you dancing?"

"It was Papa's birthday, his fiftieth. Mamma wanted the party to be a surprise. It wasn't easy, but we did it. Anton pretended to be ill, and Ricardo grumbled about doing the long delivery route alone. Papa said he'd go, just as we hoped. Mamma was excited that the food and decorations were perfect. She cried when she saw the surprise on his face. Papa had tears, too. That's Papa. He is tender-hearted."

"What else happened?"

Silence held the air while the thrill of the game slipped from Angelina's spirit, making way for a well of emotions to bubble in her heart. Tears pooled in her eyelids as the details of the evening flashed before her eyes. She greedily harbored the visions of her happy family, keeping the details hidden in her mind like a treasure.

"It was a small party, only our immediate family and closest friends. Everyone was laughing, drinking, and dancing. We were having fun. It was a happy occasion." Angelina blinked, flushing the well of tears. "But I feel terribly sad. Why? I don't understand. Why am I crying?"

She was shocked and confused by her conflicted emotions. To finally remember was exhilarating, but the deep sorrow sucked the life from Angelina's body. She wanted to curl under the blanket and sleep for eternity.

"Why am I so emotional? It was a wonderful party!"

"It's okay, Angelina. Let the details flow."

Slowing her breathing, Angelina closed her eyes and allowed the images to present themselves one at a time. Visions of her father cutting his birthday cake. Her mother's toast to *the man who made her heart whole*. Her brothers' jokes and tales of their youth. Catalina gushed over Rosario, praising the *best Papa ever*. Angelina's toast was sincere admiration for the man who provided a wonderful life for the family and molded her into a strong, intelligent woman. It was a perfect evening, but reliving it induced more tears.

Sitting on the edge of the bed, Dr. Lane offered Angelina a box of tissues. "Crying is proof the memory is authentic. A trail of tears can lead you back to your lost memories."

Angelina sat up and accepted the tissues from the doctor. She dried her cheeks and blew her nose, but another wave of emotions erupted. Each member of her family reconnected her to home, filling an empty void of loneliness. Yet, seeing her brother's faces stirred sorrow.

"What happened the next day?"

"It was harvest. I worked long, hard hours. We all did. Well, not Catalina. She always disappeared when it was time for the hard, physical labor."

"Anything else?"

"For several days after the party, we worked long days, but I don't remember specifics. The work went like it always did."

"When is your father's birthday?"

"September 15th."

"You have no other memories after the party except the harvest?"

"Nothing specific, just the usual tasks."

Dr. Lane stood and nervously searched for a pen.

"What is wrong?"

"That is enough for today. Your dinner should arrive soon. You should rest before Maximus arrives. If you haven't noticed by now, he is always prompt. You will never wait for him." Dr. Lane rambled while making a few marks on Angelina's chart. "The nurses say he is here daily at 9 am, 1 pm, and 7 pm. By the array of flowers and gifts, I see he never comes empty-handed."

Angelina dried her tears. She was too emotional to press the doctor about abruptly avoiding her question.

"Maximus creates a pattern and stays with it. He will come every day at those times and always with a gift."

"I don't mind. I enjoy his visits."

"When your memory returns, you may feel differently."

"What?"

"I said your memory is improving. Get some rest. I will see you tomorrow."

CHAPTER 54

Marcus slowly walked toward the back of the cellar, guarding the flame that cast a glowing orb around him. The one flame was not much, but it barred the shadows from lurking close. He did not need the light. After years of hauling wine cases in and out, Marcus memorized every inch of the dark cavern. The candle was for Francesca's benefit. A dark form could make her scream, drawing unwanted attention.

In the last row of the dank space, against the wall, sat a bunk made from plywood and concrete blocks. On top, a thin mattress made from three folded blankets, a pillow, and a heavy comforter kept Francesca warm in the damp space. It was not a comfortable setup, but Francesca did not complain.

"Knock-knock?" Marcus asked politely.

There was no answer.

"Francesca? Are you all right? May I come in?"

The silence clawed at his mind. Marcus was eager to scold her for disobeying him and putting everyone at risk. Yet, his warmer, more compassionate side reigned in his temper.

She could be asleep. He thought. *Or pretending to be because I followed her.*

Marcus sighed. The juggling of delicate female emotions drained what little energy he had. Aside from stale bread and cheese, the small café in Cherbourg was his last decent meal. Even then, it was a light fare and rushed. He drew a deep breath and forced back the exhaustion and hunger that gnawed at his compassion.

"Francesca! Answer, or I am coming in!"

There was no response, no moan, or shuffled movement. The only sound was the slow drip-drip of water into a puddle near his left foot. In the shimmering light, the dark, viscous fluid reminded Marcus of his comrade, Nazio.

In a surprise ambush, a piece of shrapnel hit Nazio. The deep abdominal wound seeped blood, turning his uniform dark as it saturated the fabric. Marcus tried to keep his friend alert, but the blood loss was too much. By the time the medic arrived, Nazio's heart had stopped.

Marcus closed his eyes and whispered a prayer for his friend. His hand finished the Sign of the Cross and he remembered Francesca's wound. It was not a deep plunge like Nazio's, but it was severe enough to require stitches. He was no medic, but Marcus knew to clean the space and sanitize the tools in boiling water. Though he did his best, the probability of infection was high.

The image of Francesca unconscious with a high fever motivated him to rush to her side. He did not want to lose another person he cared about. His intention was admirable, but in his haste, his abrupt movement snuffed out the candle.

"Crap!"

As he fumbled for a lighter, a blob of hot wax spilled onto his left hand. He clenched his teeth, containing his screams. Francesca's life teetering on the edge of her grave, Marcus shoved his left hand into his pocket. A surge of pain raced up his arm when the fabric grated across his fresh wound.

"Son of a motherless goat!" Shaking his hand, Marcus growled. "Barely a flesh wound."

With his right hand, he fished the lighter out of his left front pocket. Walking toward Francesca, he nimbly raced the zippo across his thigh. Once opened it, the second pass to spark a flame. Marcus could see to the end of the aisle with the space illuminated.

"No!" Marcus's heart stopped. He blinked rapidly to erase the horror. "No, no. No!"

Marcus dropped to his knees and groped the blankets.

"No! No, it can't be true! The car..."

An icy shock held him stationary while he ridiculed himself. He could have prevented this catastrophe, but his decision to remain a ghost came at a price. The chill of blame shifted to rage. Marcus glared at the empty bunk.

"Damn it, Francesca! Where are you?"

CHAPTER 55

After a morning walk around the halls of the hospital with Sgt. Stephens, Angelina settled on her perch by the window and soaked in the morning rays. She searched her mind, but her father's birthday was still the last thing she remembered. Yet, Angelina felt comfortable and enjoyed what she considered a pleasant vacation.

As the doctor predicted, Maximus appeared at the exact time each day and was never empty-handed. Along with his consistent arrival time, so was the length of each visit.

Maximus arrived freshly shaven in the morning. He wore a dark, three-piece suit with ruby-laden cufflinks that matched his pinky ring. His dazzling smile and peppy mood completed his resplendent appearance.

Today, he carried a box and two cups of piping hot espresso.

"Let me help you..." Angelina offered as she scrambled to get out of bed.

"No, no!" Maximus insisted. "You stay in bed. I don't want to choose between catching you or this precious cargo."

Angelina laughed, "I see. Then I have read you wrong. I thought you were showing off."

"This? A mere parlor trick. Although the true entertainment was getting in and out of the car unscathed." Maximus set the food on the bedside table. "A bakery two blocks away makes these fresh every day. They transform this from delicious to decadent by putting a pat of butter on top just before serving."

Maximus removed the cover and exposed a cinnamon roll as big as the plate. Angelina's eyes widened.

"Oh, my!"

"I thought we would share. If that is all right with you?"

"Yes, of course!"

The sweet cinnamon and rich coffee aroma danced in the air, overpowering the sterile smell of the dismal hospital. It was a welcomed reprieve from a monotonous reality.

Angelina held the cup to her lips and drew a deep breath.

"Mmm! The aroma to sooth my soul." Angelina took a sip and purred. "Mmm! Devine!"

"When we lived in Italy, my friend's family's business was roasting coffee beans. His mother, Rosa, brewed the best!"

Maximus told his tale from the metal chair by Angelina's bed. He carefully held the small ceramic cup in one hand while the other portrayed the story.

"The smell was hypnotizing," he hummed, wafting the air. Maximus scooted to the edge of his seat and sipped his espresso twice before completing his confession.

"One morning, when my friend was still asleep, I waited in the kitchen for Rosa. She nearly jumped out of her skin when she saw me sitting at the table, patiently waiting. I explained my desire to learn how to make espresso that tasted as delicious as hers. She waved her hands in disbelief and scoffed at me for a minute before revealing her glowing smile. I learned two things that day."

"Oh?"

"How to brew espresso like Rosa." Maximus grinned. "And the power of flattery."

"So, you are a sly fox?"

With a chuckle, Maximus shrugged. "I cannot confirm or deny the accusation, Miss."

"Very well," Angelina giggled. "Then explain how you keep the espresso so hot?"

He looked over his cup, and a mischievous grin appeared.

"It is amazing how helpful the nurses become when you tempt them with a cup."

"I doubt the coffee is what charms them!"

"You are right. It is not the coffee. The nurses enjoy their cinnamon rolls, too."

After thirty minutes of friendly banter, Maximus performed his pre-exit routine. It began with a glance at his watch as if he had no clue of the time. He stood, straightened his tie, and flexed his shoulders to adjust the fit of his jacket, then buttoned his suit coat. A quick shake of the wrist settled his watch back in place. He would say goodbye with a slight bow. His final ritualistic action was donning his Fedora.

At his midday drop-in, Maximus's appearance and mood were drastically different. The tie that was snug against his collar a few hours earlier had been slightly loosened by a finger, and an emerging stubble forecasted a full beard. His attention was focused on other matters, and his perky disposition was nonexistent. Even as he presented her with a bouquet, Maximus was tense. In a stoic tone, he asked if she enjoyed her lunch and how she felt. He ended it with a brief weather report. The fifteen-minute appearance resembled a gruff business transaction rather than a compassionate visit.

In the evening, his neck was free of the constricting tie, and the top three buttons were unfastened. The relaxed attire exposed a heavy gold chain and the voluminous jet-black hair peeking out the top of his white undershirt. His stubble had grown into a sexy scruff, which he frequently rubbed as they conversed. While pondering the answer to a question, Maximus's hand slowly combed his coal-black locks.

Their discussion flowed effortlessly for two hours as they enjoyed a box of chocolates from a local chocolatier, Russel Stover's. Maximus and Angelina's conversations were lighthearted and superficial the first few nights. Angelina craved more information about Maximus. The cavern of darkness looming behind his dark eyes froze her tongue while feeding her imagination.

She bathed in her morning Eden of sunshine. She could only think of Maximus. Mulling over stories and analyzing his non-verbal ticks became her only mental exercise. Today was no different.

A gentle rap at the door pulled Angelina back from her contemplation.

"May I come in?"

"Maximus! Please do." Her bright pink cheeks accented her enchanting smile.

"How are you feeling today?"

"Cold." Acknowledging the chill made her shiver.

"Enjoy the sunshine. My driver predicts it will rain today."

Angelina cocked her head. "Your driver?"

"Figgy. He said he can *feel it* in his bones."

The phrase made her giggle. "My mother says that too."

"Is she right?"

"I think so. What I can remember."

"No new memories?"

She slumped back. "Unfortunately, no."

Maximus extended his hand toward the empty chair next to Angelina and asked, "May I?"

"Where did you learn to be such a gentleman?"

Maximus unbuttoned his suit jacket and sat on the edge of the chair. A warm smile curled his lips as he met her gaze.

"When you meet my parents, I believe that answer will become quite clear."

"Do they still plan to visit today?"

"Actually, I have some news." He cleared his throat, jetted out his chin, then loosened the noose before finishing his thought. "News, I think...I hope will make you happy."

The sunlight danced off Maximus's heavy gold watch as he loosened his tie again. The flash pulled Angelina's attention from the windowsill. She adjusted her position enough to observe him without boldly staring. From her inconspicuous perch, she noticed Maximus had not shaven. The dark circles under his eyes completed his haggled appearance.

"Oh?" The butterflies in her stomach abruptly shifted directions in anticipation.

"Dr. Lane said I can take you home today."

Her eyes widened with excitement. "Back to my family?"

"No. Forgive me. I meant *my* home. My family's estate."

"I see." She returned to her perch, looking out the window.

The news was disheartening. Her yearning for Brusnengo grew each day. The word *home* made a wave of sadness crash over her, and she begged her tears not to fall.

"I will get you back to *your* home, I promise. In the meantime, I will take care of you."

"My family needs me, especially my Papa. He relies on me." She jabbed her thumb against her chest. "Me more than any of my siblings. I need to go back home, but you won't let me. Why?"

Maximus glanced at his watch, then at the door.

"Are you hungry? Kimmie's diner is down the way. If we hurry, we can still eat breakfast. They make the best French Toast. Their coffee is not my espresso. It is served in a cup the size of a cantaloupe."

Angelina, seething, raised her brow at his continual avoidance of the topic. This was the third time she asked why she was in America. Each time, she insisted she return home. Each time, however, Maximus evaded the question by switching topics.

Internally, she growled, an echo of her empty stomach.

"Alright, that is a bit of an exaggeration, but it is hot. It will warm you up."

"Food, the common neutralizer." Angelina sighed. She exposed the pink slippers that matched her robe. "This is a stylish ensemble, but not exactly appropriate for going out. I have searched the room for my clothes but found none."

"And you won't find them." Maximus snapped.

His agitation for her displeasure fueled her aggravation. She furrowed her brow, but before she could demand an explanation, a tap-tap at the door stopped her.

"Excuse me, boss. I got the package. Youse want me to leave it out here?"

"Wait there, Figgy." Maximus turned to Angelina and whispered. "May my driver come in?"

Hungry and slightly irritated, she shrugged. "I suppose."

"Figgy, bring it in."

With a broad smile and beads of sweat perched across his brow, Figgy bounced into the room with his arms full. He was winded, and his round face was flushed from carrying three shiny black boxes, each with a red satin ribbon tied into an elaborate bow. Maximus directed Figgy to set the packages on the bed.

"Why are you a mess?" Maximus quietly snapped at Figgy.

"I took da stairs. Doc says I need to lose a few pounds. I figured da stairs was good for me," Figgy said between breaths. "I'm okay. Just needs a second to catch my breath."

Figgy wiped his brow and filled his lungs while Maximus arranged the boxes for Angelina to open. Figgy tucked his handkerchief back into his pocket, adjusted his tie, and cleared his throat to alert Maximus he was presentable.

"Angelina, this is my driver, Figgy. Figgy, this is Miss Beretta."

"Please, call me Angelina."

"Sure, Miss Beretta! Youse even prettier than Boss said."

Maximus cleared his throat to politely reprimand Figgy.

"I mean, it's a pleasure meetin' youse. Boss said youse comin' home today. Bet youse are glad to get outa this place."

Figgy shuddered, glancing around at the sea of white. He removed his handkerchief and wiped away the anxiety on his brow. When his gaze returned to Angelina, his eyes twinkled, and his jovial spirit returned.

"Youse gonna love Boss's Estate! Ain't no finer place."

Maximus, with a menacing stair, took two steps toward Figgy, instantly silencing him.

"Would you like to open your gifts?" Maximus asked, extending his hand to help Angelina out of the chair.

She graciously accepted the assistance. Her morning walk with Sgt. Stephens and the lengthier strolls with Maximus in the evenings improved her stamina, but she was still weak.

"I hope it is to your liking. I selected it myself. If you don't like it...I had nothing to do with it." He grinned.

Apprehensive, she forced a smile of gratitude. "It looks..."

"Expensive?" Figgy blurted. "Boss only buys da best—"

A sharp glare from Maximus silenced Figgy in mid-sentence. The wordless reprimand caused the obedient driver to drop his chin in remorse.

The stunning black satin finish captivated her. She gently grazed the surface of the box. The red silk ribbon holding the top and bottom together matched the box's sheen.

"So beautiful," Angelina whispered.

Bursting with anticipation, Figgy blurted, "Wait till youse see whats inside!"

Maximus cleared his throat and glared at Figgy. The exchange resembled a nun reprimanding a small child. It achieved the same outcome. Figgy stopped his nervous dance, straightened his spine, and puffed his chest.

Angelina did not turn to watch the exchange. She could see enough of it out of the corner of her eye. The driver was a good-natured man whose actions were not intended to cause any issues. Nonetheless, Angelina understood the situation and did not wish to create further problems for Figgy.

The bow unfolded with a gentle pull of the ribbon, spilling a shiny stream of red onto the white sheets. She shivered and blinked back the odd feeling of déjà vu.

Under the white tissue paper was a black wool fabric with leopard print fur accents. Angelina smoothed back the tissue paper and admired the dress for a moment. The straight panel front and the pleated waistline with peekaboo leopard fabric were an elegant but sexy design. Even in the box, she noticed the thoughtfully placed lines that would make any woman appear to have an hourglass figure.

Angelina's eyes widened as she caressed the fur collar. The texture surprised her. She had never felt *real* fur, except the stray cats occupying the vineyard.

"Do you like it?" Maximus took one step forward.

"It's beautiful! But why?"

"Cause Boss does things right!" Figgy bragged.

Maximus, grinding his jaw, tilted his head and glared at Figgy.

"Ah, geez. I'm really sorry, Boss!" With the sigh of a whipped pup, Figgy hung his head and mumbled. "I gonna wait in the car."

"Thank you, Figgy." Angelina cried out, but the jovial driver was gone. "Please do not punish him. He means well."

"Why do you think I would punish him?"

"You are his *boss*."

"Does your father mistreat his employees?"

"No."

Sitting on the edge of the bed, Maximus locked eyes with Angelina. "Neither do I."

Unmoved by his declaration of innocence, Angelina turned her head and stepped toward the window. But Maximus gently grabbed her arm and pulled her back to him.

"Angelina, it is important you believe me. If our families are to do business together, we must trust each other."

The sincerity in Maximus's eyes pierced her soul, as did his reference to *business*. Her memory of the past few weeks may have been erased. However, her father's global dream of selling Beretta Wine in other countries was still quite vivid.

The thought of home and family created a fresh batch of tears. She looked away. Explaining her feelings would bring more to the surface. Tears signaled vulnerability and weakness. Two elements that always compromised the sale.

"Figgy is...well, Figgy." Maximus attempted to pull her gaze back to him. "The man has never met a stranger and can find the best in everything."

"That is not a bad thing." She replied, avoiding his eyes.

"I didn't say it was and didn't imply it either. You think the worst of me for no cause. Look at me, Angelina."

Maximus urged her, but she refused. Standing, he hooked her chin with his finger to gaze into her eyes. She pulled away, not wanting him to see her emotions, her weakness.

"I wish there were more people like him. The world would be a better place."

Angelina stared at the dress. Forcing a smile, she nodded.

"The dress is beautiful."

Maximus released a slow groan of displeasure.

With a light touch, she stroked the front panel. The fabric's quality was superior to any she had ever felt. She could almost hear her sister's ecstatic approval of the dress.

"I will wait for you in the hall."

"Maximus?"

He stopped at the doorway but did not turn around.

"Thank you."

With his hand on the doorknob, Maximus looked back over his shoulder but said nothing. He didn't need to. His aura of agitation expressed it all.

CHAPTER 56

"Well, well. Look who finally came home." Don Salvatore hummed. "You have been quite the little birdie floating to new and exciting places. How was France? Is the coast as smelly as I recall? What a fowl pungent place." Don Salvatore puffed his cigar as he paraded around his prisoner. "I suppose heaven can only exist in one place. Yes, my sweet Francesca, we are the lucky ones." With a grin, he blew smoke in her face. "Not everyone can live on these rolling hills, only an arms-length from God."

"Why did you bring me here?"

"To collect! Or did you forget?"

"I paid my debt! I did exactly as you asked!"

"Oh, my dear, dear, Francesca. You misunderstood. Which is forgivable. Women are...hmm. How do you say ignorant and not be insulting?" Don Salvatore rubbed his chin. "Oh, yes! I know." Smashing her cheeks with his thumb and fingers, he pulled her close to his face. "Women are stupid, weak creatures that need training!"

Francesca squirmed. He begrudgingly released her chin.

"What do you want?"

"Ah, see, you are already responding to your training, and we have barely begun," Don Salvatore cackled. He waved off the burly man holding Francesca. "Here is your fee. I will contact you when I need your services again. If my other birdies are correct, it won't be long before another package arrives."

The man caught the thin stack of cash and fanned it before stuffing it into his long black coat. With a broad grin that expanded his scraggly beard, he tipped his Fedora and backed out of the room.

Free of the burly man's firm grip, Francesca kicked Don Salvatore's groin but missed her target by a few inches.

"Now, now! Do be careful. We will need these later. But first, I have a welcome home gift for you."

"I don't want your gifts!" Francesca spit in his face.

He grabbed her golden mane and jerked her head back. "Don't test me, bitch!"

The Don whipped her head and hurdled her to the floor. She crashed with a thud against the cold marble. He sprinkled on her face the hair entangled in his fingers.

"Walk! Or I will drag you by your hair."

Hiding her expression of agony, Francesca slowly stood up, cradling her arm. She fought back the tears, but a soft whimper escaped.

"Oh, are you hurt?" Don Salvatore asked sweetly.

"I think you broke my arm!"

Grabbing her forearm with his grubby paw, he squeezed. "This one?"

A fiery pain surged up Francesca's arm and out of her lungs in a blood-curdling scream.

"A screamer! That will spice up our evening. Now walk!"

His barrel chest puffed in satisfaction, Don Salvatore hummed a tune as he waltzed behind Francesca. He smiled at his precious art as they walked along the halls. The Don noted each piece's name and value in an air of cheerful conversation.

"I must admit, my dear. Millions of dollars of art line these walls, but today, you are my most prized possession. Don't let that go to your head. Soon, I will have someone far more valuable! Turn left here."

Francesca gazed down the dimly lit hall. Half of the wall sconces were on, giving the space an eeriness.

"Why is it so dark in here," Francesca shivered.

"How can a little darkness scare *you*? Hmm? Come now, Francesca, embrace your demons for once! Make them your friends! Ah, what am I saying? Silly me, you have no friends because you betray them!"

"You didn't give me a choice."

"Now, now. That is not true. Everyone has a choice. Your husband *chose* to borrow money to free your parents from Auschwitz. Had your parents *chosen* to turn in their Jew friends, they would not have been imprisoned."

"None of those were my choices."

"One begets another. But you did choose to pay your husband's debt."

"To save my son's life!"

"And that of your own. The tale would not have a happy ending if you died and left your son in my care."

Francesca charged at Don Salvatore, but his hand connected with her cheek. The impact was powerful enough to launch her small frame into the air. She flew backward, crashing into the wall with a loud thud. Her head wobbled as she faded in and out of consciousness.

"Why do you insist on making poor choices? I am trying to bestow a lovely welcome home upon you, but you are not acting as a gracious guest."

The Don tapped his cigar above her face. The hot ashes floated down, landing on her ivory skin. Francesca snapped back awake, rubbing away the fiery embers.

"I do hope you choose to learn from your mistakes. Can you do that? Hmm? Let's start over. Forget all the hostility up to this point. You did your job well and deserve your reward. Antonio and Bruno would not have found Angelina if it weren't for you. They are stupid oafs. But with your breadcrumbs, they followed you all the way to Cherbourg. I did wonder how you were able to send those telegrams without Angelina knowing. Do tell me."

"Before we boarded the train, Antonio and I agreed that if we were separated, I would send a message back here. When I bought a new pair of shoes in Turin, I paid the lady at the boutique to send the message. In France, I used the excuse of going to the washroom." Struggling to stand, she groaned.

"Ah, you do play the sweet and innocent part well. I wonder if it is your pretty eyes. They are as beautiful as a robin blue sky on a chilly winter day. But we both know nothing is as cold as your heart." Don Salvatore cackled and extended his hand to help her. "We are almost there. Yes. The second door on the right." Don Salvatore waved his cigar, scattering ashes everywhere. "Well, it is not polite to open another's gift. Go on, open the door!"

Her hand trembling, Francesca turned the crystal-cut glass doorknob and released it. Slowly and without a creak, the door floated two-thirds open. Afraid to move, Francesca glanced at The Don.

"Well, go inside, have a look."

Hesitantly, she stepped through the threshold, but Don Salvatore pushed her deeper into the room.

"What do you think?" Don Salvatore boasted. "He looks a little frazzled now. Much better than he did when he crawled through my front door."

Francesca trembled at the sight of Antonio. His wounds oozed a sour smell, and a gurgle emanated from his lungs with each breath.

"He will live, luckily. Well, perhaps not lucky for him. He is in quite a bit of pain. Spends most of his waking hours moaning, but he is tough." Don Salvatore puffed his cigar and blew the smoke in her face.

"A devil never dies," Francesca murmured.

"Not quite sure where Bruno went."

"He is dead."

"Oh?"

"He died in the fire on the ship."

"Ha! Are you sure? Antonio did not die."

"I watched him." She shivered at the memory. "It was a horrific death."

"You watched? Your heart is more frigid than I imagined." The Don's eyes danced with delight. "Oh, well. No loss. He was an idiot who died a fool's death."

Don Salvatore tucked his cigar into the corner of his mouth and closed the door to Antonio's room.

"Antonio is not the only surprise. You are special, Francesca. Not all my guests receive gifts. But I couldn't help picking up this one." With a malevolent smile, he kissed his fingers in delight. "Now, this My Sweet, is a *real* welcome home present. A truly thoughtful gift, in my opinion." He pointed to the door across the hall. "Have a look in that room. Go ahead, I have already unlocked the door."

Francesca hesitated. Impatient, The Don shoved her forward.

"Look! Dammit, look or be beaten!"

She took a deep breath and slowly opened the door. The room's contents instantly sent a powerful wave of horror through her body. Her heart in her throat, she dropped to her knees, sobbing.

"Alberto?"

"He is a good boy. He does not eat much but is a good boy."

"Mamma!"

The young boy toddled into his mother's arms and buried his face in her chest. Francesca held him tightly for a moment. Forgetting the pain emanating from her arm, she inspected her son for any injuries. Relieved he was unharmed, Francesca embraced Alberto again. She snuggled his head under her chin and whispered words of love.

"Enjoy your visit. You have five minutes. Then you have work to do!"

Don Salvatore closed the door and locked it with a key from around his neck. Pleased with himself, he strolled down the hall, puffing his cigar. He felt a bounce in his step that had been absent since Angelina disappeared.

"Do not worry, My Little Dove, you are still the brightest gem in my collection. Had you not run, I would have no need for her. But, My Little Dove, you have awoken a dragon who must feast in your absence."

CHAPTER 57

Angelina donned the dress and ran her hands along the bodice. It fit perfectly. There was no full-length mirror to appreciate the flattering lines, but she could see a faint reflection in the window. She admired her stunning appearance and the fabric's quality for a moment until her stomach cried for food.

"Yes, yes. I know." She mumbled to her hungry stomach.

Running a brush through her hair, contemplating a way to style it, a deep sadness filled Angelina's heart. Creating an attractive hair-do was her sister's talent. A wave of nausea clung to the memory of Catalina, torturing her hair while they discussed Fernando.

Angelina clutched the porcelain sink. A chill filled her skin, and beads of sweat pearled across her brow. She splashed her face, careful not to mar her dress with any runaway droplets. The cold water eased her stomach's threat, but Angelina held her position until she was confident the spell was over. She dried her face and attempted to create a suitable stage for her leopard trimmed hat. It was not Catalina's quality, but good enough for public view.

When she opened the door, Sgt. Stephens and Maximus were gone. Angelina looked up and down the empty hallway. To her right, at the nurses' station, a woman's playful chatter with a man caught Angelina's attention. His muted, witty response turned the nurse into a flirtatious schoolgirl. Angelina rolled her eyes each time the white, stocking covered ankle and white shoe popped up.

"Blah, can you be any more desperate? You don't stand a chance with Sgt. Stephens." Angelina rolled her eyes.

The officer was handsome and had a pleasant personality. He was a fine catch, but Angelina was not interested. Sgt. Aside from not being her type, he was a married man.

As Angelina approached the nurses' station, she heard the man's voice inspiring the sappy display. His deep tone muffled words. He whispered, frequently pausing to allow the nurse to giggle. It was not how Sgt. Stephens behaved.

"Who has you so smitten?" Angelina whispered.

Curious about who the gentleman was and what he was saying, Angelina slipped off her leopard print heels and tip-toed toward the enthralled couple.

"I am free later." The nurse swooned.

The man's muffled response popped the woman's shoe up with a giggle.

"Might as well find an empty room here." Angelina groaned. "Give the guy a challenge. Be worth the chase!"

Several feet away, the owner of the voice became clear.

"Such a lovely offer from a lovely woman. Tell me, are all nurses as beautiful as you?"

The woman giggled, "I don't know."

"Hmm, if there are, I doubt there are many," he claimed.

"Are all gangsters as handsome as you?"

Angelina stopped, "Gangsters? He is not a gangster, you idiot!"

"A gangster, I am not."

"Everyone knows who you are, Mr. Fiori. Everyone! You don't have to hide your identity from me. I like a man who is a little dangerous."

Angelina wanted to vomit. The nurse's words were sickening. Maximus, eliciting the woman's swoons, turned her stomach more.

"He operates a business, you bimbo!" Angelina snipped. "A gangster, ha! Typical American!"

A few feet closer, Angelina could hear every word Maximus spoke.

"Has anyone ever told you your eyes twinkle when you smile? My culture believes such a sparkle is a sign of inner beauty."

The woman giggled, then asked, "What time you gonna pick me up tonight, Mr. Fiori?"

"I am going to be sick." Angelina groaned.

"Perhaps another night. I know where to find you."

Angelina slipped her shoes back on, fluffed her hair a bit, and inspected her body for anything out of place. She found two strands of hair clinging to her breast and one on the front of her skirt. After detasseling, she stepped into view and saw Maximus's hooked finger barely supporting the woman's chin. His charming display was precisely the exchange he had with Angelina twenty minutes prior.

Inwardly, Angelina sighed. *You fool, did you really think he differed from other men?*

Maximus made eye contact with Angelina for a brief second before releasing the nurse's chin. Smiling, he plucked the woman's hand from the desk and gently kissed it.

"It appears Miss Beretta is finally ready for a change in scenery. Ms. Danielle, is there anything Dr. Lane needs before my friend leaves?"

"I left my robe and things in the room." Angelina hesitated. "Is...there a luggage bag for me to put them in?"

"We ain't Harzfeld's, Honey." The nurse eyed Angelina.

"Miss Beretta, why don't you put your things in one of the boxes Figgy brought in. I am sure it will all fit."

The comment was an intentionally harsh verbal slap for Angelina's insult and lack of trust, especially after receiving an expensive gift. Her actions precipitated his slight, so Angelina took the demeaning comment in stride.

"That is an excellent idea! Thank you, Mr. Fiori." Angelina gave a slight nod. "Shall I meet you downstairs?"

Her innocuous response brought a look of surprise and bewilderment to Maximus's face. Though the expression was fleeting, Angelina noticed it. If she were the type to keep score, she would have placed a hash mark by her name.

"I can wait."

It was the last exchange between them that morning. Figgy tried to dissipate the palpable tension with his usual excitement, but Maximus squelched the joy.

"Figgy, take us home. We missed our window for Kimmie's Diner."

Thirty minutes later, Figgy turned onto a gravel drive. The tall solid gate connected the six-foot stonewall that appeared to stretch miles in both directions. Figgy bumped the horn three times, followed by a long honk and two more quick toots. Seconds after the last honk, the gate split in two and slowly revealed the beauty behind the cold black barrier.

Dappled in soft light and lined with tall oak trees was a long gravel road. The gentle curves of the drive and the vibrant fall leaves glowing in the mid-morning sun added to the enchantment. Every detail, including the thick, lush grass spanning far in each direction, gave Angelina a sense of tranquility.

The beauty stole Angelina's breath. She covered her mouth to hide her astonishment, but it was too late; the gasp that escaped echoed like an explosion in the small space void of chatter.

It was Maximus's turn to hide his amusement. Discretely, his fingers grazed over the thick black stubble along his chin to hide his smile. The artificially pensive cover was unnecessary. Angelina was far more interested in the splendor outside the window.

"It is so..."

"Told ya! No one can resist this place's beauty! Boss gots good taste. Better than good, if you asks me! You should see his office. Woo-wee! Ain't no finer room at that Buckingham Castle. Heck, none in any castle! He bought the wood special from Africa or sumptin. Had shipped here."

Maximus cleared his throat, prompting Figgy to make eye contact in the rearview mirror. The silent exchange stopped the driver's chatter and squelched his youthful excitement.

Angelina scooted to the edge of her seat and patted Figgy's shoulder. She opened her mouth to express a kind word, but her jaw dropped wide when the Fiori house came into view.

"Oh my! It is huge!"

Figgy chuckled, "Boss gets that a lot!"

Still mesmerized, Angelina missed another wordless reprimand. Though Maximus's glare silenced the driver's tongue, Angelina's expression of amazement bolstered Figgy's nonverbal childish excitement.

"This is your home? *You* live here... *alone*?"

"No. My family lives here as well."

The gently winding pea-gravel drive provided a brief view of the long three-story building that sat across the open field of freshly cut grass. Figgy slowed the car so Angelina could soak in the regal display that peeked through the trees.

"That's the side of the house. Youse gonna love the front!"

Utterly speechless, Angelina slid back into her seat and gently shook her head in disbelief. A quarter-mile away was a mansion the size she had never seen before. It was easily ten times larger than Catalina's large villa and far more beautiful.

"Oh, Cat. You would love this place." Angelina whispered.

The drive straightened, giving Angelina a full view of the magnificent building in the distance. One hundred yards before the wide front steps stood a three-tier fountain. At the top, an elegant winged angel held out her empty hands, sweetly welcoming her guests. Cascading from the bowl beneath the Angel of Peace flowed a curtain of water for the Grecian figures to mingle coyly behind. Rearing from the bottom tier, the front half of four stallions broke the veil of water on its fall into the arabesque shaped pool. Artistically trimmed evergreen bushes flanked the four sides. At each corner, a courageously poised stone lion balanced on its head a four-foot-wide bowl of golden flowers. The combination of vibrant flora and white masonry transformed the stunning formation into a masterpiece.

Angelina stared at the towering fountain as Figgy drove the car slowly past. Seeing her enthralled expression and receiving a nod of approval from Maximus, Figgy went around the fountain two more times so Angelina could enjoy every detail.

"I have never seen anything so beautiful!" She said, her eyes widening with each spectacular new feature.

"You think that's pretty? Geeze, youse ain't seen nothin's. Wait till you see the rest of the place. Like I said, Boss gots real good taste!" Figgy smiled broadened. "Hey, Boss. Youse want me to drive youse two around so Miss Beretta can see the stables and da lake?"

"Maybe another time. I believe Freddy is waiting for me."

"Ya, okay. Youse let me know."

Angelina stepped out of the car and slowly climbed the wide stone steps, soaking in every magical detail. From each end of the main structure, two towering wings extended forward, creating three sides of a sizeable square space. A short stone balustrade connected the wings, completing the fourth wall of the square courtyard.

Angelina was in awe of the beauty and elegance dripping from the massive structure. As she crowned the steps, Angelina admired the mirrored garden on each side of the stone walkway. The neatly trimmed evergreen bushes formed a simple maze pattern around a small tiered fountain. A stone bench sat at the beginning of each maze, and a matching bench sat at the end.

Lining the first and second stories and overlooking the maze garden was a veranda rippling out from the regal entrance. Each elegant, soft beige arch flowed from one creamy white pillar to another. Around the top story was a long stone rail, slightly taller than the one separating the drive from the garden. The grandeur, though overwhelming, was a perfect balance of artistic design and functional elegance.

Between the two creamy white pillars flanking the redwood cathedral door was a tall, slender man patiently waiting to greet her. When he moved close enough to introduce himself, Angelina jumped.

"Oh my! You startled me." Angelina took two steps back.

"My apologies, Miss Beretta. I did not mean to frighten you."

"I did not see you."

"You are not the first to overlook a simple man amidst such glorious architecture. Though, a discerning eye would infer me as a blemish on this canvas of beauty." With a slight bow, he added, "My name is Vincenzo Mustagano."

The man's formal demeanor astounded Angelina. She turned to express her surprise to Maximus but discovered she stood alone on the stone path.

"Signore Fiori had a business meeting and did not wish to rush you. This is the perfect time to enjoy *this* garden. In two hours, the sun will reach an intolerable intensity."

"You imply there are other gardens?"

"Yes, four others, each with a deep meaning. Signore Fiori does everything with thoughtful intent. When you are ready, I shall escort you to your room."

"I don't want to make you wait. The garden will be here tomorrow."

"As you wish."

Vincenzo led Angelina to her room, frequently pausing for her to soak in the superb masonry, marble floors, mesmerizing paintings, and Grecian statues.

On the second floor, Vincenzo paused for Angelina to examine the large sitting area that opened to a grand balcony. Through the set of double doors, Angelina glimpsed the beautiful view. She moved closer to the doors but stopped short.

"My apologies, Vincenzo. I should keep my curiosity on a tighter leash. Please lead the way.

"Even after five years, I find myself entranced by the beauty in this glorious place." Vincenzo extended his arm. "Your room is this way."

At the end of the wide corridor, the butler unlocked the only door on the left side.

"After you."

Angelina crossed the threshold and gasped at the opulence. Every aspect of the décor and the ornate woodwork blended into a perfect and inviting space. Her gaze gradually moved from the six-pane windows, soft white walls with raised scrolled trim, crown molding, and a shiny ebony fireplace with soft pewter accents. In front of the hearth, two matching light grey loveseats faced each other. A row of alternating burgundy and champagne silk pillows on the loveseats added to the posh furnishings.

"In this apartment, you will find everything you need. Someone will bring you lunch before long. I recommend you relax on the balcony or take a hot bath."

"Thank you, Vincenzo." Captivated by her surroundings, Angelina barely heard Vincenzo's suggestion.

Without another word, the butler backed out of the room. The door softly clicked shut, but the loud clank from Vincenzo locking it snapped Angelina to attention.

She ran to the door and turned the handle, but the glass nob would not move.

"Vincenzo?" Angelina cried, pounding on the door. "Vincenzo, you locked me in!"

There was no reply. The butler disappeared as stealthily as he had appeared downstairs. Had she believed in ghosts, she would have sworn Vincenzo was an apparition.

Angelina leaned against the locked door and sighed.

"Why would he lock me in?"

The expansive room grew smaller as Angelina realized how effortlessly Maximus had lured her into a trap. His charming behavior up to today was an act. Disappointed in herself and furious with Maximus, Angelina paced the room.

"You are deceptive, like my brother-in-law, and I fell for it! Giorgio flirted with me, then married my sister!" Angelina growled. "I should have recognized the behavior at the hospital." Angelina grumbled quietly. "Why must all the attractive men be devious snakes?"

CHAPTER 58

"Psst." Marcus whispered, hunkering low on the wine cellar steps. "Psst... Nan?"

Fernando stopped working and groaned. "What?"

"She is gone!"

Fernando glared apathetically at Marcus.

"Nan, Francesca is gone!"

"I heard you the first time. It means nothing to me? I am not a ghost leisurely hiding in the dark. I have work to do."

"She left last night. I followed her, and when I returned this morning, the car was back, but she was not. Nan, I think someone took her."

"I have work to do."

Apprehensive of being seen, Marcus glanced up and down the building's exterior before continuing his plea.

"Nan, wait! This is serious."

"A serious waste of my time! She is *your* pet. Find her or don't. I really do not care. My focus is on protecting my family! Don Salvatore will punish us if that truck of wine is not delivered and the money is collected. I refuse to give him a reason to kill my parents. They are all I have left to love."

Fernando turned to walk away, but Marcus left the shadows and grabbed his arm.

"Nan, this will affect both our families. If someone took her, then they know I am alive and..."

"Then, Lazarus, rise from the dead and do something about it. I have a delivery to make."

Fernando ripped his arm free and turned on his heels.

"I will tell you where they are."

"Who?" Fernando asked, looking over his shoulder.

"My parents. Help me, and I will tell you where they are being kept."

"Kept?"

Marcus looked around to ensure they were alone before moving closer to Fernando. In a low voice, he whispered the location of his parents.

"The nuns are taking care of them."

"So, they *are* still alive?"

"Yes."

"How do they look? Will they survive?"

"I haven't seen them, so I do not know."

Pacing, Fernando ran his hand through his hair and quietly cursed the air. His chest heaved as he fought back the emotions that threatened to explode from his core.

"Nan, what is wrong? They are alive. That is *good* news."

Fernando's agony seeped from his body in a low groan.

"I thought they were dead. Everything pointed to *that* being the truth. The night I scrubbed my best friend's blood from the kitchen floor, I prayed for them. I prayed they were alive. I prayed Rosario would stand at the top of the hill and decide exactly how to avenge his sons' deaths. That is how I felt the first week. The last several days, even under The Don's horrid rule, I prayed they were dead."

"What? Why would you pray for their deaths? What has happened to you, Nan?"

His face flushed with anger, Fernando's eyes glistened as they danced back and forth. With each word, his voice became more impassioned.

"It is not what I want, Marcus. None of this is. But you and your sisters have taught me a lesson. You showed me that *family* is the most important thing to protect. Even if that means you hurt the ones you profess to love."

"Of course, family is the most important. You and your parents *are* part of this family. Tell me you know that is true," Marcus pleaded.

"Oh, I know the *truth*. And now, I know how to protect *my* family."

CHAPTER 59

Angelina intermittently banged on the door and cried for help, but no one answered. The tick of the clock on the mantel grew louder and louder as she paced. Furious, she barked her discontent to the only person who could hear her; herself.

"You are better than this. After all the men you have met, you knew exactly what they wanted. You knew their motives. You could effortlessly guide them down a path you controlled. So, what happened to you, Angelina Rose?" she barked. "You have lost your gift. You have locked yourself out of your mind. And *now* you got yourself locked away by a *man*. A man who should have melted into putty in your hands!"

Subconsciously, she picked up a trinket, examined it, then scrutinized another. As she continued her rant, she wound the music box with an angel holding a dove in her outstretched hand. The tinkling song played while she lifted a crystal elephant the size of a grapefruit. Each piece captured more and more of her attention until she finally traded her anger for curiosity.

She did not think it possible, but the anteroom's grandness was a paltry space compared to what lay in the adjoining rooms.

Stepping through the arched doorway, Angelina gasped at the grandeur illuminated by the six-pane bay windows. Beside the bookshelves in the far corner, a pair of armchairs begged for a literary thirsty occupant to enjoy the coziness. The two-foot deep seat in the bay window, however, tugged more at Angelina's heart. An elegant, hand-carved Queen Ann sleigh bed with button-tufted charcoal fabric was by far the centerpiece. Yet, every perfectly placed item added to the room's charm and the bed's regal presence.

Another arched doorway led to a sizeable room lined with creamy-white cabinets. Every stitch of clothing a woman could ever desire, along with matching shoes, handbags, and hats, filled the cubbyholes. The floor-to-ceiling mirror and the champagne fainting chair with charcoal and burgundy pillows perfected the library of fashion.

The bathroom had two half-moon spaces flanking an oversized marble shower. The alcove on the right, below six tall windows, was a champagne gold claw-foot tub. On the left, in a similar-sized nook lined with mirrors, was a spacious vanity and a champagne chair with a round burgundy pillow. Soft white towels with burgundy silk trim and charcoal marble floors spread a dab of color around the room.

Angelina became amused by the meticulous décor. The balance of colors from the ceiling to the floor flowed effortlessly. Every trinket, hue, and decorative wall piece lent beauty to the room but did not overwhelm the eye.

"Did Maximus design this place, or did a woman with an astute eye for detail?" Angelina chuckled as she admired the miniature piano on the vanity. "Dr. Lane said he was a man of details. and Figgy did not exaggerate. This place is gorgeous!"

After her thorough inspection of the rooms, Angelina stepped out onto the spacious balcony. Under the covered portion, a small table separated two oversized chairs. A few feet to the left, next to the stone balustrade, was a bistro set. Under the pergola, basking in the sunshine, was a chase lounge chair with a smaller stone table. Spread around the balcony to add color and life to the peaceful space were several jumbo planters filled with an array of colors.

The outdoor space was larger than Angelina's room back home. The view, which seemed to stretch for miles, was more majestic than her father's favorite spot high on the hill overlooking the rolling rows of vines.

The cool afternoon air foretold the incoming storm. On the distant horizon, above a forest of dazzling autumn colors, a thick cloud bank chased the sun across the sky. Sporadic flashes of light illuminated the stacks of billowing clouds. Occasionally, a low, almost inaudible rumble reached Angelina's balcony. From her spacious perch, she watched the storm slowly encroach on the vast acreage of open fields that lay beyond the multi-tiered gardens below her.

Soaking in the fauna's beauty below and watching the storm build on the horizon, Angelina waited for someone to open the door. As time ticked by, a storm brewed within Angelina. It had been three hours since Vincenzo locked the door. Trapped, anxious, and starving, Angelina began pacing the balcony.

Figgy had persuaded Maximus to allow for a brief stop at Lamar's on their way back to the estate. It was Angelina's first donut, and Figgy was bound to ensure she had the best.

"This sugary goodness is gonna ruin youse, Miss Beretta. I sorry to do that to youse, but youse too pretty to eat the other stuff!"

On the ride to the estate, Figgy insisted Angelina try a variety of donuts. She was hungry and could not resist the driver's offer.

"This is called a Ray's Original. It's real good!" Figgy's eyes danced as he told her about each donut. "This one gots a creamy puddin' and a chocolate icin'. I think they call it a Bavaria or sumptin. It's one of my favorites. And this is a buttermilk bar. It's good with a cup of hot joe."

Angelina surprised herself by eating all three. She was not surprised that she felt sick. She slid back in her seat and prayed she would not vomit.

She had recovered from her sugar high hours ago. Angelina's stomach growled persistently as she paced. She was a starved animal locked in an enormous cage.

Dangling on the edge of pure rage, Angelina stopped at the stone railing to examine the option of jumping.

"I would surely break my leg, or worse, if I jumped," Angelina grumbled. "Vincenzo, you were wrong. This apartment does not have *everything* I need. I found no ladder or rope!"

Angelina chided herself as she kicked off her heels and resumed her pacing. Occasionally, she stopped to monitor the storm. The black wall of clouds shadowed the green fields and encroached on the gardens below. Angelina estimated it would engulf the entire estate in the rain within an hour.

A voice floating on the breeze caught Angelina's attention.

"Would you like to join me on a walk before the storm?"

Angelina squinted to see who called out to her, but they were too far away. Ultimately, she decided, *who* didn't matter. She was open to *any* chance of salvation.

"Yes, please!"

"Come down, and I will meet you at the bottom of the stairs."

"I can't. My door is locked."

"Locked?"

Angelina nodded. "For several hours. I thought some—"

Before she could finish her sentence, the man disappeared under the veranda. Angelina waited for him to return, but he did not reappear.

"May I introduce myself?" A voice asked.

Angelina looked in every direction for the owner of the voice but saw no one. "Where are you?"

"I am here! Behind you!"

She twirled around to find a young, dark-haired man dangling from one of the pergola beams.

"How did you get up there?"

The young man let go of his trapeze and landed on his feet. Before he stood, he gazed up at Angelina with a dazzling smile. His eyes danced with a mischievous sparkle as he spoke.

"You are the most beautiful creature I have ever seen! May I have the pleasure of knowing your name?"

A warm rush filled Angelina's cheeks even though she thought the gallant display silly. Based on the young man's playful tone, Angelina accepted the performance as a good-humored act.

"Angelina."

"Indeed, you are an angel!" He stood and gently kissed the back of her hand. "How long have you been here?"

"I arrived late morning and have been stuck in here ever since."

"That is an awful crime. I will see that Vincenzo is punished!"

Angelina tried to speak to him but was busy searching around the balcony for something.

"First, however, we must free you..." His voice trailed off.

"You have a key?"

The young man continued to assess the situation. He looked over the rail, off both sides, then eventually up at the pergola, giving a perplexed look after each.

"Key?" He asked absently, still inspecting the space. "If you trust me, we will not need one."

An impish giggle tickled Angelina's core. "Can you trust someone if you do not know their name?"

The young man slid the bistro table under the beam he dangled from a few moments before. He set one chair next to the table and looked up. Satisfied with the angle, he flashed Angelina a broad smile.

"Come on, I will help you up," He said, offering his hand. "You should grab your shoes. You will need them."

Angelina snatched up her shoes and accepted the young man's hand. Once she was standing on the table, he told her not to move. She questioned his plan but was quickly silenced by the young man's fluid motion. Slightly bending his knees, he pushed off the ground, jumping straight up. His muscles bulged as he pulled his torso up between the beams.

"That is amazing!"

He grinned. "Not really. This will impress you."

Balanced on the two-inch thick board, the young man slowly brought up his legs until he was in a handstand. Angelina watched in awe as he moved his body around effortlessly. His muscular form pressing against his shirt and pants left little for Angelina to imagine.

"Wow! That is impressive!"

"Now you do it." A smile pressed his cheeks.

Shocked by his request, Angelina stepped back, forgetting her pedestal was a small space. The table wobbled, sending her off balance.

"Oh, my God!" Angelina's arms flailed.

"No, you don't!"

Before she fell, the young man had a firm grip on her arms and effortlessly lifted her up above the pergola.

"You're ok," He said, holding her close to his chest.

Angelina wrapped her arm tightly around his muscular torso as he stood up.

"Why does the angel tremble?"

Angelina did not respond.

He chuckled. "I will not drop you. I promise."

Angelina held her head still. The blustery wind whistled by one ear while the lub-dub of his heart echoed in the other.

"Almost there, only a few feet to the top."

"Top?" Angelina's voice tremored.

She lifted her head to have a look around, but the young man promptly cautioned her.

"Shh! All will be fine as long as you do not wiggle about."

He did not groan or show any signs of strain for carrying her. Given his musculature, it was not surprising. The similarity between the young man and Maximus baffled her more. Both had the same strong jawline shaded with dark stubbles, onyx eyes, and thick black hair. Even the tone of their voice was similar.

"See, that wasn't so bad." He gently placed her on her feet.

"Thank you."

Angelina held his shoulder while she put on her shoes. When she stood up, he was inches from her, their lips a breath apart. The intense mutual attraction held them close together. The crack of lightning, followed by a deep rumble of thunder, snapped them apart. Angelina took several steps back. When she looked around, she nearly screamed.

"We are on the roof? How did you...?"

The young man smiled, pointing toward the row of tiles leading to the top of the building.

"You carried me up that thin line? We could have died from the fall!"

"But we didn't because you did as I asked."

The confident tone in his voice was the same as Maximus, and it infuriated her.

"What if I moved?"

"We would have fallen." He shrugged. "I could think of worse ways to die. Not everyone is lucky enough to die with an angel in their arms!"

Another crack of lightning halted Angelina from furthering the fight.

"How do we get down?"

"We don't!" He chuckled.

Angelina's temper surged. "What do you mean *we don't*? It is about to rain!"

"Are you afraid?"

Every self-assured word he spoke was precisely the thing Maximus would say. His twin was sent to annoy her.

"No! I love the rain. Being struck by God creates my fear!"

"God would never harm his angel!"

Angelina screamed at him, but a roll of thunder overpowered her voice. As the large drops of rain landed sporadically around them, he laughed.

"Now, *that* was impressive! You opened your mouth, and the sound of thunder came out!"

"It is raining! Stop playing games. I want off this roof!"

The young man continued to laugh and tease Angelina, pressing her temper. However, a voice shouting her name quickly silenced him.

"Angelina?" a booming voice echoed from the balcony below. "Angelina, where are you? God dammit! She cannot be far. She is not *that* clever!"

"I locked the door as you ordered," Vincenzo said dutifully. "There is no way for her to leave."

"Then how do you explain her *not* being in her room?"

"He ordered Vincenzo to lock me in?" Angelina fumed. "How dare he!"

"We better go." The young man whispered, grabbing her wrist. "This way."

"But you said there was not a way down!"

The young man held a finger to his lips. He waved for her to follow him. She hesitated. He gently squeezed her wrist and offered a charming smile, begging her. Another crack of lightning ended her deliberation.

They scurried to the other side of the roof.

"I will lower you down. Kick your shoes off when I tell you. You must land flat on your feet."

"What if I don't?"

"You will turn your ankle."

Angelina glared at him.

"Ready?"

"Do I have a choice?"

"Not really." He chuckled. "Good luck!"

Angelina landed with a wobble and collapsed to the floor. Writhing in pain, she grabbed her ankle.

The young man hopped off the roof, landing inches away from her. His face flushed bright red as he looked for her injury.

"Are you ok?" He asked in a panic.

"My ankle!"

"Oh shit. This ain't good! Um... can you walk?"

Angelina shot him a dirty look.

"Ok. Ok. I will get help. Don't move."

"Where can I go with this?" Angelina snapped, pointing to her ankle. "Stop staring and go for help. Hurry!"

"Right. Yes. Help." He ran his hand through his dark locks.

He sprinted into the adjoining room and disappeared. Angelina waited for a minute before standing on her feet. She slipped on her shoes and laughed.

"You are not the only one who can play a joke! I doubt you will laugh when you come back to an empty balcony!"

CHAPTER 60

Angelina peeked out the door into the hallway. The young man was gone. She slipped out of the room and down the hall toward the sound of voices shouting. Standing behind a pillar on the third floor, she looked down at the open vestibule. Over a dozen people, primarily men, nodded at an older man barking orders.

The three men she knew, Maximus, Vincenzo, and Figgy, were not in the group. However, a thin woman next to the man in charge shared a striking resemblance to Maximus. The sharp facial features, especially the prominent jawline and thick, wavy hair, meant she was his mother.

After adding her reprimands, Maximus's mother dabbed her glistening cheek. Angelina chuckled. She acted like Sofia.

Straightening her skirt, Angelina cautiously descended to the next floor. Remaining out of sight, she examined every person's face. Over half appeared to be a Fiori relative.

"You do have a big family. No wonder this place is huge!"

"And that is not all of them."

Angelina released a quiet yelp and twirled around to find Maximus standing two steps away. His scowl and cocked brow meant his charming personality had yet to return.

"I am shocked by your behavior, Angelina. Not even a guest one night, and you already caused my mother to weep."

Maximus grabbed her arm, pulling her down the steps.

"*My* behavior? What of *yours*?" Angelina snapped. "You locked me away!"

"Call off the search. I found Miss Beretta lurking on the steps," Maximus shouted to the man in charge.

Maximus's mother ascended the stairs, emphatically praising God with every step.

"You are hurting her, Maximilianus! Unhand her!" His mother flapped his hands away from Angelina. "Please forgive my son. He can be so harsh. Sometimes, I do not know who he is!" Linking her arm into Angelina's, Maximus's mother led her down the steps. "My name is Philamena. And this is my husband, Vito."

Vito waved the staff away and met Philamena at the base of the stairs. Picking up Angelina's hand, he gently kissed it.

"It is a pleasure to have you in our home. My apologies for my son's behavior. We raised him to be kind to our guests, especially my dearest friend's daughter."

Vito and Philamena sandwiched Angelina and guided her across the grand foyer.

"Did you enjoy your lunch?" Philamena asked.

"Eat?" Angelina replied.

"Yes, they were instructed to bring lunch to your room."

"Vincenzo mentioned lunch but locked me in the room."

Philamena turned around and scolded Maximus, yelling over his retorts.

"Ma! Let me..."

"Locked! Locked! With no food." Philamena's arms flew in rage. "She is already a skeleton, and you make her go without food! What is wrong with you? You will force me to an early grave. Is that what you want?"

"Philamena." Vito calmed his wife. "It is over. She is safe."

"My apologies, my dear," Philamena said, her tone instantly soft and compassionate. "Come, let me fix you something to eat. Then I will show you around the house."

Angelina and Philamena walked away, but Vito lingered to confront his son. Though Philamena chatted away, Angelina could hear part of the exchange.

"What's the matter with you? I told you to fix this mess!"

"There was a threat to her life." Maximus pointed toward Angelina. "You know I would never treat a guest, especially *her*, that way unless it was necessary!"

"A threat?" Vito sneered. "I warned you about him!"

CHAPTER 61

"Ahh, Her Royal Highness graces us with her presence." Don Salvatore snickered. "How is my favorite niece? Hmm?"

After The Don finished his customary kiss to both of Catalina's cheeks, she squared her shoulders. With her chin up, she looked into Don Salvatore's eyes. She ignored his grin of amusement for her silent postural hiss. Catalina was no longer a baby kitten for him to abuse.

"You speak as if I have not set foot on this vineyard for years. Admittedly, I took several days off to grieve for my brothers' loss and care for my husband. However, *your* meddling in the vineyard's day-to-day operations has forced me to abandon my husband's side and my rightful time to grieve!"

During her last visit, Carlos informed Catalina that Don Salvatore fired everyone but Carlos, Fernando, and Carmella. The workload of ten laborers had been reduced to three. Carlos and Fernando's workload tripled, forcing them to work eighteen hours a day. Carmella continued to cook their meals and clean the house, a job she performed with Sofia before the murders. The unfinished task mounded, forcing the sickly Carmella to forgo many household chores to maintain the vineyard. Horrified to discover the unnecessary changes, Catalina promised Carlos she would resume her old duties and help with other tasks.

"Then Lady Fortune has crossed our paths. I wonder what she has in mind for us today?"

Catalina groaned inwardly. A squabble with the Don was not on her agenda for the day.

"Why are *you* here?" She asked.

"My dear, I would ask you the same. Since you married Giorgio, you only came here to visit your parents. Have the loving Sofia and Rosario returned from their secret hideout?"

"Grief has a firm hold on their health. I do not expect they will return until Christmas. Even then, the holidays may flare their grief."

"Oh, that is truly a shame and quite sad. I was looking forward to Sofia's lavish Christmas dinner. She makes the best Lasagne Bolognese, Brasato Vitello, and Panetton. I do hope they return; it will not be Christmas without them!"

"It will not be Christmas without my brothers." Catalina's brow arched. She held his gaze for only a second. She sighed. "I pray they return soon as well, but for different reasons."

"Yes, well. If I can expedite your parents' return, do let me know."

"You are too kind."

"I *can* be!" He grinned. "So, tell me, what brings you to the vineyard today?"

"To work!"

Don Salvatore burst out in laughter, "You work? Even before your days of luxury, you did not work! Your sister, however, *is* a hard worker. Her drive enhances her beauty, though she needs no help in that area. She is a captivating creature, the radiant Venus reincarnated. Well, that was Giorgio's description of her. Though Roman at heart, I prefer the Greek mythos. Therefore, I liken your sister to Hebe, the goddess of youth." He tilted his head, watching her reaction. "Do you know about Hebe? Hmm?"

Seething at the mention and comparison to her sister, Catalina glared at Don Salvatore. It was, however, his accuracy that incited the bulk of her displeasure.

Since marrying Giorgio, Catalina did no manual labor. In her husband's opinion, Catalina needed to appear, at minimum, equal to her station as a wealthy and socially sophisticated woman. It would reflect poorly on Giorgio if her hands were coarse and her skin tan like a laborer. Therefore, he would only allow her to do the bookkeeping and issue the weekly delivery manifests.

Don Salvatore's smug expression expanded.

"No? Well, you should brush up on your Grecian mythos. I have a few books on the lore and shall bring them by the next time I visit my nephew."

Apathetic, Catalina said, "We will anxiously await your visit and the chance to learn something new."

"I have a better idea!"

"You always do!"

"While you work, I will entertain you with Grecian lore!"

Catalina rolled her eyes. She had no time for The Don's prattling. Her mission that day was to speak with Fernando, and despite Don Salvatore's accusation, she had work to do. Today's task was racking the wine.

"How gracious of you."

Her sardonic tone added zest to Don Salvatore's step and delight to his voice.

"Hebe is the daughter of Zeus and Hera. You know who they are, yes?"

"Doesn't everyone."

"One might be surprised at another's lack of intelligence. Not everyone is as wise and keen as you and me. We are in the class of people who know what others do not. Wouldn't you agree?"

An icy chill tickled Catalina's skin. The Don was hinting he knew a secret, but she had accumulated many in the past few weeks. It was impossible to know which one he had uncovered. Yet, it would not surprise her if Don Salvatore knew *all* of her secrets. He was a devilish man with spies everywhere.

"Oh, Zio, you give me, a mere woman, far too much credit," she replied, rolling her eyes.

"Perhaps you are right. But at least you know of Zeus and Hera. I would not want my great-nephew raised by an ignorant woman."

"Well, Zio, I am sure you are eager for such news, but..."

"You have been married to my nephew long enough to call me by my first name, Rodolfo. I know you intend to respect me by calling me Zio, but I believe it is time we take our kinship to a new status."

"No one calls you by your first name, not even Giorgio." Catalina's jaw gapped.

"Hmm. Surely, someone does." Don Salvatore hummed, scratching his smoothly shaven chin. "Then again, perhaps not. I guess that means you are special. In fact, only one other woman called me by my first name."

"Your mother?"

Don Salvatore chuckled. "You have me there. I suppose there have been two women."

Catalina's curiosity stopped her in her tracks. She held her hand above her eyes, shielding them from the bright sunlight blazing behind The Don's head.

"Who was the other woman?"

"Ah! My first love. But that is a story for another day. Hebe is a far more interesting tale. As I said, Hebe was a beautiful, charming goddess with a special power. Given her title, goddess of youth, I imagine you can guess..."

"The power to make one immortal." She rolled her eyes.

"You are close. Hebe made the gods youthful. There is a difference. One can be immortal as an old man, but to keep one's youth is quite a different state. Your sister emboldens the feminine grace, beauty, and charm of any goddess. As old men, your father-in-law and I agree, like Hebe, Angelina arouses the aged's youthfulness. She certainly performed her magic on me. I feel as young as my nephew. Perhaps even younger!" The Don admitted with a nudge of his elbow.

Catalina rolled her eyes again. The incessant talk of her sister grated on her nerves. Almost as much as discovering yet another man overly smitten by Angelina. It was the never-ending story of Catalina's life. A tale she grew weary of hearing and longed to end–*permanently*.

"Now, Hebe was given the job of cupbearer for the gods and goddesses on Mount Olympia. She served them ambrosia, very appropriate since it was synonymous with longevity."

Abruptly halting in his tracks, a deep, thundering roar of laughter came from The Don. Something had tickled him to the point he could barely breathe.

"What is so funny?"

Don Salvatore tried to speak, but his laughter consumed all the air in his lungs. He struggled to gain his composure. He stood up to speak, and another roar of laughter ensued.

"Can this day get any more annoying?" Catalina mumbled.

"Don't...you...see..." Don Salvatore blurted between giggles. "Hebe...and...Angelina..."

"No! I do not see and do not care!"

"No, no, no. It is too priceless. You must..."

Her patience exhausted, Catalina growled. She looked around for a way out of the painful conversation with Don Salvatore. But the drive down the hill was as barren as the last hundred feet to the cellar's entrance.

"Give me a moment. I must tell someone about this revelation. It is too rich." Don Salvatore slapped his thigh.

"I do not have all day, Rodolfo!" Catalina's brow furrowed.

Hearing his first name snapped him from his hysteria.

"Ah! You say it with the same venom and ferocity as the two before you." He remarked, wiping his brow.

After a few deep, controlled breaths, The Don composed himself enough to explain his boisterousness to the impatient Catalina.

"The similarity is quite comical, you know. Sometimes, I am so clever that I amaze myself!" He chuckled. "You see, Hebe pours ambrosia for the gods and goddesses..."

Don Salvatore's laughter returned, riling Catalina.

"Did Hebe desert her family?"

The Don ignored the question.

"Angelina, like Hebe, is a cupbearer. When customers come to visit, Angelina serves them wine! The similarity has not occurred to me until now. Oh, my!" He sighed, regaining his full composure. "Hmm...a good laugh always puts a positive spin on the day."

Catalina came to an abrupt halt at the entrance to the wine cellar. The Don's revelation may have stimulated his funny bone, but it did not tickle hers. She was done with her sister and any conversation that included Angelina.

"Thank you for your enlightening revelation about my sister." Catalina released a huff. "Now, if you will excuse me, I need to get my work done!"

"I am curious what it is you do here."

She arched her brow. "Another day, perhaps."

"Before I go, tell me what has changed?"

"My brothers are dead for one! My sister has abandoned me. Shall I go on? What has *not* changed is your bringing my brothers' murderer to justice!"

The Don flippantly waved off Catalina's comments.

"No, no. Something about *you* is different. As you stand here under the beautiful blue sky, the sunlight dancing on your skin, I am perplexed by what it is."

There *was* something different, but she was not about to tell *him* how she had changed. It would be a waste of breath.

"I am your same little 'Kitty-Cat,' Zio. I would not keep—"

"Wait, don't tell me." Don Salvatore teased. "Are you... hmm...no, you would not hide such news from me." He rubbed his chin while his eyes roved over her body. "No. I think...Oh, yes! I know. Your hair is different."

Agitated, he wasted more of her time with foolish babble; Catalina feigned a smile.

"No one can hide anything from you, can they, *Rodolfo*?"

CHAPTER 62

"How did you meet my father?" Angelina asked Vito.

Vito, gazing upon an angel, greeted her with a smile.

"Please sit. Sit with me." He patted the seat next to him. "We met during the Great War. He was placed under my command. New to the unit, Rosario was eager to please. Everything came naturally to him. He had little training, but he was a formidable soldier. Your father was a marksman's marksman. A remarkable shooter." Vito smiled at the memory. "There was no one like your father. He could focus his anger, giving him an edge over the other soldiers."

"My Papa is a calm man. Nothing makes him angry."

"That, my dear, is who he became. War changes a man in ways too difficult to explain."

Vito moved to the window and pensively stared into the distance. The mental torture caused by the memories of the war carved trenches across his brow.

"Papa would stare out the window like that."

Vito chuckled and patted her knee. "It is what old men do."

When Vito returned his gaze out the window, Angelina stepped away, giving him space to wrestle with the demons conjured by the past. His reverie, however, only lasted five minutes. With a smile, he returned his attention to his patient guest.

"How do you like it here?" Vito asked, drawing her eyes to the room with his hand.

"It is beautiful. Did you have it built?"

"Ah, I wish this were of my making. The only hand I used was being a father to my son. *He* is responsible for all of this. Maximus has many fine points. He is a good man and well-meaning. But stress can make him do odd things. I apologize for his behavior on your first day. Please do not hold it against my son." He grinned. "At least not for long."

"No apology needed. It did not upset me."

"Ah! I will ask your forgiveness a hundred more times."

Angelina placed her hand on his arm. "And my reply will always be the same."

"In your eyes, I see you are wise, like your father. The past several days, I have seen many of Rosario's traits in you." Cupping her chin, Vito added. "Only you are much prettier! Definitely, a trait from your mother!"

"Thank you."

"Maximus said you still cannot remember traveling here."

Angelina sighed. "None of it."

"You have forgotten nothing important. It is a miserable journey if you ask me."

"Vito, do not fill her head with nonsense," Philamena said, joining them. "With the proper attitude, it can be delightful!"

Vito waved her comment away with both hands.

"Blah! You can have it! I will return to Italy once more."

"Why only once?" Angelina asked.

"The day you are a bride is one I will not miss."

As they did every day, the trio sat in a spacious living room with an over-sized fireplace at one end. Two sets of windows flanked the double door that led to the main veranda and patio. The room's elegance matched the beautiful scenic view. Their effortless conversations were delightful. Angelina could not remember a time when she felt so relaxed. Vito and Philamena's hospitality quickly made Angelina forget the incident of being locked away.

Either by instruction from his parents or his own wisdom, Angelina only saw Maximus at supper. After the evening meal, he did not stay to visit. He politely excused himself.

Vito and Angelina settled in their seats, and Philamena poured the tea and placed sweets on a plate for each of them.

"I am curious." Angelina began. "The young man I met on my first day here. He did not give me his name. Is he your youngest son?"

"You have not seen him because he left." Vito grumbled.

"Because of me?"

Vito scooted to the edge of his seat. He looked at Angelina and sighed. "I will tell you what only a few people know..."

"Oh, good afternoon, Freddy." Philamena glared at Vito.

"Ma'am," Freddie replied with a slight bow.

"Would you like to join us?"

"That is kind. However, I am here for Miss Beretta."

"Oh?" Philamena frowned. "But we are having our tea. Could you come back in an hour?"

"No, Ma'am. It will be too dark."

"Too dark for what?" Angelina asked.

"Mrs. Fiori, I promise tomorrow we will get an earlier start," Freddy said, bowing his head in respect. "Miss Beretta, please come with me."

Angelina hesitated.

"It is alright, dear." Philamena patted Angelina's hand. "You are safe with Freddy. We can visit after dinner."

With a forced smile, Angelina nodded.

"Here, take a pastry. You can eat it on the way. Freddy, would you like one too?"

"Only a fool would pass up *your* pastries, Ma'am."

Philamena blushed.

"Always a pleaser, aren't you? No wonder my son loves you so well," she said, wrapping the pastry in a napkin.

Freddy and Angelina gave their thanks before walking down the long hall. Her heels clicking against the black and gold marble floor drew Freddy's attention.

"We will stop at the stables. You can change there."

"Change into what?" She looked at her shoes.

Freddy smiled. "You will see."

"Is everything a mystery with you?"

"No, Miss Beretta."

"Oh. Well, that clears things up."

Opening the door, Freddy laughed. "I will explain more soon, I promise."

They walked down a stone path on a side of the estate she had yet to visit. Her inquisitive eyes panned the area in awe of the beauty and serenity of the manicured garden. The path ended at a square patio. In each corner was a stone pillar supporting a domed roof. A stone balustrade offered support to Angelina as she moved down the left set of curved staircases. The steps made a semi-circle around a koi pond. A stream of water flowed into the pool from a replica of Zeus's face.

Freddy did not stop at the bottom of the steps. He continued down the walk toward a garden arbor covered in red roses.

"We are almost there," Freddy hollered back.

"Is there no end to this place?"

"It took two years to memorize every path. In my defense, Mrs. Fiori added a new garden or structure every few months."

"*She* designed all of this?"

"I would say she influenced some of it. If Boss has a vision for something, he will make it happen. He asked his mother to help with some details, mainly to give her something to do."

"Instead of nagging him?"

Freddy grinned. "It is healthier for the mind to be busy creating something..."

"Rather than criticizing it?"

"You have been here for three days?"

"Four."

"Boss was right."

"Oh?"

"You are very perceptive." Freddy extended his arm. "Here we are."

They emerged from the shaded tunnel into the bright late-afternoon sunshine. A hundred feet away stood a long, red barn. To the left of the barn, in the metal corral, a coal-black colt stood wobbly next to his mamma as she nudged him.

"That is Midnight," Freddy said. "Hopefully, he is as fast as his father. If not, we have two other mares ready to give birth sometime this month. Have you ever seen a horse give birth?"

"No. I don't know anyone who owns a horse."

"I will let you know if one goes into labor. It is an amazing thing to watch."

Entering the barn, the potent smell of fresh hay and manure assaulted Angelina. She covered her nose.

"You get used to it," Freddy said, handing her his handkerchief.

Freddy led Angelina to the other end of the barn, introducing her to each horse they passed.

"Boss has eighteen. Well, nineteen with Midnight. If all goes well, he will have a flush twenty-one by month-end."

"They are beautiful."

"Do you know how to ride?"

Angelina shook her head.

"I will teach you how. But you must learn something a little more practical first." Freddy pointed to the building fifty yards from the barn. "While I get things ready, go into that building. Jan is expecting you."

Cautiously, Angelina entered the two-story red and white building. To her left was a pleasant woman in jeans and a western shirt. She looked up from her desk and greeted Angelina.

"There you are. I expected you an hour ago. I reckon Freddy took the long way to get here. He says he doesn't enjoy strolling through the gardens, but he sure does it a lot. He is a teddy bear at heart. Don't believe otherwise," Jan said, leading Angelina down the hall. "Anyway, Freddy wants you to change into something more suitable. He thinks we are close in size. I think he is right, but don't tell him I said so. In that room, you'll find a pair of jeans, a shirt, and boots. No need to return them. Keep them. I have a dozen more."

With her new attire, Angelina emerged from the dressing room, frequently looking down at her outfit.

"Ah! Fits you perfectly. I will send your things back to the big house. You can go out that door down there. Freddy is waiting for you," Jan said. "Enjoy!"

Freddy was leaning against a giant oak tree, smoking a cigarette while waiting patiently for Angelina.

"It is a good look for you!" Freddy said, smashing his smoke into the gravel path with his large shoe.

"I feel silly. Like I am dressed up for a play."

"I'm guessing you have never worn wranglers?"

"Wranglers?"

"The jeans." Freddy chuckled, picking up the two bags.

Angelina shrugged her shoulders in confusion.

"Never mind. You have never ridden a horse, so am I safe to assume you have never shot a gun?"

She stopped abruptly. "A gun?"

"Didn't think so."

Freddy continued to walk, but shock held her still.

"Are you Afraid?"

Angelina nodded.

"Now, you know why I didn't tell you what we were going to do."

Freddy walked back, slipped his arm in hers, and guided her down the meandering path through the trees.

"Boss wants you to learn how to shoot."

"Why?"

"For your safety."

"Safety from what?"

"Miss Beretta, I don't know all the answers, only the information Maximus shares. As to why, I really don't know, other than I thought it was a good idea."

Freddy led Angelina to a small wooden picnic table at the edge of a wide-open field. He removed three hard-shell cases and nine boxes of ammo out of the two bags.

"First, I will teach you the basics and the rules you *always* follow. They are for your safety and that of anyone around you. No one wants to kill someone by accident. Rule number one. *Never* point this end at someone unless you intend to kill them!" Freddy pointed to the muzzle. "Rule number two *always* assume the gun is loaded."

Freddy continued with his gun safety instructions before explaining each part of the weapon, sighting in a target, and proper shooting stance. It took nearly an hour to finish the lesson and answer any of Angelina's questions.

"We have enough time to shoot one gun. Which one do you want to start with?"

Angelina smiled and pointed at the blue steel weapon stamped *Beretta*.

"Excellent choice! Now, see those bottles down there," Freddy said, pointing across the field. "I want you to sight one of those bottles in. When you are ready, give me a nod, and I will talk you through each step. Don't get ahead of me, just nice and slow, especially the first few rounds."

Aloud, Angelina repeated every step Freddy told her.

"Barrel down. Check ammo. Position feet." Raising the gun, Angelina added. "Aim. Deep breath and slowly exhale."

"Good. Good," Freddy said. He stepped behind her, placed both hands on her shoulders, and calmly told her the next steps. "Now, both eyes open. Relax your shoulders. Keep your eye on the target. Gently place your finger on the trigger. Take another breath, and as you exhale, squeeze the trigger."

The explosion emanating from the weapon in her hands rattled her to the core. The ringing in her ears was deafening. Except for her racing heart, Angelina's body became a statue only supported by Freddy's large hands.

"Miss Beretta?"

Angelina did not hear him. She was lost in her senses. Her jaw was clenched, her body rigid, and there was a tingling vibration in her palms. The loud eeeEEEeee in her ears held her hostage. Even her lungs refused to move. Freddy stepped closer to her and spoke loud enough to overpower the high-pitched ring in her ears.

"Miss Beretta? You all right?"

She nodded.

"I know the smell may be unpleasant, but you need to breathe."

The grey cloud lingering in the still air tingled her nose as she inhaled the acrid smoke. Angelina relaxed her arms to her side and turned to look at Freddy.

"Actually, I like the smell." A smile pressed her cheeks. "I liked all of it. The power, the sound, the...the...everything!"

Freddy released a boisterous laugh. "Boss was right. You are something else."

"What is that supposed to mean?" Angelina demanded with a furrowed brow.

"It means you are quite a woman. God did not make many like you. Consider it the highest of compliments!" Freddy patted her shoulder. "Now, let's have some more fun."

Angelina returned to her firing position and repeated every step aloud. Each shot increased her confidence with the weapon. When her body appeared more relaxed, Freddy stepped back for her to experience a shooter's solidarity. The mental void free of all thoughts and emotions.

"Tomorrow, I will teach you about ammo," Freddy said, reloading the gun a third time. "You are getting the hang of this faster than most, and your aim is real good, too. Boss will be pleased."

The fading sunlight gave the trees surrounding the meadow an eerie aura. The dropping temperature made their breath visible, adding to the spookiness.

Angelina rubbed her arms and bounced a little to keep warm.

"Are you cold?"

"A little."

"We can go—"

"No. I am fine!" Angelina interrupted.

Freddy chuckled and placed the gun in Angelina's extended hand.

"After this, we need to head back. Even I don't like meandering around out here in the dark."

"I wouldn't take you as a man easily spooked."

"Everyone has a weakness, Miss Beretta."

CHAPTER 63

"Carmella, this is my new maid, Margaret," Catalina said. "She will come with me each day and assist with the household duties and a few of the simpler jobs in the vineyard. Today, she can begin in the house. Instruct her on the duties you need the most help with. I need to talk with Carlos."

As they walked toward the house, Carmella, in a motherly tone, asked Margaret questions about her age, what skill she had as a cook, and if she could do laundry. The heartwarming sight was confirmation that it was a wise decision to bring Margaret to the vineyard.

"Thank you, Cat. My wife can use the help."

Catalina held her hand up to shield her eyes from the glaring sun behind Carlos. His sadness and exhaustion created heavy bags under his eyes. Though Carlos was never an overly cheerful man, he never clung to misery as he did now. He was a wretched soul consumed with the agony of loss and extreme fatigue.

"I am sorry, Rodolfo cut the staff. The season may well be ending, but the work never stops. A concept he does not understand."

"Who is Rodolfo?"

"Giorgio's Zio." To soothe Carlos's look of shock, she added, "He asked me to call him by his first name."

Carlos's eyes widened.

"Oh, stop gawking. A name is a name."

"If you say."

"Where are we on deliveries? Rodolfo told me you are behind. Is that true?"

Carlos flinched again. As if The Don's name still lingered in the air with a whip ready to strike, Carlos dropped his head and mumbled his response.

"A little behind, yes."

"How much is a little?"

"Two days behind. It was three, but a customer canceled their order because of the delay."

"Marvelous!" Catalina flung her arms up. "Another reason we need to hire workers!"

"Don Salvatore said they cost too much."

"A loss of sales costs too much! How many men do you need to catch up and stay caught up?"

"Until spring, three or four."

"Hire three. Tell them we will only keep one permanently. Hopefully, the competition will make each work harder."

"What of Don Salvatore?"

"I will handle him. Fire no one unless I tell you to do so! He thinks he can have his grubby hands in this business, but I will tell him he cannot and will not ruin my father's legacy!"

A smile formed on Carlos's lips.

"What is so funny?" Catalina asked with a hand on her hip.

"You are your mother and father all in one. Sophia's fire and Rosario's mind."

Catalina blushed. "Thank you. That is kind of you to say. Sometimes, I wonder if I am adopted because I see none of my parents in me."

Carmella reappeared in time to emphatically profess the falseness of Catalina's comment. "I pulled you from your mother myself! You are her daughter, through and through!"

"So many changes makes it tough to know one's true self."

A blaring horn from down the drive ended their conversation. The dust billowing behind the delivery truck consumed the black car trailing behind.

"Nan, what are you doing?" Catalina scoffed. "Are you trying to piss him off?"

"Is that The Don behind the truck?" Carmella fretted.

Nodding, Carlos wrapped his arm around his wife.

"What has gotten into him." Carmella trembled. "He is not my boy anymore. Ever since..."

Carlos pulled his emotional wife in close.

"It is a phase, my dear. Only a phase."

"A phase that will end in death!" Carmella sobbed.

"I will take care of this. Go inside. Don Salvatore will know your weakness if he sees you crying." Catalina placed a hand on Carmella's shoulder. "Carlos, it would be best."

"Yes, I will stay out of sight too."

Still comforting her, Carlos led Carmella into the house. From the kitchen, Catalina heard Margaret's sweet voice soothing the weeping old woman.

"Margaret, you are an angel sent to heal this place and all connected to it."

Fernando did not stop at the house. He drove up the hill to the cellar, the truck spitting gravel and dust into the air. To avoid the flying stones, Catalina covered her face and looked away. A lesson she learned years ago when Anton stormed up the drive, launching a rock that chipped her tooth. Though Anton gave her a heartfelt apology, the damage remained.

The Don abruptly stopped his car in front of Catalina. He rolled the window down and violently pumped his fist.

"Who the hell is driving that truck!" Don Salvatore barked. "I will have him hanging by his nutsack!"

"Rodolfo! Watch your language! I am appalled you would say such disgusting things in front of a lady!"

The Don's face grew redder and redder as he sat behind the wheel, silently fuming. His nostrils flared with each inhale, reminding Catalina of a bull contemplating its attack.

"Have you come to lend a hand?" Catalina asked, circumventing any other explosion of anger from him.

"Nothing of the sort! I am here to collect the money from that young man's delivery!" Don Salvatore pointed up the hill at Fernando.

"There is no money to collect today!"

Don Salvatore jumped out of the car and stood toe to toe with Catalina.

"I have had enough of your insolence!"

"Likewise!" Catalina growled. "You are not in charge here. I don't know *who* told you you were."

"I told myself!"

"Then you, Rodolfo, are misinformed! Your ignorance of the process has already cost us orders and blemished our impeccable image."

"I did nothing of the sort! Why would I jeopardize any money?"

"You did, and it will come out of *your* cut! A direct order from my father!"

"Your father said no such thing! He knows better than to challenge me! A bit of wisdom, I see you have yet to inherit!"

"We are two days behind schedule on deliveries. Something that has *never* happened in the history of this business!"

"Then, your monkeys need to work harder!"

"They are, and we have three new workers starting tomorrow!" Catalina squared her shoulders. "Do not mess with the order of things! You want to make money off this place! I will see to it you make money. If you interfere again with the operations..."

"Are you threatening me?" Don Salvatore roared.

Catalina took two steps away from him. She was trembling inside, but she also felt more alive than ever. The confrontation was exhilarating and terrifying all at once. Out of the corner of her eye, she noticed Carlos standing at the kitchen door. His comment floated through her mind again.

"I am fiery like Mamma!" Catalina thought. *"But now, what do I do?"*

The verbal battle stirred the chickens in the coup behind Catalina. The grumbling cackle from the hens queued a thought. Bickering would get them nowhere.

"Rodolfo." Catalina sweetly sang his name. "Come, this bickering does neither of us good. Didn't you say it is unhealthy for a family to fight?"

"What has become of you?" Don Salvatore adjusted his belt and made sure his shirt was tucked in properly. "Where is my sweet Kitty-Cat?"

"I am overworked, Zio. Which makes me tired. Plus, I am still grieving my family's loss."

"Don Salvatore," Fernando interrupted. Winded from his sprint down the hill, his words flew from his lips between breaths. "May...I... speak with...you?"

A scowl hardened Catalina's face.

"Nan, this is not a good time. Rodolfo is busy."

"Please, Don Salvatore." Fernando bowed his head slightly. "I believe you will find value in what I have to say."

"Of course, my boy!" Don Salvatore beamed, glad to be done with Catalina. "You look dreadful. Why so distraught?"

"May we speak alone? It is a private matter."

"Yes, of course, my boy." Don Salvatore placed his hand on Fernando's shoulder. Glancing back at Catalina with a wily grin, he added. "Speak freely, my boy. *Everything* you say will remain private."

CHAPTER 64

The next three mornings, to avoid interfering with Philamena's afternoon tea, Freddy took Angelina to the open field after breakfast. Today, her target was upgraded from several old cans to a scarecrow wearing a tattered wig of red hair, worn leather gloves, and a pair of mismatched shoes. Dangling from the target's neck was an orange tie with a giant paper heart pinned to it.

"Do you like my masterpiece? His name is Arnold."

"You made that? So much hidden talent!"

"He looks like an Arnold, don't you think?"

Angelina faked an emphatic tone. "Oh, yes! Definitely."

Freddy's expression quickly shifter her serious expression to laughter. His suppressed amusement, jiggling his belly, cracked her seriousness. They released a roar of laughter.

"You have a great sense of humor, Miss Beretta."

"I don't think your Boss feels the same way."

"He's under a tremendous amount of stress."

"Because of the threat Vito mentioned my first day here?"

"Do you know how many businesses Maximus owns?"

"One!" Angelina shrugged.

"Maximus *owns* four and is a partner in several others."

"Oh. I didn't know."

"There's a lot you don't know about Maximus. He's not the type to brag about his success or flaunt it to impress people."

"Definitely a refreshing change."

"From?"

"My brother-in-law. He is an egotistical jerk!" Angelina fired off six consecutive shots. "He could be an Arnold."

Freddy held up the binoculars and smiled.

"Very nice! Now I know."

She crinkled her brow in confusion.

"I thought wearing an orange tie was grounds for being shot. Your accuracy says Arnold is a jerk! I stand corrected!"

She laughed and emptied her magazine into Arnold.

"Here, try the 1911. I think you will like it. Has a bit more kick, so be prepared."

After performing the proper inspection steps, Angelina sighted in on Arnold but paused.

"Where did you meet Maximus?"

"We met in high school. Maximus was the new kid, fresh off the boat. His inability to speak English made it easy for some to dislike him. If he could have spoken as well as you do, his school years would be filled with pleasant memories."

"I had an excellent teacher. An extraordinary woman. She was a loyal friend to my family."

"Who?"

Angelina glanced at him with a reproving glare.

"Nice try, don't change the subject!"

Freddy grinned. "One day, a few fellas were planning to hurt Maximus. It was what the rich kids called a 'rite of passage' for foreigners. Max was in three classes with me. He seemed like a good guy. So, I found out when and where the elite planned to attack. A few of my friends from the football team showed up to even the playing field. It was a quick fight. I punched the ringleader in his nose. It exploded in blood. Another hidden talent of mine." Freddy grinned. "The guy fell flat on his ass and passed out. Before the rest of his crew fled, I warned them if they touched Maximus, they better know a good surgeon because they would be next."

"What did he do to earn your loyalty?" Angelina asked, reloading the M1911.

Freddy gave a small smile. "When my family... when *I* needed him the most, he helped me with my problem."

"Which was?"

"If you knew, would it help mend your opinion of him?"

Angelina hesitated. "Perhaps." She looked at the gun for a moment, then flippantly added. "Unless he killed someone."

"Not all men need to take a life to make a difference, Miss Beretta." Freddy admonished her. "He is different from most men in power. *Far* different from most men."

"Have you ever..."

Holding up his hand, Freddy interrupted her.

"Miss Beretta, I will not lie to you. But don't ask a question you do not want to know the answer to."

Angelina opened her mouth to repeat the question, but his intense gaze stopped her.

"Why do you want to know?" Freddy asked. "Does knowing my past make me any different of a man than I am, right here, right now?"

"Yes, it would!" She replied emphatically. "You cannot kill a human and be the same as you were before you took a life."

"You love your father, who in your eyes was a great man. Very respectable, right?"

"My father *is* a great man!"

"Your father has killed men?"

Angelina took a couple steps back from Freddy. Her face flushed with anger.

"My father never..."

"Careful, Miss Beretta!" Freddy said, holding up his index finger. "Your father was a soldier in the Great War."

"That is not the same!"

"Why? He took another's life!"

"Because he had to, or he would die!" Angelina argued.

"That is precisely my point. It is not a man's actions that make him. It is the purpose of his actions."

"I disagree!"

Ignoring her, Freddy picked up the pair of binoculars and looked at Arnold's paper heart.

"Nice job. Your cluster is tight. We may need to adjust the sights. You are consistently hitting low and to the left." Freddy held out his hand. "I will make some adjustments while you shoot a different gun."

Angelina did not press him further about his past. It was clear he would not answer. She attempted to ask other questions, but Freddy remained mute unless they pertained to guns or ammo.

"That is enough shooting for today," Freddy commanded after an hour of silence. "I have something to show you."

"What?"

Freddy gave her an expressionless glare.

"Ah! The mysterious Freddy returns!"

Vincenzo greeted them at the stone veranda.

"Fredrick. Miss Beretta. You are back early. Lunch will not be ready for another hour."

"Good. That will give us enough time." Freddy replied, handing Vincenzo the guns. "All of them go back, except this one. Leave it in my room."

"Of course, Fredrick."

Angelina covered her mouth to hide her amusement.

"And what is so funny," Freddy grumbled after Vincenzo was out of earshot.

"Nothing, *Fredrick!*"

"Cute...very cute."

His gruff tone melted Angelina's smile.

"Miss Beretta, I do not mean to upset you."

"Then don't!"

"Miss Beretta, what do you want me to do?"

"What do *I* want, Fredrick? I want to know why everyone whispers behind my back." She folded her arms. Her tone was harsher with each word. "How did I get here? When do I get to go home? *That* is what I want!"

"Somethings are not for me to say. My job is to teach you how to defend yourself."

"From what? Can you at least tell me that?"

"Sometimes, all you need is to get away." Freddy continued. "Get free and live to fight later."

"My father said the same thing."

"A wise man. Now, if Arnold came up behind you, a gun would do you no good. It is too close. He could easily disarm you. So, what you do is grate your high heel down his shin, right here." Freddy lifted his pant leg, exposing the front of his leg. "You can't see it through my fat calves, but there is a bone here that hurts like hell when you scrape it with a sole."

"You know from experience?"

"Something like that." Freddy chuckled. "Now, that only gives you a second to jab him in the ribs with your elbow." Stepping behind her, he wrapped his arm around her midriff. "Now, pretend I am Arnold."

In protest of the exercise, she tried to step forward, but his grip tightened.

"See what I mean? You can't escape unless you hit the shin."

Angelina gently scraped the front of his leg.

"Good, good!" Freddy applauded. "Follow with a sharp jab of your elbow into my rib." He pointed to his side. "Try again, but harder. I am not made of fine china."

For the next hour, Freddy worked with Angelina on techniques for breaking free of an attacker. His lessons were composed of quick and simple but effective moves that left no time for chitchat.

"Lunch is ready." Vincenzo announced from the door.

"Five more minutes." Freddy held up his hand.

"Very well. I will inform Mrs. Fiori." Vincenzo responded before disappearing.

"Let's try this again. But, hit me like you mean it."

"What? No! I..."

"I can take it, come on. I know you have it in you! Remember to stay balanced on both feet. If you are wobbly, it will be easy to overpower you."

A loud scream exploded from inside the house, followed by the sound of three gunshots.

"Stay under the veranda!" Freddy ordered. "Do *not* move from there unless I tell you!"

Angelina nodded, but Freddy was already storming through the door. In her shaded spot, she heard his feet thunder up the stairs.

From the south side of the house came another shrilling scream followed by three more shots. Angelina flinched. Carefully, she moved toward the ruckus. From the corner, Angelina looked around but saw no one until an explosion of glass rained down five yards away. A man jumped from the second-story window, landing on the soft hill like a seasoned stuntman. In a gentle roll, he sprung to his feet and disappeared into the rose garden.

Angelina looked up at the dark-haired woman with a pistol in her hand. Watching the man flee, the wind whipped the woman's long locks. In the swirling air, a cluster of leaves stirred by Angelina, drawing the woman's attention. Their gazes met, but only for a moment. The tires squealing in the distance broke the visual connection. When Angelina looked up again, Freddy, fuming, was standing in the window, and the woman was no longer in sight.

"Mother Fucker!" Freddy barked, tucking his gun back into his side holster. Turning back inside, he continued his rampage. "Who left you alone? I'll kill the damn bastard!"

Angelina returned to the terrace where she and Freddy had been practicing. Waiting for his return, she paced back and forth while a string of questions raced through her mind.

"When I tell you to stay put, dammit, stay the fuck put!" Freddy yelled as he stormed out the door. "What if that ignafuck saw you? Huh? You know how much money he would get just for knowing you exist? Everyone on this Estate has a price on their head. I will be damned if I let any of them get paid! Next time I tell you to stay put, stay the fuck put!"

Angelina took several steps back from the giant growling beast that shouted at her.

"Get in the house." Freddy roared, waving off Angelina's response. "I got to handle this mess!"

"What are you going to do?"

"What do you think?"

Freddy was gone before Angelina could plead the case for the intruder's life or inform Freddy his hunt was futile.

"Are you okay?" Philamena asked Angelina.

"Yes, I am fine. Are you?"

"We are fine. These things happen all the time. Nothing for you to worry about, my dear."

"Philamena, was that man after one of us?"

"Nonsense, it was just a robber looking for something to steal." Philamena wrapped her arm around Angelina. "You have nothing to worry about, my dear."

"That is not entirely true," an angelic voice said from the stairs. "He was looking for you, Miss Beretta."

Angelina broke free of Philamena's hug to see the woman from the window slowly walking down the staircase.

"How do you know?" Angelina asked.

The woman held Angelina's gaze as she elegantly descended the staircase, one step at a time. The sunlight danced on her dark locks, and her long slender legs peeked out of the slit of her form-fitting black dress. She was alluring and graceful in every movement.

Angelina was envious of the woman's radiant beauty and grace. But Angelina imagined she was not the first to envy the woman's looks.

"Because he tried to beat it out of me."

The halo of light behind her shifted enough for Angelina to see the growing bruise on the woman's left cheek.

"Are you hurt?" Philamena asked.

"I will be fine, Mamma. It's not the first time a man has struck me, nor do I believe it will be the last." The woman touched her jaw and winced. "But don't worry, *he* didn't leave here unscathed."

"You need to keep the swelling down!" Philamena insisted, racing to the kitchen. "I will get you some ice."

"She worries too much. But isn't that what mothers do?"

"Philamena, is your mother?"

"I am not surprised Maximus has kept me a secret. I imagine he has not told you much about our family. He thinks more than he talks." The woman criticized. With a wane smile, she added. "He has always been that way, though. He is not alone; everyone in this house is good with keeping secrets."

"Olivia, come lie down and hold this to your cheek." Philamena insisted, carrying a towel filled with ice.

"It will be fine. Now, both cheeks will match."

In her heavenly descent, the light behind Olivia cast a shadow that concealed her right cheek. Dispassionate, she allowed Angelina a glimpse at the scar that slashed through her eyebrow and extended down to her ear.

Philamena stood with one hand on her hip, the other holding the towel in Olivia's face, but Olivia waved her off.

"Either you hold it to your cheek, or I will!"

"If it will ease *your* pain, mother."

"Would you like another knot on the back of your head?" Philamena snapped. "Hold this, or I will!"

Angelina suppressed her smile. The two strong-minded women were determined to be in charge. The exchange was similar to Angelina and her own mother.

"When will he be home?" Olivia asked. "This needs to be handled *immediately*!"

"How did anyone know I was here?" Angelina interrupted.

"News travels fast, especially when others can prosper. Mamma, as much as it pains me to say it, Maximus was correct. But it appears they have accelerated the hunt for Miss Beretta." Olivia looked around the room. "Where is Freddy?"

"He went after the man who jumped," Angelina said.

"Oh, Freddy. He was long gone before you made it to the first row of trees."

"A car drove off before he came outside." Angelina sighed.

Olivia leaned back against the padded arm of the loveseat. A gold brocade pattern flowed through the deep magenta fabric . It matched the gold tone of the lace slip peeking out the slit of Olivia's dress. It was an alluring accent that few women braved to wear. Olivia's brazen persona and her stunning figure did not need the added temptation. Even with the mutilation on her cheek, Olivia was gorgeous.

"Do you feel comfortable with a gun yet?" Olivia asked.

Speechless, Angelina sat in the armchair next to Olivia. Her mouth dry, she tried to mumble a response but failed.

"It is a yes or no answer. Miss Beretta. You need to prepare your mind for the inevitable. That man *will* be back."

"How can you be sure?"

"Because he saw you!"

CHAPTER 65

"I thought we could have lunch in here today. Given the excitement, it would not be prudent to use our usual spot in the solarium," Philamena explained, leading Angelina to the small dining room. "A change of scenery from time to time does the mind good."

Angelina looked up at the ceiling extending high above the dark oak table set for six. The room was large enough for ten to dine, but the high arches, creamy-beige walls, and tall windows made the room feel larger.

"Please sit beside me," Philamena said, pulling out a chair.

Olivia settled in across from Angelina, leaving the seat at the head of the table for her mother. Philamena continued to speak as she pulled the dark blue drapes closed. Her chatter was of no importance and made Olivia roll her eyes.

"Sit up straight, Olivia."

"I am, Mother."

The pair bickered back and forth with a poisonous contempt for each other. When Freddy entered the room, they instantly went silent, neither willing to make eye contact with each other or with Freddy.

"Come join us, Freddy," Philamena said, pointing to the chair next to Angelina. "Lunch is nearly ready."

"Thank you, Ma'am. I must handle a few things first. Is everyone okay?"

"Nonsense! You can eat something," Philamena said. "Eating is important, as is what Olivia has to say."

"Ma'am, I..."

"*Sit!*" Philamena's reproving glare cut through Freddy. She was not a woman to trifle with, especially after someone invaded her home.

"Yes, Ma'am."

As Freddy settled into his chair, Vincenzo entered the dining room with a tray of food. Instantly, the aroma of the fresh-baked bread, still warm from the oven, and four bowls of steaming hot clam chowder filled the room.

"Looks delicious, Vincenzo," Philamena praised, patting his forearm. "Do tell George."

"Yes, Ma'am, I will let him know. Is there anything else?"

"No, Vincenzo," Olivia said. "We will ring if we need you."

"Certainly, Miss Fiori. I will be in the kitchen."

Olivia repositioned her bowl to meet an imaginary line and repeated the same with her utensils. Satisfied everything was in order, she delicately raised her spoon and sipped the soup.

Philamena moved like a regal queen, following every formal rule for dining. She placed a slice of butter on her plate, broke off one bite-size piece, and buttered it.

To Angelina's left, Freddy consumed his food in a far different manner. His spoon clanked against the china as he shoveled bite after bite into his mouth. Freddy's chowder was half gone before Olivia or Philamena took their first bite.

Angelina noted the diverse eating habits. Each person's facial expression revealed how they were processing the incident. Olivia was calm in her movements. Her flushed cheeks and furrowed brow showed her anger. Philamena had the perfect poker face, unmoved and stoic. However, her rigid posture spoke to her suppressed tension. Freddy, hunched over, gripped the spoon like a shovel. He attacked the food as if he were devouring the man who got away.

"Angelina, are you unwell?" Philamena gently placed the knife on her bread plate. "You have not touched your soup."

"I am fine." Angelina forced a smile.

"He was looking for Angelina." Olivia interrupted the niceties. "We must handle this before they return."

"Boss has been notified. He will be back within the hour. Once he gives the order..."

Olivia slammed her hand, rattling the dishes. Her face flushed red, and her eyes drilled a hole into Freddy.

"Damn it, Fredrick! I am giving the order. Or is a woman unqualified to make decisions?"

"That is not what I am implying." Freddy's face hardened.

"I don't give a damn what you are or are not implying. All I care about is the safety of the people inside this house. Maximus is not the only one capable of handling things," Olivia hissed. With a cocked brow, she stared at him for a moment. Satisfied her point was made, Olivia tore off a piece of bread and dunked it into her soup as she added in a tempered tone. "You know who to give this to."

Freddy did not move. His lack of response pricked at Olivia's nerves. Unlike her brother, Olivia's temper had a short fuse, ready to explode regardless of her company. Philamena would rant the same but never lost control of her temper in front of guests. A virtue Olivia did not possess.

"Fredrick, acknowledge the statement." Olivia growled, staring at her soup. "Tell me *who* needs to handle this."

"The Suit?"

"Yes, The Suit!" Narrowing her eyes, Olivia looked at Freddy, who was still sitting at the table. "Now is good!"

His displeasure for Olivia's behavior bubbled below the surface, but Freddy did not crack. He politely dabbed his mouth with his napkin before pushing back from the table. Before he could stand, Philamena weighed in.

"You can finish your lunch, Freddy. Then you can call Steven Gimmarro. Fifteen minutes will change nothing."

"Thank you, Ma'am. It's best if I handle this immediately. Olivia is right. Angelina is in danger. *They* will return soon."

Freddy did not look over at Olivia. Her grinding jaw and deadly stare were nothing new. He smiled in gratitude and bowed. He left before Phelamena could press him further.

"That was a little over the top," Philamena scolded Olivia. "Freddy could finish his meal. A man needs to eat!"

"He can miss a meal. He can miss *several* with that waistline."

"You said, *they,* Olivia?" Philamena buttered another bite of bread. "You mentioned one intruder before."

Olivia took another bite and allowed the question to linger in the air while she slowly chewed her bread. To increase her mother's tension, Olivia tore off another piece of bread and dipped it into the chowder before replying.

"Angelina heard tires squealing. Someone was waiting."

"Why assume he had an accomplice? If the intruder jumped into a car, he could easily jump into the driver's seat."

The two headstrong women continued their verbal jabs through the entire meal. Angelina wisely did not add to the argument. The bloody catfight would injure any participant.

After Vincenzo cleared away the last dishes, Angelina excused herself. The porcelain soup bowls with four tiny claw feet reminded her of the soaking tub in her bathroom.

"If I may, I would like to take a hot bath."

"Yes, of course, my dear. You should. I am sure all this commotion has you flustered," Philamena said, giving Angelina a hug. "I will check on you later."

"I am okay." Angelina smiled. "Olivia, it was a pleasure to meet you. I do hope we can visit more soon."

"I look forward to it." A wiley grin pressed Olivia's cheeks. "You will find, unlike the rest of my family, I speak my mind. Something a person in your shoes would appreciate."

Angelina stood on the balcony, pressing a towel against her hair. Despite the chaos from her first day, she quickly became comfortable in the apartment. It was a heavenly retreat to process her interactions. Today's odd comments came from every direction. She hardly knew where to start.

"A peaceful place occupied by unsettled souls." She sighed. "Olivia's words about Maximus are the opposite of Freddy's."

"Then perhaps you should make your own assessment."

Angelina whirled around to find Maximus leaning against the threshold with two glasses of wine. He was smiling, but the dark circles under his eyes, stubbly beard, and pale complexion spoke a different tale.

"I am sorry. I did not mean to startle you." Maximus handed her a glass. "This is my last bottle of Beretta wine. I thought it appropriate to share it with you."

"When did you get wine from us? I do not recall receiving an order from America."

"My father took me to meet your father at the vineyard."

"I have not lost all my memories. You and your father are a pair I would *not* have forgotten."

"Oh?"

"In a good way," Angelina blushed. "Not...Well..."

"It is good to know I would have been memorable."

"I said, you *and* your father as a pair."

"Ah! So close to gaining your respect." Maximus lamented in jest. "If I may sit, I shall tell you the story."

Angelina's cheeks flushed for her lack of hospitality.

"Yes, of course!"

"You were at the market. Your mother was eager for you to return, but we could not stay. We had business in Bergamo. Before we left, your father had a young man, I believe his name was Fernando, load a case of white and red into our trunk."

"Nan never mentioned you."

"It seems your parents did not discuss the visit either."

"Papa mentioned you and the opportunity to expand our distribution at some point. But with Catalina's wedding, he had to put things on hold. Until now." She smiled, holding up her glass in a toast. "To our future business together."

Maximus did not raise his glass. Instead, he gave a slight smile before casting his gaze down and loosening his tie.

"We must discuss business at some point. I cannot recall a few days, but I remember how to sell my father's wine."

As the sunset, the day's warmth quickly faded. A breeze stirring the leaves on the balcony chilled Angelina's damp hair, making her shiver.

"You are cold. Come inside. I will light a fire."

"After the sunset," she said, moving to the railing. "It is so beautiful from up here. My sister has a balcony off of her room that overlooks her garden. In the distance is a small mountain range. I always thought it was the most peaceful place on earth." She glanced at Maximus. "I was wrong."

"There is beauty in everything if you are willing to see it."

"Ah! The stoic philosopher who visited me at the hospital returns. I was afraid he was a figment of my imagination."

Maximus sighed and gave her a weak smile.

"Freddy said you have been under a lot of stress. I hope I am not the cause of any."

"You have brought no stress. One could argue my stress is self-induced." He reached for her empty glass. "May I?"

"Please."

The golden hues illuminating the streaks of thin clouds gradually shifted to orange and red. Angelina felt a deep sadness as if the sun's departure from the sky was a personal loss. As the final beams of light faded away, Anton's face appeared in her mind, tugging at her to return home.

"Soon, my brother. I will be home soon." She whispered.

Angelina watched the sky's second act twinkle across the deep blue curtain. She smiled, remembering her youngest brother's dream of flying.

"Will you sit with me by the fire?" Maximus asked, pulling her from her dreamy state.

Angelina looked at his outstretched hand. His soft, unscathed skin did not have the callouses or scars left by labor. She placed her worn hand in his, and a warmth radiated up her arm.

"So much of your time here has not gone as I had hoped."

"Oh?" A playfulness sparkled in Angelina's eyes. "And what had you hoped?"

"My plan was to have the pleasure of spending time with you. There is so much I wish you could experience. While you were in the hospital, I made a list of the places I thought you would enjoy." Maximus handed her a glass of wine. "Unfortunately, other issues have required my attention."

Angelina relaxed back on the loveseat, sipped her wine, and waited for Maximus to express his apology.

"Freddy informed me of the intruder today."

"Olivia said he was looking for me. She made it sound as if I had a price on my head."

"My sister can be rather dramatic. Don't let her hysteria upset you. I can assure you. You are safe here."

"Why would someone want to hurt me? Is there something that happened you are not telling me?"

"Freddy probably told you I am a man of power. Men with power have enemies. Some we make, others seek us out," Maximus said, stoking the fire. "I am a man plagued with both."

"Is that what your father meant on my first day? The threat was from an enemy he warned you about?"

"Yes. My father warned me, but I did not listen. Now, I must *take my beating,* as he says."

Maximus sat beside her, his knee inches from hers. A warmth fluttered up her core; he had never sat so close to her. Until that moment, she did not realize how strongly she felt for him. While apart, her disdain for him lingered. However, turning to see him on the balcony, all her anger for him instantly melted away. The angst in Angelina's heart was replaced with a deep desire for him to kiss her.

"There is a reason I have not told you how you arrived here. A reason I still believe trumps all others." Maximus set his wine glass on the table. He picked up her hand, cradling it between his. "I cannot prevent you from the truth any longer. My father is right. You deserve to know, but..."

With a pensive gaze, he stared at the fire and jetted his jaw forward. Every time the crackling fire popped, he flinched like a man with battle fatigue. The shadows from the fire's glow deepened the lines on his furrowed brow. Flecks of silver hair and a troubled expression added years to his looks.

Even in forty years, he will still be handsome. Angelina confessed to herself.

"Whatever is troubling you, it cannot be so terrible to tell me," Angelina professed, placing a hand on his.

The loving connection between their layered hands united them in peaceful silence. When Maximus looked up at her, his eyes glistened with tears of overwhelming sadness. Angelina resisted the reflex to lean back in dismay. It was not the look of admiration and love she expected. Behind his onyx eyes lingered the remorse of a sinner longing to confess yet wary of the repercussions.

"Maximus? What have you done?"

"You must believe me when I tell you this was not supposed to happen. None of this was to happen, at least not like it did. My intention was filled with good... with the hope of repaying a debt to an honorable man."

The urge to recoil was too strong. Angelina pulled her hands free from his, fully aware the move would destroy any chance of a budding romance.

"Are you the reason I have lost my memory?"

A knock at the door spared Maximus from her question. Out of respect, he waited for Angelina to answer the knock, but she was lost in a fury of emotions.

"Come in, Vincenzo." Maximus commanded.

"Pardon my interruption, Mr. Fiori. They are at the gate."

"Where is Olivia?"

"In the Apollo Hall. *He* is with her."

Maximus nodded his dismissal. "I will join them soon."

"Sir, there is another issue." Vincenzo hesitated, glancing at Angelina.

Maximus released a quiet growl. He raked his hand through his hair and stood to leave. Looking back at her, the fate of the sinner vanished. He was a handsome man longing for a different life with a beautiful woman.

"I know you want to return home. Though there is so much I want to share with you, it seems fate forbids it." He shook his head and exhaled his sadness. "We will leave for Italy in a few days. My mother will ensure you have everything you need for the trip."

Maximus walked toward the door, bearing life's heaviness on his shoulders. He stopped, his hand gripping the doorknob. His tortured breathing expanded his chest.

"I am a good man, Angelina." Maximus professed. "In my soul, I am an honorable man in a dishonorable world."

The deep sincerity in his voice was an earthquake that shook her heart. Angelina searched for the words to comfort him, to acknowledge his pain, or at the very least, let him know she understood. But only silence, wrapped in his musty cologne, hung in the air, piercing her heart. She moved toward him, but he walked out the door. The sorrow Angelina felt as the sun disappeared on the horizon resurfaced with ten times the intensity. Her silence injured him again.

Angelina choked back the lump in her throat and ran into the hallway. She would not repeat the mistake she made at the hospital.

"Maximus!" Angelina shouted. "Maximus!"

He stopped at the grand staircase but did not look back.

"I believe you!" She exclaimed as a tear rolled down her cheek.

Maximus looked up at her. A sliver of happiness softened his features for a moment.

"Sir, they are waiting," Vincenzo urged.

A seriousness poured over Maximus, hardening like concrete. He raised his chin, straightened his tie, flexed his shoulders, and buttoned his jacket. With a quick flip of his wrist, his gold watch slid down, slightly peeking out from the end of his cuff. The performance of his usual ticks before leaving made Angelina smile. But Maximus did not see her expression of adoration. He had already slipped into the mental prison of a man in power, forced to make decisions that obviously ripped his soul in two.

Angelina darted back into her apartment, stripping out of her robe as she ran to the closet. She dressed quickly while telling herself she needed to be with Maximus out of support, not curiosity or infatuation. Her attempt to style her hair turned into a frustrating nightmare. After fifteen minutes of tugging, placing bobby-pins only to remove them a few seconds later, Angelina gave in. She ran a brush through her hair, smoothed the fly-away strands, and parted it on the side.

"Cat, you make it appear so easy!" Angelina grumbled.

She powdered her nose and finished her beautification with red lipstick. One last glance in the mirror, Angelina admired her ensemble.

"Not bad for a moment's notice," she muttered.

Angelina, racing out the door, did not see Vincenzo walking toward her.

"Miss Beretta. I am glad to see you are dressed. Mrs. Fiori has requested you join her for dinner."

"Oh! Yes. Um... that is exactly where I was heading," Angelina lied.

Vincenzo moved to the side and bowed.

"Thank you," Angelina said with a half-hearted smile.

Trying to walk at a normal pace, Angelina hummed the Ave Maria. The soothing song helped her resist the urge to glance back to see if he was following her.

As she reached the landing, an argument between two men radiated through the front door. Angelina kept her head down, hoping to scurry past the commotion. But Olivia ran into the grand foyer, nearly mowing over Angelina. Behind Olivia was the young man who plucked Angelina from the balcony on her first day at the estate.

"Miss Fiori," Vincenzo called, bringing Olivia to an abrupt stop. "Mr. Fiori has requested you wait in the Apollo Hall."

"Vincenzo, is that who I think it is?"

"Olivia, what is all the ruckus," Philamena barked. "Oh! Hello Angelina." Philamena's scathing glare for her daughter quickly melted into a soft smile for her houseguest. "How are you feeling? Was your bath relaxing?"

"Very, thank you."

"Dinner is running a little late this evening. Shall we all have a drink? Maximus is back from his business trip. He said he has some news to share," Philamena crowed, looping her arm into Angelina's. "Olivia, join us."

Olivia didn't budge. She was transfixed on the front door.

"That was not a request, Olivia!" Philamena barked. "You too, grandson."

Vincenzo poured five glasses of bourbon while Philamena instructed everyone where to sit.

"Vincenzo, only four glasses. Vito will not be joining us this evening."

"Where is Papa?"

Philamena ignored Olivia's questions and introduced her grandson.

"Angelina, this is Vittorio. I understand you have met."

The booming voices moved into the house. With a nod, Philamena instructed Vincenzo to close the door. Before they were sealed into the room, Maximus's tone exposed his frustration.

"God damn it! This is *my* house! Things *will* go *my* way!"

Philamena gave Vincenzo another nod.

"Yes, Mrs. Fiori. I will tell him."

"Mamma, what is going on? Is that..."

"Sit, Olivia. We have a guest in this house, and we will act with respect. When your brother is ready to join us, he will. Until then, find a pleasant subject to discuss while I ask George to bring in some appetizers."

"My family is crazy, Angelina. Every one of them. There is not one thing they can do that does not end in disaster! Do you know the chaos my brother has caused..."

"Olivia!" Philamena snapped. "I said a pleasant topic. Why must you insist on causing problems!"

"See, even I create chaos. At least I am willing to admit it." Olivia rolled her eyes and leaned back on the dark green sofa. "Vittorio, come sit beside me. I will keep you safe from ..."

Before Olivia could finish her sentence, the double doors swung open. Standing slightly behind Maximus was a tall, thin man in a dark grey business suit with golden hair glowing against his flushed face.

"Peter!" Olivia screamed, racing to him. "Is it you?"

Olivia collapsed into Peter's embrace, sobbing.

"Yes, my love. I am here."

Maximus strolled into the room and greeted his mother with a kiss on both cheeks. Philamena whispered something that made him smile for a second before replying. The exchange ended with her chilling, stoic nod of approval.

"Peter, there is someone I would like for you to meet."

Angelina smiled in anticipation of the introduction, but Maximus did not look at her. His blatant rudeness flushed Angelina's cheeks and seized Olivia's attention.

Olivia, wiping the tears from her face, turned around with an expression of horror.

"Maximus, no!"

"Olivia, I think your future husband should know," Maximus replied smugly.

The darkness exuding from Maximus made Angelina nauseated. She could only assume what he was about to do, and his intention was clear.

"Husband?" Olivia cried. "Is that true, Peter? Have you come to ask for my hand?"

"I have already asked Maximus for it, and he gave me his consent," Peter declared as he showered his love with adoration. "Now, all I need is an answer from you."

Peter dropped to one knee. As he looked up at Olivia, his love for her was brighter than the sun on a cloudless day. He removed a small box from his pocket.

"You may want to wait, Peter," Maximus gloated. "My sister has a secret that, man to man, I believe should be disclosed before popping the question."

"Maximus! Why are you so cruel to me?" Olivia bleated. "Why can you not give me any peace? Peter don't listen to him. He is trying to prevent our happiness!"

Olivia's eyes bounced between her love and the man insistent on destroying her life. All the poise, grace, and beauty of the dazzling creature that descended the stairs earlier that day evaporated.

"Maximus, if you destroy this relationship for a second time, I will never forgive you!" Olivia threatened.

"Peter, do you love my sister for all that she is and all that she is not?"

"You know that I do!"

"Then, Olivia, you have nothing to worry about. But I think it only right for a man to decide if he is willing to be a father to another man's son." Maximus surmised, patting Vittorio's shoulder. "It would certainly change *my* opinion."

Olivia looked down at Peter, her cheeks stained with mascara and tears. She held her breath, waiting for Maximus's words to sink in.

"Peter..." Olivia begged. "Please, Peter."

"Is he telling the truth?"

Olivia reluctantly nodded her head.

"I was going to tell you, but..." Olivia blubbered. "But after Maximus threw you out, I thought you would never return."

"You lied to me for six years! How could you keep something like that from me?"

"I didn't lie. I didn't, Peter. When the time was right, I was going to tell you. You must believe me!" Olivia placed her hands gently on Peter's cheeks, begging him to understand. "It is not what you think. Please, Peter! Don't let him destroy us again!"

Peter pushed her hands away and shoved the ring box deep into his pocket.

"Liv, he is right. A child changes things." Peter, gripping the brim of his hat, looked into Olivia's eyes. His lip quivered. "But a lie, Liv. A lie changes *everything*!"

The pride and happiness Peter carried when he walked into the room crumbled into dust. He did not glance back at the audience, mesmerized by the unfolding tragedy. He couldn't. Humiliated, Peter put on his hat and walked out the front door, a defeated man.

Olivia collapsed to the floor, sobbing uncontrollably.

"I hate you, Maximus! I hate you with all my heart!"

"You son of a bitch! How could you destroy my mother's happiness! She was right. You are evil!" Vittorio shouted.

"Vittorio, one day, you will understand what it is to be a man. A man who must make the decisions no one else has the balls or the brains to make. When that day comes, you remember today. Because today, I did your mother a favor!"

"No! You did me no favor! You bastard! You destroyed my life! For what? Why? Please tell me, why do you hate me?"

Maximus bent down and kissed Olivia's head.

"I do not hate you, Livy. I never have."

"He is all your fault! He is a bastard because of you!" Olivia sobbed.

Maximus gently kissed Olivia's head again. Standing tall, he looked at his mother and waited for her dismissing nod. An aura of power and strength seeped from Philamena's regal stature. She withheld her assent for a moment to allow the full import of her expressionless glare to settle in.

Patiently, Maximus waited next to his sobbing sister, his hand resting on her shoulder. The powerful nonverbal conversation between mother and son filled the air with immense tension. When Philamena finally nodded, Maximus leveled his chin. He quietly walked away.

CHAPTER 66

Angelina bolted up from her bizarre dream, her heart racing and chest heaving. She rubbed the awful scenes from her eyes and steadied her breathing, grateful the bloody nightmare no longer held her captive.

"Dear God, could I have a normal dream for once?" she asked, dangling her feet off the edge of the bed.

Angelina took a drink from the glass of water on her bedside table, her eyes lingering on the brown envelope propped up by the vase of fresh flowers.

"Perhaps I could have a normal dream if I had a normal day," Angelina mumbled.

The contents of the envelope became icing to the day's bizarre events.

In Maximus's wake, Olivia collapsed against the floor, sobbing. Angelina raced to her side, but she was the only one. Philamena and Vincenzo silently left the room, and Vittorio was traumatized into a sniffling little boy. Angelina helped Olivia to her room and drew her a bath. Her intention was to sit at Olivia's bedside the entire night, but Philamena summoned Angelina.

Angelina returned to her apartment and found Maximus's mother pensively staring into the roaring fire. She admired how Philamena could hold her chin level and shoulders square despite the chaos. But at that moment, standing in the fire's orange glow, was not a formidable woman.

"You told Maximus to do it, didn't you?" Angelina demanded, her voice more forceful than she intended. "How can you be so cruel to your own daughter?"

"I am not a bad person, Angelina." Philamena eyes focused on the golden flames playfully dancing. "When you are a mother, you will understand that your child's safety is far more important than their happiness."

In the amber light, the permanent damage caused by the day's stress was written in the deep lines on Philamena's face. A single day aged her a dozen years.

Though the signs of remorse were present, Angelina refused to accept the woman's behavior. It was an unthinkable act for someone to treat a family member with such disdain. Angelina vowed to never be nor tolerate such heartlessness.

"My mother would never be so cruel."

"Then she is a lucky woman," Philamena replied. "Sometimes, it is more painful to make the right choice than to watch the chaos it brings."

Philamena looked up from the fire for the first time since Angelina entered the room. The woman's heavy sadness clung to her lips, intensifying her frown. The vibrant luster in Philamena's eyes was washed away by the tears that stained her face.

"Angelina, the difficulties of life are not obstacles strategically placed to stop you from achieving. Life's struggles are the fuel to propel you forward, to make you stronger and wiser. But most of all, the challenging times create an appreciation for even the smallest of successes in life. What Maximus and I did tonight would appear unthinkable to an outsider. But if you glimpse behind the curtain hiding all the facts, you would see the necessity of our actions." Philamena handed Angelina the envelope, a fresh stream of tears cascading down her cheeks. "This is enough money to buy your way home and back a dozen times. I hope you return for another visit soon. Leaving here with such a sour memory as your last may deter you, but I pray it will not."

Angelina's thumb fanned the money, rapidly flashing the number twenty in the upper corner. The amount of cash did not shock her. Most of their customers paid with paper money. But the crisp, untouched state made the twenty-dollar bills seem fake. Angelina shook off her concerns. American money was something she had rarely seen.

Glass shattering and a shrill from Philamena yanked Angelina from her thoughts. She grabbed her robe. Ramming her arm into the sleeve, she saw a body lying prone in the patch of grass below her open window. The waning moon cast enough light to determine it was a man, but not his identity. A lingering shadow of déjà vu exhaled a chilly breath on Angelina's neck. She shook her body to erase the sensation, but the icy trickle down her spine did not abate.

"Do not mix the scenes of your night terrors with reality!"

Her heart pounding, Angelina closed her eyes and drew in a deep breath, but the vision of a body floating down a stream snapped her eyes open. A sick feeling in her gut bubbled, and her head throbbed. She sat in the window seat, attempting to regain her composure. But another thundering echo of a gunshot negated any chance of being calm. Angelina jumped to her feet and instinctually ran to help. She abruptly stopped at her door.

"*My* gun!"

Angelina opened the top drawer of the bedside table. As she wrapped her hand around the grip, she recalled Freddy's first lesson.

"Are you afraid?"

"Terrified!"

"Good. You should be. Guns are dangerous. And when a gun is handled by someone who doesn't know how to use it, well... let's just say things get messy. Now, hold the gun like this and let your fear melt into the grip. Think of the handle as a dry sponge waiting to soak up all your fear and nervousness."

In that first lesson, Freddy told her many things, but giving her fear *to* the gun seemed like a fairy tale. Yet, at each daily lesson, Angelina understood what Freddy meant. Soon, her trembling hands became steady.

A round of gunfire followed by Philamena's wailing tightened Angelina's grip on the gun. Her thundering pulse thumping against her eardrums, Angelina flung the door to her apartment open. Her stomach lurched, and the oxygen in her lungs vanished. Instead of seeing the gold brocade rug stretching the length of the hall, she saw a frightening vision of a wide-eyed face gazing up from the cellar steps in her family home. Angelina blinked several times to push past the hallucination, but something about the vision seemed too real. The trembling woman's half-illuminated face was that of her own.

"Now is not the time to remember my nightmares," Angelina snapped. "Focus!"

Angelina registered every sensation of the present moment to bring a mental space between her and the haunting hallucinations. She consciously noted the cold marble beneath her bare feet, the flutter of her open robe as she darted down the hall, and the brisk night air nipping at her flushed cheeks.

Nearing the grand staircase, Angelina swiftly performed Freddy's mandatory pre-firing routine.

"Mag full, round in, safety green, finger long, grip strong," Angelina recited.

Both hands gripping the pistol, her eyes scanning the darkness, Angelina descended the stairs. At the first landing, she huddled close to the railing, creeping slowly down the last set of steps. To her left, the skirmish had shifted to verbal assaults and the destruction of furniture.

Angelina slowed her descent, looking around for anyone in the dark foyer. She saw no one. Halfway down the steps, the air temperature dropped significantly, and the marble beneath her bare feet felt like ice. She looked at the front door. It was slightly ajar, allowing the chilly night air to creep across the main floor.

Her hand firmly gripped the gun. She stopped at the bottom step. A sense of doubt washed over her. Could she actually kill someone? It was a valid question that zipped through her mind seconds before two shots screamed through the air toward her. Every fiber of her body froze, all but her mind rapidly flashing scenes from her life. One bullet zinged past so close to her left ear, she could feel its heat. The second shot grazed her right arm. The searing pain screamed for a moment, then vanished when another loud crash came from the Apollo room.

She heard Maximus grunt from exertion as he fought the intruder. Peeking through the slightly open door, Angelina saw a body lying on the floor. Her panic shifted to survival mode. Holding the gun up, ready to shoot, she slipped into the room and huddled behind a chair.

Her eyes darted around, taking in the scene in a matter of seconds. To the left, behind a turned over armchair, was

Philamena, unconscious with a bright red mark on her face. Through the doorway to the adjoining room, Angelina saw a body that she only imagined was Olivia or Vittorio. The frame was too small to be Freddy.

On her right, Maximus was on the floor between the sofa and the broken glass coffee table, beating the intruder's face. A solid kick to Maximus's groin made him buckle in pain. His opponent became the aggressor, landing one powerful blow after another.

The intruder paused long enough to grab a shard of glass. It was a mistake. Maximus seized the opportunity, driving a hard punch into the man's kidney. The intruder weakened, cradled his torso, and Maximus jumped to his feet, ready to re-engage.

Maximus's busted lip was swollen. Blood trailed down his cheek from the wound on his temple. Several gashes across his chest turned the white fibers of his tank top red.

The intruder cradled his broken ribs. He spit blood onto the creamy white rug covered in shattered glass. The recent blows to the man's face had yet to portray the actual level of damage. His shallow breathing and the gashes on his arms showed Maximus had delivered several mighty blows.

As the two men faced off, fists up, ready to reconvene their fight, Angelina watched for a clean shot. Despite her agitation for his antics a few hours before, Angelina did not dare risk shooting Maximus. She would prefer maiming him for his behavior rather than killing him.

Angelina snuck over to examine Philamena. Placing her fingers on her neck, Angelina palpated for a pulse. She felt nothing.

"No, no, no! You can't die!"

Angelina repositioned her fingers against Philamena's carotid artery. Closing her eyes, Angelina focused on finding a pulse. Finally, she felt a thin, faint beat.

"*At least she is alive and breathing,*" Angelina sighed.

Keeping low to the floor, she hid behind the furniture as she crawled over to examine the motionless body.

"Oh, dear God! Vito!"

Angelina clasped her hand over her mouth and glanced around the room. She was relieved her tiny squeak did nothing to attract the attention of Maximus and the intruder.

Vito laid face down with his right arm stretched out. Beside him was a growing pool of blood. Angelina gagged. The smell of blood was revolting to her. She shook her mind free from her mental paralysis and nausea.

In the short time at the estate, she had grown fond of Vito. He was carefree and lighthearted, like Angelina's father. It was difficult for Angelina to see the pseudo-father figure battered. As she crawled closer to him, she prayed he was still alive.

"Please be alive, Vito. Please!"

To remain hidden, Angelina could not reach Vito's neck. Placing her hand on his chest, she waited for his lungs to fill. She felt nothing. Her jaw tensed, and madness boiled in her gut. The intruder's destruction injured her as harshly as if it were Rosario lying motionless on the floor. She adjusted her grip on the gun. The fear of pulling the trigger had vanished. No matter what, she would shoot the man responsible for Vito. The intruder would die, and she would have no guilt. It would be justice for Vito and for the growing rage within her.

"Stop!" Angelina commanded. "I will shoot!"

Her voice immediately halted the skirmish. Both men turned to see who was shouting. Slowly, they raised their hands.

"Don't shoot, Angelina," Maximus pleaded, his hands gently waving her to put the gun down. "You don't..."

"Who are you?" Angelina demanded, holding her aim on the intruder. "Tell me!"

"Easy, lady!"

"Answer the question, unless you want to die?"

"You wouldn't shoot. Come on." The intruder took a couple steps closer to her. "Put the gun down like he said."

The intruder's foot bumped the lamp that had tumbled to the floor. In the flickering light, his face appeared familiar.

"It can't be!" Angelina muttered.

She blinked twice, then looked at the intruder from head to toe. His broad shoulders, dark hair, and olive complexion startled her. He took two more slow steps forward. Another flood of déjà vu engulfed her. His gate and the hungry look in his devilish eyes were exactly the same.

"Giorgio?" She muttered.

"Angelina?" The intruder asked.

Instantly, she raised the gun. Her hand trembled more than it did the first time she held a weapon. The intruder stepped closer to Angelina, and she took two steps back. The question of 'could she really shoot someone' rang in her ears.

"Don't come any closer!"

"You *are* Angelina!"

"Stop!" she demanded.

The intruder's next step brought his face into more light. Angelina could see his facial features clearly. The heavy bruising, broken jaw, and swollen eye no longer resembled Giorgio. A rush of oxygen filled her lungs.

"I ain't him. But I know a Giorgio." The man's pitchy voice left a slimy residue in her ears. "Be a nice kitty and put the gun down. Nobody gots to get killed over this."

"How did you know I was here?"

"Birdies chirp about a pretty day, but some sing about what one will pay for a pretty girl."

"Who sent you?"

The man took another step, but the cock of the hammer stopped him. He took two steps back, holding his hands up high.

"*Who*?"

"You know who, *My Little Dove!*"

The three words drained the blood from Angelina's heart. Her lungs stopped, and the world changed. Her carefree escape from reality instantly melted away. In its wake, Angelina's lungs expanded, and her heart thundered. The freshly oxygenated blood unlocked her memories, exposing all that her mind suppressed. The key to unlocking the bank of painful memories was Don Salvatore's pet name for her. In seconds, that which she forgot became a fresh wound oozing the burning acid of hate.

Hatred exploded from Angelina's core. She reacted without hesitation, without emotion. She heard Maximus's plea and his warning, but she was not moved. Angelina had made her decision. In a split second, life changed. It was no longer the way it was, nor would it ever be, all because of one tiny motion. Angelina's finger squeezing the trigger was the irretrievable choice that permanently stained her soul.

The world turned slowly enough for her to see the bullet sear across the room. She heard Maximus repeat her name after the round left the barrel. The gun recoiling, the acrid smell of gunpowder tickling her nose, the hazy smoke rolling from the tip of the barrel, and the man's eyes widening in shock, played frame-by-frame in slow motion.

In practice, she had a habit of closing her eyes when she pulled the trigger, but not this time. She wanted, *needed,* to see the intruder's body jolt when the bullet plunged into her target.

As the bullet tore through the man's chest, he cried out in pain, and his hand covered the gushing hole. In shock, the man looked at the blood, then back to Angelina. The intruder's face went white, and his bright blue eyes begged for mercy, but Angelina had no mercy for him, only a dark, ruthless hatred.

She didn't think or question herself. Angelina was in a trance that was only broken by the second round leaving the chamber. Like its predecessor, it found its target only inches above the first shot. This one drove through his heart, ushering a volcano of blood up his throat that oozed out his mouth. He gasped for air, but the blood had already filled his lungs.

Her hand vibrating from the recoil intensified after she squeezed the trigger again. She filled her nose with the smell of burned gunpowder, a scent she came to enjoy. Pulling the trigger again and again, Angelina's unchained hunger for the delicious vengeance devoured the man's soul with each bullet.

In that brief moment, her palm stinging from clenching the butt of the gun, sore arms, dry mouth, and heart pounding were cataloged into her memory.

The intruder collapsed, his lungs gurgling as his body lurched. The commotion jostled the lamp, and the light that illuminated his face flickered off and on, then rolled to a stop and went dark.

At some point, Freddy had entered the room from behind where Vito lay, and Olivia stood sentry at the other entrance.

Maximus, winded, held his position near the broken window. The chilly night air, flipping through the curtain, gave the events a steady cadence. Everyone remained motionless, watching Angelina as she stepped next to the dead man. With her bare foot, she rolled him over and looked down at the dead man's face. His eyes, wide open, were haunting lifeless orbs burning their memory into Angelina's soul. The world continued to move in slow motion, and the cries from Maximus and Freddy begging her to stop were muffled by her rage.

"Fuck you, you son-of-a-bitch!"

A snarl curled her lip, and she squeezed the trigger two more times, once for each eye. Instantly, the world reeled forward. The floor shifted under Angelina's feet, her stomach lurched, and she felt her grip on the gun release.

"Easy. Easy." Maximus said, catching Angelina. "You are going to be okay."

Maximus's warm hands enveloped her and placed her on the sofa. Tears streamed down her cheeks, but she did not sob. She couldn't feel, nor did she want to. If her mind validated or admonished her actions, it would destroy her, which was not an option. It was tragedy and death all over again. Angelina had left one hell only to enter another. But this hell left a deep gash from an unforgivable action. A shiver rolled down her back at the memory of her victim calling her 'my little dove.' It pushed her over the edge, hurdling her into a dark abyss that welcomed only the worst of souls, the soul of a sinner.

Angelina stayed on the sofa while the others worked to save Maximus's parents. She could hear the conversation around her and the questions they tried to ask, but she remained motionless like the body that lay a few feet away. Her eyes were glued on the rapidly expanding pool of blood seeping into the creamy white fibers of the rug.

"Did you get the other guy?" Maximus asked Freddy.

"Yes, Boss. But I wasn't as good of a shot as Miss Beretta."

Olivia checked her mother's pulse.

"Freddy put Mamma into the chair," Olivia said. "She has a pulse, albeit a weak one."

While Freddy moved to Philamena, Maximus examined his father.

"Olivia, get Dr. Lane," Maximus shouted. "He has a pulse, but he has lost a lot of blood."

"I'll get the car," Freddy replied. "We ain't got time for an ambulance."

They loaded Philamena and Vito into the black Cadillac. Olivia applied pressure to her father's wound while Freddy jumped in the driver's seat.

"Maximus, get in!"

"I can't leave her alone, Liv."

"But Papa could die!"

"She just killed a man, Liv. I know you haven't forgotten what that is like."

Nodding, Olivia looked away.

"Call me as soon as you know something," Maximus shouted, patting the hood of the car.

Maximus watched the car barreling down the drive, swerving around the fountain. In seconds, the car was out of sight.

A warm hand touched his shoulder.

"They gonna be okay, Uncle Max?"

"I don't know, Vittorio."

CHAPTER 67

Alone in the Apollo room, Angelina stared at the corpse and relived every second of her malicious act. Floating in a mental abyss, her thoughts transformed into a wicked joy. The memory of squeezing the trigger intensified the evil bliss and created an unquenchable desire for more.

Though Angelina liked the tantalizing sensation of revenge, it terrified her. She felt the powerful pull begging her to continue walking the warpath of retribution against all men, not just Giorgio and Don Salvatore. The glory and undeniable power could fill a deep hole, but it would also damn her soul. Angelina forced all justification for more destruction out of her mind. Bit by bit, Angelina closed off her emotions until she was a hollow, unfeeling shell.

In a hypnotic trance, Angelina walked out of the Apollo room, a place she now believed was cursed. An unholy vortex sucking every soul into the fires of hell. She wanted to erase the details of the room from her memory. But forgetting the place she transformed from an innocent being into a molten creature crusted in blackness was impossible.

Sitting on the edge of her bed, Angelina recalled the horrors in her home and how she felt as Carlos drove her parents to the hospital. Though she did not witness Philamena and Vito leaving, the scene had to be the same. Two battered souls struggling to survive in a car rocketing down the long drive.

A gentle tap on her bedroom door pulled her back to reality. She looked up at a battered Maximus, his jaw swollen, nose bloodied, and blood dripping from the gash on his brow. His face marred, Maximus was still handsome, but Angelina saw past his looks. She recognized the injured heart of a child whose parents lingered between this world and the realm of death. The sadness Maximus felt she, too, had felt. At that moment, Angelina wanted to comfort him as she needed when she stood in his place.

"I brought you a drink," Maximus said, offering her the glass. "It will calm your nerves."

"Thanks," Angelina mumbled.

"How are you?"

Angelina rolled the dark liquid around in her glass, searching for an accurate answer. To claim she was okay would be a lie. One could not be okay after committing murder. Yet, fear and sadness held no ground in her heart, nor did regret. The one emotion she felt was anger, but angry at whom? Maximus? Giorgio? Don Salvatore?

Myself? After all, finding Maximus was my choice. Angelina thought.

"I am sorry." Maximus moved closer to her.

Emerging from her inner search, Angelina questioned his apology.

"For?"

"It is a long list. As is my list of gratitude.".

Angelina arched her brow, intrigued. Though questions to satisfy her eagerness piled on her tongue, her systemic numbness kept her silent.

"To start with, you have been very patient."

"And?"

"You saved my life."

"Only from my own hands." Angelina narrowed her eyes.

"For that, too. You resisted a temptation many could not."

Angelina stared at him blankly, her mind resisting the urge to stand up for Olivia.

"I am referring to my sister."

"That is obvious." She slammed her drink and handed him the glass. "Don't think my silence is a show of support. What you did was cruel."

"What I prevented my sister from is cruelty."

"Ha!" The need to be angry overpowered her desire to remain calm. As the leash on her temper unraveled, her composure crumbled. "My brothers would never treat me with such disrespect and contempt!"

Angelina yanked both glasses out of his hands, spilling a little on his slacks. Looking at his thigh, she wished the liquid were an acid eating away his flesh, just like the grief gnawing at her heart.

"If you could have prevented Catalina from marrying Giorgio, would you?"

"Not *would*...I tried. But no one listened, least of all Cat."

Maximus followed her to the decanter and tossed two cubes into each glass.

"If you wish to refresh the drinks, please do!" Angelina scoffed. The evil glare on her face made him take a conceding step back. She huffed and quietly mumbled, *men are so damn controlling!*

"Why did you oppose your sister marrying Giorgio?"

"He is an egotistical jerk who thinks money is power."

"Money *is* power. It is how I amassed mine!"

"For all your character flaws, you don't flaunt it or your looks. Giorgio is obsessed with himself."

"Right before you pulled the trigger, you asked the man if he were Giorgio. Why?"

Angelina ignored the question. Sitting by the fire, she kept her gaze on the flames. She resisted the urge to cry, but a tear streaked down her cheek.

"My soul is damned," she muttered.

"No, Angelina. You are not damned. It is not *who* you kill, but *why*."

"That may let you and Freddy sleep at night, but it does not comfort me."

"He would have killed you, and my father would not have the chance to be fighting for his life right now."

Angelina's memory of cutting Rosario free from the chair rushed back to her. His body weak from blood loss, Rosario kneeled by his catatonic bride, begging her for forgiveness. It was the most heart-wrenching moment Angelina had ever witnessed. Remembering *what* happened to her father shed a light of understanding on *why* she became so enraged at the sight of Vito.

"Vito is alive?"

"Yes, so is my mother. Thanks to you."

Angelina sat in silence, sipping the amber liquid. She did not look at Maximus; she couldn't. Her emotions were too close to the surface.

Maximus placed his hand on hers, but she pulled away.

"Why?" she asked after a long silence.

She looked up at him. His face was puffier than when he knocked on the door. Instinct urged her to get a towel with ice, but she resisted her nurturing personality.

"Why were you so ruthless to Olivia?"

"It was a tough choice to make, but one, as I told Vittorio, required the—"

"Yes, yes, the *balls* to make. As if women don't make hard decisions. Balls are not magical spheres that give men a superpower."

"I said, balls *and* brains."

"Why, yes, of course!" She rolled her eyes. "Men *do* think with their bits and tackle, and they believe women are the tackle box for men to cram their shit into!"

A tear escaped, crashing against her hand.

"What happened? Did someone hurt you?"

"Did you use your balls or brains to figure that out?"

"I cannot help if you do not tell me what happened."

Angelina gripped the glass to resist the urge to throw it at him. But breaking a single glass would not give her satisfaction. She could throw a thousand glasses and still not match the hate she harbored for men.

"You should be with your parents." Angelina gripped her glass, blanching her knuckles. "No words we exchange can alter the past. You brought me here. Your hands are stained with the same blood as mine. Although, I imagine having bloody hands is nothing unusual for you."

"Angelina, God gave us free-will to choose. Though we call it *free*, it is not. All choices come with the strings of consequences attached. Accepting the consequences, good or bad, is the price we pay for the freedom of choice. You chose to shoot that man. Because of your bravery, my parents will live."

"I did not shoot that man to save you! I did it for vindication!" She slammed her glass on the side table. Her eyes twinkled with satisfaction. "My lust was for sweet revenge! But the dead man, bleeding all over your expensive rug, did not deserve to die. The man who sent him is who I want dead. That corpse is an innocent man in the wrong place at the wrong time!"

Angelina was done talking. She needed Maximus to leave before she lost control of her temper. She opened the front door of her apartment, choking back her acidic fears, and waved him out.

"Dammit, woman!"

His face red, Maximus stormed out of the room, cursing her in Italian. Angelina slammed the door shut, nearly clipping his heels.

Her back to the door, she slid down to the floor and pulled her knees to her chest as a flood of tears fell. The first tears were out of guilt for taking a life, but they quickly shifted to regret for shunning the only man who could help her achieve restitution.

What do you want, Angelina? She asked herself and swiftly replied. *To be home!*

Angelina pulled herself up and dried her tears. Wallowing in grief and guilt tied her to the past, preventing her from moving past the crippling heartache.

The crowing rooster and chirping birds trumpeted the morning sun's triumph over the dark sky. Angelina looked at the horizon, admiring the power the smallest sliver of the sun held over the darkness. It reminded Angelina of her grandmother and one of her tales of wisdom.

"Do you remember when you were a little girl and afraid of the dark?" Nonna asked Angelina. "You thought the darkness would swallow you up. That a demon lurked in the corner and under your bed, waiting for you to close your eyes. Are you still afraid of the dark?"

"Sometimes. When I wake from a bad dream."

"Dreams are a way for your spirit to communicate with you. As you get older, your dreams will provide wisdom and sometimes forecast that which is to come. Heed them and know they are a gift, not a curse." Nonna cupped Angelina's chin. "My dreams have told me you, as a woman, will be consumed by darkness. Great and powerful darkness that threatens to swallow your soul. When that day comes, remember the story of a single flame in the darkest room."

Nonna sat on her favorite marble bench in the middle of her garden. Chiseled into the base was a rosebush with nine giant blooms. Etched into the seat was Nonna's blessing, *Buono Cose Sempre*, Good Things Always.

"Come, let me look into your eyes, Principessa." Nonna smiled. "Ah! Si, your eyes look like your father's when he was your age. Tell me, you will be twelve soon, si?"

Angelina nodded.

"I will not be with you too many more years, Principessa. But I will always be in your heart. For now, my tales will have no meaning to you. They are seeds of wisdom. In time, when it is time to harvest the insight, you will recall them. It is in those moments I pray they guide you."

"I will not forget them, *or* you, Nonna."

"Good. You make an old woman feel loved."

"You *are* loved, Nonna!"

"Let me see your hands. Hmm, si, you have great things ahead of you, but you will suffer many dark, troubling days." Nonna sighed and kissed Angelina's palms. "What can the light do that the dark cannot?"

"The light can move through the darkness, but the darkness cannot move through the light."

"Very good. You do remember." Nonna wrapped Angelina's hands in her own. "When you place a candle in a dark room, the darkness does not consume the light. One day, when the darkness threatens to consume you, remember that light shines the brightest in the darkest of places. Therefore, the light God placed in you is strongest during the darkest days. And you, Principessa, have the power to move through the darkness."

With her grandmother's words ringing in her ears, Angelina understood her fate. She picked up her train ticket, suitcase, and purse and walked to the main road. It was at least a mile, but the exercise helped burn off her emotions and focus her thoughts.

Angelina still harbored hatred for men, including Maximus. In the beginning, Maximus seemed different from the men in the egotistical ranks of Giorgio. However, his treatment of Olivia proved Maximus was not a unicorn among men.

The lingering morning chill reminded Angelina of home, intensifying her desire to return to Brusnengo. She was unsure how she would get home, but leaving Fiori Estate was her first hurdle. When she reached the front gate, the men opened the door without question and cheerfully bid her goodbye.

A mile from the front gate, a young woman stopped to offer Angelina a ride.

"Where ya headin'?"

"Home," Angelina replied, flashing the train ticket.

"Well, hop in. Ol' Roobs will get you there. Toss your bags in the back seat."

The woman bent the rearview mirror down. Chomping on her gum, she fluffed her brown hair and inspected her lipstick while waiting for Angelina to get in the car. Satisfied with her appearance, the woman introduced herself.

"My name's Ruby. What's your name, sugar?"

"Angelina."

"Well, sugar, you ain't gonna make that train. And there ain't another one till tomorrow," Ruby said, slamming her foot against the throttle. "Oh, don't look so glum, sugar. I know a guy. With a little feminine persuasion, I'll get you a ticket. But I ain't runnin' no shelter house. You are on your own for a place to stay tonight. Hope you gots a few bucks."

"I have a little, not much though."

"Well, the respectable hotels only accept cash, if you know what I mean." Ruby winked, smacking her gum.

"Thank you for the lift. I was afraid I would have to walk to town."

"You is real lucky I was on my way back. There ain't many folks out this way. Only the rich can afford this land."

"Do you live out here?" Angelina asked, looking at the car's rough interior.

"Naw. I had business out this way. I got a fella who likes me to visit now and then. When his wife ain't around." Ruby laughed. "Oh, this is my favorite song!" She tapped the beat on the steering wheel and sang along. "Come on, sing, Sugar!"

Angelina gave the woman a nervous smile. Aside from Angelina's guilt for committing murder, Ruby's reckless driving put Angelina on edge.

"I cannot sing," Angelina lied, gripping the door handle.

"That can't be. A pretty Angel likes you gotta have a voice. Wouldn't be right for God not to give *you* pretty pipes." Ruby cackled.

The car swerved in and out of traffic with no regard for any other vehicle on the road. Ruby was too busy chewing her gum and prattling to be bothered by the world around her.

"Boy, you sure look like ya having a bad day. I'm starten' to think I should call you sour-puss, not sugar!"

"I have had better mornings."

"You wanna talk about it? May do you some good. The girls at the club come to me when they's in trouble. They say I give good advice. So, tell me, what's got you so doomy-gloomy?"

"It is a very long story."

"The city ain't exactly close. We got time."

"I appreciate the offer."

"Suit yourself!"

Ruby turned the radio up louder. The loud music, Ruby's awful vocals, and her terrifying driving gave Angelina a headache.

This will be a long, painful ride to the city. Angelina thought. *Mamma said don't take a ride with a stranger. Now, I understand why.*

Ruby enthusiastically dancing and her hands tapping to the beat on the steering wheel intensified her reckless driving. After the third song, Angelina was dangling on the edge of pure insanity. She inwardly talked herself out of shooting Ruby. Despite the sound reasoning that it would likely save innocent lives. Angelina leaned her head against the window, focusing her thoughts on the beautiful fall leaves. Exhausted, she tuned out the annoying pitchy shrieks coming from Ruby's vocal cords. The flashing reds and oranges hypnotized Angelina, lulling her into sleep. It was a short nap that abruptly ended when Ruby began shouting at the other drivers.

"Watch what ya' doin'! A blind monkey drunk on swill can drive better!" Ruby nudged Angelina. "Hey, sour-puss, we is in the city. I'll drop you at the buildin' over there. It's a pretty swanky hotel."

"I appreciate the ride."

Angelina was grateful, but her gratitude came from knowing the car ride was almost over.

Ruby swerved in front of a car, causing a cascade of blaring horns and screeching tires. Ignoring the shouts from the other drivers, Ruby zipped into a parking spot.

Ruby slammed the car in park but left the engine running. She stared at Angelina. It was the first full minute that she had remained silent. Angelina, reeling from the dangerous dash into the parking space, did not notice Ruby's silence.

"Honey, this ain't full service. You gonna get out or what?"

Ruby rolled her window down and tossed her gum into the street.

"Umm, yes. Sorry." Angelina stammered and collected her things. "Thank you for the ride."

"Sure!"

The woman put the car in drive, but Angelina stopped her from speeding away.

"What about my train ticket?"

"Oh ya!" Ruby grinned. "Ask for Johnny when you get inside. Tell him Ruby sent you. He will treat you right!"

"Do I owe you for the ride? I have a little, but..."

"Naw, sour-puss. Your luck looks to be worse than mine!"

"You have been very kind. I can't thank you enough!"

"Ya, ya. I ain't one to be sentimental."

The snide remark left no room for misunderstanding. Ruby was done with her good deed.

Angelina stepped away from the car. Her feet were barely clear of the tires when Ruby floored it. The abrupt jet into the street caused several vehicles to squeal to a stop while the drivers protested with their horns. Angelina shook her head and prayed she never needed another ride from Ruby.

Inside the hotel, Angelina's eyes traveled across the ornate woodwork and decorative furniture in the main lobby. At the front desk, a man in a red uniform with gold trim greeted her.

"A room, please. And may I speak with Johnny?"

Angelina opened her purse and removed the needed cash for the room. When she pulled out the bill, a small letter came with it. Her heart fluttered at the thought of it being from Maximus. She instantly chastised her whimsical emotions.

"I'm Johnny!" a young boy greeted Angelina.

His uniform was identical to the clerk at the counter. With a broad smile, Johnny picked up Angelina's bag.

"Follow me to your room."

On the elevator to the third floor, Johnny explained the hotel's amenities and recommended a few local restaurants for dinner.

"Are you gonna need a train ticket too?"

"How did you know?"

"Roob always tells people to ask for me."

"When you headin' out?"

"Oh, here. This is... well, was my ticket. Ruby said I missed the train by an hour."

"That is a shame. But don't worry, we will make sure you are on the next one," Johnny beamed, accepting Angelina's ticket. "Wow! First Class ain't cheap!"

"Will twenty dollars cover the price? It is all I have."

"I will make it work! Get some rest, and I will bring you the ticket after my shift."

"Thank you, Johnny. You and Ruby have been very helpful."

Johnny grinned, tipped his hat, and backed out the door.

The small hotel room seemed cramped compared to the spacious one in Angelina's apartment at Fiori Estate. But it was small but suitable for one-night. Angelina chuckled at her new snobbish opinion.

"Ruby, if you think this a swanky hotel, you would be overwhelmed with the glory of Fiori Estate!" Angelina mumbled to herself.

She was in no mood to admire the city, so she closed the curtains and sat on the edge of the bed. With her thumb, she spun her signet ring around her finger. Looking at the ring's details, she recalled the note with an 'F' pressed into the red wax seal.

My Dearest Principessa,

I know your stay has not been easy for you. Being far from home is difficult for anyone, and your circumstances added to the burden. You, however, carried it with grace—a true testament to your character.

Our plan was to escort you home, but fate disagreed. It is sad to know we will miss giving you a proper farewell, but we pray fate will soon bid us another opportunity.

Have a safe journey, and give your father my love. His friendship is a blessing Philamena and I cherish.

May St. Christopher be with you as you travel.

Ti auguro tanti bei giorni

Vito & Philamena

P.S.

My mother always said every woman is braver with five dollars in her pocket. Though this is considerably more, I hope it provides you with what you need and, hopefully, a few things you want.

Love,

Philamena

Exhausted, Angelina returned the money to her purse and placed her ring on the bedside table. Snuggling into the pillow, Angelina prayed her grandmother would bring her sweet dreams. Memories of sitting on her grandmother's lap, taking a stroll through the rose garden, and Nonna's magical tales filled Angelina's mind as she faded off to sleep.

Angelina's peaceful slumber flowed into a whirlwind of chaos and death. She sat upright in bed, her body tangled in the sheets and drenched in sweat. The unfamiliar room was pitch black, adding to her anxiety. She fumbled at the lamp. One yank on the chain, the dim light illuminated the bedside table.

"I wish I were an insomniac," Angelina growled in frustration. "Nonna, your dreams may have been a gift to you. My dreams are a burden!"

She stood in the shower and allowed the warm water to flow down her face. A hint of Maximus's cologne touched her nose. Even after encountering the various aspects of his persona, blemishes and all, the scent seemed familiar yet nurturing. She pushed the silly notion of it aside and wondered if she had made the right decision to leave Fiori Estate.

"It's too late now!"

Refreshed by her shower, Angelina dressed for dinner. She wasn't hungry, but she needed to eat. Sitting on the bed, Angelina put on her shoes, then reached for her grandmother's ring. It was gone.

Before she could open the curtains for more light, a voice in the shadows stopped her.

"Lose something?"

CHAPTER 68

Catalina rose from bed early. She was determined to find out what Fernando said to Don Salvatore.

"You think you can leave earlier every day to avoid this conversation? Not today. This is happening! You will tell me what you said to Rodolfo!" Catalina gripped the steering wheel on her way to the vineyard.

The people of Brusnengo, like the sun, had yet to rise when Catalina cruised through town. In the quiet darkness, she stopped once for an elderly woman walking her scraggly-haired mutt. Cat looked at her watch while she waited for the woman to lumber across the street. The lack of a bustling crowd walking to work shaved fifteen minutes off her drive.

"What has become of you, Nan?" Catalina practiced her interrogation as she zoomed past the old woman. "Even your parents think you have changed. Have you lost your mind?"

Berating him would push him further away. She argued with herself. *But a harsh lecture is what he needs!*

The sun, barely touching the edge of the horizon, tinted the sky with a soft yellow and orange glow when she arrived at the vineyard. It was enough light for her to see the delivery truck at the top of the hill.

"Ha! Caught ya!" She grinned, parking the car beside the delivery truck.

The lingering dark shadows, more than the cool morning air, prickled her skin. Age could not erase the mental scars from years of her brothers leaping from the darkness with a roar to frighten her.

"They are not here to torture you anymore." She rubbed her arms for warmth. "It is all your imagination."

Catalina grabbed her sweater from the passenger's seat. The thick fabric soothed her prickled skin, but not her imagination.

Leaning against the warm hood, she shifted her thoughts of the past to the more pressing issues.

"Nan, I know my sister's absence and my brother's death have caused you great pain. I hurt too!"

Sofia's voice entered Catalina's head, chastising her for using her own feelings to discount Fernando's. Pacing, she attempted to rephrase her argument.

"Nan, I understand you are hurting."

A movement by the cellar's entrance ceased her mental rehearsal. She strained to make out the shape lingering on the edge of the darkness.

"Hello?"

She moved closer to the shadows, but a tickle against her skin made her yelp and recoil. Catalina darted away from the car, searching for the ghostly hand that touched her leg.

"Meow...meow."

"Leonidas! You scared me!"

"Meooow...meow."

"Yes, I missed you too." Catalina rubbed the cat's head, making him purr. "But you can't scare me like that! You used to be on my side, remember!" Cuddling the loving ball of black fur, she nuzzled his ear.

"I was hoping you would come."

Leonidas hissed at the intruder and launched his body from Catalina's arms, leaving several scratches in his wake.

"Ouch! Nan, did you really have to scare me?" Straightening her clothes and hair, Catalina drew in a steadying breath. "We need to talk. I am worried about you."

"I am worried about him too."

Catalina looked up from her scratched arm. The pain inflicted by Leonidas's claws vanished when the figure in the shadows moved into view. Her heart ached. This had to be an illusion. Before she could utter his name, she collapsed.

"Cat!"

Marcus raced to her side, but her limp form collided against the dirt before he could catch her.

"Sis! Sis! Please, I didn't mean to scare you!"

"Then you should have remained a ghost," Fernando said. "She is not trustworthy. She betrayed you, me, all of us."

"That is a damn lie!" He got in Fernando's face.

"I wish it was a lie." Nan matched Marcus's aggression. "Cat is the reason Lina left! Why else would she leave this place?"

"You have stepped over the line. I have had enough of your bullshit, Nan. Either get your head out of your ass or get your ass off my property!"

"It is your head that is blinded by shit. Catalina conspired with Don Salvatore to have your brothers murdered."

"That's it. You are fucking fired!" Marcus shouted.

"No one is fired." A deep voice echoed up the hill.

Marcus's white-hot rage pushing him to punch Fernando instantly slipped away when he heard Carlos's voice.

"Carlos?" Marcus asked.

"You finally emerged from the cellar!"

"You knew?"

"There is little on this land that I do not know about."

"Nan, you were not supposed to tell anyone."

"*He* told *me* about you!"

"You are not the only one who can lurk in the dark, Marcus." Carlos grinned. "I saw you and the young lady go into the cellar your first night back. She stole the car, returned it the next morning, and left."

"Did you see anyone with her? Where did she go?"

"Easy," Carlos patted Marcus's shoulder. "I will know more soon."

"How?"

"Don Salvatore is not the only one with eyes and ears." Carlos kneeled beside Catalina and sighed. "She will wake soon, so we must hurry. Nan is correct, son. You need to remain a ghost, especially to Catalina. Give me your hat and jacket, then go back to the cellar and stay there! I will take care of Cat."

"Does Carmella know?"

"No!" Carlos and Fernando roared in unison.

"Nan, get your delivery done. We can't afford to lose any more business."

"Wait, what?" Marcus stammered. "Lose *more* business?"

"Later!" Carlos waved Marcus away. "Go. *Now*!"

The loud, rumbling engine roused Catalina. With a soft hush, Carlos told her to relax as he carried her to the car.

"What are you doing?" Catalina asked in a daze.

"You passed out and hit your head. Dr. Mariano should look at you. I will take you home."

"Wait! No. Where is Nan? Where is Marcus? I saw him come out of the cellar!"

"Marcus? You must have really bumped your head."

"No! I saw him! I saw Marcus come out of the cellar!"

Carlos bowed his head to hide his sadness.

"There have been many days I have seen your brothers. RJ in the sorting barn, Anton laughing up the steps with a case of wine. They are here." Patting his chest, Carlos sniffled. "But only in our hearts. You have yet to grieve the loss of your brothers. Carmella and I worry about you. You must take a few weeks off. Rest. Cry. Mourn."

"No, I saw him! It was him. He is alive, Carlos!"

A tear tumbled down Carlos's cheek. It was the first tear Catalina saw from him since the morning of the funerals.

"When you saw Marcus, what was he wearing?"

"A hat and a dusty jacket."

"Like this?" Carlos asked, pointing to his hat. "I was in the cellar, Cat. I would have seen him, too, but I didn't."

Recognizing the attire on Carlos, a stream of tears raced down Catalina's cheeks. She crossed her arms and frowned like she did when she was a little girl.

"Everything will be okay, Cat. Running the vineyard is difficult. It was stressful for even your father. Angelina will be home soon, and will set everything right. She can manage the vineyard, probably better than Rosario." Carlos snickered. "You have done all you can. Now, it is time for you to return to being the wife of a wealthy man."

CHAPTER 69

It was excruciating for Marcus to wait for nightfall. His conversation with Carlos, replaying for hours, intensified his unease, but the delay was necessary.

After taking Catalina home, Carlos returned to the vineyard with a package of food for Marcus.

"You were thin when you arrived and have grown thinner. Now, I see why. You pacing the floor does not cure the problem, Marcus."

"No, but it keeps me from taking my anger out on inanimate objects."

"The floor would disagree," Carlos replied dryly.

Though the man's humor was limited to dry, witty comments, Carlos always made Marcus chuckle. The weight of stress, however, squelched both of their joy.

"Do you believe Fernando's accusation of my sister?"

The allegation was inconceivable to Marcus, but Carlos's siding with his son gave it validity. Carlos was not the type to exaggerate details or spread misconceptions. The man was astute in the art of holding his mind until there was undeniable evidence. Though their conversation was brief, it was poignant. Especially the part when Carlos, with tears streaming down his cheeks, confessed that his son, much like Catalina, had changed. Both sweet, innocent souls in youth were entering adulthood as tortured souls. Catalina pined for control through power. Fernando's erratic emotions propelled him to viciously rebel against any form of control, especially by those *in* power. Catalina and Fernando's volatility dangled them off a cliff of danger, both blinded to the precarious position in which they lived.

"Carlos, do you truly believe Nan can no longer be trusted?"

"Until a couple days ago, he was trustworthy." Carlos exhaled a deep sadness. "But even then, I only saw what I wanted to see, Fernando's goodness and honor. Angelina leaving and Anton's death shattered the boy I loved. Now, I fear the man he has become."

"Dammit!" Marcus bellowed, slamming his hand on the table. "He *will* tell Don Salvatore."

"Most likely, he already has. It pains me to say, but if you were Anton, he would not reveal a Beretta son still lives."

Marcus slumped into the chair and buried his head in his hands.

"It is not the knowledge of me that is worrisome. I can disappear."

"Though I enjoy you being here, even as a ghost loading the trucks while the world slept." Carlos lifted Marcus's chin and gave him a wink of gratitude. "You would be wise to leave. In time, perhaps you can return."

"What about my parents?"

Carlos leaned closer, placing a hand on Marcus's shoulder.

"It has been hard to keep that secret from my wife and son, but it is for the best. So, Angelina, Catalina, and I are the only ones who know their location. Even with Catalina's obsession for power, she would not trade their lives for it. For now, I believe your parents are safe."

"He knows, Carlos." Marcus thumped his chest with his thumb. His eye floated in a growing pond of guilty tears. "He knows where my parents are because *I* told him."

A veil of fear enveloped Carlos. "When?"

"A few days ago."

Abruptly, Carlos stood from the table. The bottle of wine they were sharing tumbled over, the red liquid splattering on the dirt floor.

"As soon as the sun sets, you must leave!" Carlos ordered. "I will park the car close to the cellar's entrance. In the glove compartment, you will find money and travel papers for your parents. Hopefully, you will not need them. I will pack some clothes and food in the trunk."

"How will you do all of that without Carmella knowing?"

"She is a good wife and will not question my actions. Carmella understands the less she knows, the better."

Before Carlos left the cellar, he embraced Marcus. It was a hug filled with joy and grief, love and sadness, strength and fear. Marcus received the same hug from Rosario before leaving for the war. Just as he did with Rosario, Marcus soaked in the full import of the embrace.

"What will you do?" Marcus asked.

"We shall do as we always have; work hard and remain loyal to the Beretta family."

"Thank you."

Before Carlos ascended the steps, Marcus caught his arm.

"One more thing, Carlos. Have you heard from Angelina?"

"We received a telegram today. She will return soon."

"Oh, thank God! I thought she died in the fire."

"Focus on getting your parents to safety. Rosario must recover, or all of us will meet a horrid death."

On the drive to the convent, Marcus tried to recall the last time he interacted with the nuns. Their primary mission was caring for the sick and educating the young. Over a decade had passed since Marcus's last day of school, and he gratefully never needed hospital care. He wondered if any of the sisters from his school days would still be alive?

Marcus made the sign of the cross. It would require a miracle to convince the nuns to release Rosario and Sofia to a man thought to be dead.

"Jesus convinced Thomas. Maybe coming back from the dead won't seem so farfetched to these ladies."

He arrived at the convent a few minutes before midnight. Marcus swallowed his uncertainties and prayed for mercy.

"They are women of God; they have to be merciful. That is part of their creed." It was a marginally convincing point that he quickly rebuked. "But does their creed apply after hours?"

The nuns of his childhood ruled with an iron thumb and sharp tongues. Silent in prayer, they appeared angelic. However, at school, the black-cloaked angels effortlessly bent you to their will. The older students at school spun tales of the ninja nuns hiding within the walls, waiting to catch you unaware. Once captured, the nasty little children were sacrificed on the altar. The blood was drained from their limp bodies and used for communion. Since it had been centuries since Jesus's death, his body was surely depleted of blood, thus making it a believable story. These stories were passed down from older students. A tradition continued for generations. In time, every child knew the tales to be untrue.

At the front gate, a nun sat vigil on a small wooden stool. Her back was perfectly straight, her feet planted squarely on the ground, and her chin tucked as she prayed. Uneasy about disturbing the statue of piety, Marcus stood still. He was unsure if he should say something or knock on the gate.

How do you approach a praying nun? He thought.

"Good evening. Are you a child of God?" The motionless statue spoke with an eerie omnipotence. "Come closer. We do not bite." The nun lifted her head slightly, and her left eye popped open. "At least not before midnight."

The woman's eye snapped shut, and her head returned to its pious bow. Marcus's childhood fear of the nuns rushed to the surface. Some tales never die, no matter how old you get.

"I am sorry to bother you at such a late hour, Sister."

"God does not sleep. He is ready for his children at any hour," the statue intoned. "Do you need a meal, a bed for sleep?" Her head cocked and brow raised, the Nun's eye popped open again. "Or do you need to make a confession?"

It was difficult to resist the urge to hop from foot to foot under the single ogling eye.

"I...uh..." The reflexive answer leaped from his tongue, and his weight began shifting from foot to foot.

Dammit, old habits die hard. He thought.

The memory of a ruler slapping his knuckles for every *Um* or *uh* crumbled the last of Marcus's bravery. A battlefield of enemies was no match to the intimidation of a nun.

Nuns should fight wars. They would end much faster! Marcus thought.

"Do not stand there! What do you need?"

"I would like to see my parents."

"Living or dead?"

"Um...living...I hope."

"Hmm. Why would you come here, then?"

"Because they are being cared for here."

"We do not take in the ill, my child." She stood from her stool and walked closer to the gate. "They are at the hospital, where we assist the doctors. But you know this already. So why do you come here?"

"They were at the hospital, but Mother Concetta brought them here for their safety."

She cocked her head to the side, evaluating Marcus as a sergeant would inspect a private.

"You are a troubled soul. Perhaps you should spend time in the presence of God."

The nun's inspection was complete. She marched back to her post, resuming her statuesque form.

"Wait! Please, my parents are Rosario and Sofia Beretta."

The nun did not flinch when Marcus spoke their names.

"My name is..."

"To lie is a sin, my child!" Her eye popped open, and her finger extended like a magic wand toward the large stone building. "The chapel is over there."

Marcus did not need directions. He had prayed in the chapel many times. His eyes, magically entranced, followed her finger without the slightest resistance. It took a moment for his bewitched mind to break free of the nun's spell. When he looked back at her, she was once again a praying statue.

"May I see Mother Concetta?"

The question was ignored, as were the next several attempts to gain the black-cloaked statue's help. Grumbling his frustration, Marcus accepted his fate.

"Fine! I will go pray."

"Excellent choice," the nun replied as he walked away.

The bell tolled the midnight hour as he stepped inside the old stone building. The rich sound echoing through the vaulted ceiling was haunting and calming all at once. He sat in the second pew, soaking in the beautiful stained glass, organ pipes, statues, and the elaborate, hand-carved altar.

The last time he had been in a chapel at this hour was the night before his first encounter with the enemy. He was terrified of dying but more frightened about killing another soul. He kneeled all night before the altar, praying for his past sins and the ones he would commit the next day. By morning, he was exhausted, nervous, and ill. At formation, he puked on his sergeant's boots. Displeased, his sergeant told him to do fifty push-ups and report to the medic. When his sergeant reached the infirmary, Marcus had a high fever. The doctor assured him he was ill, but Marcus believed his illness stemmed from cowardice.

Marcus's unit moved on while he mended. Ten days after his comrades left, Marcus received two letters. One letter was his official transfer. The second letter contained information about the ambush that killed his entire unit. He silently wept on his pillow that night. God had spared his life, for which he was grateful, even if it meant he had to suffer from dysentery. Every year on the anniversary of the ambush, Marcus spent the evening in a church. He prayed for the souls of his friends and gave thanks to God for being spared.

In this small chapel, Marcus had prayed for his comrades. Tonight, he would pray for his family's safety. His elbows on the pew, a sense of peace fell over him. Bowing his head, Marcus began softly whispering the 'Our Father.'

The bell tolled the one o'clock hour. The deep note resonated around him, but he continued to pray. Nothing would stop him except a visit from God or his mother.

A few minutes after the three o'clock bell, he heard the shuffle of soft steps. Marcus's ears monitored the sound while the rest of him continued in prayer. As a soldier, he was mentally prepared for an attack. However, as a child of faith, he trusted the sanctuary of God's house would protect him.

"May I join you?" The loving voice asked.

"I prayed you would come," Marcus whispered into his folded hands. "I am sorry it is at such a late hour."

"No hour is too late for my child to visit."

She kneeled beside him, and together, they recited the Hail Mary. Finishing their prayers, they made the sign of the cross in unison as they always did, then sat back.

"I came to prove to you I am not dead."

"In my heart, I knew. But like Thomas, I needed to see you with my own eyes." She picked up his hands, running her finger across his palms as the tears fell from her cheeks. "Many times, I have prayed for your return."

"My heart still beats. That is all that matters."

"Why did you come? Catalina was warned of the dangers it placed on everyone."

"The young woman who friended Angelina came here to see her son, but now she is missing. I fear for her life."

"Ah! You came because of your feelings for her, not for your own flesh and blood?"

"In God's house, I will admit, I am fond of Francesca. But that is not the only reason I am here."

"And I am to believe you, why?"

"Because I am the same honest young man you helped raise. Mother Concetta, look into my eyes. Do you recognize me?" Marcus insisted, squaring his chin for inspection.

"I have prayed many nights for you while you were away at war." She cupped his cheek. "When I heard of your death, I cried as a mother would for her son."

"I was unsure if you would recognize me. There are days I look in the mirror and wonder who I have become."

"When Sister Maria Lynn told me of you, I was skeptical. Now, I know you are flesh and blood. You have changed but are still the precious young man you have always been."

"I do not blame your mother for not speaking. I, too, felt the need to take a vow of silence. Sofia needed me to be strong, as she was for me when we were young girls."

"How is my mother?"

"You must see for yourself. Sofia does not resemble the woman you once knew. I pray for her return. Perhaps, seeing you, she will. But, do not cling to false hopes."

"I understand."

"You must be gone before sunrise. Not all can resist Don Salvatore's persuasive purse. You must be careful. He is a devil and will stop at nothing. I fear even prayer will not protect you from a second attempt on your life."

"That is the other reason I am here." Marcus bowed his head. "Foolishly, I trusted someone. Now, my misjudgment has placed all of you in danger."

CHAPTER 70

Angelina whipped around to face the intruder. The dim lighting hindered her vision, but she didn't need to see. Her memory could fill in the details of the intruder's face.

From the moment Angelina left her apartment at Fiori Estate, she felt a set of prying eyes lurking in the shadows. As she walked down the long drive under the canopy of vibrant red, yellow, and orange leaves, she rehearsed her excuse for leaving. At the front gate to Fiori Estate, the guards did not ask her questions. They merely bid her a good day. She noted the oddity but was grateful for their lack of resistance. Angelina was happy to be free, even if it was temporary. There would be no escaping Maximus's lair. Like The Don, Maximus had spies everywhere waiting with their hands out.

"I wonder when you were going to show up," Angelina said. "It was kind of you to allow me time to rest and shower before you barged in here."

A hot shower and a long nap changed Angelina's disposition. She felt recharged and ready to fight for her life.

"That was the first time I woke with my memory intact. It is amazing how different you feel when you wake up fully connected with yourself." Angelina prattled as she slowly moved toward her gun.

The distinct click of the hammer stopped Angelina's migration. Staring down the barrel, she switched places with the man she killed. The fear of death raging through her body was now tinged with guilt.

This is how he felt before I pulled the trigger. She thought.

It was a compassionate notion that lasted a millisecond. The instinct to survive plowed over Angelina's moment of empathy. All that was important was discovering a suitable ploy for mercy.

Mercy is for the merciful. Angelina silently chided. *You were not merciful!*

Angelina held her hand up. She was not ready to meet her end. Faced with death, extending her life by a few seconds felt like an eternity.

"Wait! Please, do not shoot. Not yet, at least. My actions do not deserve mercy, but I pray you will answer my questions before you kill me."

In the silent purgatory, beads of sweat formed on Angelina's brow. It was cruel to dangle her off the cliff of uncertainty. Cruel but clever.

"Ask two questions."

"Thank you."

The burden of death set aside, Angelina sighed and sat on the edge of the bed. It was a relief to know she would live a few minutes longer. She needed to decide what questions might bring about her freedom.

"Ask now or die without peace."

"Yes, yes! Could you please lower the gun? I can't think with that thing pointed at me."

"Fine! Now, what is your second question?"

The pressure under the looming barrel blocked Angelina's commonsense. Her adversary was not that clever, which made her stupid mistake sting even more.

"But…"

"Tick-Tock!"

"Okay! Okay!" Angelina looked away from the gun. "Who sent you?"

"You have one question, and you waste it on who? I would have asked why. What would you ask, Johnny?"

Two feet from Angelina's left, Johnny emerged from behind the curtain. Dressed in street clothes, he blended in the dark shadows.

Angelina yelped.

"I'da asked, what do you want?"

"Yeah, that is a good question!" Ruby chortled. "You already know *who* we work for, sour-puss!"

"No, I really don't!"

Johnny pulled a telegram out of his front pocket and handed it to Angelina.

"Don't give her that!" Ruby barked. "Just read it to her. We need that! It is our ticket to get paid!"

"It's too dark!" Johnny protested. "I can't read nothin' in the dark."

"You can't read nothin' in the light, neither!"

"Can too! I ain't e-lit-trit, Roob!"

"Yes, you is. Now give me that!" Ruby took two quick steps closer to Johnny and snatched the telegram. "It says..." She held the paper up to catch the light, but the faint print was still difficult to read. "Oh, hell! It said this Salvatore man would pay a lot for you!"

"I have a lot of money in my purse! You can have all of it!"

"The fake stuff your honey prints? Hahaha, what ya take me for, a bimbo? No, no. That money ain't no good."

"I don't understand?"

"They said you was smart, but you sure ask stupid questions. I said I don't want *your* fake money. We want the reward!" Ruby grinned.

"My money is not fake!"

"Have you noticed the bills are all crisp? Like they ain't never been used?"

"Yes," Angelina replied.

"Since youse so smart, what else about that cash is odd?"

Angelina thought about the stack of cash stuffed in her purse. When she fanned through them, she registered the money's newness. An oddity she brushed off based on her inexperience in handling American money.

"Well? You figured it out yet?"

Angelina shook her head.

"Your honey prints money, American, Italian, French, he prints all of it. Mr. Fiori's government friend, some guy he met at Harvard, got him the gig during the war. A pretty sweet contract that was supposed to be permanent. When the war ended, the government, good Ol' Uncle Sam, took back the special plates. When your honey found out his friend lied about the contract, Mr. Fiori lied about giving back all the stamps. Now, your honey prints all the twenties he wants and ain't no one the wiser. Well, no one except a few of us who work the Underground."

"Underground?"

"It's what we call the dealings kept out of Ol' Uncle Sam's eyesight." Ruby stepped closer to Angelina. "Now, get your things, sour-puss."

Ruby pushed Angelina out the door and down the hall toward the elevator.

"Hurry up, sour-puss, we ain't got all day!"

Ruby and Johnny laughed together as they took turns pushing Angelina. As they passed each hotel room, she prayed someone would fling open the door and come to her aide, but no one did.

The empty corridor reminded Angelina of the dark hallways that led her into danger. It all began at home as she walked down the hall to her parents' room. At the convent, the hallway decorated with valuable art. On the train, Angelina followed Gerhart to the private cabin. The hallway on the ship where a stranger carried her away from her friend. Now, she walked down one more corridor.

"Is life a series of coincidences or a preordained path," Angelina mumbled.

"What's you mumblin', sour-puss?"

"A question asked by my tutor, Signore Lucas."

"Oh. Well, we don't need no tutorin' today! So just keep walking!"

"A tutor couldn't help either of you." Angelina could not resist the opportunity to jab at them.

"What's that supposed to mean?" Johnny barked.

"Do you want to take the stairs?" Angelina asked, glancing over her shoulder. "That might be a little less obvious." Angelina nodded at the gun.

"I is callin' the shots, sour-puss!" Ruby huffed.

"I know," Angelina replied. "That is why I *asked*."

"Well, I is already plannin' on us taken' the stairs. Ain't that right, Johnny?"

Angelina watched over her shoulder for Johnny's delayed response.

"Johnny! You best be listenin' when I'm talkin'!"

"Ya. I listen when you ain't naggin' me," Johnny grumbled. "You said we'd take the stairs."

"See. I don't need no special teacher. I was born smart!" Ruby mocked.

"How did Don Salvatore find me?" Angelina asked.

"Less yackin' and more movin'!"

"Did your source say how Don Salvatore knew I was in Kansas City?"

"That's a long story, sour-puss, and I ain't gots the time."

"Ha! You know we have plenty of time! It takes a week to cross the Atlantic." Angelina turned around to look Ruby in the eye. "Or maybe, you are not as astute as you think."

"Oh, look here, Johnny, we've got ourselves a real smarty-pants!" Ruby shoved Angelina against the wall. "I told ya, quick your yackin'."

"Back off, Roob. They said we ain't supposed to hurt her!"

The intensity of the moment felt exhilarating to Angelina. It was the same surge of excitement she felt after squeezing the trigger. The only thing missing was the sweet scent of gunpowder.

"Hurt me. Cut my face or do whatever you want." Angelina taunted. "The worse I look, the less he will pay you. *If* he pays you at all."

Ruby stepped inches away from Angelina. The odd, sour odor of Ruby's breath made Angelina's smile broaden. As Freddy had described during a lesson, it was the smell of intense fear.

"He'll pay, or I'll cut his nuts off!"

Angelina laughed, spurring Ruby's temper.

"What's so funny?"

"You have never met him, have you?"

"Who?"

"The man you *think* you are going to de-nut!"

"Oh, you think I ain't strong enough to hurt a man?"

"I am sure you hurt Johnny every time you stand naked in front of him." Angelina released a deliberate loud cackle.

Johnny tried to hide his amusement, but a snicker escaped.

"What you laughin' about Johnny?"

"Nothin' Roob."

"Enough wisecracks from you, you tiny pigeon, or whatever the hell he calls you! You wait and see, he's gonna pay me!"

"You are so naïve. For your sake, I hope I am wrong. But guess we won't know till we get there. *If* you know *where* you are taking me." Angelina chuckled.

Ruby slammed Angelina against the wall.

"What's so funny?"

"*You!*"

Ruby's temper exploded, drawing Johnny into the scuffle.

"Back off, Johnny. We girls are gonna have a chat!"

"It's my money, too, Roob!" Johnny argued, stripping Ruby's hand off Angelina's arm.

Ruby tried moving him out of the way, but he stood between them, preventing the impending brawl.

"Move, Johnny! I need to teach sour-puss a lesson."

"Back off, Roob! I ain't tellin' ya again!"

Johnny stepped forward to move Ruby away from Angelina. The duo snapped at each other, bickering over who was right and who should call the shots.

Excited to control the reigns of dominance again, Angelina continued to manipulate the pair into more chaos.

"Are we going to miss the train?" Angelina asked.

"I'm gonna rip her face off!"

"No, you ain't, Roob." Johnny shoved the gun into the back of his pants and wrapped his arms around Ruby. "Now, calm the fuck down!"

His partner wiggled and kicked like a toddler in a tantrum. Ruby was a feisty little pixy that took all of Johnny's effort to contain.

Angelina seized the moment and grabbed the gun out of Johnny's pants. It was cocked and aimed before the two could turn around.

"If you move, I *will* shoot."

"You won't shoot, sour-puss."

"Talk or die, your choice."

Ruby pranced around, mocking Angelina.

"A princess like you gonna shoot a woman? I don't think so, sour-puss! Or do you think you are gonna shoot us like your honey shot our associates?"

"Shut up, Roob!"

"Might listen to your friend. Seems *he* is the smart one. And for the record, the man that broke into Fiori Estate is dead because *I* shot him, not Maximus," Angelina sneered. "Now, tell me how Don Salvatore found me?"

"Why don't you ask the people you were staying with?" Ruby hissed and shoved Johnny toward Angelina.

Before she could process Ruby's comment, the gun kicked in Angelina's hand. The short distance between them made missing improbable, even without aiming. The bullet plunged into Johnny's chest, but he continued to career toward Angelina, blood gushing from the wound. Angelina analyzed every movement then quickly cataloged it. Her slowed, intentional thought processes allowed her to watch Johnny's body crash to the floor and prepare for the infuriated Ruby barreling forward.

"You bitch!" Ruby shrieked.

Angelina did not wait to pull the trigger. The cry of rage barely left Ruby's mouth before the bullet exited the barrel. Her aim was perfect. Though it was unnecessary, exhilaration tempted Angelina to pull the trigger again. Ruby's body jolted as the second bullet entered her chest. Blood gushing from the wounds, Ruby collapsed, gasping for air.

"Who was your contact?" Angelina demanded.

Blood bubbled out of Ruby's mouth. Intent on hearing her last words, Angelina knelt beside the woman. As Ruby gurgled an answer, the elevator dinged.

"Angelina!"

The loud bark of her name overpowered Ruby's weak voice. Angelina looked over her shoulder to watch Maximus step out of the elevator. His battered face intensified the rage in his eyes, but not as much as the barrel of his gun. With a steady grip, Maximus aimed his gun at Angelina.

"Maximus?"

"Did you really think I would let you go?"

"A girl can dream. But evidently, Beretta dreams don't come true."

"Don't move. Stay right where you are!"

Even though the Angel of Death danced in Maximus's glare, Angelina pleaded for mercy.

"Please! Wait. Before you shoot me, I need to apologize."

"For?"

"It is a long list." Angelina shifted her weight, but Maximus admonished her with a wave of his gun. "For starters, hurting you and your family."

"And?"

"For pulling you into this epic tragedy."

"You are prepared to die because of all the chaos and pain everyone has suffered?"

"Yes."

"That is admirable!" Maximus retorted, cocking the gun.

Facing the barrel of a gun twice in one day frazzled her nerves. If she was going to die, she was ready, but waiting was torture.

"Do it! Damn it! Shoot!" Angelina cried out.

"As you wish!" Maximus growled, squeezing the trigger.

CHAPTER 71

Marcus sat on the edge of Sofia's bed. It was difficult to suppress his emotions. Angelina's description helped prepare him for this moment, but it was time that ultimately saved him from losing control. Since Angelina's last encounter with their mother, Sofia's external wounds were nearly healed. Only a few signs of the tragic day remained.

He brushed her dark locks away. The yellowing bruises that emphasized Sofia's unhealthy pallor did not mare her beauty. Behind her wounds, Marcus's radiant mother still existed, giving him hope she could fully recover.

"She has not spoken a word since that day." Mother Concetta sighed.

"Does she acknowledge anyone?"

"Sofia is in a catatonic state. If she is not sleeping, she is staring off into the distance. She has said nothing since her arrival."

"Does she eat?"

"We spoon-feed her broth, but she has lost a considerable amount of weight." Mother Concetta placed a hand on Marcus's shoulder. "Her life is no longer in peril because of her injuries; it is starvation that threatens her. Every time I visit Sofia, I stand outside the door and pray God has not taken her."

"Is there anything we can do?" Marcus asked Mother Concetta.

"Pray."

Since the day he left for the military, Marcus suppressed his sadness and fear. He was a man, and men do not express tender emotions, especially not in front of their weeping mother. For her sake, Marcus cracked jokes and recanted cheerful stories of his childhood to ease her anxiety. Sofia's hug before he boarded the train nearly broke the dam holding his tears. But he remained dedicated to minimizing her agony by being strong.

Gently, he stroked his thumb across Sofia's swollen jaw. Her soft skin, usually pink with life, was cold. He plucked his mother's hand from the white blanket that swaddled her and pressed it to his cheek. The tender warmth of her love did not radiate from her palm. As Marcus's tears crashed against Sofia's leg, it was not his temper that swelled out of control but his immense grief. Marcus wept in his mother's lap. His chest heaving, he released all his sadness, all the emotions he hid from her over the past few years. His strength crumbled into a heap. The tables had turned. Now, Sofia stood on the platform, waiting for the train of death, and Marcus did not want to let go.

"Mamma?"

Marcus kissed Sofia's hand fervently, pleading for her to stay with him. He felt for her pulse; it was faint, and her breathing was shallow. Gripping her hand, the weeping little boy inside of his heart pined for his mother.

"This is how she has been, my child. I am sorry you must see such a beautiful creature reduced to an earthly purgatory," Mother Concetta choked back her grief.

"Is she going to die?"

"Everyone has a last day, but only God knows which one." Mother Concetta rubbed Marcus's back, urging the little boy to be strong. "Come now; there are a few hours left before sunrise. You should get some sleep."

"Waiting for a few hours is not wise."

"It takes time to prepare. There are things you will need to care for them."

"Carlos put some things in the trunk and glove box."

Marcus stood, but Mother Concetta gripped his shoulder.

"Stay with Sofia. Sister Juliann will fetch them."

Marcus looked up at the Nun, his eyes swimming in fear.

"All will be fine, my son. From the front gate, we can see a mile away. If anyone pulls in the drive, Sister Maria Lynn will sound the bell." Mother Concetta assured him. "If we must, we will hurry. Fear brews fear but with faith..."

"Fear has no power." Marcus finished her sentiment.

"You remembered." Mother Concetta smiled.

"I remember many of your teachings. They have kept me sane through the darkest of times."

"It was God, not me." She corrected him tenderly. "Now, get some rest."

"Thank you, Mother Concetta."

"Anything for you, Marcus. You are, and always will be, my favorite."

Marcus laid on the cot, staring at his mother. Sofia's desire to never wake up seemed to fill the air. What mother would want to wake after watching life torn from two sons.

It was difficult to imagine the torture his mother experienced and even harder to grapple with the idea Catalina had any hand in it.

"Catalina would never hurt our parents!" Marcus protested to Carlos. "She loves them! No! I can't believe it. I won't! Nothing could make Cat betray her family!"

"Marcus, listen to me. Your family has many secrets. Some I have kept for years, and new ones I have uncovered since your brothers' deaths."

"What do you mean? What secrets?"

"There is no time to explain. Carmella cannot know you are alive; no one can! You are one secret that *must* remain unknown. When the time is right, I will send for you. Until then, do not write to anyone. Do not send a telegram. You must not communicate with any of us! And, above all, Marcus, do not tell anyone your actual name! Knowledge of you can make even the pious of souls fall prey to greed."

The sun pierced through the morning fog, pulling Marcus from his sleep. His eyes snapped open, and his body jumped into motion. The same hurried nervousness he felt each morning during the war coursed through his blood. Marcus shook away his morning numbness and the words left foot, right foot. Today, he was not a soldier; he was a loving son.

"Mamma, it is me, Marcus."

Shaking her shoulders, he repeated his plea. Sofia rolled onto her back and looked up at him in a blank daze. Marcus smiled. At least she moved on her own.

"Mamma, I am home. I promise I will keep you safe!"

Kissing her forehead, Marcus drew in the motherly scent that comforted him as a child. He closed his eyes and remembered snuggling into her pillow, the smell of her hair soothing his troubled mind after a nightmare.

"It is my turn to soothe your mind, Mamma." He carried her to the wheelchair.

Marcus pushed Sofia into the hallway. A nun emerged with Rosario's room seconds later. Marcus was shocked at Rosario's pasty-white pallor and limp figure. It was difficult to see the strongest man he ever knew in a wheelchair.

"Good morning. My name is Sister Juliann."

The sound of hurried steps racing toward them prevented Marcus's response. The sister who sat vigil at the front gate ran toward them, her arms frantically waving. A few feet behind Sister Maria Lynn was Mother Concetta, winded but unrelenting in her pursuit.

"Quickly!" Mother Concetta yelled. "To the back door!"

"This way!" Sister Maria Lynn huffed, sprinting past him.

The clacking front tires, whipping black skirts, and Marcus's shoes slapping the floor echoed off the marble as they darted past the watchful eyes of the lifelike statues.

Sister Maria Lynn took a left down a short corridor that ended at two wooden doors. She unlocked the door. Marcus used the small stone statue of a cherub playing a small harp to prop it open. A gush of cool air raced into the hallway. Marcus objected to taking Sofia outside without warmer attire. Sister Maria Lynn, barking orders, ignored him.

"Sister Juliann, bring Signore Beretta over here. I will help you load him."

"Why is he taking our car?" Sister Juliann protested. "Why can't he take *his*?"

"We will put Rosario in the car. Marcus, put Sofia in. Hurry!" Maria Lynn instructed, speaking over Sister Juliann.

Marcus hoisted his mother and placed her in the front seat, careful not to bump her head. He kissed her forehead, then closed the door.

"He is here." Mother Concetta said between breaths. "You were right, Marcus. Sister Juliann, did you put everything in this car as I instructed?"

"Yes, Mother."

"Good. You will join him." The younger nun protested. With a deadly stare, Mother Concetta silenced the nun and added. "As will Sister Maria Lynn."

Both nuns scoffed at the order but silenced when Mother Concetta glared at them.

"Sisters, he will need your help in caring for Rosario and Sofia. Do as he says. I trust him, which is something I rarely say, as you well know!"

The two nuns, standing side by side, exchanged nervous looks before nodding in acceptance.

"In this envelope are instructions and all the money I could gather. Get them new clothes. I do not want anyone to know they are nuns." The sisters protested the idea but were quickly silenced after another deadly glare from Mother Concetta. "Your habits will attract attention, now shush!"

"Marcus, I will stall him as long as possible, but you must drive all night. Head toward the coast. Sister Maria Lynn knows where."

Mother Concetta made the sign of the cross on her sisters' foreheads. Before blessing Marcus, she gripped his shoulders tightly and locked eyes. The indomitable persona of a nun faded, and she spoke like a concerned loved one.

"You must not contact us. A letter or telegram will lead him back here to punish us in ways you cannot imagine. I will send for you when the time is right. Even if it takes a year, you must not reach out. Do you understand?"

"Yes."

A tear glided down Mother Concetta's cheek. In a firm embrace, she hugged Marcus. After a gentle kiss to his forehead, she transformed back into the pious woman.

"Now go. Quickly!"

CHAPTER 72

"It was foolish to think I could be more than I am," Angelina thought. *"Live as a fool and die as one."*

This was not the end she imagined. Angelina thought she would live to an old age like her grandmother. In her last decades, Angelina planned to share the many tales and lessons taught by the woman she admired the most in life. The icy floor chilled her bones, begging her to fade into the darkness. Yet, cradled in Maximus's arms, the warmth in his hand as it tenderly caressed her face encouraged her to linger for a moment longer. It was not the death she imagined, but dying in the arms of a handsome man was not a terrible end. Even if he was the one to take her life.

"Stay with me, Angelina. Don't close your eyes."

"Why did you shoot me?"

All the stress and rage that hardened Maximus's face faded. Even his sharp jawline and ominous dark stubble were softened by his compassion.

"You are really something." Maximus shook his head, chuckling. "I didn't shoot *you*."

Angelina looked down her torso, her hands searching for the warm blood she assumed was saturating her clothes. She found none.

"I shot *him*," Maximus nodded over his shoulder.

"You didn't shoot me?"

"No. I wouldn't shoot you. I *couldn't* shoot you."

Though his tone was that of an honest man, Angelina struggled to accept his words.

"You aimed the gun at *me*!"

"Why would I shoot you?"

"Because of what has happened to your family."

"They knew the risks."

A vision of Vito lying prone in the kitchen and the stench of blood lingering seized Angelina's thoughts. A pang of guilt ensnared her. She had not thought of Vito and Philamena's injuries for what seemed like days.

"How is Vito?"

"My father came through surgery, but he lost a lot of blood. Dr. Lane said it is too soon to give a prognosis."

"And Philamena?"

"That woman? Ha! She is the most resilient woman I know, present company excluded," Maximus said with a smirk. "She comes home tomorrow."

"That is a relief!"

"Did they hurt you?" Maximus asked, pointing toward the two lifeless forms lying in a growing pool of blood.

"I am fine. But..." Angelina crawled over to search Ruby's pockets. "*This* is *mine!*" Angelina smiled, holding up her grandmother's signet ring.

"We need to get out of here before the wrong people find your mess."

"Mine? That one is *your*s!"

"You shot him first!"

The adrenaline coursing through Angelina made her giddy. Despite killing two people in one day, her mental state was as carefree as any average day. There was no tension in her shoulders and no guilt to stifle her laughter. At that moment, her level of apathy bothered her more than committing murder. Perplexed, Angelina held her forehead, her mind contemplating her altercation with Ruby.

"This must be a dream." Angelina mumbled. "How...why don't I feel guilty?"

The stairwell door slammed shut. Maximus grabbed her arm, whirling her around to face him. His lips inches from hers, he ran his fingers through her dark locks. The chilly air amplified the warmth exuding from his muscular body.

"Have you ever dreamed of this?"

For a moment, time stood still. The only moving elements were their hearts beating in unison. As Maximus pressed his lips to hers, she melted, giving him the physical permission to unleash his bottled-up passion. Trapping her against the cold concrete wall, he hungrily ravaged her supple lips while his fingers plunged into her luscious hair. When he released Angelina's lips, he gazed at her longingly.

"For far too long, I have dreamed of this moment," Maximus professed. "There is so much I wish to say to you."

"These were made for kissing, not talking!"

"Then I pray my lips never leave yours." He muttered breathlessly before devouring her lips.

His right hand gripped her hair with a rugged tenderness while his left roamed the curves of her body. He groaned when his hand flowed from her low back to her hips.

"I want this moment to last forever."

The strong proclamation, though spoken softly, made Angelina pull away.

"But it can't, Maximus."

Passion and anger shared the lanes of Maximus's highway of emotions. Angelina's reoccurring rejection shifted his desire to rage. But she squelched it with a gentle nod toward the hallway.

"Oh, right!" He replied. "I forgot about them."

Angelina ran her fingers through his thick hair. All the hardened lines had faded. Instead of the aura of a troubled soul tangled in a web of chaos, he was an ordinary man, free of a heavy burden.

"I could tell!"

A ray of delight curled Maximus's lip. He tucked a strand of her black hair behind her ear, then met her gaze. He leaned in, holding his lips close to hers. The pause was exhilarating, stirring the brewing passion. When his lips finally met hers, an explosion of fireworks erupted, sending a tingling sensation through Angelina's body.

"Sweeter than I imagined," Maximus hummed. "I have never felt so alive."

He kissed her one more time then stepped away, leaving his musky cologne in his place. The arousing scent stopped Angelina in mid-step. Instantly, a shroud was removed, allowing a suppressed memory to resurface.

"It was you!"

His eyes twinkled, and a mischievous grin grew.

"You...You are the gentleman on the gangway!"

"You do have a strong grip."

"And you were the man who fought Antonio!"

"I wondered if that memory would ever resurface."

"You saved me, but not Francesca and Mar..."

Angelina choked back her brother's name and the sadness it conjured. She prayed Marcus and Francesca escaped, but in her heart, she doubted the possibility. Nevertheless, she needed to keep her brother's resurrection a secret, even if he was no longer alive.

"Why didn't you tell me?"

"I want your memories to return. Not my accounts. I am not you and do not know what happened before I arrived. If I tell you my story, you may not remember something important."

The police sirens' high pitch shrills pierced the air in the lobby when Maximus opened the door. Angelina, grimacing, resisted stepping into the public view.

"Don't panic. Walk like you own the place."

"But my dress."

Maximus looked down at the splatter of blood on the hem of her beige skirt.

"Here, put on my coat. It will cover it."

Maximus's ability to shift from one emotion to another so quickly was intriguing to Angelina. Her gut labeled it as a red flag, but her ego envied it.

"You act like all of this is part of a normal day. Is it?" Angelina asked timidly.

Maximus slipped his warm hand into hers. Interlocking their fingers, he flashed her an ornery grin.

"Which part, rescuing a beautiful woman or kissing a goddess in a stairwell?"

Angelina laughed a little louder than she intended, drawing a few reprising looks.

"Both."

"Rescuing a beautiful woman?" Maximus scratched his chin as he led Angelina to the elevators. "Not *every* day, but most. The second, however..."

Maximus abruptly stopped. He gazed intensely at her and brushed his thumb against her cheek. As the silent world around them traveled leisurely through time, Maximus pressed a gentle kiss to her lips before finishing his response.

"Never!"

Angelina allowed the tender moment to linger before adding her witty retort.

"Most, huh?"

"Most... that is what you took from my answer?" Maximus scoffed, clutching his chest. "I am hurt!"

"You are not that sensitive!"

"Good evening," the bellhop greeted them.

"Nathan, take us to the moon," Maximus handed the man twenty dollars.

"Certainly, Mr. Fiori."

Nathan removed a shiny gold key from his right pocket and inserted it into the wall. As the doors closed, a man in a business suit used his briefcase to stop the elevator.

"Sorry, sir. This is a private flight."

The man puffed his chest to bark his displeasure, but Maximus caught the man's eye. The red fury that flushed the man's face quickly drained as he backed out of the elevator, pleading for forgiveness.

"My apologies, Mr. Fiori!"

The elevator dinged as it went past each floor, but the word lobby above the door remained illuminated.

"Are we going down?" Angelina asked.

Maximus and Nathan exchanged a knowing grin. When the elevator doors opened, a hallway stretched out thirty yards in front of them. The lights hanging from the ceiling were spread far apart, leaving large patches of eerie darkness.

"Enjoy, Mr. Fiori." Nathan said, tipping his hat.

"Thank you, Mr. Nathan."

Maximus offered his hand to Angelina and escorted her down the hall.

"Where are we?"

"This hall leads to a special place where the cops won't find us."

Angelina looked at him with uncertainty.

"What do you mean by *special*?"

"In America, there was a group of people who thought drinking was wrong. Those voices finally convinced our government to shut down all the clubs and stop the sale of alcohol. As American's do, they found a way to get what they wanted. Bootleggers began discretely making and selling their own shine. Some were more discrete than others."

A tender smile curled Maximus's lips when Angelina slipped her arm into his. She returned the look, then encouraged him to continue his story.

"Despite what a minority of loud voices professed, the majority of the country wanted to consume alcohol. In came the speakeasy, an underground place for people to break the law. Drinking is no longer illegal, but the charm of a speakeasy still draws a crowd."

At the end of the hall, Maximus rapped his knuckles against the thick mahogany door. A small window at eye level opened, then closed. Several locks and chains clanked on the other side before the door opened with a screech.

"Evenin' Mr. Fiori. Miss." A tall, buff man greeted them. "Your usual?"

"I am a creature of habit."

The doorman snapped his fingers at a woman wearing a tight-fitting black cocktail dress, stilettos, and pillbox hat. "Pepper can show you to your table."

"Thank you, Drew."

From his front pocket, Maximus removed a diamond-encrusted money clip clamped on a thick wad of cash. He popped the clip, flipped through the bills, pulling out two twenties. Folding each in half, he handed one to Drew, then one to the waitress.

"Always appreciated, Mr. Fiori." Drew replied. "Enjoy your evening."

"Does everybody know you?" Angelina asked, but Maximus's response was a simple smile.

Pepper, a long-legged blonde with a slender frame, led them across the large room that was lit up like a Christmas tree. Hundreds of people mingled around, drinking their fancy drinks, laughing while playing various card games.

"Where are we?"

"My casino."

"*Yours?*"

"I inherited it from a dear friend. A man who taught me so much. Johnny would have liked you."

"You seem to have bushels of secrets. Should I be leery of finding more snakes among the grapes?"

Her accusatory tone dissolved Maximus's smile.

"More?"

"The past twenty-four hours have been very enlightening."

Maximus abruptly halted their jaunt at a crowded roulette wheel. His brow twitched slightly from agitation.

"How so?"

Angelina's comment had a purpose, to flush out Maximus's secrets. However, her timing was off. A player noticed Maximus and excitedly nudged his friend's arm. The pair were intent on learning something of value. A secret about Maximus would fetch a sizeable purse. It was a trade prevalent in every country. Angelina understood the dangers of exposing Maximus. Though she was not a snitch, Angelina held her tongue for a far more significant reason. She needed Maximus to get home.

"Let see." Angelina's playfulness instantly defused Maximus's tension. "You secretly rescue women every day, and you are invincible." Angelina discreetly nodded toward the minor injuries on his face. "But I do not know what other superpowers you have."

"There is a lot you don't know about me, but I hope we can change that," Maximus replied, his smile re-emerging.

As they resumed their walk, Angelina looked out of the corner of her eye. Inwardly, she sighed. The gamblers' begrudgingly returned their attention to the whizzing ball clicking as it soared over the numbers on the wheel.

"You are a complicated person," Angelina teased.

"So are you." He replied with a wink.

CHAPTER 73

Maximus led Angelina around the casino, showing her the different games. He explained how the machines from Las Vegas worked and which card games were most popular in a gambling hall.

At the craps table, Maximus threw down three twenties. The table attendant counted out a stack of chips and slid them, with a pair of red dice, across the table to him.

"Throw them." Maximus set the dice in Angelina's hands.

She shook her head. "No, I can't. What if I lose?"

"Then we buy more chips! Go ahead, throw them."

Hesitantly, she accepted his generosity.

Opposite the table from Angelina, a tall lady with a white fur stole wrapped around her shoulders gasped. Maximus looked at Angelina, and his eyes widened. Her arm was cocked, ready to throw the dice like a baseball. The woman was the catcher's mitt. Maximus grabbed Angelina's wrist.

"No! Wait!" He cradled her hand. "Toss from the wrist."

The dice bounced off the backboard and tumbled to a stop, sending the people around the table into a cheering frenzy.

"Why are they clapping?"

"Roll them again," Maximus chuckled.

The excitement from around the table became contagious, washing away any of Angelina's trepidation.

"You are good luck!" Maximus said.

"Is my amnesia contagious? Have you forgotten my recent tragedies?"

"See these chips? Each one is worth money. Money we did not have when we started." Maximus separated a small stack of chips from a dozen towering pillars. "This is what you started with, and this is what you have won!"

"Really? But I did not understand what I was doing!"

"Beginner's luck," He winked. "We should celebrate your winnings with a drink. I can't let you bankrupt my casino."

Maximus waved over a gentleman wearing a black suit with small gold poker chip buttons down his black shirt. The man nodded and gathered up the chips in front of Angelina.

"Cash us out, please." Making eye contact, Maximus handed the man the dice. "We will be in the bar."

"Very well, Mr. Fiori."

"What is he doing?"

"He is going to get us our money."

"You trust him to bring it to us?"

He chuckled. "Come on, I think both of us need a drink."

"Just one?"

"You robbed my casino. Now you want to drain my bar?"

He slid his hand into hers and led her through the smokey room, past the dazzling lights and chiming bells. Seven musicians dressed in shiny black suits with deep burgundy shirts stood on a raised stage. The drums' soft tssh-tssh and the bass's deep thub-thub gave a steady beat for the saxophone's riffs. Two trumpets and a piano rounded out the ensemble's jazzy tone. The brass musicians, while playing an animated intro, performed choreographed dance moves. After each instrument showed off a fancy riff, the brass softened their sound and parted like a curtain. A plump woman wearing a lacy black dress and a single burgundy flower in her hair, stepped up to the microphone. Her buttery voice filled the room.

She sang, *"I got a man that's more than eight-foot tall. Four-foot shoulders and that ain't all. King-size papa..."*

"Have you ever heard jazz music?"

Angelina shook her head.

"They say jazz started in New Orleans but grew up in Kansas City." Maximus grinned and slipped his arm around Angelina. "Kansas City's music is distinctly different from the blues and jazz of Chicago and New York. The lady singing is Julia Lee. Her saxophonist, Nathan, studied under the best, Charlie 'Bird' Parker. The 'Bird' plays the sax in a way that no one else can. Nick is the pianist behind Nathan. I love hearing him tickle the ivory keys. Jazz is soothing for the soul."

Angelina tried to listen to Maximus's explanation of jazz and his affinity for the style of music. However, his unbuttoned shirt exposed the thick gold chain resting in a forest of black hair. His seductive scent filled her nose, and a vision of him, shirtless with a bushel of grapes on his shoulder, consumed her thoughts. The golden sunlight shimmering off his sweaty torso lured Angelina deeper into the dreamy vision.

The summer breeze rippled the hem of Angelina's white cotton dress. She admired his muscles rippling as he walked down the row of vines. A small hand slipped into hers. Maximus looked at the child with an adoring smile. She glanced down at the dark, curly-headed boy who strongly resembled her youngest brother, RJ. A bubbling joy filled her heart, and a wave of peace washed over her. Maximus set the basket down and embraced the child. When he looked up, it was no longer Maximus. The loving face shifted to one of terror, asking, "Where are you, Lina." It was Fernando's face. She gasped.

"Angelina?" Maximus gently squeezed her hand. "Are you okay?"

Reluctant to look up, Angelina nodded.

"What would you like to drink?" He nudged her again.

"I need to go." Angelina reached for her purse.

"Angelina. Look at me!" Maximus wrapped his warm hand around hers, but she did not respond. "You must look at me. This is shock you are feeling. What you have felt until this moment is adrenalin!" He pulled her chin up to keep eye contact. "I hoped I could get a drink or two in you before your adrenaline ran dry. Do not feel guilty about your actions today. You did what you had to do."

"It is not the act but the reason to act." Angelina's face hardened. "Isn't that how you and Freddy think?"

Before he could reply, Angelina was standing with a glare of determination. Maximus grabbed her wrist and pulled her back into the booth.

"We can't leave just yet."

"I need to go. I do not feel well!"

"The stress you have gone through in the past twenty-four hours mixed with not eating will make you feel unwell."

Holding Angelina's face in his hands, he stared into her eyes. "You are my girl, Angelina. That means you must persevere through tough times. Only the strong win wars. Back home, you have a war raging, but I cannot let you return until I am sure you can overcome anything life throws at you. Do you understand what I am saying?"

A tear streamed down Angelina's cheek as she nodded.

"Good." Maximus gently kissed her forehead. "Now, I need you to drink this and eat. Our night is not over."

Angelina protested, but Maximus shushed her by putting a shrimp in her mouth.

"Eat and drink. That is all you get to do right now."

She brushed the tear off her cheek and did as Maximus said. The food helped her stomach, and the scotch calmed her nerves enough to enjoy the music again.

"That's my girl," Maximus winked. "I am sorry for the tragedies you have experienced, truly I am. With all my soul, I believe God puts us through events to strengthen us. A never-ending training camp for the battles he needs us to fight. Our experiences and the people we meet change us in unimaginable ways."

Maximus swirled the ice around in his glass. After a moment of silence, he slightly raised his glass and took a swig.

"If I can teach you anything before you leave, it is a lesson from Johnny. Everybody has a weakness. Find yours and know what triggers it. It is the key to making a strategic response, not a reaction spurred by insecurity. *Responding* is a controlled action. *Reacting* places a bright spotlight on your fears, showing your enemy how and where to strike."

"Why are you telling me all of this?"

Maximus sighed and shook his head. His brow furrowed. In one swig, he drained his glass, washing down the painful words on his tongue. He waved for the waitress to f another round.

"Finish that drink," Maximus nudged Angelina. "You will need a fresh one to hear what I have to say next."

"What do you mean?"

Maximus sat in silence, staring at her glass.

Eager for his response, Angelina slammed her drink. The amber liquid warmed her throat but did not sting. It was smooth with a hint of sweetness edging an undertone of oak. A harmonizing blend that made Angelina pause in recognition of a well-crafted spirit.

Preparing for his news, Angelina squared her shoulders and elevated her chin. She would bear whatever he had to say with the regal command of a queen over her subjects.

"You need to return home. I know this, and so do you. With your memory in tack, you know what waits for you, as do I. What happened at my house was not a botch job. Yes, they wanted to take you. But they wanted to make sure I did not return with you."

"What? How can you be sure?"

Maximus waved away her question.

"For the second time, I underestimated Don Salvatore. My father warned me about him, but I didn't listen. A mistake that may cost my father's life."

In a daze, Maximus stared into his drink and ran his hand through his hair.

"You do that when you are stressed." She nodded toward his head. "Every time you do not want to say something. Did you know that?"

A grin of approval for her astuteness lasted for a second before melting away. "A telegram came from Brusnengo."

Rosario's face appeared in her mind first, then her mother's, followed by Catalina's. The thought of losing any of them wrenched her gut.

"What does it say?"

Maximus pulled the yellow paper from his breast pocket.

"It is marked urgent."

Angelina waited until the waitress walked away before she accepted the piece of yellow paper from Maximus. Her hands trembled as she unfolded the telegram.

"Vincenzo said it arrived right after you left this morning," Maximus said remorsefully. "As much as I want to keep you here, you must return immediately."

Angelina, you are needed.
Please return home at once.

"If he has hurt her, I will kill him!"

"Easy." Maximus whispered. He placed his hand on hers. "Angelina. Look at me. You may not feel guilt right now for those lives you took, but you will. Adding another name will only cause you more agony."

"Fine, then *you* can kill him. I will enjoy watching!"

He hooked her chin with his finger and gazed into her soul.

"I would love nothing more than to fight your battles for you, slay every dragon that dares draw near. I will forever be your St. George." Maximus's eyes danced to the tune of a lover's devotion. "Right now, I cannot leave my family vulnerable. There is a traitor in my ranks, and I must find him... or *her*."

"Her? *Olivia*? She wouldn't betray you! For all her failings, she loves your family."

"Love is like the sun, warm and radiant at its peak, cold and absent in the darkness."

"There is always light in the dark. Don't give up on Olivia, Maximus."

"Is that how you feel about Catalina?"

"Yes. Cat only sees what the devil tells her. Once she is free of him, she will behave like my sister again."

"Will she? Or will taking the man she loves deepen the divide between you?" Maximus relaxed back with a sigh. "You must convince her before, not after."

Angelina stared into her drink, the ice cracking to the same beat as her heart. Maximus was right about Catalina and leaving his family.

"I know Giorgio did something to you." Maximus gently stroked her shoulder. She flinched. "It doesn't take a mind reader. The look on your face before you pulled the trigger was evidence enough."

"I will kill him."

"In time, yes." Maximus urged her to look at him. "Every man that has crossed me paid for his transgression, but on *my* timetable. A man is not born powerful; he must strategically gather it. Your day will come, but I beg you to wait until I can join you in the fight."

"I am to become a puppet?"

"That is not what I said."

"For how long? How long must I pretend?"

"What happens if you make wine from a grape picked too soon?"

"It spoils the wine."

"Then wait to harvest your victory." Maximus slammed his drink. "Now, there is one more thing." He held out his hand. "May I have this dance?"

Her heart was numb to the tenderness in his touch. Half of her clung to the life raft of reality, the other her rage stirring the sea that threatened to engulf her. The tears welling in her eyes crashed against Maximus's suit.

"I know you are afraid, but you have a strength inside you that you do not even see. It is that fire that enchanted me."

Maximus grinned and kissed the back of her hand. He pulled her in close and effortlessly moved them around the dance floor. His ability to dance was not lost on Angelina or any other woman watching in awe. She melted into him and allowed him to whisk her around the floor. It was soothing to be cradled in his firm yet gentle embrace.

"Angelina, I will be your St. George. I will help you weaken your foe, but in the end, it is you who will lead the meek dragon around like a whipped dog on a leash." Maximus pressed his lips to her forehead, drawing in her scent. "Tesoro Mio, by the time you return home, *no man* will be able to overpower you."

CHAPTER 74

A bitter breeze nipped at Angelina's cheeks as she stepped off the train, but she did not wince. She was warmed by the bottle of wine she had consumed and energized by the letter Maximus slipped into her purse.

After what seemed to be an eternity, she finally returned to the place where her journey began. She drew in the familiar aroma of what her heart knew as home. The baking bread, simmering pots of tortellini with prosciutto, and the sweet, buttery panettone laced the air. The most soothing smell, however, was the brewing espresso at Bella Vita Café across the street. She filled her lungs with the seasoned air and remembered the last time she stood on this platform. On that day, she left her hometown a caterpillar, drawing all her energy inward to survive. Now, in the warm sunlight, Angelina stood magnificently transformed. Her time away, though stained by blood, taught her how to defeat her enemy.

From the end of the platform, Carlos waved his hat. He looked tired, but the smile on his face was one of pure joy for her return.

The porter set three suitcases down beside Angelina, waiting for his gratuity while Carlos hugged her. Impatient, the porter cleared his throat, breaking the reunion. Carlos reached in his pocket, but Angelina stayed his hand and retrieved a sizeable tip from her purse.

"Thank you, Signore," Angelina smiled.

The porter, pleased with her generosity, removed his hat and bowed several times as he retreated to the train.

"Angelina, are *all* these bags yours?"

"Yes. A gift from the Fiori family. Everything I have brought home is from them." Smiling, she twirled to show off her expensive dress. "Do you think Catalina will approve! I brought her home a few things I think she will love."

Carlos's cheerful disposition faded. He donned his hat and picked up the heavy suitcases, avoiding Angelina's inquisitive eyes.

"We should go," Carlos muttered.

Angelina placed a hand on Carlos's arm, stopping him.

"Carlos? What is the matter?"

"We must not talk here. Especially about *her*."

Angelina glanced around the station, catching several men gawking at her. Unintimidated, she gave each a fierce snarl that snapped all but one man back in line. She noted his long dark coat, the silk burgundy band around his new fedora, and polished shoes. The man's attire was strikingly higher class than anyone at the station.

You dress like an aristocrat, but your scraggly beard and dirty nails are that of a hired hand. What message shall you deliver to your boss? She questioned in silence.

When the man looked up, Angelina was still watching him. She made eye contact and flashed a vixen smile. He did not shy away, nor did she. Her message was unmistakable; *I see you and know why you are here*. Angelina gave the man a brief wave, then turned to join Carlos at the car.

In trepidation, Carlos looked around before he whispered, "Do you know who that is?"

"Don Salvatore's spy," Angelina replied louder than usual.

Carlos winced. He opened the car door and shooed her in.

"All is well, Carlos." Angelina cupped his chin with her black-gloved hand. "Things will be different now that I am back. We will *not* live in fear."

"After you learn all that has transpired since you left, you may not feel as confident."

"Confidence is a choice, Carlos."

As he pulled out of the station, Angelina removed her hat and sighed. She was tired from her trip, but she needed her stamina to last a little while longer.

"Take me to see my parents."

Gripping the wheel, Carlos nervously glanced between Angelina and the road. His tongue tripped over every word.

"That is...well...not possible."

"What do you mean, *not possible?* I need to see my father."

"Rosario is not... um... where he was."

Angelina shifted to make eye contact. His inability to meet her gaze and nervous speech were unsettling.

"They were not to be moved!"

"It was... a *necessity.*"

A sinking dread pulled on Angelina. Her imagination posed potential reasons for moving her parents. The worst and most prevalent thought turned her saliva to sand. She swallowed, but the desert within remained dry.

"Are my parents... *alive?*"

"I believe so."

"Believe so?"

"I have not seen them for several weeks. To protect the sisters and your parents, Mother Concetta barred visitors."

"That is understandable, as well as wise. But why were they moved?" Angelina noticed Carlos's blanched knuckles gripping the wheel. "Where are they?"

"They are no longer under the care of Mother Concetta."

"I gathered that! Why were they moved?"

"Don Salvatore was informed of their location."

"Who informed him?"

"It is hard to say."

"When I left, three people knew of their location. You, Catalina, and I."

"And Francesca."

A vision of Francesca lying across the threshold, bleeding to death, stirred Angelina's emotions. The possibility of her friend surviving never entered her mind. If Francesca survived, perhaps her brother did too. A hopeful flutter tickled her heart, but Maximus's voice cautioned silence.

"You are the keeper and gather of all information," Maximus insisted. *"Divulge nothing to even the most trusted person. Knowledge is the privilege of power, and you have the power to create a narrative or destroy it."*

It was similar to one of her father's lessons. Rosario trusted Carlos with his life. But, some secrets could be entrusted to no man.

"Carlos, how do you know of Francesca?"

"She is your friend."

"That was not my question. How do you know *about* a woman I have never introduced to you?"

"You did not introduce her. I learned from someone else."

"Who?"

"I...I...hesitate to say. There has been so much betrayal."

"Trust must begin somewhere. My father trusted you, and you know he trusted *me* more than anyone. Now, untie your tongue and tell me who betrayed us?"

"Very well, I will tell you, but if I am wrong..."

"That was the turn for the vineyard. Where are you going?"

"There is something you must see."

"Can it wait? I need a shower and a hot meal."

"It is not wise to wait," he replied mournfully.

He glanced in the rearview mirror, then to Angelina. For the first time since she arrived, Carlos finally met her gaze. She gasped when she read the turmoil he was hiding.

"By the look on your face, this isn't a surprise homecoming party."

"Carmella wanted to have one. Given the current state of... *everything*, I thought it would not be wise. I hope you agree."

Upset, Angelina stared out the window. Her happiness for being home was dwindling rapidly.

"How was your trip?" Carlos asked.

It was a blatant attempt to shift the conversation to a more enjoyable topic. She flashed a disgruntled glare and huffed.

"Exhausting."

"But was it fruitful?"

"A wise man always finds a bountiful harvest, even in the desert of silence."

Relaxing his shoulders, Carlos smiled, and his pallor improved. He sighed and loosened his grip on the wheel.

"It is good to have you home. You have been missed."

"As your telegram implied."

Carlos nearly ran off the road. A horn blared, snapping him back into his lane. One eye on the wheel, he looked at Angelina again.

"What telegram?"

CHAPTER 75

A clap of thunder greeted Maximus when he climbed out of the car. The dark bank of clouds churned into a growing thunderhead. Intermittent flashes marked its distance.

"Youse think it's gonna be another ice storm, Boss?" Figgy asked with a shudder. "Sure feels like it."

"It's Missouri, Figgy." Freddy pulled his collar up. "The weather is like a mistress. Fiery hot one minute and a frozen bitch the next."

"Ain't that the truth!"

"Boss, you want some company?" Freddy asked.

"No!"

An icy wind sliced through Maximus's coat. He popped up his collar and grumbled his displeasure for the cold as he hustled up the steps.

"Alright. See youse tomorrow!" Figgy hollered.

The warm air and the smell of a crackling fire greeted Maximus's senses when Vincenzo opened the door. Deep in thought, Maximus ran his hand through his hair and grunted a mostly inaudible hello.

"Good evening, sir. How was your trip?" Vincenzo asked, helping Maximus out of his coat.

"Long."

"May I get you anything?"

"Peace and quiet."

"As you wish, sir."

Before Maximus reached the stairwell, he glanced over his shoulder and barked an order to his butler.

"Vincenzo, have dinner brought to my North Wing office."

"As you wish."

He made it up three steps before a movement caught his eye. In a fluid motion, he removed and cocked his gun.

"Will you shoot your sister?"

"My sister knows the dangers of lurking in the darkness."

"I am not lurking, dear brother."

Olivia stood on the landing above Maximus. The moonlight popped out from the clouds, pouring silvery light through the cupola. Half illuminated, Olivia descended the stairs, her spine rigid as her long fingers grazed the railing.

"Did you enjoy your vacation?"

"It was not a vacation."

"Two weeks away, while our father lingered on the cliff of death, sounds like a vacation."

"Olivia, I have not been gone for two weeks."

"No? Wishful thinking then."

"Why did you do it, Liv?"

"What was that? Are our parents okay?" Olivia held her hand to her ear. "Why yes, brother. Our parents survived. Mamma is back to her usual self, and Papa." She slinked down the stairs. "Oh, listen to me. I shouldn't bore you with details you care nothing about."

She stopped on the step above Maximus. Even elevated, she was still an inch shorter than him.

He eyed her pale features. "You look tired, Liv."

"So do you."

"Stress will do that."

"I live as a princess. What stress could I possibly have?"

Maximus tucked a strand of her hair behind her ear, exposing her beautiful eyes. The dark circles beneath them were more prevalent, either from the poor lighting or stress.

"Why did you betray me, Liv?"

She looked away, exposing the scar on her cheek. It was her way of reminding Maximus of his part in her tragic tale.

"Liv, your scar does not hurt me, not anymore."

"It should. It should pain you as it does me."

"Is that why? To punish me?"

"Always about you, Max, isn't it?" Olivia scoffed and stepped around him.

"Why did you betray me?" Maximus growled, grabbing her arm. "You put our entire family in danger. You knew he would send someone, and you led him into our house!" His voice boomed around the open space. "Our house, Liv! Where our parents sleep. Where *your* son sleeps! How could you be so selfish? Punish *me*, Liv. For the rest of my life, punish *me*. But leave our family out of it!"

"You really think I would put *our* family in danger, don't you?"

Maximus ground his jaw and squeezed her arm tighter, but she did not wince from the pain.

"You do!" Olivia chuckled. "You hate me enough to blame me for *your* crime!"

"*My crime*?"

"Yes, Max! Papa almost died because of your arrogance! *You* brought her here! *You* baited Don Salvatore into a fight! Why else would you go to such lengths? It certainly isn't out of love. Your stone heart is incapable of love!"

"Enough!" Maximus shouted, throwing her down the last few steps. "Enough of your patronizing, Olivia!"

She tumbled down, only yelping once before turning her pain into a maniacal cackle. Strips of her black hair hung across her face, and her eyes glistened with tears of rage.

"Does beating a woman make you feel strong?" Olivia sneered as she regained her feet. "You have been trying to make up for your lack of manhood ever since this happened." She pointed to her scar.

"I was eight years old!"

"And you watched as they raped me!"

Maximus's temper snapped. He stormed down the steps and grabbed her hair. This time, she yelped, but he had no sympathy for her.

"I swear to God, Liv if you continue to fight me..."

"What? What else can you do to me? You already ruined my life!"

Maximus loomed over her. The veins along his temples throbbed, and his grip tightened as he berated her.

"Look around you, Olivia. You live like a princess, remember? Your life isn't ruined because of *me*! If you are miserable, it is your own damn fault. I have done everything for you! Everything!" Maximus drug her up the steps. She resisted, but he overpowered her. "You and your son get whatever you desire. Why? Because I slave day in and day out.

I make the sacrifices. I take the risks. I put my life and my reputation on the line."

At the top of the staircase, Olivia twirled out from his grasp and slapped him. The fiery sting burned his cheek.

"You ungrateful bitch! You want for nothing, dammit! I give, and you take!" Maximus's fury radiated from his pores. Beads of sweat rolled down his throbbing temples, and his nostrils flared. "You want a vacation from me?"

Olivia took several steps back, but he stormed toward her. He grabbed her wrist and flung her over his shoulder.

"No! Maximus, put me down!" One of her slippers flew off her foot, and her silver nightdress flourished with each kick she made. "Stop! Don't hurt me! Please!"

"I have *never* hurt you, but God knows I have had plenty of cause to beat you!"

Olivia pounded her fists on his back, but Maximus did not flinch. He tolerated her verbal abuse for two decades. Tonight, he would allow her the chance to inflict physical pain. But her petite frame could leave no deeper scars than the ones he already acquired.

"Maximus! Maximilianus! Let me go! Vincenzo! Papa!" Olivia cried. "Maxie, put me down!"

"As you wish, *Princess* Olivia!" Maximus tossed her onto her bed. "You shouldn't have betrayed me, Liv. I tolerated you directing your anger at me, but betrayal is unforgivable!"

"No, no, no! Maximus, I didn't. I didn't do it! Wait!"

Maximus slammed her door shut. He removed a key and locked her door seconds before her hand landed on the knob.

"Max! Maximus, wait! I didn't betray you!" Olivia cried, jiggling the doorknob. "I swear, Maxie. I didn't do it! Please!"

As Maximus walked away, he heard his sister's pounding fists fade as she slid to the floor, sobbing. He picked up her wayward shoe and hurled it against her door. The shoe hit its mark, and a loud pop echoed through the halls.

Maximus stormed toward the stairs, pausing long enough to bark orders at a speechless Vincenzo.

"She stays in that room! Stays! No one visits her. *No one!*"

CHAPTER 76

"Carlos, I am going to ask you a question, and I need you to answer me without hesitation!" Her commanding tone left no room for any resistance from Carlos. "What do you know about my trip?" Before allowing him to respond, Angelina placed a cautioning hand on his arm. "Consider this a conversation to prove *your* loyalty!"

Carlos's olive complexion faded.

"I did not know *where* you went until my cousin, Andrea, visited me. The day you left, she was working the ticket counter at the train station. She heard you ask for a ticket to Turin. With that information and our conversation the night of your brothers' funerals, I knew *who* you sought to find. Your father said the Fiori family lived in America, but that is all Rosario told me. My informants are good at collecting bits of info but nothing to the level of finding someone in a foreign country. I would not know where to send a telegram."

"Did your cousin tell you anything else?"

"Andrea said the cobbler's wife boarded the train, as did Antonio and Bruno. I feared for your life." Carlos's voice cracked. He looked away, blinking back his emotions. "I kept what I knew a secret from everyone, including my wife. Until your telegram came, I didn't know if you were alive."

"I apologize for putting you through undue stress."

"It was wise not to reach out." He cleared his throat. "The Don came every day to the vineyard looking for you and..."

"And what? Your hesitation is becoming agitating!"

"Every day since you left, Don Salvatore came to the vineyard to collect the money from the deliveries."

"Where is Catalina? She knows not to trust The Don. She should be collecting the money before that bastard has a chance!" Angelina fumed.

"I tried to tell her this, but she does not like being told what to do. She never has." Carlos nervously scratched the back of his head. "That is not the worst of it. We are behind on all the bills. And with no one but Fernando and I, we have fallen behind on deliveries too."

"Then hire someone!"

"I have tried. No one wants to work for him. With you—" Angelina held up her hand in disagreement.

"My being home does not fix this mess!"

"It does for a simple man. You are the closest thing to your father. In everyone's eyes, if you are running the vineyard, your father is running the vineyard."

"Then spread the word, I am back. Hire as many men as you need. But make sure every single one is loyal to my family. There are enough snakes among my father's vines!"

"How will I pay men to work? We have no money?"

"Leave the money to me."

Angelina opened her pocketbook, and her heart twirled at the sight of Maximus's note. She resisted removing it and re-reading it for the hundredth time. She had memorized every curve of every letter, partly from infatuation but mainly because she needed to destroy the evidence. She touched the note, and her heart sang a phrase from Maximus's letter.

"My darling, do not forget me or my love. I will defeat every dragon if only to hold you in my arms once more."

Her lips tingled, remembering his passionate kiss. Angelina suppressed her arousing memories. She could not be the dreamy schoolgirl lost in the fantasy of a crush.

"Will this cover what you need?" Angelina asked, removing a thin stack of bills from her pocketbook.

Carlos's eyes widened. "Yes, more than. Where did you..."

She held up a hand. "Spend it wisely. Tell no one about it."

Angelina snapped her pocketbook closed and reached for the door, but Carlos stopped her. A sadness lurked behind his dark pupils and the heavy burden he longed to share filled the bags beneath his eyes.

"Is there something else?" Angelina asked.

"Si. Marcus brought Francesca to the vineyard."

A flood of emotions raced to the surface, but Angelina kept them hidden. It was an answer to a question she dared not ask. She steadied herself.

"Go on."

"She left in the middle of the night, and Marcus followed. But *she* did not bring the car back. That well-dressed man at the station returned the car."

"Where is my brother now?"

"I sent him to the convent to warn Mother Concetta. If he did as I said, he and your parents are on their way to safety."

"You have done well. Do not hesitate to tell me what you know. We are the only ones left to protect my father's legacy." Angelina patted his hand. "Your advice is invaluable to me."

A tear escaped and raced down Carlos's cheek.

"My silence is not to displease you. I wish to protect you."

Carlos held the hospital's front door open for Angelina. As he crossed the threshold, a heavy sadness pulled on his shoulders. Angelina had felt the same the last time she was here. She chased after the doctors and nurses rushing her parents to surgery. Her best friend, Maria, was one of the nurses fighting to save her parents. They pushed them through the doorway to the surgical ward. Maria, her white dress stained with Rosario's blood, gave a reassuring expression. The hope in Maria's eyes provided Angelina the strength to wait hours for news of her parents' condition.

"Carlos, who are we here to visit?"

"I am sorry, this is the first person you see on your return." Carlos fiddled with the brim of his hat. "Maria is making sure everything that can be done is done. She is a good friend."

"She is my *best* friend!"

A pair of nurses walking toward them eyed Angelina before exchanging whispers. Their look of contempt as they walked by plagued Angelina. They were the fourth pair of eyes to look down upon her.

"Carlos, why is everyone glaring at me?"

They stopped outside of room 1026. Carlos kept his head low, unable to meet Angelina's gaze. He sighed.

"Many things have changed. Too many. They stare because Cat spreads rumors. She has said terrible things."

"Why? Because I left her in the jaws of a wolf? I offered. No, I begged her to come with me!" Angelina growled. "After everything I have lived through since our brothers' deaths, my own sister is against me?"

"No, no. Catalina did not speak out against you until two days before your telegram arrived."

"What happened two days before?"

"The Don began spreading the rumor of your return—"

"That I am to be his bride?"

Carlos abruptly looked up. "Yes. How did you—"

"It has been his plan all along."

Carlos shook his head and sighed.

"Such news is what spurred Catalina's tales of you. Out of jealousy, she pushed The Don's hand, and then..." A lump caught Carlos's throat. He clutched his hat and steadied himself. "Then this happened." Carlos nodded toward the hospital room. "I am sorry. I tried to stop it..." His voice, laced with tears, trailed off for a moment. "I would go in... but, I cannot bear seeing the body."

Angelina placed her hand on Carlos's shoulder.

"I could use some coffee. Why don't you go find both of us a cup?" Her delicate tone and the compassionate pat on his back soothed Carlos enough for him to nod. "And Carlos. There is nothing for you to apologize for. I can see you have done the best you could."

"You are your father's daughter." Carlos smiled slightly. "I am grateful to have you home."

Angelina watched the man plod away. His head hung low, shoulders slumped, and his feet shuffled like a man twice Carlos's age. A pang of guilt stabbed her chest. Her absence placed more on Carlos than Rosario ever would have done.

As the door closed behind her, Angelina gasped. She understood why Carlos did not want to enter the somber room. In the dim lighting, the badly beaten body covered in white reminded Angelina of a tragic scene in a Shakespearean play.

She uncovered the hand, exposing the purple and black splotches. Her heart hardened with each beat. If she could see her own soul, she imagined it would be as battered as the flesh before her. They were kindred souls, one battered on the outside, the other inside.

"If I had stayed, none of this would have happened," Angelina's voice trembled with regret. She did not bother wiping away the tears that streamed down her cheeks; the flood would continue.

"I tried to run from my inescapable fate. I should have stayed. I was foolish, and for that, you suffered his abuse."

Angelina placed the bruised hand against her cheek. She bowed her head, and her tears crashed onto the white linen.

"You are not the only one who has paid a heavy price. In our time apart, I, too, have suffered." The piercing gaze from the crucifix hanging above the bed fed the festering guilt in her soul. "I am no longer an innocent girl."

"*They* made me a wolf." She pounded her chest. "They made me a wolf just like them!"

Frothing at the mouth, lungs gasping for air, she growled an unearthly cry of hatred that left its mark on her throat. "What I have done. Who I have become are perpetual evils that lurk in my every thought. I have done horrible things. Things that God *cannot* forgive."

Holy water, blessed by the Pope, could not cleanse her bloodstained soul. She was a sinner now, just like the wolves that tore the flesh of her family apart. Angelina gripped the sheets and allowed her pain, her victimhood, and her sorrow to escape.

As the nearby chapel bell tolled in the distance, a quake of pain reverberated through Angelina. Her inevitable future lay in front of her. But what stung more was knowing she was not done committing sin. What she had to do next pulled her deeper into the darkness. She feared she would become lost, unable to return to a life of love and happiness.

"*Do not give away your power! You are the master of your life,*" Sofia's voice echoed in Angelina's mind.

"You are right, Mamma." Angelina sniffled. "I will not give the wolves the satisfaction of knowing the damage they inflicted. They cannot - *will not* control me!"

Angelina removed a white lace handkerchief from her sleeve and cleared away the stains from her temporary collapse of emotions. By the final gong of the bell, Angelina had tucked her feelings and her handkerchief away.

She brushed a strand of hair from the swollen eye and exposed another long gash. Angelina bit at her free hand to suppress the overwhelming urge to curse the bastard who inflicted these wounds. She snarled, and her nostrils flared as her gaze swept down the body entombed in white linen. Her rage even silenced Maximus's calming voice. There was no rationalizing the fury that boiled inside her blackened heart. She despised the men who conjured the evil demons into her life.

"They *will* pay for this! For *all* of this! For all they have done to our families, I will make them *suffer*!"

"Perhaps God put you here so you would not see what I have become. But what I have become is a necessity. It pains my heart that we cannot seek vengeance side by side." Angelina placed a kiss on the battered hand before tucking it under the white linen. "Seeing you here, I understand... I understand what I must do to vindicate our families. But I promise, Francesca. I promise with all my being, I will savor it enough for both of us!"

Outside Francesca's room, Angelina rested her head against the door. This was not the life Angelina desired but the one God handed her. She would rise to the occasion and prove to everyone, she was not a victim and bent to no man's will.

"The tweet-tweet of a birdie is so sweet-sweet!"

Angelina spun around to find Don Salvatore standing a few feet away. With a grin, he removed a large stack of money from his breast pocket.

"A pleasure, Signore," Don Salvatore beamed.

Angelina's jaw dropped. She could not believe it. A man she was sure would never work for The Don smiled at his reward.

"You work for *him*?" Angelina fumed. "How could you betray me like this?"

"What is the last thing I told you?" Gerhard asked.

"Trust no one..."

"Trust no one, *not even me*," Gerhard corrected Angelina.

"But..."

"Signorina, you knew my services are purchased with money. Selling information is my way of making a living, just as yours is crushing grapes. Everyone must eat, and I am a big man!"

Spitting at his feet, Angelina glared at Gerhard.

"Then, I hope you choke on your next meal!"

Gerhard tipped his hat and bowed his head.

"Auf Wiedersehen dir auch."

"Should you desire a permanent position, I am in need of someone with your skills," Don Salvatore coaxed. "I can assure you, you will never go hungry!"

Stuffing the folded stack of cash into his breast pocket, Gerhard gave The Don a nod of gratitude.

"An offer to think on, Signore."

"You know where to find me," Don Salvatore replied.

Furious, Angelina mumbled an Italian curse.

"Now, now, My Little Dove," Don Salvatore snickered. "You cannot begrudge a man willing to work."

From around the corner, a woman cried out for her freedom. The consternation made The Don chuckle.

"Ah! He found her. Good. Perhaps she can shed some light on where your parents have been taken." Don Salvatore grinned. "Unless you care to tell me? Hmm? Or did your travels give you amnesia?"

Angelina flinched.

"Yes, yes. Did you think you could really travel out of my reach? You will quickly learn, My Little Dove, that everyone is a puppet searching for his master. I, as a skilled marionette, can step in and effortlessly pull any man's or *woman's* strings."

"Unhand me!" Mother Concetta cried. "Unhand me this instant! It is a sin to badger me so!"

Brazenly laughing, Giorgio rounded the corner with Mother Concetta's arm firmly in his grasp.

"She thinks I am worried about my soul," Giorgio cackled, gouging the barrel of his gun into her side. His grin broadened when he noticed Angelina. "Well, well. Look who finally came home!"

"I see you are barely limping." Angelina's eyes narrowed. "I thought it would take you longer to heal."

"Dr. Mariano doesn't like me, but..."

"Despises you is more accurate!"

"But follows the doctor's oath to the letter!"

"What would you know of oaths!"

Exerting his displeasure for Angelina's tone, Giorgio squeezed the nun's arm, making her knees buckle from the pain.

"Be nice to the nun, Giorgio. You may need her to pray for your soul." Don Salvatore snickered. He stepped close to the nun and hissed. "Mother Concetta, would you like to confess your sins first, or shall Angelina begin?"

"Let me go, this instant!" Mother Concetta barked, ripping her arm free. "I confess to God and no one else!"

"Oh? Well, then, feel free to shoot her, Giorgio. Unless My Little Dove is willing to talk."

"Leave her alone!"

"See, Giorgio, not everyone hates the nuns."

"What do you want?" Angelina stepped forward.

"What I have always wanted, your parents to die a painful death!"

"My father did not kill your brother!"

"So, *you* say, but my birdy tells me otherwise!"

"I am flattered, sister. I thought you forgot the night we bonded," Giorgio cackled.

Don Salvatore rounded on Giorgio, his eyes darting with rage. "What did you say? Are the rumors your wife spreads true? I told you not to touch her!"

"Well, well. For the first time, Giorgio, you didn't brag about your latest fuck. I am truly honored." Angelina jeered.

Pushing the nun aside, Don Salvatore grabbed Giorgio by the throat. "You insolent brat! I told you she was *mine!*"

"At the vineyard, you said if I played my cards right, I could have both of them!"

Don Salvatore slammed him against the wall and growled. Grabbing Giorgio's face, The Don squeezed until his nephew whimpered like a little boy.

"You worthless piece of shit! After all I have given you!"

"But Zio…"

"Shut up! Shut up!" The Don released his death grip and backhanded Giorgio. "You ungrateful leach!"

"Stop it! Stop! I command you to stop!" Mother Concetta cried out. "To fight in a hospital run by the church is as sinful as fighting in God's house."

Don Salvatore, hunched like a predator, slowly marched toward Mother Concetta. He snarled, making her jump.

"What did you say?"

"Stop, please!" Mother Concetta cowered against the wall.

"It is a good thing you work for God and not me!"

Don Salvatore grabbed the back of her veil and yanked it off, exposing more than her graying locks. The Don's eyes narrowed.

"I wondered what rock you crawled under! Your pious garb kept you hidden from me the whole time. Clever, clever. I'm impressed. But then again, you were a cunning creature."

"Please, please. Don't hurt me." Mother Concetta slumped to the floor under The Don's ominous form.

"That isn't what you said to me thirty years ago!"

Angelina tenderly placed her hand on Don Salvatore's shoulder and whispered in his ear. Instantly, he released the nun's habit and looked into Angelina's eyes.

"You would do that to save this tramp? Do not let the black fabric fool you. She is dark to the core! Aren't you, *Cetta*?"

"Leave her!" Angelina stood tall, with her chin level and shoulders back. "You came for me, not her."

"My Little Dove, what delicious confidence you have! I shall enjoy devouring it with a bottle of the family wine! What do you think, red or white?" The Don's cackle echoed off the barren white walls. "Out of respect for your purity, I had planned white. Since my nephew has taken that jewel." He twisted Giorgio's ear. "I think red shall be more appropriate!"

"Angelina, no! You do not know what you are sacrificing!" Mother Concetta protested, clambering to her feet. "Don't do this, Rodolfo. Angelina is good and pure…"

"Shut up, bitch!"

In a flash, The Don backhanded the nun, sending her into the air. She slammed against the wall with a yelp and crumpled into a sobbing heap of black fabric on the floor. He marched toward her, his chest heaving with anger.

"Good and pure? We were good and pure!" Standing over the whimpering nun, The Don snarled and spit on her face. "I will finish the job I sent Mario to do!"

"Please, no!" Mother Concetta pleaded.

"No?" The Don released a boisterous roar of laughter. "You confess to God, but you beg me to have mercy? How ironic!" Angelina placed a calming hand on The Don's shoulder, stopping him from hurting Mother Concetta. "I will deal with you later, *Cetta!*"

Giorgio seized the opportunity to slither away. Cautiously, he stepped out of reach. But the movement was enough to grab Don Salvatore's attention.

"As for you, Giorgio." The Don's cackle of victory shifted to a growl. "Run to your little bitch of a wife and pray I do not tell her of your sins!"

"Zio, I am not a leach. I did *everything* you told me to do."

Don Salvatore slapped Giorgio. "And that which I told you not to do! Don't forget that part, you brat! Be grateful you are still my blood, or I would gut you right here! Never forget, *you* are indebted to *me*. Now go before I change my mind!"

Giorgio lept to his feet and reclaimed his arrogance by straightening his disheveled shirt. A mirror could not reflect a more perfect replica of a young Don Salvatore. From his snarl to the huffs of displeasure, Giorgio was a taller version of his uncle, inside and out.

As he marched away, Giorgio leveled his shoulders and chin. He did not look back. His pride would not let him.

Don Salvatore, however, did not watch his nephew storm away. His attention, like a child playing with a boring toy, flipped from Giorgio to Angelina.

"My Little Dove, you have been treated poorly and betrayed by so many." Don Salvatore purred. He tucked Angelina's arm in his, gently petting her hand as they waltzed down the hall. "But all that is over now. In my home, you are a queen! You will be the center of my attention and affection -always! *If* you obey."

On their way to the front door, Angelina noticed Carlos down the hall. She shook her head to shew him out of Don Salvatore's sightline. As they walked past Carlos in hiding, Angelina spoke loud enough for him to hear.

"I will do *whatever* it takes to protect those I love."

"Ah! See, such a good attitude. 'Tis really a shame Francesca did not share your mindset. I had grand plans for the three of us. No matter. We will raise little Alberto as our own. That is until you provide me an heir. I must admit, I am weary of raising other men's sons. To be fair, Mario raised Giorgio. But that is what I paid the man to do."

Don Salvatore stopped at the front desk to hand the young woman three bills folded together.

"You did well, my dear. Here is a little extra. Buy yourself something nice, hmm?" The Don flashed a smile and winked. "Do tell Carlos I appreciate him picking up my bride at the station. I will see she gets home safely."

The young woman glanced at Angelina and gulped before nodding to Don Salvatore. Angelina took a second to peek back at Carlos. A tear rushed down his cheek.

"I will be okay." She mouthed.

"Shall we, My Little Dove?" The Don said as he put on his hat. "Where was I? Oh yes, Giorgio." Don Salvatore rambled as he escorted Angelina to the car. "My nephew has outgrown his usefulness to me. He is blood, so to honor my brother, I will see the boy doesn't starve. But that will be the end of my generosity."

CHAPTER 77

"Well, forget the prodigal son, for here is the daughter!" Catalina emerged from the corner of the room.

As she slowly approached Angelina, the black satin trim on her crushed velvet dress shimmered in the fire's warm light.

"Catalina! Oh, Cat. I have missed you so much!" Angelina was surprised yet relieved to see her sister. She reached out to hug her but was rejected.

"I wish I could say it is good to have you home, dear sorella. But you are the only liar in the family!"

Catalina's harsh tone sent a wave of sadness crashing against Angelina's chest. Their time apart was not long, but the distance traveled magnified it into a lifetime. Their appearances had not changed, yet each had evolved into a nearly unrecognizable person.

Leary of prying eyes, Angelina glanced around the cozy parlor. The empty pieces of furniture relaxed her shoulders. She released a quiet sigh of gratitude for the private moment with her sister.

"Cat, please? We cannot fight! We must work together to defeat him!"

"Tisk-tisk, sorella!" Catalina stumbled toward Angelina. "Tisk-tisk!"

"Are you drunk?"

"On felicity for your safe return!"

"The empty bottle and your empty glass tell a different story." Angelina took a calming breath and lowered her voice. "Cat, I am grateful we have a private moment together. I thought he wouldn't allow us any time together, especially not so soon after my return home!" Angelina nervously glanced over her shoulder. "Maximus and I formed a plan. If we work together—"

"A month-long vacation did not change you, did it? You still need to be in control of everyone and everything! No apologies for your absence or for your *betrayal*! When Giorgio told me you were returning, I was angry. But when Carlos said I was doing a terrible job running the vineyard and *you* would fix what I broke. I was furious!" Catalina stepped toe to toe with Angelina. "I was not surprised. You have fooled him. You have all of them fooled. But not me, Lina. I know what you have done. You will not win. *I* won't let you!"

Maximus's calming voice urging Angelina to maintain control changed to the agitating tone of a bleating goat. The high-pitched fueled her temper, but Catalina's false accusations ignited Angelina's rage.

"Giorgio has filled your head with lies!"

"My husband has opened my eyes to your treachery!"

"And you believe him over blood?"

"Constance confirmed his accusations." Catalina reached for the empty bottle. "I can't believe you would betray me! Actually, I *can* and *do* believe it! Did you ever care about any of us, Angelina? Or was it always your plan to take over Papa's business and boot the rest of us out?"

"That is not true, and you know it!"

"Really? Well, the evidence says it is true!"

"What evidence?"

"Ah! There is my loving husband! Where have you been?"

Giorgio strolled into the room. His eyes trained on his bride. His composure and blatant disregard for Angelina's presence was a deliberate slight.

"My Zio and I had a little business to discuss." Wrapping his arms around Catalina, he kissed her with the passion of a long-lost lover. "You are so sweet, my love," Giorgio hummed.

"Not near as delicious as you." Catalina gazed longingly into his eyes. "Oh, my apologies for the blatant display of affection. I so easily forgot about you, Lina. It is rude to rub *our* love in *your* face."

Angelina rolled her eyes. "Rude is not the word to describe *your* love!"

"I suppose it would be hard to understand something you have never known. Pitty, really. Nan is such a kind soul."

Giorgio hooked Catalina's chin and gently kissed her lips again. His teeth held her bottom lip for a second.

"Have you told her?" Giorgio asked.

Catalina tap-danced her fingers up Giorgio's chest.

"Don't be silly. I wouldn't spoil the surprise!"

"What surprise?" Don Salvatore bellowed.

"Well, dear Zio..."

Catalina's eyes danced between Giorgio and The Don.

"Dear God, no!" Angelina's knees buckled.

Catalina glared at her sister as she stepped out from behind the dark carmine and black sofa. She lifted her chin and straightened her shoulders. Locking her gaze with Angelina, she revealed a devious smile.

"We are expecting!" Catalina beamed, gently rubbing her abdomen. "Isn't it grand! The Salvatore Legacy will live on! We will, of course, name him after you, Rodolfo!" Catalina gushed.

The Don's face flushed red as he glared at the happy couple. His displeasure seething, he stormed toward them. Giorgio wrapped his arm around Catalina, but The Don shoved the two apart and marched toward the villa door.

"I am thirsty! Where is the damn maid? Amalea!"

Catalina wrapped her arm in Giorgio's. "Angelina can pour us drinks. After all, she is the most proficient at opening a bottle of wine! I believe, Rodolfo, you likened her to the goddess Hebe who was forced to slave away, filling everyone's cup...but her own."

Don Salvatore's nostrils flared. "Your pregnancy does n—"

Angelina gently slipped her arm into Don Salvatore's, instantly calming his temper.

"Doesn't mean you should drink. You must be careful not to over imbibe, dear sister. Remember, Isabella? She consumed too much and lost the sweet babe."

"Dr. Mariano said I could have a glass of wine!"

Angelina plucked the glass from her sister's hand.

"Then it looks like Amalea will need to bring you some juice. As for the rest of us, if it pleases Don Salvatore, I will gladly open a fresh bottle. We should toast to the joyous occasion."

"My Little Dove, you have had a long journey. A hot bath and a good night's sleep are all the efforts you need to exert.

Tomorrow, the four of us shall have dinner to celebrate the newest members of the Salvatore family."

"Member-*s*?" Catalina scoffed.

"As we discussed, My Little Kitty-Cat, Angelina needs a suitable husband. I intend to be it." Don Salvatore grinned at Angelina. "Though I have yet to make my official proposal, at the hospital, My Little Dove whispered her acceptance."

Catalina's lip quivered.

"He is a wolf. Any sign of weakness will entice him to sink his teeth into you," Giorgio whispered. "Our time *will* come, be patient My Love."

"You are marrying *him*?"

Angelina yawned, then rested her head on Don Salvatore's shoulder. "I am exhausted. Which way is our bedroom?"

"Giorgio, you remember the way out. I must attend to Angelina's needs. Amalea will call you tomorrow to make dinner arrangements."

Giorgio remained calm as he bowed slightly and bid his goodbye. A seasoned performance by an actor that frequently played the part.

Catalina did not hide her true feelings. Her balloon of abundant joy had been popped by Angelina—*again*. Catalina slammed the wine bottle on the sofa table and released a high-pitched huff. She glared at Angelina for a moment before turning on her heels to follow her husband.

A mixture of emotions rumbled inside Angelina. She was deeply saddened by her sister's attitude yet felt a warming rush of victory twirl through her core. She won this fight. Angelina's triumphant feeling quickly faded when Catalina glanced back with a snarl of hatred. The sisterly bond they shared as children had instantly vanished, making Angelina question if it ever existed.

"Before you leave, Cat, give me a hug. I have missed you. But now that I am back from my frivolous travels, we can make up for the lost time." Angelina embraced her sister and whispered in her ear. "This is not what I want for either of us."

"Do what you must to survive." Catalina did not engage in the hug. "You taught me that, and that is what I will do."

"I can't lose you too. Please!" Gripping her sister tight, Angelina fought back her tears. "Please! We must—"

Catalina broke the embrace. "You should have thought about that before you seduced my husband!"

The void of love in Catalina's eyes crushed Angelina. Out of survival, her sister did more than accuse her of adultery. She declared them enemies.

BOOK CLUBS & MORE
Ask The Author

Dear Reader,

Have you ever wondered how or why the author wrote the story? What inspired them to use specific names and locations? Do you believe the tiniest detail has a deeper meaning? I will tell you the answers to these questions and more. Simply invite me to your next meeting!

Visiting with readers is one of the best parts of writing. It gives you a chance to learn more about me and the reason behind the novel. (I use lots of symbolism, and most details are not happenstance!) I, too, benefit because I ask you questions, too! Learning what inspires you, why scenes ensnared you, and what you think will happen next are all gratifying and help stir my creativity. Who knows, you may find yourself in my next novel!

Writing is more than telling a story. It is a conversation that doesn't end on the last page. I look forward to the next chapter in our discussion! Connect with me through social media or www.theitalianrose.com. Please be sure to like, share, and leave reviews!

Very Truly Yours,
Christina R Mitchell

Get YOUR NAME in my **NEXT BOOK!**
FOLLOW on Socail Media or Subscribe for one entry
WRITE A REVIEW for two entries.

All Subscribers will receive the
'Who, Where, and Why for The Sinner.'

🖒 **TheItalianRose**

📷 **TheItalianRose**

ⓣ **@TheItalianRose**

🌐 **TheItalianRose.com**

🌐 **papillonebooks.com**

LEGAL'S NOTE

Though some names are family names, the character traits and actions do not reflect those individuals. This story, in its entirety, is pure fiction.

Yours Truly,
David R. Mitchell, Esq.
www.MitchellandAssociates.com

AUTHOR'S NOTE

Please leave a review on the website on which you purchased this book. Like, share, and follow us on all social media platforms.
@theitalianrose
The few seconds it takes to do this provides tremendous, lasting support, plus encourages me to type faster. ☺
I hope you enjoyed the book!
Want the 'Who, Where, and Why, for this book?

Get YOUR NAME in my **NEXT BOOK!**
FOLLOW on Socail Media or Subscribe for one entry
WRITE A REVIEW for two entries.
See your name in print!
Subscribe at www.theitalianrose.com.

For more inside scoops, invite me to your book club!
It has been a pleasure to entertain you!

Buono Cosa Sempre'
C. R. Mitchell

Join the family at www.theitalianrose.com.

C. R. MITCHELL

C. R. Mitchell's author journey began in 2008 when her husband encouraged her to channel her natural storytelling talent to inspire others. Intrigued, she began writing. In 2014, an illness drastically changed her life, turning her from a workaholic and active in the community into an unemployed hermit.

Despite feeling broken, she clung to her faith, convinced her life path shifted so she could inspire others by writing. From her personal experience with chronic pain and depression, she wrote a nonfiction book on managing these invisible monsters to encourage others to embrace a victorious mindset.

Her debut novel, The Italian Rose Mafia Series, honors the formidable women in her life, particularly her mother, who triumphed in the sexist Italian culture.

Mitchell excels at crafting vivid scenes with realistic characters that readers can fall in love with or despise. She believes that a novel achieves an artistic level when it evokes strong emotions within her during the final read-through.

She and her husband started GolfWithLiz.com – The ODP Foundation, after their daughter died in a car accident. Ten months later, they hosted their first golf tournament. With the help of family and friends, their annual golf tournament, held the first Sunday in May, raises money to fund annual scholarships for young women. In three years, the foundation has awarded over $20,000 in scholarships.

Christina is a member of P.E.O., Chapter KH. P.E.O. has awarded over $435 million to support women's education.

Mitchell resides in Blue Springs, MO. She cherishes time with her husband, children, family, and friends. She enjoys snuggling with her Papillon puppy, Enzo, playing the piano, and the occasional faceplant into chocolate.

Learn more about C. R. Mitchell at www.theitalianrose.com.

www.ingramcontent.com/pod-product-compliance
Lightning Source LLC
Chambersburg PA
CBHW020631020726
47494CB00001B/143

www.ingramcontent.com/pod-product-compliance
Lightning Source LLC
Chambersburg PA
CBHW020631020726
47494CB00001B/143